DEATH IN VALLETTA

LYNNE MARIE TAYLOR

BLOODHOUND
— B O O K S —

For Colin

CHAPTER ONE

Valletta, Malta. Monday, 5 July 1880

'The admiral's body is this way, Doctor.'

Dr Vittorio Bonnići tried to keep pace with young Sergeant Galea, using his cane to help negotiate the dark path through the renowned gardens of Villa Porto. It was close to midnight. The skies were clear, with just a faint light from the pared slice of a new moon. Stone statues loomed up at regular intervals, silently observing their progress. Tall palm trees in raised flower beds appeared aloof, turning away from the night-time intrusion. The cool air throbbed with the chirr of tree crickets.

'Do we know what happened?' he asked, as they approached the back of the villa.

'Only that the admiral fell from the roof terrace. He had gone up to smoke his cigar.'

Villa Porto was an elegant neoclassical building, three storeys high, built around the turn of the century. Lights glowed through the windows on the first floor, revealing faint silhouettes of people inside. The accident had caused an abrupt end to a select gathering – a soirée. As he drew near the terrace, Bonniċi could just about make out two men, deep in murmured conversation. He gripped the handle of his medical bag tightly. This was the most important task he had ever faced as police physician. Admiral Lord Collingwood, former Commander-in-Chief of the Mediterranean Fleet, lay dead and he had been called to determine the cause.

As he approached, the shadowy figures broke apart, revealing themselves to be Captain Borġ, superintendent of the Maltese Police, and Lieutenant Carstairs, aide-de-camp to the governor. Captain Borġ's black eyes glowered from under his heavy brows.

'Ah, Dr Bonniċi, at last,' he said. 'We have been waiting for you. Where have you been?'

'I got here as swiftly as I could,' Bonniċi replied. 'I had work to do, at the hospital.'

'You should have been here sooner.'

As usual, his tone grated. Bonniċi was the most qualified police physician in Malta, but Borġ refused to acknowledge his abilities. Perhaps it was the privilege associated with the Bonniċi family name. Or perhaps it was the weakness in his left leg, which caused him to walk with a limp. Whatever the reason, Borġ regarded him with sneering disdain. However, Bonniċi knew better than to rise to the bait – he would let the excellence of his work speak for him instead.

'Good to see you, Doctor.' Carstairs stepped forward to shake his hand; a smart young man, he was always ready to smooth the waters. 'It's a terrible situation. Sir Thomas is deeply concerned.'

Bonniċi could imagine the consternation with which the governor had received the news. Admiral Lord Collingwood was highly regarded in Malta, much decorated for his role in the

Crimean War. The death of such a distinguished resident would cause ripples through the tight-knit community.

He put down his medical bag and approached the body, which lay close to where the men were standing. Three police-issue lanterns had been set nearby, flickering in the slight breeze. They revealed a sight more disturbing than Bonniċi had expected. He knew Lord Collingwood by sight: a man who exuded authority; tall, spare and vigorous. Now the admiral lay broken on the stone ground, his left arm pinned underneath him, his right arm reaching forwards as if for support. His neck was bent back at a sickeningly unnatural angle, his eyes wide open and his mouth darkly ajar, as if registering the horror of his last moments. Sticky black blood pooled around him. It was still spreading, millimetre by millimetre, towards the edge of the terrace.

Bonniċi took a moment to detach himself and focus on the task ahead of him. Calmly, he knelt down to feel for a pulse. There was none. The admiral's body was cool to the touch, his skin a bluish-grey, lifeless and eerie in the wavering light.

He called to Galea to bring the lamp closer. The young man sprang forward, lifting the lantern above the body with intense concentration.

Bonniċi began a close examination of the body. The back of the admiral's head appeared to be the source of the haemorrhage; the grey hair matted with thick blood. Carefully, he inspected the wound under the hair, feeling for signs of fracture. He found that the occipital bone at the back of the head had been crushed, broken pieces depressed into the brain cavity.

'Skull fractured on impact,' he commented.

He turned Collingwood's face further towards the ground, noticing slight red mottling at the top of the neck.

'Did you note this, Superintendent?' he asked. 'It could be bruising.'

Borġ grunted in response, but made no move to view the corpse more closely.

Bonniċi felt gently along the limbs, identifying fractures in the collarbone, humerus, hip bone and femur, all of which were on the left side of the body, indicating how it had landed. He looked up at the roof terrace, at least thirty feet high. It would have taken less than two seconds to reach the ground. *Death must have been virtually instantaneous.*

He stood up and pulled out his pocket watch. 'Death confirmed at eleven forty-seven. Cause of death appears to be a fractured skull, with multiple injuries sustained by the fall.'

'Thank you, Doctor,' Carstairs said. 'Question is, how the hell did it happen? Was he drunk, d'you think? Did he somehow trip over and fall?'

'Difficult to say,' Bonniċi said. 'We'll find out more from the post-mortem examination.'

'Or was there someone up there with him, someone who pushed him over the edge?' Carstairs peered at the body on the ground. 'I don't like the look on his face. Never seen anything like it.'

'Have your men searched the roof, Captain Borġ?' Bonniċi asked. 'Did you find anything?'

'No. We have looked. Nothing there,' Borġ said. 'Nobody at the party saw anything. They were all in the reception room. I think it was an accident, he was too close to the edge, he–'

'Superintendent,' Galea interrupted, his voice high with excitement. 'Have you seen this?'

He pointed to the ground, where his lantern had caught a reflection from a blue and green glass brooch, not far from the admiral's right hand. Bonniċi picked it up and held it in the light. It was an oval shape, approximately two inches across: a peacock eye set in silver filigree.

'It is the Evil Eye!' Galea exclaimed. 'The admiral has been cursed!'

Bonnići raised an eyebrow at the young man's superstitious beliefs. 'It's just a piece of jewellery,' he said. 'But it could be important evidence.'

He turned it over to examine it. The clasp was undone. Had the admiral ripped it from the coat of an assailant?

'I will take that,' Borġ said. 'Give it to me.'

As he handed it over, Bonnići thought he caught a glint of recognition in the superintendent's eye. *Was there something he was trying to cover up?*

Borġ put the brooch in his pocket. 'Nothing more to do here,' he said, brusquely. 'Sergeant Galea, get the body taken away to the mortuary. I will notify the magistrate. Dr Girello can carry out the post-mortem examination in the morning. Dr Bonnići, you are done here. You can go.'

Bonnići drew in a deep breath, wanting to say something, but feeling there was little point. He dusted his trouser legs with a handkerchief and wiped traces of blood from his hands. Picking up his bag, he made his way back to the side gate, looking up at the villa before leaving the gardens. He could see the party guests gathered by the windows, in their elegant evening wear, their idyllic society life shattered by this moment of violence. He closed his eyes, picturing the body tumbling down; the sudden, terrifying moment of impact. A feeling of disquiet settled on him. The role of the police was to discover the truth and restore order, but he had no faith in Captain Borġ's abilities. One thing he did know, however: the British would want to be in control.

Sir Thomas Grant was feeling tetchy. He hated this time of year; it was so damned hot one could hardly breathe. The windows in his vast office were all open, but it was airless. He had been Governor of Malta for three years, yet he still could not get used to these intense weeks in July and August, when there simply was no let-up to the heat. His head was aching. He yawned, and thought how good it would be, at the end of the day, to sip an ice-cold gin and tonic.

He picked up the top sheet of paper from his in-tray. The Colonial Office in London had written to him again about the Collingwood case. The inquest had been inconclusive: not enough evidence to prove accidental death, homicide, or even suicide. The inquiry was still ongoing, but the police had made no progress. The Colonial Office was deeply concerned and wanted him to sort the situation out as soon as possible.

A knock at the door. His aide-de-camp, an excellent young man.

'Yes?'

'Lady Collingwood to see you, Your Excellency.'

'Admiral Collingwood's widow? Ah, fine. Carstairs, do show her in.'

Alicia. A force to be reckoned with. He had known her for years. He braced himself as she swooped into the room. Tall and imposing, she always made him feel a little on edge. Her mourning clothing accentuated her dark hair and piercing blue eyes. She took off one black glove and proffered her hand.

'Thomas.'

'Alicia. How are you?'

'Bearing up, but it's a nightmare. It really is.'

'I know, I'm sorry. It must be terribly tricky for you right now.'

'You do not know the half of it, Thomas. The lawyers are having a field day. We can do nothing about the estate unless suicide can be ruled out. And you know as well as I that Edward would never have taken his own life!'

'But Alicia – the police report is quite clear. There is nothing to suggest anything other than a fall, but neither can the other verdicts be ruled out.'

'Really, Thomas! It's obvious the police have made up their minds. If that police superintendent says one more time, "A tragedy, a terrible accident"... I'll ... well, I don't know what I shall do.'

'Captain Borġ is the best man for the job.' He tried to sound convincing.

'Thomas, there's something here that isn't right. My husband would not "fall" from the roof terrace. Somebody did this to him. It must be an outsider, a foreign criminal. Don't you see? We're none of us safe now, with a killer around. I demand you get someone else in to investigate. A real detective. They must send someone from Scotland Yard! I have to know the truth, Thomas. I *have* to.'

Sir Thomas reflected for a moment. He could not face the idea of Scotland Yard tramping over the island. Truth be told, he really could do without the whole thing being blown up out of proportion; he could not bear the thought of the scrutiny. Affairs in Malta had been stable for forty years, with a light-touch approach that seemed to work well. He knew better than to rock the boat.

On the other hand, he recognised that Alicia would not stop until she had what she wanted. He could tell from the determined set of her chin. *Perhaps there was another way. A compromise.* He could ask his former colleague Murdoch, from the Edinburgh Police. Murdoch would understand. They had served together as young officers in the Highlanders. Yes, he felt sure George could spare someone for a few weeks, a token effort to give the appearance he was taking action. He picked up his pen in what he hoped looked like a purposeful way.

'Why don't you leave it with me, Alicia? I'll see what I can do.'

'Please do. I am relying on you, you know. I need you to do this for me, and for Edward. He was a national hero.'

'Indeed.' Sir Thomas nodded solemnly to acknowledge the sentiment.

Pulling on her gloves, Lady Collingwood stood up to leave, stopping at the doorway. 'It's entirely within your power as governor, Thomas. I expect a detective to arrive here in Malta within three weeks.'

Sir Thomas rubbed his temples. His head was absolutely pounding. His wife was currently out of the country. She could not bear the summer heat, preferring to stay at their house in Farnborough. So, he was free to slip away and spend time with whomsoever he chose. There was a certain charming lady who mixed the best gin and tonic on the island. Her hands were always cool, and she was adept at soothing away the fiercest of headaches.

He called Carstairs back and dictated a letter to the Colonial Office. Then he wrote a quick note for Murdoch. That should surely be enough for one day.

CHAPTER TWO

Edinburgh, Scotland. Monday, 19 July 1880

Detective Inspector Sam McQueen strode along Cowgate, bowler hat jammed on, hands deep in his jacket pockets. The pavement was narrow and filthy, and he had to step into the road to dodge a milk cart. He had been summoned to speak to Superintendent Murdoch in his chambers. If he had calculated it right, he should get to Police Headquarters just before nine thirty, but he had to keep up the pace.

He turned left into Fishmarket Close. The tenements loomed high above him; their stones were blackened by soot. This was his shortcut, but it meant a scramble up slippery cobbles and stacks of stairs. He heard shouts from an open window – a woman's voice, chiding her bairns. He smiled at the colourful language, then dodged a cascade of dirty water.

The close opened out onto the grand buildings of the High Street, by Parliament Square. He swung left into the main entrance of the office and took the steps two at a time up to the third storey. Once outside Murdoch's office he stopped and took out his pocket watch. Nine thirty exactly. Excellent. He took a deep breath, removed his hat and rapped on the door.

He was not sure what to expect from the meeting. He had a good relationship with Murdoch, who had mentored him throughout the ups and downs of his career. McQueen had a reputation as a good detective, but he also had a knack for falling out with his peers.

He heard Murdoch's deep voice saying, 'Come in,' and stepped inside.

'Morning, sir. Is this about Johnstone?' McQueen asked. 'I've heard he's out.'

His former colleague Inspector Johnstone had been sentenced to two years' hard labour – on McQueen's evidence – after accepting bribes from a well-known gang of swindlers. A corrupt detective was the lowest of the low. McQueen had had no compunction about standing up in court and attesting to the meetings he had witnessed and the money passing hands. Morale among officers had been difficult for some time afterwards and was not yet fully restored. Johnstone's return was bound to cause the superintendent some headaches.

Murdoch gestured for him to sit down, tapping his pipe contents into an ashtray.

'Yes, Johnstone is back in town,' he said. 'You'll need to watch your back.'

He took a wad of tobacco, pressed it firmly into the bowl and struck several matches to light it. He took a few quick puffs to get the pipe going, then leaned back in his chair.

'But I also have something to discuss with you,' he said. 'Something out of the blue, you might say.'

He rooted around on his desk and held up an official-looking paper.

'I've had this letter from the Colonial Office in London,' he said. 'They're looking for a detective inspector to go to Malta. They've asked for you.'

McQueen sat forward. 'Malta? The island?'

He tried to recall what he knew about the place. It was in the Mediterranean Sea, somewhere off the boot of Italy. People stopped there on their way to India.

'Yes, home to the Mediterranean Fleet,' Murdoch said.

'What's the problem there?'

'The former Commander-in-Chief Admiral Lord Collingwood has died after a fall. Suspected murder. It's of great concern. They need to find out who's at the bottom of this. A matter of national security.'

'Indeed?'

'Their police force is small, as you can imagine, with no trained detectives. The Governor of Malta has requested a detective inspector to take charge. I know him; we served together in Crimea. Very upright man, you know the sort. Proper Scottish Presbyterian. I suggested you, told him of your Free Church background.'

McQueen laughed. 'Oh aye? Is that right?'

He had long ago stopped speaking to his father, renowned minister at Fountainbridge Church. He was everything that his father railed against; smoking, and drinking being just two of the vices that had seen him cast from the family home.

He took the letter, glanced through it and handed it back. 'This has to be a joke,' he said. 'You can't seriously be expecting me to take on a case like this.'

Murdoch drew on his pipe and a fug of sweet-smelling smoke settled around him.

'I think you should consider it very carefully,' he said. 'It will be a challenge for you, a change of scene. You can do things your way for once.'

McQueen turned his bowler around in his hands. He hated

travelling. It would be hot and uncomfortable, and he would be surrounded by English colonials.

'I don't know, sir,' he said. 'I'm not sure I'd be the right man for the job.'

'Well, to my mind, Inspector, you are the perfect choice. And, let me remind you, your actions have not left you many friends here.'

The meaning was clear to McQueen. It would be better for all if he disappeared for a while. He started to get up, in a rush of irritation.

'I need to think,' he said. 'I've things to do here...'

Murdoch put his pipe down and stood up to shake his hand.

'Don't take too long, son. They need to know in a couple of days.'

McQueen turned at the door. 'Warmer than Siberia, at any rate,' he said.

He pushed his hat down firmly. He had a lot of thinking to do.

———

At the end of the day, McQueen ducked into the low doorway of the Fountain Inn. Once inside, he was hit by the smell of sawdust, tobacco and stale beer, and the customary din of loud voices and laughter. The light was murky and he stopped for his eyes to adjust. The inn was packed with men who had finished long shifts at the nearby factories. He recognised a couple of faces, blackened by smoke and shining with sweat. Naturally, they ignored him.

He shouldered his way to the bar.

'Pint of heavy – and a whisky.'

The barman, short and wiry, gave him a curt nod as he handed over the drinks. McQueen drained the pint, asked for another, then took the tankard and the glass to his usual corner table. He sat down heavily.

He tipped the tankard towards him, staring into the white froth on top of the beer. *Could he really leave Jeannie at this time?* He sighed. Perhaps it would be for the best. Things had been difficult between them recently. He had hardly been at home; he had been neglecting her. She deserved better.

He pushed the beer to one side and took a swig of his whisky. The warmth of the spirit felt good as it travelled down his throat. He twisted the whisky glass around as he placed it back on the table, watching the door and waiting.

It was not long before it opened, admitting a tall, awkward character who looked anxiously around until he saw McQueen, then loped over and sat down.

'Why do we have to meet here?' he asked. He wore wire spectacles, which had steamed up, and he took them off to polish the lenses. 'You know I can't abide these drinking dens.'

He looked around myopically, taking in the raucous banter and laughter around him. 'These people are wilfully turning away from the Word of God!'

He put his spectacles back on and sighed.

McQueen laughed. He had expected nothing less from his older brother.

'You'll not be wanting a drink yourself then, Andrew?' he asked.

'I will not! Just tell me what this is all about and let me get out of here.'

'I have some news,' he said.

'What is it?'

'I have been requested to leave Edinburgh.'

'What do you mean?'

'I'm being sent overseas. Exiled to an island, like Napoleon.'

'Where?'

'Malta.'

'But, Samuel,' said Andrew. 'You can't go there. It'll be swarming with Roman Catholics!'

McQueen laughed again, enjoying the look of utter disbelief on his brother's face.

'That's the least of my concerns,' he said. 'Look, Jeannie can live with her brother in Leith. I'll send money, but I can't go unless I know she will be all right. Could you look out for her, for me?'

'Very well. If I must. For your sake.' For all his funny ways, and his dedication to the Church, Andrew was a good soul and would never let him down. 'But why do you have to go, and when?'

'They want me to solve a case – a murder. It won't be for long. I'll be back in a few weeks.' McQueen drained his whisky glass. 'Tell Ma I'll write.'

'But... Mary and I – we wanted you here for the baptism. Wee Jonathan. We hoped you could be godfather?'

'Not a chance, Andrew. Renounce the devil, me? Sorry, brother, not this time.'

Andrew cast him a dour look, nodded in acceptance, and left the way he had come. McQueen reached for his pint.

Before he could take a sip, a loud crash heralded the arrival of trouble. He recognised the freckled face of young Reid as the constable tried to stop a flailing, cursing figure from entering the inn.

'Sir, it's Johnstone!' Reid shouted. 'He's looking for ye, and he's awfy boozed up.'

Within moments, a scarecrow of a man glowered before him. Still with the same black hair and scrawny beard, trying to mask a pock-marked face.

'McQueen, ye bastard! I said I'd bloody find ye, an' I have.'

'Come on, Johnstone, take it easy,' McQueen said, hoping to calm him.

But Johnstone, none too steady on his feet, was already squaring up to him, ready to strike.

'Ye've cost me ma job – ma whole life. Ye should have held yer tongue.'

McQueen dodged the punch, grabbed Johnstone's arm and pulled it up behind his back. Johnstone toppled forwards, pulling them both over. The beer went flying.

Johnstone rolled over and kicked out, catching McQueen in the face. Drinkers gathered around, cheering at the sight of two detectives tussling. McQueen got to his feet and pulled Johnstone up by the lapels. He went for a swift jab with the left, then a strong uppercut with the right, watching his opponent's face change from drunken determination to shock and bewilderment. Johnstone went flying backwards, landing on a stool with a loud cracking and splintering of wood.

Sergeant Reid looked at the mess and shook his head.

'The superintendent's no' going to like this, Inspector,' he said.

'Get him out of here,' McQueen answered, nodding towards Johnstone. Then he went to the bar to get himself a replacement pint.

Murdoch was right. Time for him to book a berth to the Mediterranean.

CHAPTER THREE

Mediterranean Sea. Saturday, 31 July 1880

T en days cooped up on a steamship had taken its toll. McQueen had spent most of the time pacing the deck or reading *Godwin's Guide to the Maltese Islands*. The Bay of Biscay had been terrible; nearly the whole ship was brought low with sea sickness. And after they had passed Gibraltar, it had steadily grown hotter and hotter. Each day had seen the temperature rise, above and below deck. It was torture for McQueen. Unused to the heat, he realised he should have bought himself a linen suit, but there had been no time and they were damned expensive.

He could not bear his cabin. With no windows he felt hemmed in, unable to breathe. He had to share it with a sour-faced Italian, some twenty years older than him, whose rasping snores drove him up to the cooler top deck. Here, he could spend the dark hours leaning on the rail, smoking, and watching the steady progress of the ship through the gentle waves of the Mediterranean Sea.

They would reach their destination in less than two days, the ship tracking the north coast of Africa. Many other travellers had sought the same night breezes, some even sleeping on mattresses brought up from their cabins. The steady thrum of the ship's engine had a hypnotic effect, only slightly disturbed by whispered conversations, quiet coughs and the sound of throats clearing. He was thinking about Jeannie. He pictured her smoothing her hair down, tucking a stray curl behind her ear, before tackling the pots at the kitchen sink. She would be worried that she was not doing enough to earn her place in her brother's home. He thought he would write to her, assure her that it would not be for long, that he would soon be back home.

A tall young Army officer approached and stood next to him, offering him a cigarette from a small tin. McQueen took one readily and lit it. Any chance to have an imported cigarette was welcome. *Egyptian tobacco,* he thought, *hand-rolled.* He generally made his own cigarettes, using a tobacco pouch and ripped-up paper. A habit picked up from fellow police officers; Army veterans who had returned from the Crimea.

McQueen had noticed the officer around during the voyage and they had exchanged a few words. The young man had introduced himself as Lieutenant Greening. He was on his way back to Malta after a short period of leave.

'Getting close now,' the young man said, his face pale grey in the blue light of the early hours. He was clean-shaven with high cheekbones and a full, almost feminine mouth; the kind of upper-crust good looks that McQueen judged would only ease his path through life. Yet he was not arrogant, his tone naturally friendly and sincere. 'Soon be back to work. Do you have business in Malta?'

'Business of a kind,' McQueen replied. 'I'm with the police. Did you hear of Lord Collingwood's death?'

The lieutenant tensed slightly, taking a moment to flick the ash of his cigarette overboard.

'Ah, indeed I did,' he said. 'I know the family a little. A terrible thing.'

Greening appeared to be choosing his words carefully.

'I'm on my way to investigate the circumstances around the death,' McQueen explained. 'Can I ask what you know about Collingwood?'

'The admiral? I know his reputation.'

'Good? Bad? Highly regarded?'

Greening was quiet for a while, but the hushed atmosphere on the deck seemed to encourage him to confide his thoughts.

'A hero, yes. But somewhat fearsome. Bit of a tyrant.'

'In what way?'

'I've heard some tales, you know.'

'Go on. It won't go any further,' McQueen prompted.

Greening hesitated. 'As ship's captain, he was known for his absolute intolerance. He'd have men whipped for the slightest thing. Cat o' nine tails – thirty, forty lashes for being caught gambling, or being drunk. God help you if you were guilty of anything worse.'

He dropped his cigarette over the side of the boat and took out another from the tin he kept in his jacket pocket. Again, he offered one to McQueen, who shook his head, despite the generous offer.

'A cruel man,' Greening continued. 'No compassion – you know? I heard of a young sailor. He'd just found out his baby had died. Slipped off ship at Portsmouth to see his wife. Late back the next day. Collingwood had him starved in the brig for a week, then flogged. A hundred lashes.'

'Jesus. Did he survive?'

'Only just.'

McQueen thought of his masters at school, and on occasion

his own father, meting out punishments he had known to be unwarranted. He hated the kind of man who enjoyed abusing their power over others.

'And in Malta? What do people think about Collingwood now?'

'Put up with him, on the whole. Not a man of great charm. His wife, Lady Collingwood, is seen as a good sort, I'd say.'

'And when he died? What was the reaction?'

'Well, gossip, you know. Shock. But – put it this way – I heard there were a great many people at the funeral, but not many mourners.'

Greening lit his cigarette and lapsed into silence.

They stood watching the faint yellow light begin to appear on the horizon, as the boat continued to chug through the water. McQueen wondered what he was heading into. *How many people wanted the admiral dead?*

———

When the island of Malta finally came into view, McQueen was waiting on the port deck, bag packed, impatient to get off the ship. He mopped his neck with his handkerchief and watched the city of Valletta come into focus as the steamship *Nepal* slowly glided into the harbour. The sky was a clearer, brighter blue than he had ever seen, the sea glittering as the sunlight caught every slight movement of the water. The shoreline was dominated by high walls and fortifications, seeming to grow naturally from the limestone rock. He was struck by the attractive arched frontages of stone buildings as they approached the landing point, and the incongruity of a single English-style church spire, rising above honey-coloured flat-roofed houses. He itched to take out his sketchbook and capture the lines.

Once the steamship had anchored, the passengers stood waiting, bags at their feet, until an officious man in spectacles had looked over the papers and declared the boat clean. Then calm turned to chaos as they clambered over one another to disembark. It appeared they all had to be ferried across to a landing stage on tiny boats, brightly painted with blues, greens, yellows and reds. McQueen had read about these water taxis called *dgħajsa tal-pass*. The boatmen vied with each other to get custom, shouting at full volume, standing up in their boats and manoeuvring them with two long oars.

McQueen pushed his way through the melee, threw his bag into a *dgħajsa* and climbed in. The boat rocked alarmingly in the water as the ferryman rowed to the landing stage. It was bright and hot, and he could hardly see against the glare as he finally stepped back onto solid ground.

Immediately, his senses were assaulted by the noise of the teeming harbour and the stench of seawater, ordure and rotten food. Beggars clamoured around him, tugging at his clothes as he walked up the steep steps from the landing stage. He brushed them away, unable to understand a word they were saying.

At the top of the stairs he stopped, disorientated by the heat. The ground seemed to be lurching towards him as if he were still onboard ship. He put his bag down for a moment while people pushed past. His plan was to find somewhere to stay for the night and to explore the city. He would take one evening to get the lie of the land before starting his investigation. He took his hat off for a second so he could mop his brow.

As he did so, a short, shabby man appeared in front of him, peering up from under a battered black cap. An insincere grin revealed sparse, jagged teeth.

'I take you where you want? You want buy lace for your

lady? Gloves? You want hair cut? You want cigars, tobacco? I take you, yes? Come, come with me.'

The man hovered around, standing too close. There were endless "guides" harassing the passengers and this one did not look worse than any of the others. McQueen gave in.

'Very well,' he said. 'Hotel?'

'Yes, yes, good hotel. English hotel. Come, this way.'

He followed the bobbing head up a steep road flanked by steps, then along a twisted route that took them through narrow streets. Wooden balconies jutted out from tall town houses, painted in greens and reds. Life-size statues of saints seemed to appear on every corner. Cats slunk ahead of them, while dogs lay in doorways, dozing in the shade. He tried to memorise the way, but he was finding it difficult in the heat. He felt his shirt getting damp under his woollen jacket and sweat began to drip down his head from the rim of his hat. He brushed the stinging salt out of his eyes.

'How much further?' he asked. He was not sure he trusted the guide, who had a sharp, furtive way about him. It was the kind of look McQueen recognised from city folk used to living on their wits.

The guide called back over his shoulder. 'Very close, mister. Follow, follow.'

They turned into a street as narrow as any of the Edinburgh closes, and the guide stopped suddenly. 'See, hotel,' he said, giving McQueen his strange gappy grin and holding out his hand for a tip.

Indeed, it was a hotel. The sign next to the door read *The Crown Hotel, 67 Strada Stretta*. McQueen gave the man a penny and went in. It was cooler inside than out, with a reassuringly calm British feel about the place. Perhaps he had misjudged his guide. Yet, he noticed out of the corner of his eye that the man did not leave straight away; he stayed in the doorway, watching the reception desk, as McQueen booked in for the night.

After he had unpacked his bag in his room, changed his shirt and cooled down, McQueen went out again to get his bearings. He retraced his way back to the harbour, the centre of activity. The *Nepal* was one of three P&O boats anchored there, surrounded by *dgħajjes*, water barges and coal lighters. He watched as passengers who were still onboard threw coins into the water for local boys to retrieve. The ship would soon be on its way to Bombay, the Indian staff bustling around the decks in their white uniforms.

After a while, he set out to look for a telegraph office, finding one at Marsamscetto Street, opposite the landing stage. He went in to send a message to Murdoch, to say that he had arrived, that the heat was fearsome and that he was hoping to meet the governor the next day. Then he penned a note to the governor and sent it via a message boy, saying he would report in at nine o'clock the following morning. The telegraph office was teeming with people, bodies damp with sweat in the oppressive heat.

Valletta was built on a rock peninsula with two harbours on either side: Marsamscetto Harbour to the north-west and Grand Harbour to the south-east. McQueen had memorised the layout described in his guidebook: ten streets running lengthways, traversed by eleven streets, connecting the two harbours. He began to make his way back towards the centre, keeping to the shade under the projecting balconies of the town houses and noting street names to make a mental map of the city.

At the corner of Strada Vescova and Strada Zecca, a woman crossed in front of him. She appeared to be covered from top to toe in a long cloak with a starched hood framing her face. He guessed this must be the *għonnella* described in his guidebook – unique to Malta. It was made from flowing dark material, designed to protect women from the sun – and, it was said, from unwanted glances. It gave her a mysterious allure as she swept away from him. He felt compelled to follow her, to find out where she was going.

She disappeared between ornate wooden doors into a church. Curious, he stepped in after her. It was dark, the entrance blocked by a heavy curtain. McQueen took off his hat and waited for a moment in the cool of the church interior. He fanned himself with the hat brim and loosened his collar. He could not see anything, but he could hear a monotonous low chanting, in what he assumed must be Latin, broken up by the occasional quiet ting of a bell. A Roman Catholic Mass. He stood listening for a moment. It was the first time he had heard the ancient liturgy and he felt the draw of its thousand-year history.

When his eyes had adjusted to the dark, he pulled the curtain carefully to one side to look for the woman in the *għonnella*. She had stopped before a statue of the Virgin Mary, lit by a multitude of votive candles. He watched as she reached for a taper and used it to light a candle. She had dropped the hood of her cloak, her face now revealed beneath a black lace veil. She was not young, but she had a natural, dark beauty. She was concentrating, deep in thought as she watched the wavering flame. Glimmers of gold flickered across her eyes, which held a depth of blackness, an impression of emptiness and loss. He watched, mesmerised.

There was a noise behind him; the heavy wooden door opened then closed with a thud. The woman in the *għonnella* looked in his direction, her devotion interrupted. He saw her face harden as she noticed him staring at her. He backed away, almost knocking into a tiny elderly woman behind him, who shot him an angry look as she brushed past to join the service. He left, feeling like the stranger that he was, plunging once again into the stifling heat outside.

———

After his dinner McQueen headed out of the hotel into Stretta Strada. The best way to learn about a city was to get talking to people, ask some questions. As far as he could tell, Stretta Strada was the drinking centre of Valletta. The further he walked along the narrow street, the more bars he encountered. It was cooler now it was dark, bringing out large numbers of British soldiers and sailors looking for a lively night. Raucous groups spilled out of tiny taverns, sloshing beers and singing bawdy songs. Like a Saturday night in Edinburgh Auld Town, but louder and with more colour.

A group of four soldiers pushed past him, dressed in red tunics and tartan bonnets. He stopped to ask them their regiment.

'First Royal Scots, pal. Ye'll nae fin' better!'

Their accents reminded him of home. He followed them into a crowded bar, bought himself a beer and sat in the corner. The young Scots were soon joined by a pair of brightly dressed local girls who sidled up next to them. He watched, amused, as the soldiers vied with each other for the girls' attention. One of the lads, who was tall, dark and built like a prize-fighter, paired with the bolder of the two girls, who had been making eyes at him. Two of his pals joshed with the youngest looking of the group, trying to get him to approach the other girl. The youngster's pallor betrayed his lack of experience as he went along with their banter.

McQueen watched the girl responding to the soldiers, noticing how weakly she smiled as she tried to flirt. She was leaning in towards the young lad, showing herself to her best advantage, but he glimpsed a hesitancy that betrayed her reluctance. She reminded him of Jeannie, of how she was when he first met her, doing what it took to survive in an uncaring world. A gentle but damaged soul.

He sighed. Finishing his beer, he went back to the bar, where a multitude of bottles sat on the shelves. Not a single label he recognised. He longed for the range of whiskies he would find at home, the single malts alongside the popular blends.

He tried to get the attention of the bartender. He was a burly man with a cloth draped over his shoulder, who was leaning on the bar carrying on a loud conversation with a Maltese customer. It took several loud raps of a coin before he deigned to look over.

'What have you got in the way of whisky?' McQueen said loudly, to make himself heard over the noise.

The man reached behind him for a bottle with a red label. He gave the impression of easy-going untidiness: greying hair in need of a cut, a scruffy apron tied over a large belly. But his coal-black eyes were constantly dancing around, reading the room. He was clearly not keen on serving this customer. McQueen peered at the label.

'I said whisky. Not rye-flavoured water! Have you not got any Scotch?' he asked.

The bartender shrugged. 'All we have,' he said, getting out a glass. 'Want to try it, or not?'

'Go on then. Fill it up.'

He tried it. *Filthy stuff, but it would have to do.*

'Busy tonight,' he said. 'Is it mostly military you serve?' He knew there were 6,000 troops in Malta, as well as the many sailors spilling off the ships moored in Grant Harbour.

The bartender grunted, showing no interest.

McQueen persevered. 'Do they give you much trouble?'

At that point there was a crash from the corner as the young soldier slipped off his stool, too drunk to walk, his friends laughing at him lying prone on the floor.

A look of irritation crossed the bartender's face. Moving surprisingly fast from behind the bar, he grabbed the soldier by the neck and deposited him outside the door, swiftly followed by the rest of the group.

'There is your answer,' he said, returning to the bar.

'It's the same in Edinburgh, where I stay,' McQueen said. 'Down by Leith docks. Sailors are the worst. Scots sailors can drink anyone under the table.'

The bartender shrugged.

'I'll take another dram, sir.' McQueen pushed his glass forwards.

The bartender poured the drink.

'What brings you to Valletta?' he asked.

'A job,' McQueen replied. 'Going to be here a week or two, working with the police.'

'Oh, yes?' The bartender stared at him intently, polishing the bar with a less-than-white cloth. 'What kind of work?'

'Oh, this and that.'

'Hear that, Ġwanni?' the bartender called over to his Maltese friend. 'He's with the police.'

The friend gave out a sharp 'Ha!', smirking over the top of his drink.

'I told Ġwanni you was trouble. Could see soon as you walked in.'

'You've got me wrong.' McQueen swallowed the whisky and put his glass out for another. 'I like a quiet life.'

The bartender poured him a larger measure.

'Quiet life, eh? So, what do you want, here in my bar?'

McQueen raised his hands. 'Nothing! Just getting to know the city. Where the good people go, where the bad people hide.'

The bartender called out to his friend again. 'Hey, Ġwanni – he says there are bad people here, what do you say to that?'

Ġwanni shook his head with mock solemnity and said something in Maltese. The bartender gave a harsh laugh then turned back to McQueen.

'Listen,' he said. 'I have licence, I serve good drinks. I have no trouble with police.'

'Costs a lot does it, this licence?' McQueen asked, picking up on a slight tension in the bartender's words. 'Police keep a close eye on your place?'

Another black look crossed the bartender's face. He leaned across the bar, his jowly face uncomfortably close, his breath warm and rich with garlic. 'Be careful, Mister Policeman. Do not ask too many questions. Somebody won't like it.'

'Oh, aye?' McQueen said. 'Who?'

'You will find out.'

A new crowd of soldiers pushed their way to the bar and the bartender turned away to deal with them.

McQueen took his glass and went to sit at a table, alone.

A few whiskies later, he made his way back to the hotel. As he went to get his key at reception, he noticed someone creeping away from the entrance.

'Who is that?' he asked the elderly man at the desk. 'It's that fellow who brought me here, isn't it? What's his name?'

The hotel clerk shrugged, feigning indifference as he handed over the key. 'I do not know him. No idea.'

He would wager a hundred guineas that the old devil knew fine well. 'Well, if you see him again, pass on my regards.'

Trying not to stumble on the stairs, he made his way up to his room, his mind whirling with images of dark churches, packed bars and strangers watching his every move.

CHAPTER FOUR

Valletta, Malta. Tuesday, 3 August 1880

A t nine o'clock sharp, McQueen handed over his papers to a bored-looking subaltern at the reception desk in the Governor's Palace. His guidebook had assured McQueen that this former palace of the Grandmasters was "sumptuously fitted up", so he was ready to be impressed. It certainly was built on a grand scale, taking up one side of St George's Square in the heart of the city. An outsized Union Jack flapped proudly on the roof, a declaration of ownership of the islands.

The young officer disappeared with his papers then came back and handed them over without changing his expression. 'Wait here,' he said. McQueen stood in the grand hall, watching the disciplined toing and froing of the military staff. After a few minutes, a slight, harried-looking man came hurrying up to him, holding a sheaf of papers. A few years younger than McQueen, he was clean-shaven except for a neat moustache, his hair short and parted at the side. Awkwardly tucking his papers under his arm, he held out his hand.

'Ah, Inspector, how d'you do? Evelyn Carstairs, Second Lieutenant, aide-de-camp.'

His clipped English vowels made McQueen want to use his broadest Scots, but he resisted the temptation.

'Detective Inspector Sam McQueen. Here to see the governor.'

'Ah, yes, well.' A flicker of worry crossed his face. 'How can I put this? I wish you'd told us you were arriving today. We're – er – not quite ready. It's a bit, you know, busy, and the governor isn't actually here.'

He pulled out his watch from his pocket and his eyes widened in alarm.

'I say, can you follow me to my office?' He set off at a fast pace down a broad corridor, speaking over his shoulder. 'Only I've just got a few minutes before I have to leave for a meeting with the Ladies' Guild. I'll do my best to give you a briefing.'

It was, at least, several degrees cooler than outside. McQueen walked behind Carstairs, taking in the grandeur of his surroundings. Their footsteps echoed on the fine marble floor, as they walked past portraits of the Grandmasters of the Sovereign Military Order of Malta. The ornate ceiling was painted with swirling, richly coloured scenes from the Bible. Suits of armour lined the hall and he could imagine them creaking to life and marching down the corridor in front of him, holding their pikes and spears. The palace spoke of centuries of history, of times of opulence, wealth and power under the Knights of the Order of St John of Jerusalem. All now owned by the British colonial government of Malta.

Reaching a small room at the end of the corridor, Carstairs opened the door and indicated that McQueen should go inside.

'This is my office. Do sit down. Excuse the mess.'

He sat at a large desk, swamped with papers. McQueen sat down opposite him and found he was looking up at a portrait of a portly man with huge white whiskers and an excessive number of military medals.

'Yes, that's the old boy, the governor,' Carstairs said. 'He's away a great deal, keeps himself terribly busy. Of course, that means that everything lands on me.' He smiled suddenly, revealing slightly protruding front teeth. 'Not that I mind. What have they told you, about why we need you here?'

'Lord Collingwood's death. Someone to investigate, find out what happened.'

'Absolutely. Lady Collingwood's got a real bee in her bonnet,' Carstairs said. 'She's convinced the admiral was murdered. Much easier for everyone if he wasn't. The police are absolutely sure that it was an accident.'

'Aye, but what do you think?'

Carstairs looked a little taken aback at being asked his thoughts. He reflected for a moment.

'I don't know. I saw the body and the look on his face was most alarming. I'll never forget it. But I can't think anyone would... you know – want to murder him. Lady C. absolutely refuses to believe it could be accidental, that he could simply fall from a roof.'

He sorted through his pile of papers. 'Let me just find... ah, here we go,' he said, pulling out a few pages. 'Here's the report from the police. You should find everything here.' He started to read it out. '"Late night, towards the end of a soirée, Lord Collingwood goes to the roof for a smoke. The housekeeper hears a scream, body's then found on the terrace below, with a fractured skull. No sign of a struggle."

'According to them, he had leaned too far over, under the influence of too much wine and port. Head smashed in, poor devil.'

He looked up and handed the papers over as he finished. 'Make of that what you will, Inspector.'

McQueen took the report and glanced through it. Just three pages, scant on detail. Very little description of the body, how it was found, and the lead-up to the event. He thought of all the procedures that would have been put in place at home. Statements from every person at the party. Any evidence of intoxication, the state of mind of the deceased. There would be so much to do to unearth the detail, and it was a month ago already by now.

'This is a poor piece of work, Lieutenant. The superintendent will have to give me better answers than this.'

'Ah, well, you might want to tread carefully there.'

'I need to see him, straight away.'

'Certainly, but I would warn you – he's not exactly overjoyed that you're coming.'

'Well, he'll have to get used to it. Do you have a warrant for me? I was told there would be one.'

'Yes, yes, here it is, from the governor,' Carstairs said, handing over another paper from his desk. 'Gives you authority while you're over here.'

McQueen cast his eyes over it.

'Hang on, I've got some money to give you, somewhere.' Carstairs rooted around in a drawer before pulling out a fat paper envelope. 'Expenses and all that. It's easy to get around. Just jump into a *karozzin* – that's a Maltese carriage – it's the way everyone travels. Expect you'll sort things out in no time. You'll like it in Malta; everyone does. It's an unusual place, a little bit of England really, with the hot sun thrown in.'

He hesitated a moment, looking at McQueen's woollen suit. 'Ah, one other thing. Hope you don't mind me saying this, old chap, but you'll need a new suit, a better one for the climate. You'll be far too hot, dressed like that. This time of year, it's brutal.' Carstairs' own suit was a light khaki linen, smartly pressed. 'I can recommend a tailor – go to Ellul's – best by far, and he won't charge you a fortune.'

'I'll see,' McQueen said. 'I'll not want to waste any money. I may not be here long enough to warrant it.'

Carstairs made a sound somewhere between a snort and a laugh. 'You can't say I didn't warn you, old boy,' he said. 'Now then, what else do you need? Oh yes, lodgings! We've secured you a room. With *Sinjura* Caruso, a widow. Very respectable. You'll be comfortable enough there, I dare say. Here's the address – Number 44 Strada Ponente.'

He looked at his watch again and jumped up.

'Heavens, must go.' He picked up his hat and put it on as he walked briskly out. 'This way.'

McQueen kept hold of the papers and followed Carstairs, who set off at pace through a courtyard. It was a quiet sanctuary of shady orange trees, ferns and classical statues. He could hear birds chittering over the murmuring of a water fountain. Despite the shade, he was beginning to feel the heat again. It seemed to wrap itself around him, causing him to break instantly into a sweat.

They emerged through an archway into blinding sunlight, on the other side of the square. He raised his hand to shield his eyes. They were on a busy street, full of people out on their errands or stopping to talk to acquaintances. At least half appeared to be British, including soldiers in uniform and ladies with parasols. Of the Maltese, there were priests in black robes, women wrapped in *għonnielen* and small children running around with bare feet.

'Strada Reale,' Carstairs said. 'Valletta's main thoroughfare.' He pointed across the road. 'There's the police office, part of the law courts at the Auberge d'Auvergne.'

McQueen remembered from Godwin's guide that this was one of the seven grand houses known as the Auberges, belonging to the different nationalities within the Knights of the Order of St John. They were built in the sixteenth century in a time of great wealth. Less grand than the Governor's Palace, this building had just one main entrance, with awnings across the front affording some shade to the windows at street level.

'I'll leave you here, Inspector,' Carstairs said. 'Good luck. Listen, why don't you join me tomorrow night at the mess? I can introduce you to Colonel Arbuthnot, a friend of Lord Collingwood's. I'll send you a note.'

He veered off without waiting for an answer and headed up the street.

———

At the Auberge d'Auvergne, McQueen was directed to the office of Police Superintendent Captain Borġ. It was an expansive space, with wood panelling, arched casement windows and cool marble floor tiles. A large mahogany desk dominated the room, at which Borġ sat writing. On the wall behind the desk was an enlarged photograph of the superintendent in full uniform, receiving some kind of award from the governor. McQueen cleared his throat, but was met with no response. Eventually, the superintendent stopped, looked up and scowled. He was short and broad with a dark, fleshy face and matt black hair. 'Inspector McQueen?' he asked, looking him up and down. A deep voice, heavily accented.

'Indeed,' McQueen answered. 'Superintendent.'

He held out his hand in greeting. Borġ stayed seated, glaring at him, ignoring the gesture.

McQueen sat down at a chair by the desk and crossed his arms, assessing the police chief. Borġ was wearing a black uniform with gold buttons and swirling silver embroidery on the sleeves. No doubt he thought he looked very fine.

'I am not happy you are here, Inspector,' Borġ said. His eyes were unfriendly. 'You've come to investigate the admiral's death? There is no need. It was a tragic accident, that is it.'

'But there has not been a conclusive verdict,' McQueen said. 'Lady Collingwood believes it requires further investigation.'

Borġ sighed. 'Typical of the English. They don't get the answer they want, they change the rules. The Maltese police are not good enough for Lady Collingwood, she runs to the governor, and now we have you. What can you do that we can't, hey?'

McQueen leant forwards. 'Well, one thing you need to get straight, Superintendent, is that I am Scottish, not English. I am from the Edinburgh police force. Let's be clear on that. I have my job to do. It's your job to provide me with answers.'

He dropped the police report onto the table.

'I've had a look at this, and it seems to me to be sadly lacking in detail. I have many questions. Perhaps you can enlighten me?'

Borġ raised his hands, an unpleasant smile on his face. 'Go on then, Inspector, ask.'

'Let's start with the list of guests that were there that night. Why have you not got statements from each of them?'

'We got as many as we needed. Why would we involve everyone? They were at a party; they didn't see anything.'

'But you don't know that if you don't ask. And look,' he turned the page and tapped the relevant section, 'there is nowhere near enough detail on the state of the body and where it was found. I would expect at least two pages on that alone.'

'Little to say. He was there, on the ground. Easy to see how he died.'

'And what about evidence of intoxication? You haven't

established how much the admiral had drunk during the evening.'

Borġ picked up a heavy paperweight and looked at it before putting it down again.

'Enough, Inspector. I don't need you to tell me what we should do. It is done. Case closed.'

McQueen held up his official letter.

'I beg to differ, Superintendent. I am here to investigate further. This warrant from the governor gives me authority. And I require your assistance to get to the truth.'

Borġ slammed his hand down on the desk.

'Sergeant Galea!' he roared.

The door opened immediately. A young man in police uniform stepped smartly in and saluted. Clearly on standby to obey orders, he looked every inch the keen young officer. 'Sir!'

'Inspector McQueen is leaving now.' Borġ lowered his voice to a growl. 'I am too busy for this... this *inkonvenjenza*. Sergeant Galea will take you to see Lady Collingwood now. You will soon find the truth is very simple.'

He waved his hands to dismiss them. McQueen stood up to leave.

'I need the post-mortem report first,' he said. 'I am going to see the police physician, to ask him about the findings. *Then* I will go to the villa.'

'I don't care what you do! Just leave; go. Galea, get him the report, then take him away.'

'Touched by your welcome, Superintendent.'

He left the office, Borġ staring at him with open hostility. *Not the best start to the investigation, but at least it was clear where they both stood.*

CHAPTER FIVE

D r Bonnići had just half an hour before his clinic to
prepare a mixture for one of his patients. The man –
Farruġia – was a bar-owner, a large bon-viveur in his late forties.
He had come in complaining that no matter how much he ate
and drank, he was constantly hungry and thirsty. He was tired
all day, up several times in the night and finding his vision was
blurry. Bonnići was concerned. He had tested the patient's
urine and from the sweet smell of it alone, there was no doubt
that he had diabetes mellitus. These were worrying symptoms,
and the only treatment was for Farruġia to cut back on food and
beer.

The medicine Bonnići was preparing was a tincture of
opium, to which he added fifteen drops of digitalis. The digitalis
was to strengthen the heart's contractions; the opium would
counteract it. Together these had been proven to reduce
appetite, and unless Farruġia took this, his impulses would lead
him to a drawn out death. Blindness and then loss of limbs
would gradually make his life difficult to endure. Bonnići did
not want Farruġia to join the nineteen patients on the diabetes
ward at the hospital. He belonged in his bar, with his loud laugh

and infectious good humour. Bonniċi finished counting the drops and wrote out the label.

A loud knock at the door made him look up. 'Come in.'

Sergeant Galea appeared, his youthful face full of self-importance.

'Dr Bonniċi. This is Inspector McQueen. Captain Borġ asked me to bring him to meet you.'

A sturdy figure stood behind him, appearing to fill the whole doorway. *The Scottish detective.* Bonniċi's heart lifted. Now, at last, he could share his thoughts on the Collingwood case. He had been looking forward to the arrival of the inspector from Edinburgh. Not only would he be an experienced detective to work with, but perhaps he would know some of the scientists from the renowned medical school, leading the way in forensic medicine. Bonniċi had so many questions he wanted to ask. But as McQueen moved forward to shake his hand, he felt something of a sense of disappointment.

The inspector was rather dishevelled in appearance. He was clearly far too hot in his tweed jacket and bowler hat, a ridiculous choice of outfit for the climate. His handshake, although strong, was warm and damp. Bonniċi surreptitiously wiped his hand on a cloth by his desk.

'Doctor,' McQueen said, a rolling "r" at the end of the word.

'Inspector,' Bonniċi said, thinking that the detective looked more like a farmer than a policeman. He had been expecting someone a little more refined. This person looked as though he would be more at home striding out across the fields with his clumsy big boots. *And brown clothes? Whoever wore thick brown clothes like that?* Bonniċi was fastidious about his own suits, which were well-fitted, pristine and black. He considered it the only colour that should be worn by a gentleman.

'Inspector McQueen needs to talk to you about the post-mortem report from the Admiral Collingwood case, Doctor,' Sergeant Galea said.

'Very well. Leave him with me – wait at the entrance until we're finished.'

Galea disappeared, leaving the two men alone.

Turning away, Bonniči opened the top drawer of his document cabinet and pulled out a brown folder. When he turned back, McQueen was roaming his eyes along the shelves, looking at all his bottles and potions. Casually, the detective pulled out a bottle of clear liquid and started reading the label. '*Idrossido di sodio concentrato*. What's this, then? Is it dangerous?'

'Put that back!' Bonniči snapped. 'It's sodium hydroxide. Causes severe burns.'

McQueen raised his eyebrows. 'Och, don't mind me,' he said, putting the bottle back on the shelf. He continued to turn a few of the bottles around, looking at their labels.

'Leave them. None of these bottles should be touched by anyone other than me, or my fellow dispensers.'

McQueen held his hands up. His casual air was irritating. Bonniči sensed a lack of respect. *Did he think he was some kind of provincial, dim-witted quack?*

'Here are my post-mortem examination notes,' Bonniči said, trying to keep his voice even. He placed the three pages, written in Italian, on the bench.

McQueen peered at them, then opened the report he had brought in with him. 'I have the English translation from the police office,' he said. He started to read from it: '"Admiral Lord Edward Collingwood. Seventy-four years old. Height, 5ft 10ins, weight 11 stone 8 lb, distinguishing marks – scar on right shoulder from old wound. Cause of death, fractured skull. Internal injuries – rupture of spleen, multiple rib fractures.

Pelvic fracture and fracture of femur." What you might call a mess.'

He looked up. 'I believe you saw the body in situ?'

'I did. I was the physician attending.'

'What did you find? I want to know all the details.'

Bonniċi felt as if he were being tested. He thought for a moment, taking his time. 'The admiral's body had descended from the roof at the back of the villa. Landed on the stone terrace below. Death would have been virtually instantaneous.'

'The position of the body. Was it as you would expect with a fall from that height?'

'Yes, absolutely. He landed on his back, skull fractured.'

'How soon did you get there?'

'By my calculations I arrived around one hour after the death. The blood was just starting to coagulate.'

'And when you examined the body, did you observe anything unusual at all? Anything that struck you as out-of-keeping?'

He hesitated slightly. 'Well, yes. There was one thing.'

'Go on, man.'

'It was his neck. His bow tie was disordered, loosened. I thought I could see some red marks, some bruising.'

'What? Did you not think to check this in the post-mortem?'

'Of course we did!' Bonniċi said. *Did he think they were fools?* 'Dr Girello is the chief surgeon. He performed the examination with my assistance. We looked closely at the neck. As well as the bruising, the hyoid bone was broken. An uncommon injury. It could have been caused in the fall, but it is unlikely. It's in my notes.'

'No, it's not,' McQueen said. 'I've read the report and there's no mention of the hyoid bone.'

'But it is there!' Bonniċi scanned his papers and thrust one of them under McQueen's nose. 'There, see! *Osso ioide – rotto.* Clear as daylight.'

McQueen looked at the notes, then looked back at the report he was holding.

'Well, it's not in this version.'

'Give it to me!'

Bonnići grabbed the English translation and checked it several times.

'I don't believe it. This translation has left out the whole section about the injuries to the neck.'

He felt sick. He also felt appalled, insulted. His and his esteemed colleague's work had been disregarded. It looked as though they had been careless, less than thorough. *The detective must see that this was not the case.*

McQueen sat back, arms behind his head. 'Well, well,' he said. 'We do seem to have found something interesting, don't we?'

Was the inspector mocking him?

'I have nothing to do with this! You can see that, surely!'

'I can see there has been a cover-up, that's for sure.'

Bonnići threw the papers down on the bench. 'You have to believe me! I have photographs – of the body.' He had not meant to tell him yet, but he felt goaded.

'Oh, yes? Captain Borġ didn't tell me anything about photographs.'

'I asked the photographer to come to the post-mortem, to record the victim's injuries.'

'Where are they? I want to see them.'

'They are at my house. Captain Borġ refused permission to use them at the inquest. He said there was no need.'

McQueen looked at him sharply. 'Are you sure? The superintendent withheld your evidence?'

'He did,' Bonnići said, trying to keep his tone neutral. He

had to be careful not to reveal too many of his thoughts about Borġ. *Not yet, anyway.*

'I need to see those photographs. Now.'

Bonniċi started to clear away his bottles. He was a police physician. He was not going to be spoken to in such a way.

'I regret, Inspector, that I don't have any more time to help you. I have a clinic to run.'

'But you have to show me the photographs.'

'Later,' he said, thinking quickly. 'Come to the Windsor Castle Hotel at five o'clock. I will bring them. And can you leave me the police report? I need to check some details.'

'Fine,' McQueen said. But his tone suggested he was less than happy.

Bonniċi put away the report, changed into his white coat and picked up his hat and his cane. He ushered the detective out of his laboratory and locked the door behind him. Then he made his way down the hospital corridor to his clinic, doing his best to disguise the weakness in his left leg.

CHAPTER SIX

The heat seemed to be mounting with every hour; the sun was white and intensely hot as it climbed the sky. It must have been ninety degrees when McQueen arrived at Villa Porto, the young sergeant in tow. He shaded his eyes as he climbed out of the *karrozin*. The home of the Collingwoods was situated on a hill in the village of Kalkara, the opposite side of Grand Harbour from Valletta. Almost white in colour, the grand frontage featured two rows of elegant columns and arches. Battling the heat, McQueen resented the long set of steps leading up from the street to the entrance. If the ornate fountain in the front garden was meant to impress, today it was lost on him.

They were met at the door by a woman in a black dress, grey hair pulled back sharply from her lined face. A chatelaine of keys hung from her waist; the housekeeper, he assumed. Galea spoke to her in Maltese – McQueen managed to pick out the words *polizija* and *spettur* – and she turned away, her face showing no emotion. She showed them into a drawing room and went to fetch her mistress.

The room was light and cool, with glazed tiles on the floor.

A fine Persian rug lay in the centre, with a plush green sofa and three armchairs of varied design around its edges. McQueen walked across to the fireplace to study the painting of a white-haired gentleman in full admiral's regalia: braided epaulettes, a red sash and at least ten medals. He had a tri-corn hat in one hand, the other hand was resting on a crimson chair. He read the plaque: *Admiral Lord Edward Collingwood, Commander-in-Chief of the Mediterranean Fleet 1858*. The deceased, then. Collingwood's eyes seemed to look down from the painting with scorn; his bearing suggesting that he considered himself worthy of high regard. Even without knowing of his reputation, McQueen felt he and the admiral would not have been the greatest of friends.

It was not long before Lady Collingwood appeared, with a young man by her side. Expecting a subdued widow, McQueen was surprised by her commanding presence. She was tall, sturdily built, wearing a mourning dress of rustling black silk. A cameo brooch was pinned to her collar and she held a black shawl around her shoulders. Her dark hair was piled up into neat curls. He judged her to be a great deal younger than her late husband, with an intelligent look and an attractive face possessed of well-defined, symmetrical features.

Ignoring Sergeant Galea, Lady Collingwood greeted him. 'Inspector McQueen?' She looked at him searchingly with sharp blue eyes. Judging by the minuscule movement of her mouth that passed for a smile, he did not think she was impressed with what she saw. He felt conscious of his damp collar and tweaked it away from his neck.

'I am so glad you're finally here,' she said. 'I've been waiting weeks. I've had so much trouble with the police; they simply won't listen to me.' She turned her eyes to Galea. 'You can wait in the kitchen, Sergeant.' He disappeared rapidly through the door.

Lady Collingwood introduced the young man by her side. 'This is Edmund,' she paused, 'now Baron Collingwood of Dereham, of course.'

The new Lord Collingwood looked nervous. He was tall, with the slight stoop of someone used to always bending down to speak to others. His light blue eyes blinked rapidly as he attempted a polite smile.

'How do you do?' he said.

McQueen had no idea how to address these English aristocrats. Perhaps he should have checked before setting out.

'Aye, well,' he said. 'Now I'm here, we'll get on, shall we? I need to know everything that happened in the lead-up to the admiral's death.'

Lady Collingwood indicated he should sit on the sofa. She sat firmly at one end and looked expectantly at the other, as if to keep him as far away from her as possible. He sat down and took out his pocketbook and pencil.

'It was the fifth of July, yes? Could you run through what happened on that night?' he asked.

'Well, Inspector, it was one of my soirées. We had twenty people here.'

'Nineteen, Mother,' said her son.

'Oh, yes – there's a list somewhere–'

'Who were these people?'

'A mixture really. Society people. Lord Davenport with his wife and daughters. They were on tour, staying in Malta for three weeks. And there were the Browns, and their daughters... Henry Arbuthnot and several gentlemen from the Chamber of Commerce, with whom my husband liked to discuss business.'

She stopped for a moment, to pull a lace handkerchief out from a pocket, under her shawl.

'There were also some Maltese guests. Wonderful Michele Tanti who owns the *Malta Post*, with his sister. His daughter

Maria came along – and her fiancé, the young lawyer. That strange priest Father Filippo, who I find rather depressing. He is always fawning over that rich widow *Sinjura* Spiteri, poor dear, she can hardly walk. And then there were some officers. Who were they, Edmund?'

'Lieutenant Simmonds, Captain Rushton and various others from the Royal Artillery, I believe.'

'We were a little low on ladies, which I was concerned about. There were only five who could play or sing, but then of course that didn't matter–'

'What happened, exactly, during the evening?' McQueen asked.

'The usual. We served the wine, we had conversation, and then we gathered to listen to the music.'

'Do you know at what time Lord Collingwood left the party?'

'Not exactly. Around ten thirty? When Lady Aurelia started to sing "Die Forelle". Edward really wasn't an admirer of Schubert. True to form I saw him slipping out of the room. It was his habit to go up to the roof to smoke a cigar, so I imagined that was what he was doing.'

'What was the interval between his departure and when he fell?'

'I have thought about this quite carefully and I think it may have been around half an hour. We had heard six Lieder – two songs from Lady Aurelia, three from Beatrice and one from Catherine. One of the officers was going to play a Beethoven sonata. He was just settling down and putting the music out when we heard this terrible screaming coming from the garden. It was the housekeeper. My God it was awful, I've never heard such a sound.'

She paused, her fingers tightening around the handkerchief.

'Some of the gentlemen rushed outside. They tried to stop

us from going out, but we did. We saw his body, just lying there on the terrace, in a pool of blood.'

She faltered and looked at Edmund. McQueen watched her carefully. The horror of the memory was momentarily reflected in her expression, but she quickly composed herself again.

'Well, there was no doubt he was dead,' she said. 'I looked up at the roof. I couldn't help but think someone must have been up there, but I couldn't see anything. It couldn't have been anyone from the soirée. They were all in the room when it happened. I remember thinking it was such a terrible, sudden way for him to die. After all the risks he took for his country.'

'What happened next?' McQueen prompted.

'Someone sent for the police, but it seemed to take forever for them to turn up. I think Henry sent a message to the governor, and that young man of his arrived – Carstairs, isn't it?' She looked to her son and he nodded.

'Captain Borġ and Carstairs dealt with everything from then on. The doctor came to certify the death, and eventually they took Edward's body away. On a cart, Inspector! Can you believe it? On a cart.'

She was silent for a moment, then shook her head as if to clear the image.

'After that, there were all the reports, and the inquest. That Carstairs was very useful and terribly polite, but the way he and the police have assumed it was an accident, it made my blood boil. It can't have been, Inspector, it just can't. Somebody did this to him, they must have. I need to know the truth.'

Her voice cracked slightly. McQueen was impressed by her composure, given the experiences she had gone through, but she could not quite hide her anger.

'There's something I wanted to ask,' he said. 'You said that everyone was in the room when it happened. How do you know that? How can you be sure?'

'I remember looking around, as we left the room. I couldn't swear to it, but I have a good memory. The only person who left the room, I'm sure, was Lord Collingwood himself.'

He noted this down in his pocketbook.

Edmund sat forward. 'Inspector, what are your plans?'

'For a start, I'll need that list of guests, and then I'll want to speak to everyone in the household. And naturally, I'll have a look outside.'

Lady Collingwood gathered herself, making it clear the interview was coming to an end.

'Keep me informed of your progress, Inspector,' she said. 'You can write to me here. I assume you know what you're doing.'

McQueen got up from the sofa.

'Just one more question,' he said. 'Did your late husband have any enemies, anyone who you think might have hated him enough to...?'

She looked at him sharply.

'My husband was a much-admired man,' she said. 'Any person in public life has enemies, but he certainly did not deserve any. There might have been some who wished him ill, but no one I know who would want to murder him. It must be someone from outside – an undesirable, I'm sure.'

She stood up, wrapping her shawl more firmly around her shoulders. 'My housekeeper will take you out to the garden. My butler Williams can gather the servants in the kitchen – ask him, will you, Edmund? And give the inspector that list.'

McQueen felt he had been thoroughly dismissed. For a moment he had glimpsed the real woman behind the haughty façade, the wife devastated by her husband's sudden death. But now she was retreating behind a wall of reserve. *Did she even believe he could solve the case?* She was not displaying much confidence so far. He snapped his pocketbook closed. The reputation of the Edinburgh Police rested with him. He looked forward to the challenge.

———

The new baron Edmund led him into the library and sat down at a heavy mahogany desk. McQueen took the seat opposite him and studied his face. He found that the young man could not look at him directly. He was exceptionally well dressed in a formal black suit, his fair hair brushed back from a high forehead. However, he did not look well; there were faint green-blue smudges under his eyes, and his skin looked grey.

'Let me find that list,' he said, pulling open a drawer and handing over a piece of paper with the guests' names on it, neatly written in perfectly formed letters.

McQueen cast his eyes over it. 'What can you tell me about these people?' he asked. 'Who did your father talk to on that night?'

'Well, at one point I heard him with Henry Arbuthnot. They were talking about some business deal or something. Didn't look like it was going very well.'

'So, they were arguing?'

'Er, I wouldn't say arguing exactly, but Arbuthnot was not at all happy.'

McQueen noted this down.

'Go on,' he prompted. 'Any other conversations you recall?'

'Umm, well there was Michele Tanti, the editor of the *Malta Post*. He was telling everyone how unfortunate it was that the Maltese aren't allowed to buy any of the new railway shares. He was getting quite het up, and Father told him he should be grateful for the opportunities the Maltese *do* have. Tanti's daughter Maria stepped in to try and lighten the mood, as she always does. Mama was very grateful.' Collingwood smiled a little at the memory. 'She gets a little vexed when her soirées don't go well.'

It did not sound as though the admiral was popular with his guests.

'And did you talk to your father at all?'

'Not really. He made me take over from him in a game of whist. He'd lost several hands. Said I should win back the family honour. I said I'd try, and I did win for a little while. But then I lost again. He was watching all the time, which was rather off-putting. Told me I wasn't bold enough, that I hadn't a clue how to play. Luckily, we were called over to listen to the music.'

'At which point your father went out of the room?'

Collingwood nodded. 'Yes, I saw him leave, but I thought nothing of it.'

'Who else was playing cards?'

'Lieutenant Simmonds, Captain Rushton and the lawyer, Micallef.'

McQueen made a few more notes.

'One more question. Did anything out of the ordinary happen at all on that day, either before or during the soirée?'

Collingwood went quiet, seeming reluctant to answer. He picked up the paper knife and twisted it in his hands. It had a short brass blade, clearly not sharp, as he ran his fingers down the edge. Eventually, he admitted, 'There was something, yes. An envelope was delivered to my father, earlier in the day. He opened it and glanced at the note, but he very quickly put it away again. I didn't see what it was, but he seemed momentarily rather annoyed.'

McQueen sat up straighter. 'Did you tell the police about this?'

'I did, yes.'

He wondered where the envelope was. *Had it been on the*

body? Did the police have it? Why had this not been in the report?

'What did you think was in the envelope?'

'I don't know.'

He could see Collingwood was holding something back. There was a slight hesitation before he answered.

'Come on, man. Don't tell me that you had no idea at all!'

'I, er, thought, perhaps a woman. I wanted to spare my mother, so I didn't tell her. She has enough to worry her.'

'Do you know for a fact he had lady friends?'

'I believe so, yes, but I have no proof.'

'And you have no idea who this woman was?'

'No.'

Collingwood sighed and put the paper knife down.

'Look, he wasn't perfect, but my father was a national hero. He was knighted for his part in the Crimean War, when he captained HMS *Agamemnon*. There was nobody braver, they said. I think he found it difficult to settle into normal life, after all his time at sea.'

He paused and McQueen prompted, 'In what way? What do you mean?'

'In all honesty, I barely knew him. And he could hardly bear to be around me. So, I have very little I can tell you.' His voice had a bitter note and McQueen was sure he had not meant to say so much. This unguarded, disillusioned side of him would be useful. McQueen decided to press the admiral's son on his feelings, using something of his own experience.

'I think I know what you mean,' he said. 'I've known for years that my father is disappointed with me, with my choice of profession. He was so much happier with my brother, who could do nothing wrong. Was that the problem with you and your father? What was your relationship with him like?'

Edmund looked up at the ceiling, somewhere above McQueen's head.

'Um, I wasn't exactly... I didn't exactly... well, let's just say that I didn't quite cut the mustard. I had to follow him into the Navy, but I didn't make it past the lowest rank. I was requested to leave, so you see, he couldn't quite forgive me for that. Not exactly following in his footsteps. My older brother, Richard, was the heir. He was very much like my father, a huge credit to him. He did go through the ranks and made it to captain. But he died in India, five years ago. Cholera. My father found it hard to accept that he had gone, that I was the only son he had left.'

He stared at McQueen, his pale eyes turning red and watery around the edges, as if daring him to say something. Clearly, he had spent his whole life feeling sorry for himself. McQueen doubted Edmund would have the gumption to even think about getting rid of his father, but nothing was impossible. *Could a fit of resentful rage have led to the father's death?*

McQueen stood up and walked over to a large globe on a brass stand. He spun it round and stopped it, looking to see which country was under his fingertips. Canada. Northwest Territories.

'So,' he said, slowly. 'You see your father receive a message, and you look the other way. You overhear him arguing with Colonel Arbuthnot, and you witness his exchange with Mr Tanti. He belittles you over the card game, and then you see him leave the room.'

He spun the globe again. Africa this time. The Cape Colony.

'Seems to me,' he said, 'as if you might be – relieved – at the news that your father had this accident? Is it not the case that you were rather pleased that he had been killed?'

'No – ah – absolutely not! It was a terrible shock.'

Collingwood shook his head and swallowed several times, his Adam's apple jumping up and down in his throat.

'I was thinking of my mother. She's suffered so much already. I wanted to protect her.'

'Indeed,' McQueen said. It seemed to him that the new Lord Collingwood was much better placed to look after his mother's interests now that his father was deceased. He would keep his mind open, perhaps ask some more questions about the young baron.

'Thank you, Lord Collingwood,' he said briskly. 'If you could show me out to the garden, that will be all for the moment.'

Outside, McQueen looked up at the villa, shielding his eyes from the blinding brightness of the sun. He could hear an incessant rasping sound from what sounded like an army of cicadas. Hard to believe they could make such a racket. There were gardens on all sides of the villa; formal designs with straight paths, raised flower beds, trees, classical statues and fountains. A terrace was wrapped around the house – around ten feet in depth – fashioned from blocks of limestone. He walked around it slowly, working out the layout.

Three sides of the villa featured first- and second-floor verandas. Doorways from most rooms meant that family and guests could step out onto a veranda to admire the gardens and the view. The first floor offered shade from the sun, the second floor the more impressive view from a height. The roof terrace would offer the best view of all.

Only the back of the villa did not have a veranda, just a flat wall between the terrace and the roof. From any other side, the admiral would have landed on the veranda just ten feet or so below him, rather than on the ground. McQueen looked up at the stone parapet on the edge of the roof. *How high was it? Would it be easy to lean forward and topple over by mistake?*

Sergeant Galea had come outside with the housekeeper, Mrs Trapani.

'Does she speak English?' McQueen asked. The sergeant spoke to her in Maltese. She shook her head and said something in reply.

'Only a little,' Galea said.

'You're going to have to translate.' He turned back to the housekeeper. 'Tell me what you heard and what you saw.'

As she told her story, she looked earnestly from one man to the other. Galea explained, 'She says she was in the kitchen when she heard a loud cry, then a heavy sound, like a sack of grain landing on the ground. She ran outside and found the admiral here on the terrace. Blood was coming out from his mouth. She screamed and people started coming out from the party.'

'Who were the first people out?' McQueen asked.

'Colonel Arbuthnot, *Sinjur* Tanti and *Sinjur* Micallef.'

He noted down their names. 'Then what happened?'

Mrs Trapani continued her account, making the sign of the cross several times as she spoke and wiping her eyes with her apron.

Galea continued, 'Tanti took everyone back inside. Colonel Arbuthnot stayed with the body. Then Lady Collingwood and Edmund came out and saw what had happened. They were shocked, very shocked. Police came.'

Mrs Trapani's face was drawn and there were dark circles around her eyes. McQueen guessed she had not been sleeping well since the incident. She watched him anxiously, her fingers fluttering at the sides of her apron.

'What else can you tell me?' he asked, sure she was holding something back.

'Nothing,' she said in English. 'I not know more.' He noticed her looking back towards the house. He made a few notes, saying to Galea as he wrote, 'Tell her that she can go, that we will leave it for now, but that I will be back with more questions soon.' He watched her face as Galea translated. She swallowed and nodded, a little miserably, before turning and going back indoors.

McQueen examined the terrace where the body had lain; he could make out a faded but distinct reddish stain on the ground. He picked up a few small stones, balancing them in his hand. He stepped back and looked up at the roof.

'Sergeant Galea,' he said after a few moments. 'What do you think about where the body landed?'

The young man paused, thought a little and then said, 'I don't know, sir.'

'Well, we need to measure the distance from the wall to this stain on the ground.'

He stepped to the side of the staircase.

'Hold this.' He took his surveyor's measuring tape out of his pocket, gave one end to Galea, then walked to the house. 'Eight feet from the wall.'

He went back to show the sergeant. 'Agreed?'

Galea nodded. 'Yes, sir.'

'We need to check from the roof, but it seems to me that a body falling by accident, losing balance and toppling over the parapet, should hit the ground somewhere between four and six feet away from the wall. Do you follow me?'

Galea nodded again, but without conviction.

'Well, the fact that it is this far from the wall indicates to me that there was some force propelling the body from the roof. I cannot believe this was not obvious to the police.'

'I don't know, sir. Perhaps we didn't...'

Galea tailed off, looking down at his feet.

'You might well look unhappy, sergeant, because by my reckoning it's already looking as if Lady Collingwood is right; we have a murder on our hands.'

CHAPTER SEVEN

McQueen and Galea made their way up through the villa to the roof. Here there was no shade, no escape from the sun. McQueen felt sweat prickling around the rim of his hat. From the back of the villa, he looked out over the edge and down to the terrace thirty feet below. The ground swam up towards him and he rested his hands on the parapet. Given what Bonnići had said about the likelihood of strangulation, perhaps there had been a struggle. He imagined himself in the position of an assailant, wrestling with the admiral and forcing him, conscious or unconscious, over the edge. The parapet was no more than thirty inches high; in McQueen's opinion it would not be impossible to manhandle a person over it.

He looked around for any indications of a scuffle, but there were none. He stood for a moment, thinking. He felt sure the admiral would not have stood to the rear of the roof, in the darkness. For a relaxing smoke, he would have wanted to look out over the water. McQueen walked across the rooftop to the front of the villa, where there was a fine view across a creek, then along to the right, where he could see Grand Harbour. *This was where Collingwood would have stood.* He checked the terrace floor, along the parapet, and turned up several discarded cigar ends, partially covered with dust. He picked them up, rolled them into his handkerchief and handed them to Galea. 'Keep those for me, will you?' he asked, thinking to check them later. 'They might well be significant. Even more reason to believe the admiral did not accidentally fall. He clearly stood on this side of the terrace, not at the back.'

He looked out at the view of the harbour. Around twenty ships were currently anchored there, with dozens of small boats clustered around them. 'Big business, supplying the Navy,' he commented.

'Yes, sir,' Galea said. 'My father and my uncle sell oil for lanterns. It is an important market for them. All the Army barracks as well.'

Across the creek, fortified walls and a colossal fort guarded the docks. To the right, McQueen could see Grand Harbour and the city of Valletta. The entrance to the harbour was not far away, and beyond that lay the open sea. It gave him a sense of how important the island was, situated on the main sea route along the Mediterranean. Now, with the Suez Canal, all sea trade and warships could get through to the Middle East and India. Almost all had to stop at Malta's port to take on coal and provisions. No wonder the British Navy was obsessed with protecting it. A man like Admiral Collingwood represented the very pinnacle of power on the island. *What had he done – who had he provoked – to lead someone to murder him?*

Suddenly, a loud boom cut through the sound of the cicadas buzzing. Across the harbour a thin plume of smoke rose up into the azure sky.

'The noonday gun,' Galea explained. 'People go and watch from Upper Barrakka Gardens.'

Just like the one o'clock gun from Edinburgh Castle, McQueen thought. Keeping the regiments in line and making sure everybody's clocks and watches were set to the right time. It reminded him of how hungry he was.

'Let's go and talk to the servants,' he said, keen to get out of the sun.

In the kitchen, the servants were gathered gloomily under the eye of Williams, the butler.

'Ah, here he is,' Williams announced portentously, in a rich Welsh accent. A stout figure, he was in tails, with a white shirt and a white bow tie. His hair was just starting to go grey at the temples and he had bushy dark whiskers and eyebrows. His authoritative air was slightly marred by a wandering eye, which kept drifting off to the left.

'The servants are all here, Inspector.'

'Thank you, Mr Williams,' McQueen said, trying to ignore the drifting eye. He quickly scanned the people in front of him. As well as the housekeeper there were ten other servants. Mentally, he assigned them their roles: the smartest and most self-important would be the lady's maid and the valet, then there were two footmen in uniform, the cook with her big apron, the kitchen and scullery maid, and finally the lowly housemaids and the houseboy, a smudge of blacking on his cheek.

'I am Inspector McQueen, and this is Sergeant Galea,' he said. 'We are here to talk to you about the night of the fifth of July. The night the admiral died. How many of you were on duty during the soirée?'

'If I may, Inspector,' Williams interjected. 'The younger ones were not on duty later that night – that's Camilleri, Farruġia, Agius and Mifsud. They are Maltese – they probably won't understand you.'

McQueen gritted his teeth at the butler's high-handed attitude.

'Right – you four go with Sergeant Galea,' he said.

He watched as three of the maids and the houseboy went over to join the sergeant. The houseboy was clowning around, pushing and shoving the girls. Clearly, he loved the distraction from normal duties. One of the maids, a tiny girl with huge dark eyes, seemed to be trying hard not to be noticed. She kept her eyes well averted from McQueen, hiding behind another girl. He made a note to talk to Galea about her later.

'Sergeant, take a statement from each of them. Ask them if they heard or saw anything that night.'

Galea nodded. 'Yes, sir.'

After they had gone, Williams said, 'The rest of the servants apart from Mrs Trapani are British, so you won't have any problems with us.'

'I'll be the judge of that,' McQueen said.

One by one, he interviewed the members of the group, and one by one they told him that no, they had not heard anything until the housekeeper screamed, that it had all been as normal during the soirée, and no, they hadn't seen the admiral go up to the roof. One of the footmen had seen him leaving the drawing room when the music had started. He said Lord Collingwood had nodded at him and put his finger to his lips as he slipped out of the room, as if to say, "don't tell anyone". When asked how much the admiral had been drinking, the footmen said they hadn't noticed, maybe one or two glasses of wine and a port? Not much more. They were all shocked by what had happened.

The butler knew exactly how much his master had drunk during the evening: four glasses of wine – the Beaune 1874 – and then two glasses of Ramos Pinto port. 'That was very much his usual, Inspector. Lord Collingwood appreciated a good burgundy. It was no more and no less than his habitual amount.'

'How did he seem when last you saw him?'

'I was on my way up from the cellar when I saw him at the foot of the stairs. I assumed he was on his way up to the roof for a smoke. It was around that time in the evening. He was completely steady. He did say something to me, but I cannot remember exactly what. Something like, "There'll be the devil to pay…" I think he just meant Lady Collingwood would be displeased that he left the room early.'

'What time was this?' McQueen asked, making notes.

'Ten thirty exactly,' Williams replied. 'I know because the longcase clock in the hall chimed on the half-hour.'

'And did you see anyone else leave the drawing room after the admiral?'

'Well, no, Inspector, but I was occupied with making sure the footmen were doing their jobs, keeping the glasses replenished. Gentlemen do drink a great deal, you know. But I am certain that everybody was there when the admiral's body was found.'

McQueen had difficulty knowing whether Williams was looking at him or somewhere over to the left. He also had no idea whether the butler was speaking the truth or not, but on the face of it the story tallied with Lady Collingwood's account. He closed his pocketbook. 'That will do for now, Mr Williams,' he said. 'Now, what does a man have to do to get a bite to eat around here?'

As McQueen tucked into some bread and cheese laid out by Mrs Trapani, Galea returned, looking highly pleased with himself.

'So, Sergeant, how did you get on with your interviews?' McQueen asked, through a mouthful of bread. 'Did you find out anything new?'

'Yes, sir! I think so. The houseboy says he saw someone in

the garden, just as he was going off duty. You think it could be the killer, sir?'

God damn it, why was this coming out now? McQueen despaired. *The police had not even thought to interview all the servants. It was downright incompetence.*

'Tell me more. What time was this? What did this person look like? What did they do? This is important, man!'

Galea consulted his notes. 'It was around nine o'clock. The boy saw a person going across the garden to the kitchen door, trying not to be seen.'

'Why did he not say anything before?'

'He said he had gone outside for a smoke, which he is not allowed to do. He didn't want to get into trouble.'

'Bring him here, now!'

The houseboy was around twelve or thirteen, on the brink of adolescence. He had a cheeky air, which he was having trouble subduing. He looked at the policemen with bravado, highly aware of the importance of what he was saying.

'Ask him his name,' McQueen ordered. 'And get him to tell you exactly what he saw again.'

Galea translated the boy's responses. His name was Pawlu, and he was sorry he didn't say anything before, but nobody asked. It was dark, too dark to see well. But it was a stranger, a man, with long hair. A bit wild looking. He ran across the garden and into the house through the kitchen.

After giving his account, the boy stood smirking, as if waiting to be congratulated. But McQueen was far too irritated that this essential, hugely significant piece of information had only just been revealed. He stared at the lad fiercely.

'You'd better be telling me the truth, young man,' he warned. 'If I find you've made any of this up, you will be taken to the magistrate. As it is, we will have to tell Mr Williams what you have been doing. Let's hope he will be lenient with you.'

The boy had the grace to look a little more subdued as he was led away by Sergeant Galea.

When they were about to leave, McQueen remembered the young maidservant he had noticed, who had gone out to speak to Galea. 'Who was the young lass who looked like a frightened mouse?'

'That's my cousin,' Galea said. 'Her name is Ċensa.'

'Did you get a statement from her?'

'No, she wouldn't talk to me. Not a word.'

'Go and fetch her,' McQueen said. 'I want to speak to her.'

Galea disappeared and came back after a few minutes with the maid. She looked no more than fourteen or fifteen. Her dark hair was pinned up underneath a white cap. She wore a plain black dress covered by an apron, hanging from her tiny frame. Galea said something to her and she sat down reluctantly. He did not seem to think much of her, judging by the dismissive way he said, 'She does not speak English, sir.'

'Just ask her again if she saw anything that night,' McQueen said.

She shook her head vehemently when Galea asked the question. He did not think she was going to say anything, but then a torrent of words came spilling out, at the end of which she twisted away and ran out of the room. McQueen looked at Galea questioningly.

He shrugged. 'She is a silly girl. Makes no sense what she says. She does not know if she saw something or not.'

McQueen was unimpressed. 'Go and fetch her back again,' he said. 'Tell her she has to talk to us.'

Galea went after Ċensa and brought her back in, pulling her by the wrist. She was crying and hiding her face. He sat her down again. 'She is a strange girl, sir, her mother always says so. I do not think we should take notice of her.'

'Nonsense,' McQueen said. 'Ask her again if she saw anything. Give her a handkerchief and tell her to pull herself together. It's important that we hear the truth, whatever it is.'

She listened to Galea and mopped her face. Then she sat upright. Staring straight in front of her she intoned her story, then she gave Galea back his handkerchief, a sullen look in her eyes.

'She says she was in bed the whole time and she didn't hear anything until the scream. She looked out of the window, but she didn't see anything. She was too scared to go downstairs so she only found out what happened when Mrs Trapani came up later.'

Why all this palaver when there was nothing to tell? Was she frightened? McQueen was frustrated by the language barrier, convinced he was not being told the whole story. He would have to revisit the household, to find out more about what was going on. A long-haired stranger seen crossing the garden and going into the house. Surely *someone* knew who it was? He would need some leverage, a way to prise the truth out of them. *This could well be the person who threw the admiral from the roof.*

'All right,' McQueen said, dismissing Censa with a wave of his hand. 'I think we have done all we can here. Are you ready to go back?'

'Yes, sir,' Galea said. 'It's nearly siesta time now. Nothing will happen until four.'

As the *karozzin* pulled away, McQueen turned to look back at the villa. On the second floor he saw a shadowy face – it looked like Mrs Trapani – watching them at the window.

After a swift beer, McQueen picked up his bag from his hotel and set off for Strada Ponente. All the shops and houses were shuttered up and the streets were deserted. Beggars and ne'er-do-wells lay curled up in the shade of walls and under benches. A sense of torpor hung over the whole city. As he trudged along, McQueen felt sweat trickling down his back, as well as the sides of his face. He cursed his heavy suit.

Eventually, he found his lodgings at the end of a terrace of four-storey town houses and knocked at the door. He stood waiting, noticing how well the brass knocker was polished, listening for sounds of life inside. Finally, he heard someone approaching and the door was opened by a weary woman who was holding a tea towel, flour on her hands. She was dressed plainly, all in black, dark hair pulled loosely away from an attractive face. She stared at him blankly for a moment. Then, seeming to recognise him, she stepped back slightly, her hand tightening on the edge of the door. He realised with a jolt that he had seen her before, the previous evening, lighting a candle in the church.

He felt like a fool. His new landlady, and he had already got on the wrong side of her. He remembered the harsh look she had given him. He held up the scrap of paper from Carstairs and tried to sound reassuring.

'*Sinjura* Caruso? I'm Sam McQueen, from the police. Lieutenant Carstairs sent me, he said you had lodgings?'

She stared at him without speaking. He could understand how strange he must seem, first appearing out of the blue at the service, and now here on her doorstep. He decided to brazen it out, as if the moment in the church had never happened.

'I'm just here for a wee while, working on a case. I'll not be any bother. You have got a room for me, yes?'

She still did not say anything and he wondered if he had got the whole situation wrong.

'You do speak English, don't you?' he asked, finally.

This snapped her out of her silence.

'Yes, of course,' she said in a quiet, flat voice. At that moment she seemed to make up her mind, reluctantly opening the door wider to allow him in.

'I do have room. Come in, please. This way.'

She led him up two flights of stairs to the third floor of the building. She moved with a light step, making McQueen aware of his heavy boots. She showed him into a room at the front.

The room had an enclosed wooden balcony, projecting out over the street. McQueen wandered over to the balcony window and looked out. To the right, he could just about glimpse the sea. He turned back towards *Sinjura* Caruso and put his bag on the floor.

'This will do nicely, thank you,' he said.

The room was large and bare, but clean. The floor was pleasantly tiled with an intricate pattern of yellows, greens and pinks, the walls a whitewashed stone. The bed had been made and a washbasin and jug stood on a chest of drawers, with a pile of cotton towels next to them. The silence was unsettling, as *Sinjura* Caruso stood there, looking anywhere but at him.

At that moment, the front door slammed and there was the sound of someone rapidly running up the stairs. A child's voice was calling out, '*Ma! Ma!*' followed by a stream of Maltese, in which McQueen thought he could hear "*Ingliz*". A boy came careering around the corner into the room, saw McQueen and stopped short. He stared up at him with big round eyes. Around ten years old, he had untidy black hair and was wearing a white shirt and brown knee breeches. His feet were bare and grubby.

McQueen offered the boy his hand.

'Sam McQueen,' he said. 'Not English, Scottish!'

'My son, Antonio,' *Sinjura* Caruso said, nudging him

forwards. Antonio shook McQueen's hand and thought for a moment before saying in careful English, 'How do you do?'

'How do you do?'

McQueen reached into his waistcoat pocket and gave him a sweet, left over from his journey. 'Now, this is for you. It's called tablet, and it's from Scotland, which is my country. Try it – eat!'

Antonio looked at his mother for approval and when she nodded, he tentatively nibbled the corner. Instantly, his face lit up with a huge grin.

'I like tab-let,' he said. 'Thank you, Mister–'

'McQueen.'

'Mac – kveen?'

'Yes, indeed. And where am I from?'

'Uhh... Scot-land?'

'Yes! Well done, lad. I can see we're going to get on famously.'

Sinjura Caruso placed her arm on the back of Antonio's shoulders and started to lead him out of the room.

'Thank you,' she said with the beginnings of a smile. 'We leave you – it is time for rest. Dinner is at seven.'

Antonio poked his head back as he was going out of the door. 'Goodbye, Mister Mac-kveen' he said. 'I learn good English, yes?'

McQueen laughed.

'Yes, lad, I'll teach you – and you can teach me Maltese.'

When they had gone, without even unpacking his Gladstone bag, he dropped onto the bed. In an instant he was fast asleep.

CHAPTER EIGHT

McQueen awoke two hours later, feeling groggy, wondering where the hell he was. It took a full five minutes and a splash of cold water for him to remember about his meeting with Doctor Bonnići. He had only a quarter of an hour to get to the café. Grabbing his jacket and hat, he headed out, the extreme mugginess of the air hitting him as soon as he stepped outside the front door.

Already familiar with his route, he started walking up Strada Arcivescovo. He was surprised to see how many people were out and about. At one o'clock the streets had been all but deserted. Now, there were Maltese men appearing from all directions, heading towards the city centre, chatting loudly to one another and passing around printed sheets. From close by, he could hear the unmistakeable sound of a gathering crowd. It was a low drone like a swarm of bees, with occasional shouts and laughter breaking through the buzz. His senses prickled; something was in the air. He picked up his pace.

Turning the corner, he saw that Saint George's Square was filling up with hundreds of people. A rostrum had been set up on the north side of the square, and a crowd was gathering in front of it – perhaps it was a political gathering? A thickset man in a black cap and shirtsleeves bumped into him and muttered '*Scusa*'. McQueen stopped him. 'What's happening?' he asked, nodding towards the rostrum.

The man thrust a leaflet at him. '*Partito Anti-Riformista. Grupp politiku,*' he muttered, before disappearing back into the crowd. McQueen glanced at the sheet and read *Il Diritto di Malta*, written in Italian.

The café was on the other side of the square. He found Bonniċi sitting inside at a corner table, sipping a coffee. As he sat down opposite him, he was amused to see how immaculate the doctor looked; his collar starched and white and a diamond pin in his smart grey cravat. His hair was shiny with pomade and his face smooth as if he had recently shaved. McQueen even caught a whiff of cologne as they shook hands. Very different to the police physicians he had worked with in Scotland, who took more of a plain and practical approach to their appearance. Perhaps the occasional scrub with some carbolic soap, but that would be it.

'What's going on out there?' he asked. 'Is it a rally?'

'It is,' Bonniċi said. 'I don't think it will last long. It's a new political group, calling themselves the Anti-Reform Party. They are angry because they say the British want to stop us using the Italian language.'

McQueen knew from his guidebook that the day-to-day language for the islanders was Maltese, but the language of the wealthy, the law courts and the university was Italian, and had been for over two hundred years.

'Is that something new?' he asked.

Bonniċi shrugged. 'There is a recent report recommending that English should be taught in all our schools. It makes good sense to me. But part of the population is getting agitated. They don't like change, and they don't like being told what they can or cannot do.' His tone was neutral, neither friendly nor hostile.

McQueen wondered if Bonniči was going to be more helpful than he had been when they'd met earlier. He felt they had not got off to a good start.

'Thank you for meeting me,' he offered.

The doctor smiled slightly. He seemed calm, very much in control. He called the waiter over and ordered more coffee and some pastries. Then he put an envelope on the table.

'I have brought the photographs,' he said.

He cleared some space, moving cups, spoons and sugar out of the way. He opened up the envelope and pulled out four photographs, 8½ by 5¼ inches, laying them carefully out on the table. There were four close-up images, showing the cadaver's head and shoulders from different angles.

McQueen took his time, studying them. He felt strangely removed from the situation; here he was looking at a body that had once been alive, yet it meant nothing to him. Collingwood lay on the autopsy table, stripped of clothing, eyes disturbingly open, white hair pulled back by gravity from his face. An old man, grey and lifeless. Nothing to connect him to the haughty personage portrayed in the drawing room painting.

'Here,' Bonniči said, handing McQueen a magnifying glass. 'You should be able to see some marks.'

McQueen held the glass over the neck on the first of the images. There were faint smudges on each side that looked like they could be bruises, and a dark shadow over the Adam's apple. It was indeed possible that two thumbs had been used to throttle the victim.

'Most useful,' he said. 'I've not seen photographs used in this way before.'

'I think it is eminently sensible to use photographs to record injuries. I am intrigued by the work happening in Paris, where they are beginning to photograph murder victims. Normally, as you know, photographs are only used to keep a record of criminals' faces.'

'Well, I agree with you that this does suggest foul play. Captain Borġ should have allowed these photographs as evidence.'

He put them back in the envelope, aware that other people in the café would be able to see the grisly pictures.

'There's something else that's bothering me,' he said. 'Wasn't there anything that struck you as strange about where the body landed?'

Bonniċi thought for a moment. 'No, I have seen this kind of accident any number of times,' he said. 'Usually when people have been drinking. Only last year there was a British soldier killed when he fell from the roof. It is always the same, so many bones are broken. Either the head fractures or the heart simply tears apart and ceases to function.'

'But how did he end up so far from the building? Think about where the edge of the roof is, and where he landed. This is a fair way out, so he must have been thrown off with some force. He *cannot* simply have toppled over.'

Bonniċi looked to be considering the facts. 'You may have a point,' he said, after a short pause. 'I was only interested in physical causes of death, not how he came to land in that particular place.'

'I've worked it out here,' McQueen said, pulling out his pocketbook. He opened it to the page where he had sketched out the back of the villa, mapping out the body's trajectory. 'Look, he weighed eleven-and-a-half stone, yes? The height of the building is thirty feet. The body landed eight feet away from the building.'

He tapped his pencil over his calculations.

'I believe the force needed to reach this distance suggests he was pushed or thrown from the roof.'

He thought he caught a glimmer of approval in Bonniċi's eye when he looked up from the pocketbook.

'Interesting,' the doctor said. 'But difficult to prove.'

'Aye, but I've also talked to the butler and the other servants, and they have given statements saying the admiral was not drunk. I think we can make the case that this was most likely to be foul play.'

The waiter appeared with the coffees and pastries, and Bonniċi moved the envelope to make room on the table.

'Borg does not want to do any more investigating,' Bonniċi said, dropping two lumps of sugar into his coffee and stirring it. 'He would prefer to keep the inquiry closed.'

McQueen copied Bonniċi, then tried the coffee. It was disgustingly bitter with a strange flavour, unknown spices floating on the surface. He pulled a face and added more sugar.

'Too late for that,' he said. 'Is he covering something up? Or is he just lazy?'

Bonniċi cleared his throat. He put the police notes on the table. 'I am afraid he is covering something. There is other evidence we found at the scene, which does not appear in this report.'

'What?'

'Sergeant Galea found a brooch, near to the body. It had the eye from a peacock's tail on it. There is no mention of it here.'

'This is ridiculous! How the hell can I do my job if Borg won't even share significant evidence? He will not get away with this.'

Bonniċi looked at him sharply. 'Be careful,' he said. 'Borg is a powerful man. It is not a good idea to cross him.'

McQueen took a bite out of one of the pastries. It was savoury, filled with soft cheese, and very good. It made a mess, flakes of pastry falling everywhere. He licked his fingers before wiping them on a napkin.

He relished the idea of a challenge. He could see how the police chief could have delusions of grandeur. *A big fish in a small pond.*

'Aye, well,' he said. 'Maybe it's not a good idea to cross *me*. I'm here to find out the truth, whatever that takes.'

'You don't know how things work in Malta, Inspector. You'll find Borġ has a lot of influence,' Bonnići said.

So far, McQueen felt he was not going to get much help from anybody. He had to assert his position, set up a team for the investigation. The police physician could be useful. He seemed at least to be willing. Certainly, he was more amenable than the last time they had met.

'I'll go and see the magistrate and request he officially opens up the inquiry again, and allows me to see all the evidence. I'll ask him to keep you on the case.'

Bonnići gave him a card. 'Here's my address,' he said. 'Send me a message, either at the hospital or at my house, if I can help.'

The noise from the square was getting much louder. McQueen could hear drumbeats and chanting. He felt his instinct as a police officer to go and see what was going on.

'Thank you,' he said. 'Are we done here?'

'Yes,' Bonnići said. 'You can keep the photographs.' He paid the waiter and McQueen grabbed the last pastry from the plate as they left.

While they had been at the café, the crowd had trebled, if not quadrupled in size. McQueen estimated there were over a thousand people packing out the square. Nearly all of them were men, dressed in brown cotton trousers, white shirts, waistcoats and black caps. A few women, cloaked in black *għonnielen,* looked on from the sides. The drums were being played by a group of boys. They played the same rhythm over and over, a cue for the crowd to call out, 'Rizzo! Rizzo!'

'They are calling for Francesco Rizzo,' explained Bonnići. 'He is the leader of the Anti-Reform Party. Come with me. We can watch from over there. I'd like to hear what he has to say.'

They skirted around the crowd. It was a little cooler, but still a residual heat rose from the pavement. There was no breeze and a smell of food and perspiration hung over the square. This, combined with the sound of the drums, made McQueen feel uneasy. He was glad to have Bonnići with him as they made their way to the front of Main Guard – the building opposite the Governor's Palace. It might help him to make sense of what was going on.

They stopped behind one of the pillars in front of Main Guard. A group of thirty British soldiers was standing nearby, wearing blue uniforms with white pith helmets. They were holding rifles by their sides, but they did not seem overly concerned. Every now and then one would make a comment to his colleague, as they watched what was happening. They looked young to McQueen; young, pale and very English.

The noise from the crowd grew louder and he watched as three men approached the rostrum and stepped up onto it, to a resounding cheer. The man in the middle raised his hand to acknowledge them, then stepped forward. Short and stout, he made an unlikely leader. He had an avuncular air about him, with his formal, smart clothes and bushy dark moustache. But when he spoke, his rich, booming voice gave him real presence.

'Rizzo is a well-known lawyer,' Bonnići said. 'Good at persuasion.'

Naturally, McQueen could not understand what Rizzo was saying, even though he was speaking in Italian as well as

Maltese. Noticing this, the doctor translated as Rizzo declaimed:

'People of Malta. Have you seen that the governor wants to stop us using the Italian language? The language of the law, and medicine, the foundation of our society? Have you seen that the British propose to teach only English to our children at our schools?'

There was a pause as the crowd shouted, '*No! No!*'

'*Come osano?*' Rizzo continued.

'How dare they?' Bonniċi translated. 'We must stop this. Malta is our country; we should be able to determine the language we want to speak. We love the Maltese language, but we also love the beautiful language of Italy. It is our heritage, it places us where we are meant to be, next to our neighbours in Southern Europe.'

McQueen scanned the faces of the men in the crowd. Animated and in thrall to the speaker. Some were holding banners and flags, which they waved enthusiastically at each pause. Rizzo was a good orator, keeping them in the palm of his hand.

The speech went on for a good while, but eventually the leader stopped with a flourish, holding up his hands. '*Chiediamo i nostri diritti!*'

'What did he just say?' McQueen asked.

'We demand our rights,' Bonniċi explained. 'We demand a greater part of government, and we demand our voice.'

Rizzo stepped back to great applause. Then a younger-looking man took over. Much less smartly dressed, he had a ferocity of manner very different to the leader. He stood right at the front of the rostrum and raised his fist. '*Malta e' dei Maltesi, non degli Inglesi. Fuori lo straniero!*' he cried.

'Malta belongs to the Maltese, not to the English. Out with

the foreigners.' Bonniċi repeated the words, with an awkward sideways glance at McQueen.

The young man had long unkempt hair and wild eyes. McQueen felt the mood changing immediately, as though people had been waiting for this younger firebrand to raise the stakes. Men at the front of the crowd followed his lead and started chanting in Maltese. *"Neħilsu mill-barranin!"* Gradually, the call spread until the whole square resonated with the cry, *'Neħilsu mill-barranin!'*

Conscious that he stood out because of his height and colouring, McQueen stepped back into the shadows. Bonniċi was alert too, looking around with an air of concern. The soldiers tensed, responding to the change in atmosphere. One of the senior officers came out of the guardhouse. 'Hold back for now,' he ordered. 'Do not do anything unless I give the signal.'

The young man jumped down from the rostrum and started mingling with the crowd, moving amongst it, shaking hands and giving out leaflets. The gathering started to dissipate, men walking away, reading the sheets and talking loudly. But around Main Guard, a group of young men had turned their attention to the soldiers standing guard. They baited them, calling out *'Hej, Ingliżi!'* The soldiers refused to be drawn and stood stock-still, eyes front. The youths grew bolder and started to throw stones, some of which hit their targets. McQueen got ready to intervene, but before he could step in, the commanding officer took charge. 'Rifles at the ready!' he ordered. They raised their weapons and aimed at the youths.

'If you proceed any further, I will order my men to fire,' shouted the captain, who had gone red in the face. There was a little more posturing and shouting from the youths, but then they backed away and sloped off, throwing black looks behind them.

Bonnići pulled McQueen's sleeve and motioned him to move away.

'Let's leave them to it.'

As they started to walk back towards the south of the square, they heard a shout of 'English pig!' behind them, and McQueen felt a thud as a stone hit him in the middle of his shoulders. He whipped around, ready to lay into whoever had thrown it, but at the same time Bonnići stepped forwards, holding up his police badge.

'Leave him!' he called out. 'He is with me, with the police.'

They saw a couple of youngsters turning tail, then running away, laughing.

'It's all right,' Bonnići said. 'They are only boys.'

'I'm glad you stopped me. I'd have walloped them for calling me English.'

'Why? Do you dislike the English? I did not know that.'

'Oh aye, our countries have a long history. Have you had trouble like this before?'

'Not for a long time. Not since the governor tried to cancel Carnival over thirty years ago. I am surprised.'

As they reached the end of the square, McQueen looked behind him again. A scuffle had started in the middle of the remaining crowd. Four police officers in uniform had grabbed the young man who had stirred up the crowd. He was shouting and struggling as they marched him away. McQueen wondered what he would be charged with.

Malta was not proving to be the quiet island paradise he had been expecting. The anger felt by the Maltese people against the colonial government was palpable. He had also seen the Army ready to suppress the protesters. *Would they have fired on them?* Unlikely, but there was always the possibility. Instinctively, he did not want to ally himself with British imperialist control, but he could not pretend to know or understand the Maltese people yet. It was an uncomfortable position to be in.

The atmosphere was still charged as he parted company with Bonniċi, but it was beginning to calm down.

'I'm going to see the magistrate now,' he said. 'Strike while the iron's hot.' He jabbed his thumb back towards the square. 'Interesting afternoon entertainment.'

Bonniċi smiled slightly. 'Indeed.'

McQueen watched as the doctor walked away, only occasionally using his cane, his hat placed most exactly on his head. *An intriguing man*, he thought. Perhaps there was more to him than he had first imagined.

He headed for the police office. As he stood in the foyer, he saw the young speaker being taken to the cells, still struggling and cursing. A voice behind him said, 'Oh dear, tsk, tsk.'

He turned around to see Captain Borġ. 'That young man is always getting himself in trouble,' the superintendent said, his lips curled in amusement. 'Now, Inspector, what can we help you with?'

'I'm here to see the magistrate. I have new evidence to present, to restart the inquiry.' McQueen held up the envelope of photographs, enjoying the flash of anger that crossed Borġ's face, wiping his smile from it.

'He cannot be disturbed. You will have to come back in the morning. And you'd better have something good; he will not be happy.'

McQueen went back to his lodgings for dinner. *Sinjura* Caruso had prepared a pungent rabbit stew. He was not sure if he liked it, but the bread was good. He sat alone in the dining room. It was dark and sombre, with just one oil lamp to light the room.

The table was heavy mahogany, with a lace cover over a plain felt cloth. On the sideboard opposite him, he could see a large silver crucifix, next to a family photograph in a black frame. He went over to have a closer look: *Sinjura* Caruso was seated, baby Antonio on her lap and her husband standing by her side, one hand in his pocket. A handsome young man, pride etched on his face.

When *Sinjura* Caruso came in to collect his plate he nodded towards the photograph. 'Your late husband?' he asked. 'He looks like a good man.'

She stopped, looking down. 'Yes, he was good,' she said. 'A ship's captain. It is sad. Lost at sea. Antonio was three when he died. He does not know him, *jaħasra*.'

'My condolences. It must be difficult.'

She picked up his plate. 'It is,' she said. 'Every day I look at Antonio, I think of my husband and worry about what will happen.'

McQueen felt sorry for her as he watched her go back into the kitchen. She moved elegantly, closing the door behind her with a swish of her skirts. *A fine-looking woman. She should not have to fend for herself.* He reached for the bottle of wine. It tasted of filth, but he poured himself another glass and downed it. He sat drinking until the bottle was empty.

CHAPTER NINE

Wednesday, 4 August 1880

Doctor Bonniċi hesitated on the steps leading down to the cellar. The odour from the street was bad enough, but he feared it would be even worse inside. He pulled out his handkerchief and held it over his nose and mouth. He had to go in; there was no one else who could help.

He had been interrupted at breakfast that morning by a rapping at the door. He heard his housekeeper remonstrating with someone – a woman – who was clearly in distress. He came out of the dining room, brushing crumbs from his jacket with a napkin. 'Sorry to disturb you, *Dottore*,' said his housekeeper. 'I am explaining to this person that she needs to go to the hospital and wait for you there.'

The woman, dressed in a ragged grey gown, had pulled away from the housekeeper and thrown herself at him, clutching at his hand.

'*Duttur*, please come quickly, it's my husband. He has the fever.'

The wretchedness of her condition and the desperation in her voice had cut right through him. 'All right,' he had found himself saying. 'I will come.'

At the bottom of the steps, he went in cautiously through the doorway. It was so dark that at first, he could make nothing out. He could hear children pushing each other around and whispering, on one side of the room. As his eyes adjusted, he could see there were four or five of them, all very small. The woman took him over to see her husband.

The sick man was lying on a filthy bed of rags. The floor was tacky, with an overwhelming smell of sewage. A pail stood nearby, uncovered, full of human waste. Bonniči almost vomited. He held the handkerchief even tighter against his mouth. He forced himself to focus on the patient.

The man was clearly extremely ill. His eyes were rolling upwards and he was delirious. He muttered constantly, twisting from side to side in pain.

Bonniči took out his stethoscope and listened to the man's heart. It had a weak and irregular beat.

'How long has he been like this?' he asked.

'Close on two weeks, *Duttur*. I thought he was getting better, but last night he got much worse.'

'Has he been coughing?'

'Yes.'

'Stomach ache? Headache?'

'Yes.'

'Why have you not got any water?' he asked. 'It's important to have fresh water. And you need to take this waste away.'

'The pump is at the end of the street,' she said. 'I haven't got the strength to carry the water or the pail.'

'There should be a courtyard, with water supplied in a tap!'

'It is not working. I know it is bad.' She showed him the

courtyard, which had become a stable, home to a pair of goats. It stank of ordure, the drains clearly blocked and out of action.

Bonnići went back to her husband and gently palpated his stomach. The man yelped with pain. Sweat poured down his forehead. Bonnići pulled out a bottle of laudanum and gave the patient a small quantity, tipping it into his mouth.

'It is typhoid fever. Your husband must go to the hospital. There is nothing I can do for him here. He needs to go to the isolation ward.' He found he could not meet her eyes. 'I am so sorry, sinjura, there is little hope. You need to look after yourself and your children. Unless you can get back on your feet, it will have to be the poor-house.'

She collapsed to the ground, sobbing. He suspected she had not been feeding herself, saving any bread for her children. Now, the enormity of the situation – the fear of losing her husband, and the worry of how she could look after the family – was too much for her. She was too weak to cope.

'Stay here,' he said. 'I will send some help.'

Bonnići reported immediately to the police office, so a cart could be sent to take the husband to hospital. He asked his housekeeper to find someone to clean the cellar and to carry water for the family. He paid for this help, and for enough bread for a week. He was angry at what he had seen. These common dwelling houses – kerrejja – were new. Sold off by the government, these buildings, large enough for a family of five or six wealthy people, were instead being let out to upwards of fifty. Families with many children were crammed into single rooms with no sanitation. Water was too often barely accessible, requiring long trips to taps or pumps. Cellars and courtyards were being used when they were unsuitable for human habitation. And the authorities wondered why there were so many deaths from typhoid!

The greed of landlords was beyond his understanding. How

they turned a blind eye to suffering, intent only on lining their pockets. He did not know how they could live with themselves. Questions had been raised at the Council of Government by the elected members, representing the Maltese people, but they were outnumbered eight to ten by those appointed by the Queen. The governor and the chief secretary were notorious for never wanting to rock the boat, and the crown advocate was very clear that there was nothing wrong with the existing system. Bonnici knew there was a group of businessmen that had a heavy influence over the crown advocate. As uncomfortable as it made him feel, he had his suspicions that Captain Borġ and his brother were amongst those involved.

———

Meanwhile, McQueen's meeting with the magistrate, the lugubrious Signor Cassar, had gone well. The magistrate's office was on the first floor of the Auberge d'Auvergne. It was an impressive room with tall, shuttered windows and a cool, black-and-white tiled floor. Gilt-framed paintings of biblical scenes hung on the walls. Signor Cassar sat at his desk, which was piled high with legal papers. He took a good half-hour to study McQueen's evidence – his sketches of the body's position, the calculations of the trajectory of the fall, the photographs and the two versions of the post-mortem report, as well as the description of the brooch found at the scene. Then he looked up, the bags under his eyes looking larger than ever, and announced that yes, there was sufficient evidence to re-open the magisterial inquiry. And that he hoped McQueen would very soon find the perpetrator of this crime.

McQueen had been shifting impatiently in his seat, waiting for the verdict. Finally! Now he had full authority to run a murder investigation. The magistrate called for Captain Borġ, who came in, casting his eyes from one face to another. Reading the situation, he stood with his arms folded, while Signor Cassar expressed his disappointment at the withholding of evidence from McQueen, and the redacted report – a "bad decision" on the superintendent's part. He instructed Captain Borġ to give McQueen total co-operation, including the use of an office and full-time support from a police sergeant.

'Yes, yes. We will do this,' Borġ said, a hideous smile on his face. 'I regret any errors, *signor*. The inspector will be given every assistance.'

Once outside the magistrate's office, Borġ called over his adjutant, a sloppy-looking individual with a heavy black moustache.

'Cauchi, take the inspector to the filing room,' he ordered. He turned to McQueen. 'The only room we have, Inspector. Please, make yourself at home.' His voice dripped with sarcasm. McQueen itched to pick him up by his silver-embroidered tunic and shake him until his teeth rattled.

The filing room at the end of the corridor was small and oppressively hot, with a musty smell of old papers. The only windows were high up, near the ceiling, and looked to be sealed shut. Filing cabinets were crammed around the walls, with one desk in the middle of the room and just one decrepit chair. McQueen sat down, seething. *The case was his, it was officially re-opened, but he was on his own.* He was going to get no help from Captain Borġ. The adjutant left, closing the door behind him. McQueen picked up a book from the desk. It was written in Italian – completely useless. He threw it as hard as he could. It made a satisfying thud as it hit the door.

By the time Sergeant Galea reported for duty, McQueen had clambered up onto the filing cabinets to open the windows, using brute force to prise the frames from the sills. He had taken his jacket off, loosened his collar and rolled his sleeves up, but sweat was still running down his face.

'Ah, it's you, Sergeant. Welcome to our new home. There must be a pole for opening and closing these windows. Sort it out for me, will you?'

'Yes, sir,' Galea said.

'And is there a blackboard somewhere here? I need one, now, with some chalk.'

'Yes, sir.'

Galea disappeared and came back a few minutes later, struggling with the weight of a large slate board on an easel. McQueen helped him set it up in the middle of the room.

He looked at the young sergeant more closely. Uniform pressed, shoes shined. Smart, fashionable moustache. He had pleasing manners and appeared to possess the willingness to do whatever he was asked. Yet, he seemed to be holding something back. His guard was up. He was not going to commit wholeheartedly, probably under instructions from Captain Borġ.

'Now, Sergeant,' he said, 'this is a big opportunity for you. We officially have a murder investigation. If you do well, and help me to solve the case, who knows where it will lead?'

'Yes, sir,' Galea said, but the light did not go on in his eyes. McQueen sighed.

'Let's start with what we know.' He wrote on the blackboard:

> *Time of death 11pm.*
> *Who? Collingwood family, 19 guests at the party.*

Servants. Or unknown assailant – stranger seen in the garden.

Why? Unknown. Check will & beneficiaries.

How? Strangled? Thrown from roof.

Evidence: Cigar ends. Photographs of the body. Brooch found at the scene.

'Pay attention, Sergeant; we have two things to follow up on at this point. Firstly, we need to continue talking to the people who knew Lord Collingwood well. We've spoken to his family and the servants. We can speak to Mr Tanti later, and I'm seeing Colonel Arbuthnot this evening. Secondly, we have those cigars Collingwood was smoking. We can find out what make they are. Do you have them?'

Sergeant Galea felt all his pockets, a pantomime effort of looking for something that he clearly knew was not there. 'Sorry, sir, I have lost them,' he said, eventually.

'You *what?*' McQueen could not believe his ears. 'I gave you those cigar ends when we were on the roof and asked you to keep them. You cannot have lost them!'

'I am sorry, sir. I don't know where the handkerchief has gone.'

Damn it, this was inexcusable. The young man had lost vital evidence!

'And where's that brooch, the one found at the scene? Do you know where it has been stored?'

'Sorry, sir. I don't know. The superintendent has kept it.'

McQueen studied Galea for a moment. The lad looked downward, avoiding his gaze.

'How long have you been sergeant?' he asked.

'Six months, sir. I was very lucky, sir. Captain Borġ is my

uncle and he said I was the best. I passed the exam with top marks.'

He said this with such a guileless, earnest expression, McQueen inwardly groaned. *What on earth was he supposed to do with him? The youngster seemed to have nothing between his ears.*

'Your uncle, eh?'

'Yes, sir. He's a great policeman. He knows everyone. Everybody respects him. He is the best superintendent we ever had.'

No wonder Galea had been assigned to work with him, thought McQueen. *Uncle Ricardo, eh?*

'Listen, I don't care who your bloody uncle is. You are reporting to me. You'd better get your act together, my lad, or we are going to fall out. Go on, get out of my sight. Don't come back until you've decided whose side you're on – and make bloody sure it's mine. You hear me?'

Galea jumped and hurriedly left the office.

It was too hot to do anything. McQueen gave up and went in search of a beer.

CHAPTER TEN

After siesta, McQueen set off to interview Michele Tanti, the editor of the *Malta Post*. Weaving his way through the busy streets, as shops re-opened their doors and shutters, he was grateful for the slight drop in temperature. The newspaper offices were at the foot of Strada San Giovanni, with steep steps leading down to the glittering blue water of the harbour.

Tanti was first on the list of guests from the soirée, apparently one of the few Maltese who had been accepted into the top circles of British society. Galea told him that he was "one of the best", a successful entrepreneur who knew everybody and everything that was happening in Malta. McQueen, who had mixed experiences of working with the press in Edinburgh, would have to be convinced. Newspapermen could be as charming as you like when they wanted a story from you, but they would not hesitate to destroy a reputation to sell a few more copies. He tended not to give them any information unless he absolutely needed their help.

He found the home of the *Malta Post* behind a crimson-painted shop front, with oil lamps in the window. Tanti came to the door, a short man with an open, friendly countenance. He looked middle-aged, but energetic, with bright inquiring eyes. A spot of ink was smudged on his cheek above his grey-speckled beard.

'Come in, come in,' he said. 'Excuse me, I am busy – working on a big story. Did you see the rally yesterday? I have to finish a piece about it – we go to press on Friday.'

McQueen introduced himself.

'Ah, Inspector, of course. I knew you were on your way. You are from Edinburgh, is that right?'

He led McQueen into his office, which was crammed full of bookshelves, desks and tables, all covered in piles of books and papers, and seemingly ready to topple over at any minute. Through a glass door at the back, McQueen could see an old printing press and a shadowy figure working at a compositor's machine. A far cry from the massive steam printing machines, which churned out 20,000 copies of the *Edinburgh Evening News* every day.

McQueen leant against a desk, crossing his arms.

'You were at the villa on the night Lord Collingwood died,' he said. 'Could you describe what happened?'

'Well, Inspector, I don't have much to tell. I was there. I did speak to him. We had a few words about the railway shares, nothing much. But that was early on.' He picked up his pen and used it to scratch his head. 'Like everyone there I only found out what had happened to him later when there was all the screaming and noise outside. Of course, when we went out to see, there was nothing we could do. I took Lady Collingwood back inside and asked my daughter to look after her, while her fiancé went to fetch the police.'

McQueen checked his pocketbook. 'Is that Giorgio Micallef?'

'Yes, he offered straight away. He is such a fine, dependable young man.' Tanti smiled. 'Just what Maria needs to settle her down.'

'So, what did you think had happened to Collingwood?'

'I suppose I thought it was an accident. But it was strange. Perhaps he jumped, I don't know, but if he was unhappy, he hid it well. He seemed to be his usual irritable self when I spoke to him.'

'How well did you get on with the admiral?'

'Well, Inspector. Lord Collingwood and myself, shall we say we enjoyed sparring with each other?'

'Over what?'

'He was a friend of the governor, and rather forthright in his views,' Tanti said. 'He believed the Maltese people should not be included in local government, that we aren't capable. He also said we should not be able to invest in businesses in our own country. And, of course, he firmly supported the compulsory teaching of English in all schools.

'In principle, I agree with him about learning English, because of the opportunities it gives us. I have written about it in my paper. But he deeply offended many people. Look, I have this letter he wrote, published in our rival newspaper – the *Standard* – it has a British editor. Here, read it and you will see why.'

Tanti rummaged around on his desk and handed over a piece cut out from the *Malta Standard*, a long column featuring a letter from the admiral, signed *Collingwood, GCB, GCMG, KCH*. McQueen quickly scanned it. The tone was distinctly patrician. Collingwood stated that while they persisted in using Italian as their official language there could be no place for the Maltese in their own government. That the British had every right to expect all Maltese to speak English, as the right and proper language for business, the law and indeed all the professions. If the people would buckle down to learn the British way of doing things, then after some considerable time, say twenty years, they might stand a chance of some form of integration. But it all had to start with learning some discipline – and the English language – at school.

McQueen whistled. *This was no way to make friends.* 'When was this letter published?' he asked.

'About a week before his death,' Tanti said. 'Don't misunderstand me, Inspector, I personally did not mind his manner. I found he enjoyed a good argument. I think I could have persuaded him to understand the Maltese people a little better.'

He stood up, as if to show McQueen out. 'After all, in early Roman times we were living in a civilised, cultured fashion, when the British were still running around waving spears, blue paint on their faces.'

McQueen laughed. He had warmed to this plain-speaking newspaper editor.

'I am sorry, I have not got more time for you now.' Tanti handed him a card. 'Please, come and dine with me and my family tomorrow night. I would like to show you the Maltese hospitality for which we are famed throughout the world.'

'Thank you. I would like that.'

The streets were dark as McQueen walked back up the stone steps. He wondered how it had come about that he, who had a deep distrust of the English elite, had been assigned to this case. It seemed Lord Collingwood had made no friends amongst the people of his adopted country, and he could not feel much sympathy for a man with such an imperious attitude. Yet here he was, thousands of miles from home, trying to find out who had pushed this arrogant admiral to his death. He needed a drink. He went in search of a bar.

After a swift beer in a crowded bar in Stretta Strada, he set off for his meeting with Lieutenant Carstairs and Colonel Arbuthnot. He made his way to the Auberge de Castille, described by his guidebook as "the largest and finest of all the knights' palaces". It now housed the Officers' Mess of the Royal Artillery and Engineers. Walking along the main street after dusk, McQueen found it was calm and cool. There was a warm yellow glow from the gas lamps, lighting up the cafés, the bars and the shops selling fancy goods from Paris and London. The British officers were out and about, parading with their fashionable wives. The only Maltese he could see were those serving drinks or driving carriages.

The Auberge de Castille was indeed large and fine. He climbed up the steps to the tall arched entrance and was granted access by a young guard in uniform. The Officers' Mess was on the first floor, reached by a grand marble staircase with pure white alabaster banisters. Inside, the floor was a shiny, polished wood. Huge potted palms were placed around the tables and chairs, which were packed with officers in uniform.

McQueen tried to find Carstairs through all the noise and the smoke. With waiters scurrying around carrying trays of drink, this was a far cry from the spit and sawdust interior, the rough clientele and the dour barman at the Fountain Inn. Another world he was not familiar with, the world of the British military abroad.

He felt a tap on his arm and a waiter pointed out Carstairs to him, who was waving from a table by the window. He made his way over. Carstairs, wearing a red tunic, was sitting at a table with an older military type. 'Good evening, Inspector,' he said, sounding very clipped and formal. 'Let me introduce you to Colonel Arbuthnot, otherwise known as Buffy. He's probably Collingwood's closest associate – known him for many years.'

Arbuthnot, white-haired with a florid complexion, stood and shook his hand. 'How d'you do?'

McQueen sat down next to Carstairs, who asked him what he would like to drink. 'I would advise the beer, of course. It's imported from England – not bad, if I say so myself. The wine is also imported. I really wouldn't recommend the local stuff; it strips your insides.'

'Beer, please,' McQueen said. 'And I'm not much of a wine drinker, but if there is a chance of a Scotch...?'

'Well of course,' Carstairs said. He called over a waiter and ordered.

McQueen turned to Arbuthnot, whose bloodshot pale eyes and red cheeks suggested a significant intake of alcohol already that evening. 'Could you tell me about Lord Collingwood?' he said. 'About his life in Malta?'

'He'd been back just over eighteen months,' replied Arbuthnot, drawing on a pipe. His grey bushy moustache was stained brown at the ends. 'Twenty years he had been away. '53 to '58 he lived here. Back then he was absolutely in his prime. Top of his game. Admiral, Commander-in-Chief. Strong leader, you know the type. Did things his way. Top brass didn't like him because he didn't follow orders. Politicians loved him because he got the job done.' He waved his pipe stem in the air. 'I always said to him, "Collingwood, you are an absolute beast, and you have the luck of the devil." I was in the Army at that time, but I stayed on after my posting. Couldn't bear to leave the old island.'

'So, how did you feel about him coming back to Malta?'

'Over the moon, old boy. Over the moon. Thought we'd have time to relive the old days at the club. Children grown up, wife looking as lovely as ever. I always told him I'd run off with his missus, wonderful woman.'

He seemed to realise he might have said something

untoward, fumbling around for the right words.

'Course I didn't expect anything like this to happen. I absolutely wouldn't... you know.'

He went back to puffing at his pipe, eyes glazing over.

'And do you think he was happy to be in Malta?' McQueen prompted.

'Well, I don't know that he was,' Arbuthnot said after a moment. 'He was all right for a good few months, but those last weeks he was decidedly ill-tempered, would hardly give me the time of day.'

'Is there anything you know about that could have put him out of countenance?'

'Not a thing, old chap, not a thing.'

The waiter brought the drinks to the table and McQueen drank half his beer. It was an Indian pale ale, light coloured and cool. Just what he needed.

'What about the night he died?' he asked. 'Did anything happen that was out of the ordinary? Did you argue with him?'

Arbuthnot's eyes sharpened for a second. 'Yes, we *did* have words. He was a bit harsh with me, I have to say. Business, you know.'

He picked up the whisky bottle and poured a dram into each of the glasses.

'But I was shocked as anyone when he fell from the roof like that. Shocked as anyone.'

'I don't believe it was an accident,' McQueen said. 'I've been to the magistrate; the case is officially re-opened.'

'Oh!' Carstairs had raised his glass, but he abruptly put it back down, his eyes wide. 'Are you sure? Only the governor had hoped, you know... quick result and all that.'

'Yes, I am sure. Collingwood did not fall, and it was most likely he was pushed or thrown.'

'Well, it can't have been anybody from the soirée. I asked

questions when I got there. As far as I could make out everyone was accounted for, all the guests, so it must have been an outsider.'

McQueen thought of the stranger in the garden, but said nothing.

Carstairs' face flushed with excitement. He leaned forwards, lowering his voice.

'I say, Inspector, did Borġ tell you? He's been under a great deal of pressure recently. There've been so many immigrants, particularly Sicilians. Forced out due to Italian unification. Some of them are dangerous. Borġ is trying to get on top of the situation, but it's difficult. They operate in different ways, think nothing of killing a man. Wouldn't surprise me if it was one of them, you know. If I were you, I would look no further.' He picked up his glass again and took a swig, nodding sagely.

First thought, always: blame the foreigner. McQueen decided to stir things up a little.

'I don't know,' he said. 'It's a wide field. There are plenty of Brits here as well. 6,000 troops for a start, let alone all the sailors in port at any one time. Could have been any one of them.'

Arbuthnot had sunk back, as though barely able to follow the conversation, but at this point he sat bolt upright, moustache quivering. He pointed his nicotine-stained finger at McQueen.

'Absolutely not. No. Couldn't possibly be anything to do with the Army or the Navy, I guarantee you. The man was a hero. Medals all over the shop.'

McQueen laughed. He glanced around the room, taking in the loud English voices of the officers, the privilege so clearly on display. There was nothing that grated on him more than the arrogance of entitlement, assumed rather than earned. *Of course,* he thought, *they will all close ranks to protect each other.* It had been a long day and he felt a headache coming on. He raised a glass. 'Gentlemen. *Sláinte mhar.* Good health.'

CHAPTER ELEVEN

Thursday, 5 August 1880

McQueen's head was pounding, despite the headache powders he had taken late at night. He had fallen asleep quickly, then woken up a few hours later, pillow and nightshirt damp with sweat. There was no air in these houses. *How on earth did they sleep?* He had tried one position and then another, for what seemed like hours, getting more and more irritated. Finally, he had given up, thrown on some clothes and gone for a walk.

He turned right from the lodging house and headed down towards the sea. The water in the harbour was flat and still. The air was cool and he could hear the shushing of the waves. A faint yellow glow was appearing on the horizon, beginning to lighten the sky. A thirty-foot wall reached down from the road to the sea, and he leant over it trying to work out how he could get down to the rocks below, wanting to feel the coolness of the water in his hand.

He heard a soft sound behind him and turned to see a small

figure approaching. Black tousled hair and a dark face, which broke into a grin. 'Mister McQueen. It's me, Antonio.'

The landlady's wee lad.

'What are you doing up so early, young man?' he asked.

'I like it. Is quiet. See there?' Antonio pointed towards a row of dilapidated shacks near the rocky shore. 'My father showed me fish. Men catch in boats. Long time ago.'

He felt a pang for the lad. Losing his father at such a young age. 'How do you get down to the rocks?'

'You go through Sally Port – over there. I show you!'

They walked down a stone staircase and through an archway, emerging by the fishing huts, where the breeze brought with it the distinctive odour of the sea. They stood watching the water in silence, tall fortifications standing high above them, looming over the rocks.

McQueen felt the strangeness of being there, on a tiny island, so far from home. He had to find ways to understand more about the Maltese, to get familiar with the streets and the families who lived here.

He was struck by a thought.

'What would you say to earning a bit o' money, lad?'

Antonio looked up at him, excited. 'Me? Get money? How?'

'Do you go to school?'

The boy shook his head. 'No, but I can nearly write my name!'

Again, McQueen felt sorry for him, looking at his scruffy clothes and his bare feet. *When this was all over, maybe he could give the wee lad a hand, find him a place at school.*

'Well, you could help me, as a message boy. We have laddies at home who do this. I'll give you a shilling a week. You have to be quick, and I have to trust you, yes? Do you think you could do this?'

'Oh, yes!' Antonio said, jumping up and down on the spot. 'Messages, yes, I run very fast!'

'Come on, then. Let's get to work. Breakfast first, then I have to go to the police office.'

As they walked back in the semi-light, a baker's shop was opening up its wooden shutters, preparing for the day's business. They stopped for some bread.

Later that morning, McQueen stood at the blackboard. He had written down various names with a note next to each.

> *Edmund – opportunity?*
> *Tanti – motive?*
> *Arbuthnot – argument – opportunity?*
> *Staff – motive?*
> *Trespasser – who?*

He heard a hesitant knock at the door. Sergeant Galea poked his head in. The young man was even more smartly presented today, his black hair smoothed down, his moustache neatly waxed, turned up at the ends.

'Sir?'

'Yes, come in.'

He walked in and saluted. McQueen stifled a smile and sat down at the desk, waving at Galea to sit opposite.

The sergeant reached into his tunic pocket and pulled out a handkerchief, tipping the cigar ends onto the desk.

'I found them, sir.'

'Come to your senses, have you? Where were they?'

Galea stared straight ahead. 'In my pocket, sir. Sorry, sir.'

It seemed to McQueen that the young police officer had decided which side he wanted to be on. From now on, Galea would follow *his* directions, not those of his uncle.

'Excellent. A wise decision.' *Brave, too.* He scooped the cigar ends back into the handkerchief and handed it back.

'Well, you'd better get out there and find out what brand they are, hadn't you?'

Galea stood up, scraping the chair back. His face was a picture of conflicting emotions: embarrassment, relief and hope.

'Yes, sir,' he said, hesitating. 'Shall I go now?'

'Yes, Sergeant, now! Go on, get away with you. Come back later when you have something to report.'

Galea stood awkwardly in the middle of the office, opened his mouth as if to say something, then thought better of it and left the room. The youngster had made the right choice – there was hope for him yet.

McQueen put his feet up on the desk, hands behind his head, thinking. He needed to take stock. *What would he be doing if he were back in Edinburgh?* He would be out and about, talking to people, finding out who knew the victim and who stood to gain from his death. Was his life insured? What was in his will? Who was his lawyer, his executor, his banker? *He needed more information.* Carstairs was his best hope, his link to the British establishment.

He tried to put himself in the mind of the murderer. *To throw a person from a rooftop was not a guaranteed way to kill them – people had survived falls from that height. So, perhaps it was not calculated, it was something that happened on the spur of the moment. The broken bone in the throat and the marks on the neck suggested pressure, strangulation. Had the admiral blacked out during a struggle? Did the assailant panic, pushing him off the roof to make it look like an accident? Who was the assailant – the stranger seen in the garden? Or someone that knew the admiral, either from the household, or an invited guest? Whoever it was, they would now be living in fear that they would be found out.*

The answer surely lay at the villa. He decided his next step should be to go back, talk to Lady Collingwood again and go through the admiral's papers. In his experience murders were either crimes of passion, carried out in the heat of a moment, or motivated by money. He needed to find out what was going on in Lord Collingwood's private life and with his financial affairs. He wrote a note to Carstairs asking him to join him, then went outside to find Antonio. The lad was waiting on a bench opposite the Auberge d'Auvergne with some other messenger boys. He came scampering up straight away.

'Here, laddie – take this to the Governor's Palace. A message for Lieutenant Carstairs.'

———

As McQueen was sinking his teeth into a second cheese pastry, Captain Borġ came into the café and sat down at his table. The police chief put his cap down and looked around for a waiter, who hurried over to take his order.

The superintendent's fleshy face rolled over his collar as he settled down in his chair. He sat silently waiting for his coffee to arrive, then stirred sugar into it before slurping it down, all the while watching McQueen.

'You like your office?' Borġ said, finally. His smile made McQueen think of a bull terrier, baring its teeth. 'So sorry we have nothing better. Nothing grander for the great detective. We are just poor policemen, yes? We mop up drunks, check the wine isn't watered down, is that right? We have no idea how to solve real crimes.'

McQueen shrugged, moving his plate, with its mass of

crumbs, to the middle of the table. 'I merely told the magistrate the facts,' he said. 'I was asked here to look at the case. Even from my first investigation I can see you've made many mistakes, covering things up, failing to ask the right questions.'

'Nobody liked him. Nobody misses him. What difference does it make if he was pushed or if he fell? My way, it is all tidy. He is gone and buried; we get on with our lives.'

'Yes, but that's not right. It is not the truth. And it means that someone is out there who has got away with murder. Can you not see that?'

Borġ leaned forward, speaking in a low voice.

'I know everything that is happening in Malta, Inspector. I don't need you here.'

'Is that right, Superintendent? You have it solved already?'

'It will be the person who was in the garden. There is no great mystery. I will find out who it is. It will be a vagrant, a nobody. A foreigner. They will be dealt with.'

So, Galea had reported back after the visit to the villa and the superintendent knew about the stranger.

'I am warning you,' Borġ continued. 'You do not need to look anymore. There is nothing to find. I will inform the governor that you are wasting time on useless activity. You will be out of here in no time, Inspector McQueen. In no time, understand? You are not welcome.'

With that, he stood up and clapped his hand on McQueen's shoulder. In a loud voice he exclaimed, 'Good, good, Inspector. I am happy you like it so much here. I will see you later, yes?'

He walked off, hailing people left and right as he went.

McQueen called for the waiter and asked for a double whisky, despite the early hour. The superintendent had got under his skin. He felt unsettled, irritable. *How did he end up in this situation?* Here he was, on this hot, oppressive island, entirely alone. He felt out of place, not knowing the people or how to work with them. He wondered if this was a case he might not ever be able to solve.

Not that things were much better back home. Everyone said they valued integrity, but he was regarded as a traitor. No one trusted him, and he trusted no one in return. If he did not keep his wits about him, his former colleagues would find a way to discredit him. They might even get him drummed out of the force. He had a vision of himself in one of the bars in Edinburgh, worn down with drink, following errant husbands and wives, or shady insurance swindlers, getting ever more disreputable as the years went by. His father would be right to feel shamed by his disgrace.

The whisky arrived and he drank it slowly, feeling it settle his nerves.

CHAPTER TWELVE

M aria Tanti caught sight of her aunt passing the doorway
to her room.

'*Zija* Paolina!' she called out. 'What do you think of my new gown?'

Her aunt came into the bedroom and watched Maria admiring herself in front of the mirror. She frowned. 'My dear, why did I not see this material before you ordered it? It's so bright, Maria. And the neckline, it is a little – you know – low. Do you really want to draw such attention to yourself? What will Father Filippo think? It's very nice, *ħanini*, but–'

'Oh, *Zi*, you will worry yourself to death; it's fine! I like to wear bright colours and I'm perfectly well covered. Besides, I'm respectably engaged now. Giorgio will be dining with us tonight and I have to look well.'

To say Giorgio's name, to think that he would soon be her husband, made her feel proud. The thought that he had chosen her when he could have had any of the young ladies of Maltese society. Everyone knew he would be a wealthy man. He was establishing himself as an excellent lawyer. Also, he had been the ward of Count San Pietro. He had the look of an aristocrat about him, and there were whispers that perhaps he was the count's natural son.

Yes, Maria was pleased that she had caught his attention. She was by no means a classic beauty; her nose was too big, and her mouth was too small. But she knew she had a nice smile, and she had used it to her best advantage. She loved to tease Giorgio and jolt him out of his seriousness. She did not think anyone had joked with him before; it made her laugh to see his eyes cloud with confusion when she provoked him.

She felt doubly excited that evening. Not only was she going to see her fiancé, but also, the detective inspector from Scotland was coming for dinner. Maria was not ashamed to admit to herself that she had found the death of the admiral rather thrilling. She felt sorry for the family, of course she did, but the idea that someone may have actually murdered him, well, that was the most exciting thing that had ever happened. As the daughter of a newspaper editor, she had dreams of becoming a journalist. This was her chance to find out more about the story, to find out what the detective knew already. She would offer to help him; after all, there was little she did not know about Maltese society.

Her father and fiancé were standing together in the parlour when she finally went downstairs – discussing politics, no doubt. She loved to hear Giorgio's voice. He always spoke softly, persuasively. She could imagine that as a lawyer, he knew how to get people to say more than they intended.

'Maria, my angel,' her father said. He put his arm around her waist. 'What a pretty gown!'

How lucky she was to have such a caring, adorable father. She had no memories of her mother, who had died when she was young, and he was everything to her. She kissed his cheek, which felt soft, smooth and cool. 'Thank you, Papà.'

Giorgio took her hand and held it to his lips, his dark curls tipping over his forehead. When he looked up, she was struck anew by the unusual colour of his light-green eyes, so attractive and yet somehow difficult to read. She found his attentive behaviour amusing. He was so polite and correct. It made her want to unsettle him and make him laugh.

'Well, what have you two been plotting?' she asked. 'While I have been making myself beautiful?'

'Maria!' her aunt said. 'Please, the sin of pride... Father Filippo will be here any minute.'

'Oh, who cares what Father Filippo thinks?' she said, at the very moment when the priest appeared in the doorway. Quickly, she flicked open her fan and hid her face behind it, trying to suppress her laughter at her aunt's mortified expression.

The priest came bustling forwards apologising for being late. He had left the cathedral and he had seen *Sinjura* Spiteri on the Strada Reale. She had needed help because she had lost her glove, and they had gone all the way back inside to look for it... and eventually they had found it – in her bag all the time – and now here he was. Poor *Sinjura* Spiteri, she was getting so forgetful!

He came close to her, and Maria stepped back very slightly. 'Ah, *sinjorina*,' he said, bending over and taking her hand to kiss it. As always, she felt repulsed by his yellow teeth and the dandruff scales lying on his shoulders. Her every instinct was to pull her hand away, but she had to put up with his fawning. Her aunt was always asking him to the house, in the belief this would help her reach Heaven, and he was the bane of her existence. She would have to confess to her rudeness the next day and receive a suitable penance.

She stood by, bored to distraction, as they discussed the Festa of San Duminku, which was taking place at the weekend. Father Filippo was declaring that he hoped the new priest at San Duminku would manage the blessing of the statue without any mishaps, when there was a knock at the door and the final guest came in. The detective had arrived! He walked in, still holding his hat. Big and awkward, he seemed to fill the room. A servant came scuttling up to retrieve his bowler. Maria had to stifle a laugh. She had imagined somebody officious and correct in his dress and demeanour. This man looked so out of place with his brown suit – *goodness, was it made of wool?* It looked so thick and uncomfortable. *Was it really the best he had – his evening wear?*

Her father greeted the inspector warmly and brought him over to meet everyone. She thought he had the look of a man who perhaps used to be of athletic build, but who was now a little bulky. His hair was a reddish light brown, and untidy, and his beard could do with a trim. She did not think he cared much about his looks. His collar was not exactly white and his necktie looked limp and creased. But he had a quiet assurance about him that was appealing, and – she decided – kind eyes. He greeted them all with a soft accent that made it difficult to pick out what he was saying.

After initial introductions, they went in to dinner. Giorgio escorted her. McQueen, she noticed, had to be the odd man out, walking in alone. Clearly her father had invited him after her aunt had already made all the arrangements. No wonder *Zija* was eyeing this Scottish visitor with such disapproval. They sat down at the table. Maria was next to McQueen, with Giorgio on the other side of her. She could not resist asking the detective straight away about the investigation. 'Are you allowed to tell us what you have found out so far?'

He smiled. 'Indeed not,' he said, with a quiet tone and in

that intriguing accent. 'Strictly speaking you are suspects because you were there when the admiral died.'

'No, we're not!' she answered. 'We were all together in the drawing room, weren't we, Papà?' She looked to her father, who was sitting opposite her, for corroboration.

'Yes, indeed we were. We were listening to the music. Everything was completely normal until Mrs Trapani screamed from the garden and we all rushed outside.'

'Yes, there he was on the ground by the steps and there was all this blood beginning to seep around him.' She tried not to sound too gleeful.

'Oh please,' *Zija* Paolina interrupted. 'Let us not talk about this now. I have had nightmares about it ever since. It was so horrible.'

'I apologise,' McQueen said, holding his hands up. 'I'm afraid I do bring unfortunate subjects to the dinner table.'

One of the servants brought in some dishes and put them down on the table.

'Baked macaroni,' said her father. He cut McQueen a generous portion and put it on his plate. She watched, suppressing a laugh, as the detective picked up his fork and poked at it, unsure of what to do. He watched the others, tentatively tried a bit. He seemed to like it, as he set about clearing his plate with gusto.

'Tell me about yourself,' she said.

'There's not much to tell. I have been with the police for over fifteen years, always lived in Edinburgh. It's a fine city.'

'What's Edinburgh like? And what do you think of Malta so far?'

'Compared to Malta, Edinburgh is very cold. It's grand in places, very poor in others – you know. I am still trying to find my feet in Malta. It's certainly very hot. I think I need to buy a new suit!' he said ruefully, looking at his jacket.

'Oh, I'm sure we can help with that, can't we, Giorgio?' She turned towards him. 'Can you give him the name of your tailor?'

Giorgio looked a little cold in response. *Perhaps he felt his tailor was far too good for this foreigner?*

'Of course,' he said, in his most polite voice. 'It is Ellul's on Strada Reale. Do mention my name and he will give you a good price.' He gave McQueen a card.

The servant came in to clear the plates, then brought in some squid stew. She could see McQueen eyeing it suspiciously and decided to have some fun.

'Have you never eaten squid before, Inspector McQueen?' she asked. She picked out a ring with her fork. 'Look, this is his body sliced into rings, after you pull the insides out.' Then, finding a tentacle, 'He has eight tentacles, which we chop into pieces, after we have cut off his beak.' McQueen raised his eyebrows and brought his napkin to his mouth, which made her laugh.

'Maria, really!' *Zija* Paolina said. 'I am sorry, Inspector, do not pay any attention to my niece. She is always teasing. Please eat, you will enjoy I am sure.' McQueen still looked unconvinced, poking the squid before trying it, but he did manage to eat what was put in front of him. *He had a good appetite, that was for sure.*

'Tell us, Inspector,' her father said. 'Do you have any plans for seeing the wonderful sights of the island?'

'If I have the time, perhaps, but I am not likely to be here for long. But do tell me what I should see if I can.'

'Malta has a rich past and there is much to see. If you are interested in ancient history, there are ruins of Megalithic temples at *Ħaġar Qim*.'

'And you must see the Grotto of Saint Paul, at Rabat,' *Zija* Paolina said. 'There is an underground church there. Father Filippo, tell him about Saint Paul.'

The priest looked flattered to be asked to speak. 'The blessed Apostle himself came to our island. He was shipwrecked on the way to Rome, and he sheltered for three months in the grotto. It was he who brought the Word of God to Malta. The grotto is a sacred place. The stone from its walls is said to protect you from poisonous bites, and fevers.'

'And there are catacombs there – miles and miles of them,' Maria added. 'They are still finding new sections, even now. Hundreds of bodies were buried there from Punic, Roman and Byzantine times.' She waved her fork at McQueen. 'Watch out, though; they are haunted. Most of the catacombs are walled up now. A school party went there, many years ago; thirteen children and a schoolmaster. They got lost in the tunnels. Never seen again. People say they are still there. Spirits wandering through the underground maze–'

'Maria! Why do you always need to make everything so dramatic?' *Zija* Paolina interrupted. 'Please, let us change the subject. Father Filippo – will you be at San Duminku on Sunday?'

While the others were talking about the festa, Maria decided to ask McQueen the question that was uppermost in her mind. 'With the investigation, Inspector, is there anything I can do to help?' she said in a low voice. 'I know a lot of people. I work with my father on the newspaper, you know.'

McQueen thought for a while, chewing on his food. 'What I want to know,' he said, 'is what people really thought about Lord Collingwood. I need to understand more about him.'

'Well, I can tell you something, Inspector. He could not have been more unpopular here in Malta. You should have heard some of the things he said about the Maltese people! He treated us like children, as though we're completely inferior.' She pushed her plate away from her. 'I only used to go to the villa because I liked his wife. Have you met her? She is quite a character. Lady Collingwood has done a great deal of charity work and has even set up a fund for Sicilian refugees. But Lord Collingwood – well, there are a lot of people who are becoming quite fanatical, anti-British. I think they might well have wanted to make an example of him.'

She suddenly realised she was the only person speaking, and that everybody was looking at her, as though horrified by what she was saying.

'Now, Maria,' said her father, sternly. 'It's not your place to come up with theories. That's a job for the inspector.'

She rolled her eyes. 'Well, I am only telling him how it is.'

For the rest of the meal, she kept quiet, politely asking McQueen if he would like some fruit and cream for dessert, and passing him the plate. He talked to her father about the *Malta Post* and all the recent news.

As she ate her peaches, Giorgio chose a moment to lean in towards her, speaking so softly only she could hear.

'I'm not sure you should be offering to help the inspector,' he said in Maltese. 'As my fiancée I would prefer it if you didn't give him any of your time. There is no need, and it is not becoming.'

She looked back at him blankly. *What did he mean?* All she had said was that she might be able to help. *Why was he listening to what she was saying to the inspector, anyway?*

'Don't worry,' she said. 'You know I can't go anywhere without *Zija* Paolina by my side. I only want to help; I want to find out what happened.'

'English, please,' interrupted her father. 'We want to make the inspector feel welcome at our table.'

'Sorry,' Maria said. 'Have one of these cakes, Inspector. You will love them; they are sweet with honey.'

Ignoring her fiancé, she continued to talk to McQueen, trying to find out more about his job. He told her of a journey he had once made to Paris, on the trail of a swindler who had married not once, not twice, but four times, every time running off with each wife's savings. He had tracked the bigamist to a hotel and sat at the café opposite, watching and waiting. The manager had insisted there was no one of that name or appearance staying there. Indeed, no one appeared for three days. Then eventually, McQueen arranged for a note to be delivered to the manager warning that the French police were on their way to raid the place. He caught the miscreant climbing out of the window at the back of the hotel, arrested him and took him back to Edinburgh for trial.

'Hurrah!' Maria said. 'He got what he deserved!'

She wanted to ask for another story, but her aunt stood up at that point. 'Come, Maria, it is time for us to leave the men to their port and cigars.'

Maria was furious. All she wanted to do was stay with the men and hear more about the world beyond her small island.

'Well, I hope you will come and see us again soon, Inspector,' she said as she got up from the table. 'I have so enjoyed learning about the life of a detective!'

'Thank you for making me feel so welcome here,' McQueen said, with such sincerity to his tone that she blushed. 'I certainly hope we will meet again before long.'

She threw a quick glance at Giorgio as she left. He was lighting a cigar, stone-faced. She had to admit to a certain feeling of glee at the thought that the burly Scotsman seemed to enjoy her company.

CHAPTER THIRTEEN

Friday, 6 August 1880

A decapitated head, in a shrine?
        The carriage swayed around the corner and McQueen caught sight of Christ's head – complete with crown of thorns and dripping blood – displayed in a niche on the corner of a town house. He turned around to stare. At home, religion was more of the mind. You read, you thought, you listened to learned discourse. His father regularly had 800 people turning up to hear him read and discuss the works of John Bunyan. Here, religion was tangible – you could reach out and touch the saints. Objects and icons had magical properties to protect and save you. He was not convinced by either.

'I've seen everything now,' he said, sitting back. 'Jesus Christ in a box.'

'Oh, you'll find that everywhere. The more gruesome and lifelike, the better,' said Carstairs, who was next to him in the *karrozin*, rooting around in his attaché case. 'I shouldn't do this in a carriage, I'm beginning to feel a bit green around the gills. Ah, here it is.'

They were heading for Villa Porto, to look through the late admiral's papers. Carstairs pulled out a large sheet, folded with a seal. 'It's a copy of the will, from the solicitors. Got it yesterday.'

'What does it say? Anything of interest?'

'Nothing remotely unusual, Inspector. The son inherits everything. Lady Collingwood gets a lifetime allowance. No special bequests.'

McQueen thought of Edmund, his blinking eyes and mild-mannered exterior. *How well he had done, following the removal of his father.*

When they arrived at the villa, the housekeeper met them at the door. They followed her to the drawing room. McQueen caught sight of the little maidservant scurrying away across the hall, as if trying not to be seen. It was the girl Censa who had given such confused evidence on the last visit. He made a mental note to try and speak to her again before he left the villa.

Lady Collingwood looked even more imperious than the first time he had seen her. She took them into the admiral's study and indicated the writing bureau across the room.

'His papers are all in there. Lieutenant Carstairs looked at them weeks ago. Why do you have to look through them again? You will not find anything, I'm sure.'

'That's as may be,' McQueen said. 'But it has to be done.'

'Don't worry,' Carstairs said. 'We'll be discretion itself. We're looking for anything that may help the inspector with the investigation.'

'Very well. Here is the key. I will give you two hours. And

mind that you put everything back exactly where you found it. I'm not having you making the admiral's study untidy.'

McQueen raised his eyebrows as the widow swept out of the study. They went over to the writing bureau, a small, fine-looking piece of furniture made of smooth, brown walnut wood. Carstairs unlocked a door at the side, revealing four drawers within, each with a brass handle. He opened the top two drawers and gave one pile of papers to McQueen, keeping one for himself.

'I have had a quick look through these papers before. What do you want me to look out for this time?' he asked.

'Anything that defines the admiral's financial status and concerns. Anything that links him to people or places you don't know about. I am trying to form a picture of the man and all his dealings. There will be something here we can follow up, I am sure.'

McQueen noticed that despite his normally distracted air, Carstairs set about the task with an impressive concentration. He sat at the admiral's desk, reading the papers and sorting them. All that could be heard in the room was the rustling of papers and an occasional throat-clearing.

McQueen looked through his own pile of documents and letters. There were bills from tailors, milliners and haberdashers, wine-merchants, grocers and coal providers. All the normal expenditure for a wealthy household. He stopped for a moment when he picked up a bill from a stonemason in Dereham, Norfolk. The creation of a headstone for "Richard Collingwood, Captain of Her Majesty's Navy, 1849 to 1875". How hard it must have been to bury his eldest son and heir. Perhaps not surprising that the admiral still held on to this poignant record.

He moved on to a large clutch of letters embossed with the House of Lords seal. It seemed the admiral had been an active member, presumably up until he left the country. There was even a letter from Prince Alfred, Duke of Edinburgh, wishing him a comfortable retirement "in the glorious surroundings of the magical island", with the royal seal at the bottom. Collingwood was a man at the very pinnacle of achievement, mixing with royalty and the top echelons of society. McQueen had known this, but somehow seeing the correspondence made it seem more real.

The shutters of the study were closed and the windows open, so the room was shady and relatively cool. Occasionally, a breeze would lift the edges of the papers, but it was not strong enough to move whole sheets. He could hear the loud ticking of a clock on the mantlepiece. It took a good hour, but eventually they had emptied all the drawers and each had a pile of papers in front of them.

'What have you found?' McQueen asked.

'Well, I've got all the letters from his bank and as far as I can make out, there's nothing untoward. He has been living off an annual capital of £2,000, from various investments. Railways, ship-building and steel primarily.'

All very well for the privileged, McQueen thought. *Those who have money can make more money.* It was a far cry from the world he knew. He had never given a thought to his own future, had always lived hand-to-mouth. He was surviving on £250 a year. His needs were simple, and that just about covered it, but... *Perhaps it was time to start thinking about making some investments?* He threw the idea out as soon as it occurred to him.

A quick totting-up of all the bills he had found suggested that Lord Collingwood was living within his means.

'So, I've not got any surprises, what about you?' McQueen said.

'No, I don't think so. I mean to say, I'm not entirely au fait with all the ins and outs of his accounts, but it looks to be, shall we say, all above board.'

McQueen felt dissatisfied. *There should be more. Where was Collingwood's private correspondence?*

'I think there must be something else – hidden away,' he said. 'A separate compartment. Let me have a look.'

Taking the key from the side lock of the bureau, he opened the curved lid in the front, revealing a writing slope underneath that could be tilted up to a 30-degree angle and fixed with a wooden support. He laid it back down flat. Above it he found two drawers and pulled each of these out, revealing some more papers, which he passed to Carstairs.

'Social engagements,' Carstairs said, leafing through them. 'Not of any interest, I don't think.'

McQueen continued looking for clues to a hidden compartment. He removed the wooden pen tray from its holder, but there was nothing revealed underneath. It was the same when he took out the sand-holder and the inkwell.

Perhaps there was a section he could get to from the top? He ran his fingers around the raised edge. Invisible to the eye, he could feel the tiniest of cracks. He assessed the size of the bureau. *There should be more space within, but how to get to it?* He started looking for a hidden spring mechanism. Working out where it would most likely be positioned, he half-pulled out the drawers above the writing slope and felt around for a catch. Almost immediately, his fingertips felt the edge of a piece of metal. He pulled it towards him.

'Here we go – got it!' he said, as the top of the bureau sprang upwards, revealing a whole new storage area. He looked inside and saw an intricately carved ivory letter rack, with ten different sections for keeping correspondence.

'Well done, McQueen!' Carstairs said, peering over his

shoulder. 'I say, I am impressed. How on earth did you work that out?'

Tucked inside were dozens of letters in cream envelopes. McQueen reached for one and pulled out a sheet of paper. Written in a beautiful, looping hand, it was a short note, signed, *"Yours lovingly, Sarah"*. He started to read it.

'What have you found?'

A harsh voice from the doorway made him turn around, letter in hand. He saw Lady Collingwood standing stock-still, her eyes travelling from the writing bureau to the letter and then to him.

'Is that a letter to my husband?' she asked.

'Aye, it is.'

'Give it to me.' She took the letter from him and scanned it, then looked at the number of envelopes stacked in the hidden compartment. The corners of her mouth tightened. She gave it back to McQueen without meeting his eyes.

'Come with me, Inspector,' she said, her features impassive. 'You don't mind do you, Lieutenant Carstairs?'

'Absolutely not,' Carstairs said. 'I'll just – you know – carry on here, put everything back in its place.' He set to work smoothly and quietly, replacing the papers in their correct drawers.

He will go far, McQueen thought, *a true diplomat.*

He followed Lady Collingwood out of the study and along the hallway. She led him through the French windows at the side of the house, onto the veranda, and stood looking out into the garden. The sound of cicadas swelled around them. Behind them, the air was cool in the shade. Where they were standing, warm air was nudging at them, bringing a scent of dry grasses and sandy soil. He could feel his face turning red. Beads of sweat were forming on his top lip. He waited for Lady Collingwood to speak.

'I am not a fool, Inspector,' she said, her eyes focused on a palm tree at the bottom of the garden. 'I was aware that my late husband may have taken a mistress from time to time. You must understand, it is common for a man in his position. He was away a great deal, you know.'

'Of course. I understand.' He wanted to keep her talking; he needed to find out how much she knew and how it had affected her. A fly landed on his hand and he brushed it away.

'I was hoping that nothing like this would come out,' she said. 'I hoped to God that he had been discreet. Look, Inspector, before you ask, I do not know who this woman is, or any others. Take the letters away, do your detecting, and find out all you can. But please, could I ask you... as a gentleman, if it's not relevant to the case, if it's not directly linked to the murder... could you keep this away from public scrutiny? I still want to preserve his memory, to protect my family.'

McQueen had sympathy for her; she must have had a difficult time. She would have known about the culture she was marrying into, but that did not necessarily make it any easier. He felt a surge of animosity towards the admiral, for thinking it was completely within his rights to keep a mistress, when he had a wife and a family at home. *But what were Lady Collingwood's true feelings towards her husband? Her seeming acceptance of his dalliances could be a pretence; she could be hiding a relief to be rid of him.*

'I cannot make any promises, you know that,' he said. 'It will likely all have to be included in the report. But can I ask if you thought he still had someone – you know – someone he was seeing, here in Malta?'

He watched her face as she answered. She thought for a moment, then sighed.

'I didn't think so, no. If anything, of late he seemed to be treating me with greater than usual consideration. I thought perhaps, in the twilight of his years, we might grow closer. Well, what can I say? We got on tolerably well together, you know.'

Her eyes as well as her voice seemed to soften, although she gave nothing else away. *Either her regret was genuine, or she was a damn good actress.*

'I have a great deal to think about, Inspector,' she continued. 'I love living in Malta, but no doubt I will have to return to England. It will all take some time. The sooner you can find out the truth about what happened to my husband, the sooner I can begin to rebuild my life.'

She turned around and he followed her back inside the villa. They went into the drawing room, where Carstairs joined them, a sheet of paper in his hand. Before they could resume their conversation, there was a loud knock at the front door. They all listened to the sound of the butler, Mr Williams, remonstrating with somebody, then he appeared at the drawing-room door. 'I am very sorry for the disturbance, Your Ladyship,' he said with obvious disapproval. 'It is the police sergeant. He says he must speak to Inspector McQueen.'

McQueen followed him out into the hall, where Sergeant Galea stood, eyes lit up with excitement. 'Inspector!' he said. 'I have a message from Captain Borġ. He has identified the stranger in the garden and charged him with the murder. It's the man at the police cells, the agitator.'

The sound of a moan drew their attention to the kitchen door, where Mrs Trapani was standing, hands over her face. Before everyone's eyes, she slumped unconscious to the floor.

'Ah,' said Mr Williams. 'That will be Mrs Trapani's son Guiseppe.'

CHAPTER FOURTEEN

'What do we know about this young man?' McQueen asked Galea.

'Guiseppe Trapani. He's been arrested many times. Captain Borġ gave me this for you.'

Galea handed him a sheet listing the charges against Trapani: affray, trespass, incitement, sabotage. All during the past twelve months. *And now – murder.*

McQueen remembered the flicker of amusement in the superintendent's eyes as he watched the young agitator being taken away at the police office. If Borġ had to accept Lord Collingwood's death as murder, McQueen could see how Trapani – a thorn in his side – would make a good suspect. *Why had he been at the villa that night?*

'Could you keep Mrs Trapani in the kitchen?' he asked Williams, who was hovering around them in the hall.

'Go and look after her there,' he told Galea. 'When she has recovered, find out all she knew about her son being here on the night of the murder. I am going back to the police office.'

Carstairs travelled back with McQueen in the *karrozin*. He was almost bouncing up and down with excitement.

'What do you think, Inspector?' he asked. 'Do you have your man? It's him, isn't it? He was there, on the scene.'

'Yes, he was,' said McQueen, 'but I don't see it. Why would he do it? Why would he want the admiral dead?'

'He's well known – a firebrand. He must have killed Collingwood to make a point. About us, the British. An attack against the Crown.'

McQueen shook his head. 'Too extreme. If it were a political act – an act of terrorism – then his party would have acknowledged what he had done. There would have been a full statement about why the admiral had been killed. No, I'm far from convinced we have our man.'

'Oh,' Carstairs said, disappointed. 'Too good to be true, eh?'

'Unless there's another reason. I will interview him. Soon find out the truth.'

'Ah, hang on.' Carstairs opened his attaché case and started rummaging around. 'Just remembered, old boy. I found this – thought it might be interesting.'

He pulled out a sheet of headed notepaper emblazoned with the mark of Coutts Bank. 'It refers to a standing order, revoked a couple of months ago. It appears that on the fifteenth of June the good admiral requested that his annual payment of £100 to a specified account be stopped forthwith. The bank is writing to confirm the request, but it's not clear who the money was being paid to.'

McQueen took the note and looked it over. 'Interesting.'

'Shall I contact the bank and find out who was dealing with it? I can do that; I know people. My cousin, he works there. Shall I send a message?'

Carstairs and the English establishment. *Should he trust him?* It might just be the quickest way to find the information.

'All right,' he said. 'You do that. It could be important.'

They continued the journey in silence. When they arrived back on Strada Reale, Carstairs jumped down from the carriage. 'Have to go,' he said, loudly. 'Meetings and all that, paperwork, you know. Cheerio!' He scuttled off, clutching his attaché case to his chest as though it were a baby.

———

McQueen went straight to Captain Borġ's office. He found him sitting at his desk, leaning back in his chair, looking pleased with himself.

'Ah, Inspector,' the superintendent said. 'You received my note?'

He nodded. 'Aye, I did. I left Sergeant Galea to take a statement from the housekeeper, Mrs Trapani.'

'Well, I think we can close the case for you now, Inspector. While you were gone, I had – shall we say – a little word with young Trapani. I have a statement from him. He admits he was at the villa of Lord Collingwood. He even says he was on the roof and pushed him over the edge.'

'You *what*?'

'I have a sworn statement saying Guiseppe Trapani pushed Lord Collingwood off the roof.'

'With what authority? The case is mine! He is my witness. I've come to interview him now.'

Borġ shrugged, holding his hands out wide in front of him. 'Well, I regret, Inspector, that I cannot help it if, in my enquiries about Trapani's involvement in civic unrest, I happen to find information about your case. I have been instructed to be helpful, no?'

McQueen wanted to reach across the desk and throttle him. *The bastard. How dare he?*

'Take me to him now.'

'I don't think this is a good time. He is resting.'

'Take me to him *now*!'

Borġ looked a little taken aback, but did nothing.

McQueen was not going to let the superintendent get the better of him. 'Now. I insist,' he said, slamming his hand down on the desk.

Borġ sighed. 'All right.' He shouted an order and a police constable appeared. 'Take the inspector down to the cells.'

As they were leaving, he said, 'You should be grateful to me, McQueen. I have done your job for you.'

McQueen swung back towards him, ready to strike, but checked himself just in time. 'You won't get away with this, Superintendent. I will see to that.'

He strode after the constable, furious. When they got to the cells and the desk sergeant opened the door to reveal Trapani sitting on the slatted bed, his worst fears were realised. The young man raised his head, his right eye swollen shut, the skin stretched and a shiny crimson. His long black hair was bedraggled, his clothes disordered and torn. He looked weary and in pain. McQueen ordered the constable out of the cell and sat down next to him.

'Och, man,' he said. 'What have they done to you?'

Trapani shook his head, looking at him warily.

'That shouldn't have happened. It should have been me interviewing you.'

Trapani did not seem to understand what was being said to him. His lip was bleeding. He wiped the blood away with his sleeve, wincing as he moved. McQueen suspected a cracked rib. He was not likely to be willing to speak to another police officer after the treatment he had received.

'Look, I'll get you a lawyer. We'll sort this out. Do you know someone? I'll get them here, now.'

He pulled out his warrant from the governor and showed it to Trapani. 'I'm a detective inspector from Edinburgh,' he explained. 'I'm the one in charge of the investigation into the murder of Lord Collingwood. Borg shouldn't have talked to you. You have to trust me.'

Trapani continued to look at him blankly, to the point that McQueen wondered if he could even understand English.

'Can I get anyone else in to help you?' he asked. 'Do you need water?'

He opened the cell door and shouted, 'Some water, now!'

The constable came back, somewhat surly in demeanour, slopping water over the brim of a cup. McQueen took it from him with a sharp look and gave it to the prisoner.

After taking a couple of sips, Trapani finally spoke. 'Marsat,' he said, his voice croaky, as though he had not used it for some time. 'Marsat. Lawyer.'

'Right,' McQueen said. 'I will return. I'll get you your lawyer, and then I'll be back.'

He marched out of the cell and up to the magistrate's office. He would have Borg's guts for garters.

———

Il Magistrato Cassar called McQueen and Marsat to appear before him in his office.

'What exactly is your complaint?' he asked. He looked at them as if they were small children, whose ball game had smashed his window and interrupted his afternoon snooze.

Marsat was small and round, with strands of black hair carefully combed over his balding head, and a pugnacious attitude. 'The prisoner, Guiseppe Trapani, has been detained without a lawyer, he has been subjected to police brutality, and he has been coerced into giving a statement,' he said. 'The

123

inspector here has told me the statement should be withdrawn so that he can interview the suspect himself. Trapani is willing to comply with this request.'

The magistrate looked at McQueen with raised eyebrows. 'Inspector, can you confirm this?'

'Yes, indeed. Captain Borġ has gone beyond his responsibilities. He has interrogated the suspect in my investigation, and he has used violence to get the answer he wanted, for his own convenience.'

Cassar was quiet for a few moments. He had a heavy way of breathing that was getting on McQueen's nerves. He could feel himself getting impatient, dying to say, 'Get on with it, man.'

Finally, the magistrate spoke. 'I do believe that the police superintendent is acting within the law,' he said. 'The Order of Council, dated fourteenth of April of this year, gives the police full authority to detain people suspected of spreading dissidence, without legal assistance and for an unlimited time. The police may also use methods of interrogation – up to a point – to obtain answers from said suspects.'

'But this is nonsense!' Marsat exclaimed, gesticulating as he spoke. 'The governor's approach is draconian. He uses Orders of Council to change the law to suit his every whim. He does not like it, this new unrest from the people. Oh no, the Maltese should behave themselves, be like the slaves he thinks they are.'

McQueen added emphatically, 'This is *my* investigation. The confession is not sound. I need to speak to Trapani myself.'

'Exactly!' said Marsat. 'The superintendent can interview Trapani about the rally, but not about the murder. Trapani has been charged with murder without Inspector McQueen's consent.'

The magistrate thought again.

'Inspector, do you wish to charge Trapani with murder?'

'Not at this point, no,' he replied. 'I need him fed and

watered. I need him cleaned up, and for a doctor to look at his injuries. And I need to interview him again to get a new statement. I do not believe he was involved in the death of the admiral, but I do think he has important evidence.'

'*Signore*, you must quash the statement if he is not going to be charged for this murder. You must allow the inspector to speak to him,' Marsat said.

The magistrate sighed, his long face looking increasingly like that of a sorrowful donkey.

'Very well,' he said. 'Get me Captain Borġ.'

When the police superintendent emerged to join them, his face dark with suppressed rage, McQueen watched in amusement the storm that unfolded. They spoke in Italian, too fast and furious for him to understand, but he could nevertheless interpret the body language and tone of voice. For all his bluster, Borġ was clearly being forced to concede. He argued forcefully, but after a full and angry exchange eventually he threw his arms up in the air and left the room, giving McQueen a filthy look on the way out.

———

Later that afternoon, McQueen and Galea went back to interview Trapani in a separate room, together with the lawyer. He looked better, stronger, his wound had been dressed, but he was not willing to make eye contact. McQueen knew Trapani would still feel wary, concerned that this could be a trap.

'Look, I regret what happened to you earlier,' he said. 'I am not here to put words in your mouth, and I have no interest in your political activities. I want you to tell me exactly what happened–'

'He doesn't speak English,' Marsat interrupted. 'I will have to translate.'

The lawyer relayed McQueen's words in Maltese, whilst Trapani stared up at the ceiling.

'We know you were there, at the villa. The evening of fifth of July. You were spotted by the houseboy.'

He mumbled a few words in reply, shaking his head. McQueen felt a rising frustration.

'Tell him this from me: you cannot claim you weren't there, man. You have to tell me what happened, or there's nothing I can do about your murder charge. What were you doing at the villa?'

Marsat and Trapani exchanged words, the younger man getting more and more agitated. At one point, he stood up abruptly, looking around him as if working out whether he could escape. His chair fell to the ground behind him with a clatter. McQueen readied himself to intervene, but the lawyer picked up the chair and pushed Trapani gently back down, continuing to speak in a reassuring tone.

The young man put his head in his hands, staring at the floor, his hair hanging down in twisted strands.

'It's all right,' Marsat said. 'He understands the situation. He will explain.'

After a short while, Trapani looked up, pushing his hair away from his face. He looked McQueen in the eye, a deep crease forming between his dark eyebrows. Light from the tiny window accentuated the gaunt cheekbone on his left side, then as he turned slightly, the purplish swelling above and below his right eye.

'I can speak English,' he said, his voice heavily accented. 'I don't like to, but I can. Yes, I was at villa. I visit my mother. It was her birthday.'

'What time did you arrive?'

'Nine. She was busy. She make food for the rich English while the Maltese they have nothing. It make me sick.'

'Keep the politics out of it,' McQueen said. 'I told you I'm not interested. What did you do?'

'I wait in her room until she is free – late. Then we talk. I give her birthday gift. I tell her about plans for the protest. About how we involve all the people. The people of Valletta and the people in other towns and villages. I am printing leaflets, newspapers. I tell her about it.'

McQueen cut in. 'I don't doubt it. Once again, I am not interested. What happened at the time when the admiral died?'

'There is window in my mother's room,' Trapani said. 'You can see the garden. I am opposite my mother and I see something drop. It was hard to see because it is dark, but it look strange. We hear a sound, heavy, it hit the ground. I tell my mother to wait and I go outside.'

He took a sip of water, and then continued. 'I see a shape on the terrace, and I go to see what is it. It is Lord Collingwood. I check to see if he is breathing, but he is dead. My mother is behind me, and she scared. We agree I get away fast. I not meant to be there. She waits then she make alarm. That is what we did.'

'Do you know what time exactly he fell from the roof?'

Trapani shook his head.

'How long did your mother wait?'

'Five minutes.'

'And was there anything else you noticed either before or after that happened?'

'No. Listen, I hate the man. He talk about our people as if we are animals. Yes, many are poor, but is not their fault. We have to pay wheat tax – more and more – and bread is only food we afford. Pah! But I would never, never do such a thing. Only a coward kill like that, and I am not coward. Do with me what you want – I don't care!'

With these words, he sat back with his arms folded across his chest, staring at McQueen with intense dark eyes.

McQueen was convinced. The young man was quite the firebrand, but there was not much to suggest he had anything to do with the admiral's death.

'Very well,' he said, standing up. 'Sergeant Galea will write down your new statement.'

He took Marsat outside and said he had no further interest in Trapani. The lawyer shook his hand and said he would attempt to get his client released on bail at his court appearance the next day.

As he walked away, McQueen thought about the implications of Trapani's story that the murder had happened a few minutes earlier than everyone had believed. Lady Collingwood had been adamant every guest was in the room when Mrs Trapani raised the alarm. *But perhaps someone had slipped back in, unnoticed? Did this open up the list of suspects?* He felt as though he still had a long way to go with the investigation.

CHAPTER FIFTEEN

M cQueen went back to his office to plan his next move. There were the business dealings and financial matters to delve into more deeply. He could do with talking to Arbuthnot again, now he knew there had been five minutes between the murder and when Mrs Trapani had sounded the alarm. It might have been a noble act on her part, but it made the investigation more complex. Anyone who was at the soirée could have slipped away, gone up to the roof and got back again to the drawing room unnoticed. He had to go through that guest list and scrutinise everyone's movements on the night. Then, there was the maidservant at the villa. He felt sure she had something she was hiding. He must go back and see her again. But the first step must be to identify the admiral's mistress – who and where was she?

He found the stash of letters from the admiral's writing bureau and began to read them. There were sixty in all, arranged in date order. He started with the first, which was dated fourteen years ago, from an address in Fareham, Hampshire. He checked it against one of the later ones. Yes, it was the same handwriting. *So, the old goat had at least been consistent then*, he thought. He felt a surge of anger on behalf of the admiral's wife, who for all those years would have been doing everything to make her husband's life comfortable, while he spent time and money on another woman.

The letters – signed "Your Sarah" – were full of thanks for Collingwood's help. She was happy in her little cottage; she loved the little puppy he had sent her; she was excited that her gardener had planted some delphiniums, her favourite flowers. McQueen grew increasingly irritated by her sentimentality. She referred to Collingwood as "my dear heart" and looked forward to his every visit "with exquisite anticipation". No wonder he was smitten, with all that gushing adoration.

He picked up a few letters from the middle of the pile. The same address, the same light tone. Perhaps a little petulance creeping in? Asking for a little more attention, an account with the milliner so she could have the latest fashion. She wanted him still to admire her, and how could she with so little pin money to spend on herself?

Finally, he looked at the latest batch, all sent to Collingwood at the Royal Malta Yacht Club. He saw that she had moved to Malta as well, to a town called Sliema. He looked at the dates. Four months after the Collingwoods had arrived, there she was thanking him for the lovely little apartment, telling him how blissful it was in the warm climate, and how wonderful that she could keep seeing him. McQueen wondered at her cleverness. *How had she managed to keep one man dangling on the end of her line for so long? How special was she, for the admiral to take the risk of installing her near him, on the tiny island where it would be almost impossible to maintain a secret?* There was no address beyond Sliema, and no surname. But he did not think it would take much to find out who she was.

Sergeant Galea came into the office.

'Sergeant!' he said. 'I have a job for you. You will like this one.'

'Yes, sir?'

'See these letters? They are all from the admiral's lady friend, who it appears is called Sarah and lives nearby, in Sliema. Can you go to the P&O offices and ask if you can access the records for all arrivals in Malta in March and April 1879? You need to look for details of women travelling on their own, first name Sarah. Follow them all up. Find out where they are staying, what they look like, and their circumstances: if they are married, single, widowed and so on. That should take you the rest of the day. Go on, off you go! You can report back tomorrow morning.'

He enjoyed watching the range of emotions reflected on the young man's face. He looked both pleased and daunted at the same time.

'Yes, sir, P&O offices, March and April last year – I am going.'

Surely even Galea could not make a mess of such a simple task, could he? McQueen was looking forward to seeing how he got on.

He scribbled a note to Carstairs saying he would meet him later. He went outside to look for Antonio, who soon came running up.

'Can you take this message to Lieutenant Carstairs at the Governor's Palace?'

'Yes, Mister McQueen.'

Note in hand, Antonio continued to stand in front of him, looking as if he were itching to say something.

'Come on, then, lad – out with it! What d'you want?'

'Please, Mister McQueen – I want to ask you. On Sunday it is festa. There is a band and they carry San Duminku in the streets. Shall I show you? It is the best night of the year!'

McQueen had no idea what Popish nonsense this was, but the lad seemed so excited. 'We'll see,' he said. 'What time?'

'It will be six o'clock,' said Antonio, jigging up and down. 'Can we go? Can we go? Ma says I can go.'

'Perhaps,' McQueen said, amused at the boy's antics. *It would be a chance to see the local culture, soak up the atmosphere.* 'Now, off with you!'

He had sufficient time to go and see Colonel Arbuthnot again. He wanted to question him about his argument with Lord Collingwood at the soirée. He headed to the Union Club, where Arbuthnot had said he could be found every afternoon. It was at the top of Strada Reale, in another old palace, the Auberge de Provence. After a fast walk through the blazing sun, McQueen arrived and sought refuge in the cool of the bar upstairs. The place impressed him with its wooden beamed ceiling and richly painted walls.

He found Arbuthnot in a seat in the corner, a gin and tonic in front of him. The old man looked up somewhat blearily as McQueen approached. His eyes were red-rimmed and watery.

'Oh, it's you,' he said, picking up his glass and swirling the contents.

'Mind if I join you?' McQueen asked, calling over a waiter and asking for a whisky.

'Be my guest, old boy, be my guest.' He was slurring his words.

'I have some more questions for you.'

'Ah, yes, the admiral. Yes. Poor chap. Fell off the roof. Saw him. On the ground. Blood everywhere.'

'Yes, I know.' He frowned, wondering how much sense he was going to get from the colonel in this state. Clearly, he was three sheets to the wind. 'Tell me again about your argument with him that evening.'

'Argument? Oh, yes. Harbingers.'

Arbuthnot took another sip from his glass. McQueen's whisky arrived, watered down with some melting ice. *Not the ideal way to serve it, but still, it was cool.*

'Lord Collingwood. Harbingers?' he prompted.

'Thing is, old sport, I'm in a bit of a tight spot.'

Arbuthnot drank down the rest of his gin and gestured to the waiter to bring him another.

'I had it all worked out. I took out a loan – I won't tell you how much. Enough to make your eyes water. I invested in Harbingers. Steel, you know. Collingwood said they were a sure-fire winner. Bought 300 shares. Spread the word, got others to invest. He told me to. Man's word is as good as his bond, isn't it? Gave me all the confidence I needed. Sank everything into it.'

He stared gloomily at the table until the next drink arrived.

'What happened?' McQueen asked.

'Weeks later, he pulled out. My old friend – we went back years, you know. He pulled out. I couldn't believe it. He was a director. Whole thing was bogus. Sold the company, took the profits. Nothing left, no orders, nothing.'

'So, you've got the shares, but...'

'But those bloody loan-mongers want their interest and I've got nothing to pay 'em with. Shares aren't worth anything if I sell 'em. Don't know what I'll do.'

Hands shaking, he took a long drink, then leaned forwards. 'It's the others. Keep thinking of the others. I told them to invest, you see.' He grabbed hold of McQueen's arm. 'Collingwood didn't care, but I can't bear to think of the others.' Tears formed in his eyes and he sank back into his gloomy haze.

McQueen stood up. 'Don't let him drink any more,' he said

quietly to the waiter. 'Can you get a cab to take him home?' He handed over some coins.

As he left the club, McQueen wondered if there could have been a confrontation when Arbuthnot had found out about the investment. *Could he have toppled his erstwhile friend from the roof in a fit of rage? Was this drunken stupor the effect of guilt, for a deed much worse than poorly advising his friends?* He needed to find out more about Harbingers, and Collingwood's involvement. It was time to talk to Carstairs. He headed back to the Governor's Palace.

Waiting in the reception hall, McQueen was surprised by the speed at which Carstairs appeared, and the concerned expression on his face.

'I say, McQueen,' he said, somewhat out of breath. 'The governor wants to see you, sharpish. No getting out of it, I'm afraid. Captain Borg's been to see him and he seems a bit rattled.'

So, he was finally going to meet the governor. Now, he could see where the power rested – about time, too. Carstairs led the way up to the first floor at breakneck speed.

'That'll be about our friend Trapani,' McQueen said. 'Two cases, one suspect. I could tell the superintendent wasn't too happy.'

'Well, I think you'll be all right. It's... you know, Borg is not used to anyone standing in his way.'

They stopped outside an ancient-looking wooden door at the end of the marble floored corridor. Carstairs knocked loudly then went in.

'Inspector McQueen, Your Excellency,' he said.

The room was commanding in size and overwhelmingly

red: red velvet chair seats, red wallpaper, red curtains bedecking the windows. The governor sat behind an outsize desk, two rows of chairs with gold frames set at angles in front of him, as if he had recently dismissed an audience. Despite being seated, McQueen could tell he was tall, and his considerable white whiskers – and eyebrows – gave him an imposing presence. He stood and shook hands with McQueen across the top of the desk, then motioned to them both to sit down.

'Pleased to meet you, Inspector,' he said. McQueen could not hear any hint of a Scottish accent. One of those Scottish families who send their boys to English boarding school and then dispatch them into the Army. *Probably only lived there fifteen summers or so in his whole life.* He looked like a tough old boot, his leathery, lined skin a record of many years in hot climates. Although very upright, he moved stiffly. McQueen suspected this was the last job the governor would be carrying out in Her Majesty's service before retirement.

'How is the investigation going? I hear you've been ruffling some feathers.'

'It's difficult to work with Captain Borġ. He's been obstructive, he has withheld evidence, and I don't like his manner.'

The governor frowned. 'Let's be clear on this, McQueen. Borġ answers to me. He's a good man – you should give him time. I agree he has been a little, shall we say, over-zealous, but he was carrying out what he thought were my orders.'

He stood up abruptly. 'Have you seen the Tapestry Chamber?'

'No.'

'Follow me, then. Carstairs, let's show the inspector around.'

They made their way along the corridor, the governor pointing out the Grandmasters of the Order of St John, depicted in a sequence of portraits. Finally, they turned into a room on the right.

'This is where the governing council meets,' the governor said, indicating rows of velvet covered chairs and neat desks, and a throne embroidered in gold with the Royal Arms of England.

It was stiflingly hot and McQueen felt oppressed by the opulence of the surroundings. The wooden ceiling was painted with gold and bright colours, as were the friezes along the top of the walls. The windows were covered in red curtains. In addition, all four walls were hung with ten-foot tapestries.

'I can see where the chamber gets its name.'

'One hundred and seventy years old. They were the gift of one of the Grandmasters, made especially for this room as a copy of the Indian hangings in Versailles.'

The governor swept his arm around the room.

'Look at all the wealth they have in this country. We are the custodians, McQueen, not the owners. We tread a fine line.'

McQueen walked around slowly, looking at the pictures of exotic animals in jungle settings. He went closer, to inspect an animal he thought to be a white tiger, sinking its jaws into a striped horse.

'Your point is, sir?'

'My point is, Inspector, that I need to maintain order. You are here for one purpose only, and that is to find out who is responsible for the death of Lord Collingwood. I don't want you pushing your weight around, undermining Captain Borg's position.'

'You gave me the authority to run this case – it was Borg who overstepped the mark.'

'The superintendent is sure he found the murderer, Inspector. He believes the young man to be dangerous. If

Trapani gets released tomorrow, and anyone else gets hurt, your head will be on the block.'

'It is not him. He has no motive and his mother has given him an alibi... which Borġ would know if he had followed the correct procedures. Trapani is a zealot, but he's not a killer.'

'You had better be right.'

They headed out of the chamber and the governor stopped at the stairs leading back down to the palace entrance. The interview was clearly over.

'One final thing, Inspector. I have to impress on you that this investigation needs to be cleared up as quickly as possible. Tell him why, Lieutenant.'

'We have just had news that the Duke of Edinburgh, Prince Alfred, will be visiting Malta on the fourth of September,' Carstairs said.

'Indeed. That's less than a month from now. This is a real headache for me. I will give you one more week, McQueen. If you have not solved the case by then, you will be sent back to Edinburgh. One week, or you go back home.'

CHAPTER SIXTEEN

'Next, please.'
Doctor Bonnići ran his clinic at the Central Hospital along organised lines. At least twenty people were waiting outside in the corridor. He had just ushered out an elderly widow with severe bronchial difficulties, clutching a bottle of cough syrup. He knew this could do nothing to help her in the long run, but it could at least make her more comfortable. By the time patients reached him, the best he could do was treat the symptoms. Cures were not easily come by.

He left the door open and went back to his desk. A few seconds later a young couple came in, the girl looking shamefaced and nervous, the youth adopting a kind of swagger, but probably equally unsure of himself. Bonnići had seen it all before and tried to put them at ease.

'Please, sit down. What can I do for you?' he said.

The young man was small and wiry, the smartness of his middle-parted hair spoilt by a squint. He was aggressive in his manner, reminding Bonnići of a terrier, but he was so young it was almost comical. He could not have been older than seventeen. 'It's my fiancée. She's been feeling ill. Sickness. But she's hungry all the time. It's her stomach. Can you give her something for it, Doctor?'

The girl looked at him pleadingly, her eyes wide. She was a tiny thing, four feet ten inches at the most, with no weight on her at all. He guessed she knew exactly what was wrong, but that her suitor refused to believe her.

'May I ask her some questions without you in the room?' he said to the boy. 'I'll call you back in.'

The young man reluctantly left the room, looking behind him as if it were a conspiracy against him. Bonniċi explained to the girl that he had some difficult questions for her. She looked at him, terrified. He asked if she had been intimate with her fiancé, and she nodded, flushing red. Then he asked her if her menses had ceased. Once again, she nodded.

'How many weeks ago?' he asked.

She looked down, and said, her voice barely over a whisper, 'Six or seven.'

'Then I don't need to examine you. You already know, don't you?'

She nodded again.

He got up and went to the door, calling her fiancé back in.

He confirmed the news. He could see how devastating it was for the couple. The young man turned pale. 'Are you sure, *Duttur*? Are you sure? What is she supposed to do?' The girl started crying, silently. 'She's in service. They'll throw her out. And her family's in Rabat. She won't be able to tell them.'

'Well,' Bonniċi said carefully. 'There are mother and baby homes, run by the nuns. I can ask them to take you in for a few months. They will look after you when the time comes to deliver the baby. I'm sorry, there's nothing else I can do.'

The girl jumped up, shaking her head, panicking. Her fiancé put his arm around her. He seemed to make a decision, there and then.

'Thank you, *Duttur*,' he said, leading her away. 'It's all right, Ċensa, don't cry. We can get married straight away; I will marry you. You won't have to go to the home.'

As they went out of the room, he could hear the young man continuing to reassure her. 'We'll get some money. It'll be all right.'

Bonniċi shook his head. *How could this happen, time and time again? What chance did the couple have? They were children themselves.* The young man was full of bravado, but there was a desperation about him that did not inspire confidence. This was the part of his job that Bonniċi hated, the times when he could not help people. He could hand out pills and powders, but unless they had good food, clean water and decent living conditions, their chances of a healthy life were limited. Like the family he had visited, with seven people living in one room. When illness arrived, like the sudden, swift onslaught of typhoid fever, it would often claim the lives of several family members.

He rubbed his eyes, finding it difficult to concentrate. He knew that as a medical practitioner he did not encourage confidences. He could be distant, not the warmest of people, but he did feel a genuine sympathy for his patients. A day like today made him feel low in spirits. There were those who wanted children and yet could not have them. And then there were those for whom a baby was a nuisance, another mouth to feed, or worse, in society's eyes, a grievous sin because it was born outside of wedlock.

It was thirteen years now since he had lost Liena to tuberculosis. They had never had children. He could not help thinking of her sadness, her quiet acceptance of the fact she would never hold her own baby in her arms. He sighed and called in the next patient.

After the clinic, Bonniċi went back to his laboratory, where he could lose himself in his work. He was deeply concerned about the typhoid case. *Was the infection local to the family he had visited, or was the water supply itself contaminated?* He had taken samples from the cellar and from the nearest water pump. The pump water was supplied from a large tank; if that had been contaminated, he feared there would be a major outbreak throughout the city.

He felt the weight of responsibility. He had spoken to the Chief Medical Officer, promising to provide an answer by the end of the day. It was essential that he carried out the work with absolute thoroughness. He started with the cellar water. Not only was it discoloured, but it had a noxious smell. He tested it for chlorine, nitrates and ammonia. Positive results from all. The water was contaminated with sewage, known to be a cause of typhoid.

He got so angry when he thought about Gabriel Borġ. *The man was unscrupulous!* The dwelling places his company had created were unfit for human habitation. There were clear guidelines on window sizes, provision of a clean water supply and ceramic sewage pipes to take dirty water away. Yet none of them had been adhered to, because there was no requirement by law. They only cared about profit, above all else. The families living in the cellars were given nothing. It was as though they had been abandoned, no one caring whether they lived or died, simply because they were poor.

He did not know why he had not been more vocal, speaking up for the causes he believed in. It was as if he had given up fighting. He needed to use his anger to better effect.

He leaned back in his chair, rubbing his temples. He glanced over at the photograph of Liena on his desk. As always, she looked at him kindly, encouraging him with her gentle smile. He missed her, every day. Their marriage had been short, just five years. He knew he had let his grief affect him too deeply, shutting himself away.

He had become lonely and the long hours he spent in the laboratory were beginning to affect his health. He was forty-five now, not young anymore. Recently, he had started to battle with weakness and pain in his joints and muscles. There were times when he fell asleep in his chair, overwhelmed by fatigue. He was beginning to think he would have to take better care of himself.

Liena would have told him to get out more, to go hunting. He used to like that: the early start, the fresh air, the open landscape away from the city. *He would get a hunting dog, a companion.* For a fleeting moment, he found himself dreaming about doing something pleasant, something he would enjoy.

But for now, he needed to finish this task. He set to work analysing the water taken from the pump.

A short while later, he heard a knock at the door. He picked up his cane and limped over to open it. A small boy gave him a big smile, asked if he was *Duttur* Bonniċi, and gave him a note. The bold, dashed-off handwriting told him it came from the Scottish inspector even before he saw the signature. McQueen needed to meet him at his home at seven o'clock that evening. *Interesting.* He wondered what the detective wanted to discuss. The boy waited cheerfully for an answer, looking around the laboratory with interest. On an impulse Bonniċi gave him a penny with his message. The lad disappeared with a grin, seemingly amazed at his good luck.

When Bonniċi arrived home that night, he found McQueen sitting on his doorstep, holding a bottle of whisky.

'Medicinal,' the detective explained. 'Wholesome and good for the stomach.'

'You had better come in,' Bonniċi said, smiling as he opened the door.

On entry to the house, he had a room to the left which was his home laboratory, and a room to the right which was his library. The parlour was straight ahead, with the kitchen off to the right. He was pleased to see that his housekeeper had laid out some food on the table.

'Have you eaten?' he asked.

McQueen shook his head and the two of them sat down.

Bonniċi wondered what had made the detective decide to visit him. He knew he must have something particular to talk to him about. He busied himself with serving out the pasta and pouring out a glass of local wine.

'Have you heard what happened today?' McQueen asked, tucking straight in to his plate of food.

'No, I've been busy. I had a clinic today, then I was in the laboratory.'

'Captain Borġ tried to charge Guiseppe Trapani with the murder. The young man who was arrested at the rally.'

'What?'

'Trapani has admitted he was at the villa that night, but he's not our murderer, I'm sure of it.'

'Why would he want to kill Lord Collingwood?'

'Well, exactly. Borġ's theory was that he wanted to make an example of him. My theory is that Borġ feels he will curry favour with the governor by solving two crimes in one: the murder and incitement to violence.'

Bonniċi felt uneasy. This was not the world that he knew anymore. Things were happening that did not feel right. Up until now the Maltese had seemed relatively happy with their government, proud to be a British crown colony. Now there were murmurings, tensions and plots.

He got out some whisky glasses.

'The worst of it,' McQueen said, through a mouthful of food, 'is that he beat a so-called confession out of Trapani and expected to get full credit for solving the case!'

'Were you able to do anything about it?'

'I got the magistrate to void the statement and Trapani's now up for bail. The superintendent is not talking to me, the magistrate objected to being prised out of his afternoon snooze and the governor has rapped me on the knuckles. Hence the medicine.'

Bonniċi opened the bottle and poured them both a generous measure. He was not one for strong drink, but this occasion warranted it, and he took a big swig. The smokiness and the alcohol burnt his throat and he choked, which made McQueen laugh.

'Look, I want to know what it is with the superintendent,' McQueen said. 'Why did you warn me about him? What did you mean about "how things work in Malta"? I'm never going to get anywhere unless I understand.'

'What's this whisky?' Bonniċi asked, looking at the bottle. 'I've never tasted anything like it.'

'It's an Islay malt. Ardbeg. The best in the world,' McQueen said, rolling his Rs. 'The smoky flavour is from the peat. It cannot be beaten.'

It felt to Bonniċi like it was stripping his throat, but he went back for another one to try it again.

'Captain Borġ,' he explained, 'thinks he is the most important person on the islands. Apart from the Bishop of Malta, and the crown advocate, he most probably is. He has business concerns everywhere, he knows everyone. His brother

Gabriel sits on the government council. All the wine shops and bars pay the superintendent money, so he allows them their licences. The brothels, the gambling shops, they are all under his control.'

'I suspected as much,' McQueen said. 'It's the way he sits there looking as though he's so powerful, thinking there is nothing anyone can do to touch him.' He downed his glass in one and topped it up again.

Bonniċi drank the remains of his whisky, starting to feel its effects. 'The governor thinks Borġ is a strong police chief who has control over crime by dint of good policing,' he said. 'But it's nothing but bribes and corruption.'

He was surprised how much he was divulging to the detective. There was something about McQueen's solid presence, the way he seemed to care about how things were done, that made him feel bold.

'There's more,' he said. 'There are common dwelling places, *kerrejja*. The situation is so bad, and it's all because of the corrupt system. Two days ago, I had to visit a family, to see a patient with typhoid fever. The rooms, in the cellars. There's no water, no sanitation.'

The scene appeared before him: the stench, the dying man on his bed of rags, the wife crying, thin as a rake. That feeling of powerlessness. The only help he could offer was short-lived. And yet it was so simple: all they needed was clean water, good food, fresh air. He shook his head as if to rid himself of the memory. He was almost in tears. *He should not have accepted that drink.*

He got a grip on himself. Took a breath.

'A new company has been buying government property to develop as common dwelling places for the poorest of the city. They are supposed to adhere to guidelines – provide ventilation, sanitation. But they haven't done any of it. In many cases, they have crammed families into dark rooms, with nothing in them at all, not even a window. I don't know for sure, but I believe the man behind it is Gabriel Borġ – the superintendent's brother. They are in it together, up to their ears in money-making property deals. I am ashamed, Inspector. Ashamed that it should be like this in my country, and no one is doing anything about it!'

McQueen was listening intently. 'I know what you mean,' he said. 'I've seen the same in Edinburgh. The old slums. Not fit for animals. Better now, a lot better, but still. Landlords have a lot to answer for.'

'There's fault everywhere,' Bonniċi said. 'The government, for selling off property without enforcing the contracts, the property developers for their penny-pinching, the landlords – and me, for not doing anything about it. I've been hiding away. At the hospital and in the laboratory. I know I have. I have never spoken out, *never.*'

There was a silence after this. Bonniċi could not believe how much he had revealed about himself. McQueen was considering how to respond. The detective reached for the bottle again and poured them both another.

'Well,' he said, after a moment's pause. 'We can change that. Everyone has their moment. Think about it. I've already unravelled some of Borġ's scheming. The magistrate – and the governor – now know he tried to hide evidence. When I solve the case – and I will, with your help – perhaps we can shake things up at the same time and see what comes rattling out.'

He held up his glass, as if proposing a toast. 'What do you say, Doctor?'

Bonniċi felt a glow of hope and optimism – *or was it just the alcohol?* He could not help smiling as he raised his glass and clinked it against the detective's.

'I will drink to that!'

CHAPTER SEVENTEEN

Saturday, 7 August 1880

'I know what make the cigars are, sir.'
Sergeant Galea came into the office looking pleased with himself. 'I took them to the tobacconists on Strada Reale.'

McQueen was sitting back in his chair, feet on the table, feeling the worse for wear. There had not been much left in the Ardbeg bottle by the end of the night.

'Oh, aye?' he asked, amused at the young sergeant's pride. 'So, what are they?'

Galea pulled out his pocketbook. 'They are Nostrano del Brenta, an Italian make – very expensive.'

'Good. And did the tobacconist know if Lord Collingwood smoked them?'

'He smoked Cuban cigars. There were only two main customers for these.' He checked his notes again. 'Professor Attard from the University of Malta, and Count San Pietro. One of the *notabile* from Città Vecchia.'

'Excellent. Progress – at last.'

This youngster was beginning to have his uses.

'And, sir...'

'Yes?'

'I have found out where the mistress lives.'

'Bravo, Sergeant! Tell me everything!'

Galea had found three possible passengers on the P&O lists and had managed to find out the details of each of them. There was an elderly widow visiting her sister, married to an Anglican vicar, a governess returning to the family of a Navy captain based in Valletta, and Mrs Sarah Hawthorne of the New Imperial Hotel, Sliema.

'Aha! Sliema. That has to be our woman. No time like the present,' McQueen said, rubbing his hands together. 'Let's go and find her.'

Sliema was a new, fast-growing area on the other side of Marsamscetto Harbour. They took a water ferry across from the foot of Strada San Marco and made their way to the hotel. Finding Mrs Hawthorne's apartment on the first floor, they knocked at the door. They were shown by a young maidservant into a bright, sunny room with a view over the harbour. McQueen handed over his card and wandered over to the window while they waited. The Valletta skyline was now a familiar sight, even though he had been in Malta for less than a week. He noted the landmarks he could now recognise, the bastions of St Michael and St Andrews, the Anglican cathedral, and to the left, Fort St Elmo.

It was only a matter of moments before the door opened and Mrs Hawthorne entered the room. McQueen had been expecting a frivolous creature from reading the letters, but the person before him was anything but. Small and compact, Sarah

Hawthorne was cool and poised. She had fair hair, worn in a simple style, and piercing blue eyes, which regarded him with intelligence and a hint of mischief. She had the kind of sharp features that required animation to make her attractive. In repose, he thought she could look quite pinched and cold-hearted, but here, in front of him, she flashed a smile that was most beguiling.

'Police, indeed – goodness, a detective inspector! I feel flattered. I wondered how long it would take you to find me. It's about Lord Collingwood, I suppose?' The tone of her voice was low, measured. McQueen imagined many men would find it alluring.

'It is, Mrs Hawthorne. We're investigating his death. We would like to ask you some questions about your relationship with him, and, in particular, when you last saw him.'

'Do sit down, Inspector, and you–'

'Sergeant Galea, madame.'

McQueen was amused to see how hard Galea was finding it not to gaze at her, open-mouthed. She knew how to draw attention to herself, making a show of sweeping her skirt to one side before sitting down elegantly. Cornflower-blue sprigs adorned her dress, bringing out the blue of her eyes. She held a fan in her right hand and used it to great effect, her eyes wide above the top as she deftly fanned the air onto her face.

McQueen liked the look of her. *She was a little older than him*, he thought, *and looking well for her age*. A few faint lines by the corners of her eyes. Clearly, she took good care of herself, but then that was probably her chief occupation. He had encountered many fallen women in his work, but not many high-class courtesans or kept women. *Did she even think of herself as such?* She intrigued him. He took out his pocketbook.

'How did you find me, Inspector? Let me guess, was it my letters?'

'It was. We found them in his writing desk – hidden – going back over ten years.'

'Oh dear, I told him so many times to get rid of them. He was far too sentimental. I knew it was a bad idea for him to keep them, though I did try to be very careful in what I wrote.'

'What exactly was your relationship with Lord Collingwood?'

'Well, Inspector, you can't possibly expect me to divulge any details. Let's say we were very good friends, and that Lord Collingwood would visit me – not so very often, perhaps every fortnight or so – to reacquaint himself with me and to discuss our joint interests.'

McQueen allowed himself a secret smile at her playful way with words.

'I was so sad to hear about his death,' she went on, her tone a little more serious. 'Of course, nobody knew to tell me, so I found out through the newspaper. Can you imagine how I felt, reading about it in the *Malta Standard?* I was, genuinely, heartbroken.' She looked down at her fan, then back up at him, with eyes that were cool and unreadable.

'When was the last time you saw him?'

She thought for a moment. 'It was a while ago. I was getting a little concerned. I think perhaps two weeks before he died. It was the middle of June, around the twentieth? I seem to remember the weather was about to turn hot.'

She fanned herself again.

'And how did he seem when you met him?'

'Well, Inspector, I am going to be honest with you here.' She dropped her voice a tone. 'He seemed slightly upset about something. Which is unknown for him. Normally nothing ever, ever disturbs him. Disturbed him, sorry.'

'What do you mean?' prompted McQueen. 'In what way did he seem upset?'

'It's difficult to say. He was a little distant. And he wouldn't be drawn at all on what was bothering him. I did try. I asked several times if everything was all right. In the end he snapped at me, and he even left early. Not my finest hour.'

McQueen could sense her scrutinising him as he wrote a couple of notes. He looked up and found himself caught in her gaze.

'I know what you're thinking, Inspector. You are wondering if Lord Collingwood was all that stood between me and destitution, if I relied upon him for my rent, my food, my everything.' He raised his eyebrows.

'Well, let me tell you that I am not such a fool. I am an independent woman with my own income of 500 pounds a year. There are other gentlemen who value my time, two of whom are also in Malta. They know of one another, but they also know I hold a special place in my life for each. I hope they will stay unnamed. But I can assure you that I did not need Lord Collingwood. The others are already pleased that I have more time for them.' She smiled, showing small, even, white teeth.

'Very reassuring,' he murmured. This "lady" seemed unusually secure of her position in life and confident of her abilities. There was a promise in her eyes that he found attractive, but he also sensed she was far too clever and manipulative to be trusted.

There was a sudden sound from Galea, who had tried to swat a fly and slammed his hand down on a side-table, apologising profusely. It broke the tension in the room and they both laughed.

'Tell me,' McQueen said. 'How did you and Lord Collingwood first meet?'

'Oh, that was over ten years ago. I used to run these soirées when I lived in Portsmouth, for gentlemen in the Navy to discuss culture and current affairs. You'd be surprised how popular they were. I used to run them with my late husband, before he so sadly passed away.'

She looked at McQueen, eyes full of merriment, daring him to say what he thought.

'I'm sure your Navy gentlemen had a delightful time.'

'Lord Collingwood certainly did. Dear Edward. We had so many happy years together.'

How did she do it? Her voice was so soft, and conveyed such a promise, he very nearly believed her. He stood up abruptly and moved over to the fireplace.

'You lived in Fareham, in Hampshire.'

'Indeed, I did.'

'Why the move to Malta?'

'It was his suggestion. You see, he could not bear for me to be far away from him. Quite a determined gentleman. And the climate really does have its attractions.'

McQueen pulled his damp collar away from his neck. He was not sure he agreed with her. He looked back at his pocketbook.

'So, you're staying here in Sliema, you've been here just over one year, and the last time you saw Lord Collingwood was around the twentieth of June. Is there anything else you can tell me about his state of mind? Did you form any impression of what was concerning him? Business matters, perhaps? Or family?'

'I knew next to nothing about his business affairs. He had interests in ship-building I believe, and a steel company. He was very astute. I don't think anything would ever cause him to lose sleep over money matters. As for family, he spoke very little about it. I hear his wife is quite the society lady. Committees to help refugees, schools for the poor and that kind of thing. I'm not sure I would care to meet her. And his son Edmund. Well, he spoke about him most dismissively, I'm afraid. I've never met him, so I have no idea what he is like.'

She sat up even straighter on her chair, looking down as she smoothed the material of her dress over her knees.

'Strangely enough, for all the time we spent together, I can't say that I knew Lord Collingwood well, Inspector. Edward arranged his life to please himself. My place was to offer a diversion, an escape from the tedium of the everyday.' Her lips curved upwards slightly as if a memory amused her. She threw him a direct glance. 'And how about you, Detective Inspector McQueen? Are you married?'

He was not surprised by this move on her part. Flirting was second nature to her, he was sure. 'That's not at all relevant, Mrs Hawthorne,' he said. 'But no. No, I am not.'

He thought fleetingly of Jeannie. *Should he have married her? It could never have happened. She would not have been accepted in his world. But still. It might have been the right thing.*

'Well, I am sure you will find plenty of pleasant distractions during your stay in Malta,' she said, arching her eyebrows.

'I've no need of distractions. I have a job to do.'

'Of course, and a very important one. I understand, and if there's anything I can do to help, do let me know. I am nothing if not discreet, Inspector.'

McQueen looked over at Galea, who was gazing out of the window, pretending he could not hear the conversation.

He picked up his hat. 'Let's go, Sergeant. I think we have plenty of information to be going on with.'

Mrs Hawthorne stood up and gently shook the creases out of her skirts, before offering him her hand.

'Do come back, Inspector, any time.'

On their way out of the apartment, Galea caught McQueen's eye and nodded his head towards a large blue vase in the corner of the hallway. Curling majestically from the rim were at least ten peacock feathers.

'This is strange,' he whispered. 'It is unlucky to keep peacock feathers in the house. They bring bad luck.'

'Interesting,' McQueen said, once they were out on the street. We should keep an eye on her. I'd like to put a watch on the apartment and see who comes in and out. Who else has she been seeing? We need to know.'

After his meeting with Sarah Hawthorne, McQueen felt even more conscious of his heavy woollen suit. He felt weighed down and exhausted. It was Saturday afternoon, post-siesta. Taking Antonio with him for company, he strolled along Strade Reale, looking for a tailor's shop. All the world and his wife appeared to be out shopping. A pastime he detested. He checked the card he had got from the Tantis. "R.P. Ellul," he read, "Fashionable Merchant Tailor – First Class Work". That was the name Carstairs had recommended, too, so they must be all right. The word "fashionable" worried him, though. A detective had no need to be in fashion. It was much more important to blend in with the crowd. He admitted to himself, though, that a heavy suit in summer was most certainly not doing that.

He found the shop and stopped outside. He was not looking forward to going in.

'Right, lad. Wait here. You'll not want to have any part in this fiasco,' he said to Antonio, giving him a penny. 'Go and buy yourself an ice or something.'

Then he drew a breath and stepped inside. A bell rang to announce his arrival. Immediately, a sales assistant approached him. He held up his hand to keep the man at bay while he took in his surroundings. On the left-hand side of the shop were shelves laden with yards of folded up material. Samples of suits hung on a rail in front of them. On the top of the shelves were tall piles of hat boxes. Over on the right-hand side there was a counter with samples of gloves, ties and cravats on display. Behind that counter, shelves of shirts in cardboard boxes. He walked towards the suits.

'Can I help you, sir?' asked the assistant.

'How much for a new suit?' McQueen asked. He pointed randomly at one of the light linen jackets. 'Like this one? To fit me?'

The assistant, a slight elderly fellow who barely came up to his shoulder, answered with exaggerated politeness. 'For you, sir, made to measure, this garment would be perhaps five pounds... and four shillings.' Something in his tone made McQueen think he had to calculate much more material than was usual.

As he stood pondering, thinking this was too much of an outlay, the bell rang. He looked over to see the handsome young lawyer Micallef walking in. Impeccably turned out, with a close-fitting morning suit in dark grey pinstripe, he immediately made McQueen feel conscious of his bulk and his ill-fitting clothes.

Micallef nodded at him. 'I see you are taking our advice.'

His cool, superior demeanour was more than a little irritating. *He was too pleased with himself by half.*

'I may or may not,' McQueen said. 'Not sure I'll be staying long enough to warrant it.'

Micallef walked over to the counter, taking his gloves off. 'I'm looking for a new pair to replace these,' he said, loudly. 'They're getting a little worn.'

'Excuse me,' the assistant murmured, running over to deal with the lawyer. Obsequiously, he pulled out several sets of gloves, describing the merits of each pair. They discussed them at some length, until they had agreed on the most suitable purchase, while McQueen looked at each of the suits on display.

Micallef was on McQueen's list of people to interview. He decided he might as well strike while the iron was hot.

'As you are here, can I ask a few questions to do with the case?' he asked.

Micallef affected an air of boredom.

'Yes, certainly,' he said, as though his patience was about to be truly tested.

McQueen took out his pocketbook. 'I have read your statement and I believe you went to fetch the police on the night of Lord Collingwood's murder?'

'I did,' Micallef replied. 'I knew that would be the most efficient way, and I had not been drinking, unlike most of the officers.'

Of course not, thought McQueen. *God forbid that he should loosen up and enjoy himself a little.*

'Can you relate to me what happened.'

'I ran from the villa down to the marina, where I found a police constable. I told him what had happened, then I went back to the party. The police arrived around thirty minutes later.'

'And did you know Lord Collingwood well?'

'I only knew him through my fiancée Maria Tanti. She is friendly with Lady Collingwood. I barely spoke to Lord Collingwood. He did not have much time for Maltese people, even those who are the most successful... although he seemed to like my prospective father-in-law.'

'Is there anything you remember about that night? Anything you found unusual?'

Micallef thought for a moment.

'Not really,' he said. 'I did hear him say to Colonel

Arbuthnot, "I couldn't care less what state your finances are in."
I thought that was unnecessarily harsh. Arbuthnot did not look
happy.'

McQueen made a note.

'Did you see Lord Collingwood leaving the room?' he asked.

'No, I believe I was talking to Miss Tanti at the time. She's a
lively girl, as you may have noticed. We're to be married very
soon, you know. In a matter of weeks.'

There seemed to be something of a warning note in his
voice, as if marking his territory.

'I congratulate you,' McQueen said. 'I hope you will be very
happy.'

He feared that Maria would soon have her liveliness
quashed by this stuffy prig.

'We will be, Inspector, I am sure of that. Will that be all?'

'Indeed. Thank you for your time.'

On his way out of the shop, Micallef picked up the sleeve of
the suit McQueen had just been considering.

'You know, I'm not sure that style would suit you, Inspector,'
he said. 'Perhaps on a younger man?'

McQueen decided he was not going to order a suit just yet.
He tried on a few different hats, settling on a wide-brimmed
straw affair. Something to shade his red face from the sun.

CHAPTER EIGHTEEN

Maria was fighting a sense of injustice. She had begged her father to be allowed to go to the monthly board meeting, but he had refused. She had pushed him too far. Normally, she knew precisely how to get her way. How else was she going to learn, in readiness for when she took over the *Malta Post?* This had been her greatest ambition, ever since she had heard the Ladies' Guild talk about women in business. There was a Swedish woman – Louise Flodin – who printed her own newspaper in Stockholm. *If this woman could do it, why couldn't she?* But her father had stood his ground. There was no way that a young woman, however intelligent, could attend such an important meeting. The board members would not stand for it. She was not yet ready, he had said.

So, here she was in the still muggy afternoon air, walking through Barrakka Gardens with her aunt, like all the other citizens of Valletta who could think of nothing better to do. Granted, some young couples looked happy and in love, but most people were simply passing the time, dressed in their finest after their afternoon rest, hoping to meet friends and acquaintances and exchange the latest gossip.

They were walking past the fountain, where the fine mist rising from the cascading water created a slight coolness in the air, when she saw Inspector McQueen standing at the iron railings, looking out over Grand Harbour. He was holding an artists' sketchbook in his left hand and drawing the scene in front of him, deep in concentration. A small boy was by his side talking nineteen to the dozen, but the detective did not appear to be paying him any attention. She noticed with some amusement that McQueen had a new straw hat.

'Oh look, Zi,' she said, with a rising sense of excitement. 'It's the detective! What's he doing here? Shouldn't he be out somewhere, you know, detecting? Let's go and talk to him.'

'I'm sure he won't want you disturbing him, Maria,' her aunt said.

'Nonsense! I want to find out what he's doing. There might be something I can help with.'

She linked arms with her aunt and walked over to stand behind him, trying to see his sketch of the harbour. He was using a piece of charcoal, sweeping it across the page to create a rough outline, then drawing the rooftops and church towers on top. He seemed to be aware of her, but he did not acknowledge her presence.

'Not bad,' Maria said. 'You didn't say anything about being an artist.'

'That's because I'm not,' he said, hardly bothering to look up. He carried on sketching, but with a smile.

'I'm trying to work out the geography of the area,' he said. 'I find it helps me if I draw it. This, by the way,' he nodded at the boy next to him, 'is Antonio. Sometimes known as Ninu. He's training to be my assistant. Right now, he's showing me around the city.'

The boy looked at her shyly. She was not used to children. She liked them – very much – but she never knew quite how to talk to them. She always felt she spoke over-brightly, not quite hitting the right note.

'Hello, Ninu,' she said. 'Are you being helpful?'

He nodded, his eyes looking serious and wary at the same time.

'He's telling me what all the landmarks are,' McQueen said.

'Oh, I can help you with that!' Maria said.

She noticed Antonio hanging back and looking a bit put-out as she moved closer.

'That area there is Kottonera,' she said, pointing straight ahead. 'Known as the three cities – Vittoriosa, Senglea and Cospicua. They're like three fingers of land separated by French Creek, Dockyard Creek and – over there – Kalkara.'

She watched him sketching in the ancient stone fortress on the opposite side of the harbour.

'That is Fort St Angelo,' she said, 'and over there, that's Fort Ricasoli. Forts everywhere! Would you ever guess we had a fear of invasion?' She laughed, but he did not respond.

He started writing in some names of the landmarks as she pointed them out, such as the rounded domes of the churches. She liked the way he wrote, in emphatic caps, pinning the names of the buildings to their rightful places. She could tell that he liked to create a sense of order. Perhaps she got a little too close as she peered at the page. Her aunt coughed and said, 'Come now, Maria, we need to move on. Leave the inspector to his work.'

'Oh, *Zi*, don't fuss so. I have got a few things to ask Mr McQueen. He's nearly finished, haven't you?' she said. 'I'm sure he won't mind walking with us for a little while, will you, Inspector?'

McQueen closed his sketchbook and put his charcoal away in his waistcoat pocket. 'A walk will do just fine,' he said, looking amused. Antonio slipped away, watching them from a distance, a frown wrinkling his brow. But she was not going to miss out on this chance to find out what was happening, from the detective himself.

Maria had heard about the arrest and subsequent release of Guiseppe Trapani from her father. She knew Trapani's mother through her visits to Villa Porto. She liked *Sinjura* Trapani very much and had chatted with her on several occasions in the kitchen. She felt it was a shame that such a gentle, good woman should be saddled with a wild, rebellious son like Guiseppe. She had seen him once and taken an instant dislike to his long hair and his insolent manner. He had a sharpness about his looks that made her think of a lean dog, hovering on street corners, ready to run out and snatch scraps of food. She wanted to quiz McQueen on why he had been allowed to go free.

'Inspector, you know I told you about the Anti-Reform Party, the ones who are against the British? My father says one of their members has been suspected of the admiral's murder – Guiseppe Trapani?'

'I'll not admit or deny that,' McQueen said.

'Well, I'm concerned that the police have let him out again. I've heard he's dangerous. Who knows what he might be planning next?'

'We will be keeping an eye on him,' was all McQueen would say.

'I'm sure I can find out when the Anti-Reform Party is meeting again. There will be someone who can tell me.'

She began to think about different people she could ask. There was her friend Sonia, married to a clerk in Dr Marsat's office. Marsat was known to be a supporter of the Anti-Reform Party, a right-hand man to Francesco Rizzo. She would start there.

'Shall I do that? Shall I find out and send you a message?'

She looked at McQueen expectantly. 'Perhaps we could find someone to infiltrate the meeting and report back afterwards?'

He narrowed his eyes, as if considering where she had got these ideas from. Then he shook his head.

'It's not a good idea, Miss Tanti,' he said. 'You might stir up some difficulties. I am sure your aunt will agree that it would be better to leave this matter to the police.'

He was treating her with condescension, like so many other people in her life. She felt her cheeks go red as she realised he was not taking her seriously.

'Dearie me, yes,' *Zija* Paolina said. 'You really mustn't interfere, *ħanini*. Come along, now, we need to walk back home.'

'Very well,' she said, in a rush of irritation. 'Let's walk home, shall we? It was very pleasant to meet you, Inspector. I wish you every success with your investigation. I'll go home and practise my drawing, shall I? See if I can do as well as you? It's all us women are capable of, clearly!'

She knew her waspish air did not become her, but she could not help it. *Everything made her so wild!* She left McQueen looking a little perplexed at how their conversation had ended.

Maria felt that the island of her birth was far too small for her. She had such energy and so many ambitions. She often looked out across the sea, imagining how exciting it would feel to land on the coast of Italy, and to travel up through the rest of Europe. She was attracted to Giorgio because he had been to university in Padua, and he had promised to take her to Italy – and Germany and France – after they were married. She longed to see mountains and lakes, to see famous buildings and art, and to try all different kinds of food. *Imagine, roaming around the sights of Rome and Paris!* The thought made her stomach knot with excitement. *It would not be long; just over a month.*

In the meantime, she was determined to help with the

investigation. She would find out more about the Anti-Reform Party, whether McQueen wanted her to or not. She felt sure she could uncover important information that would help to unlock the case. She would be the star reporter, disclosing the truth in her father's paper. And as for stirring up difficulties, well, she was not afraid of anyone in Malta, not any single person.

———

The same evening, Maria went to call on her friend Sonia. They had known each other all their lives and had shared music lessons at Maria's house. Now, Sonia was respectable and married. With a gentle, patient demeanour and a nicely rounded figure, she had caught the attention of an ambitious young clerk called Roberto Bolero, and they now had a six-month-old baby boy. Maria had to sit and admire the baby for a good half-hour – how very strong he was, how well he was sitting up, how he was taking to solid food – before she could get around to asking her question.

'Sonia?' she started, tentatively. 'You know how fond I am of my father.'

'Yes, and how you run rings around him! You are always making him do what you want.'

Maria laughed. *It was good for him, kept him on his toes.*

'Well, this time there's something I want to do for him. You know that your Roberto works for Dr Marsat, the lawyer?'

'Ye-es...'

'And you know Marsat is involved with the Anti-Reform Party?'

'Ye-es...'

'I need to find out when they are next meeting. I am convinced it will be at Marsat's offices. Could you find out from Roberto if that is the case, and let me know when it's happening? I'd like to know who they all are and what they are plotting. It's important – it will help my father so much to know. For a story in the paper. Do you think you could do that for me?'

'I don't know, Maria. Roberto needs to be careful. What if Marsat found out he'd passed on information? He could lose his position there!'

'Oh, it wouldn't come to that. No one will know.'

'But they might! What are you planning, anyway? You've got that look in your eyes; you're up to something.'

'Nothing! I just need to know when the meeting is. You don't have to worry about anything. It will be fine. Please, Sonia?'

Eventually, and reluctantly, Sonia agreed to send her a message, but only if Roberto agreed. Maria felt a familiar pang of guilt. She had always been able to persuade her friend to do anything she asked. Sweet Sonia, who was so willing to help, and who never questioned her motives.

CHAPTER NINETEEN

Sunday, 8 August 1880

I
t was Sunday morning and McQueen felt restless. He had
been thinking about Sarah Hawthorne. He felt sure she was
central to the investigation. Who were the other gentlemen she
was seeing? Either one could have a motive for wanting
Collingwood out of the picture. Two constables had been tasked
with watching her apartment around the clock, but he could not
wait to get answers. *Would she tell him more if he went back to
see her alone?* There was a certain appeal to the thought of
seeing her again. He shrugged on his jacket and left his lodgings.

After the mugginess of the past few days, he was surprised
to find it breezy outside, with a few wispy clouds in the sky. The
wind flapped his trousers and the water in the harbour looked
choppy. He decided to walk rather than take the ferry. It would
do him good to stretch his legs.

The walk to Sliema took him high along Valletta's fortified
walls, looking down over Marsamscetto Harbour. No
steamships: the Nepal was gone, the next P&O not due until the

next day. Then the road dipped steeply down into a marina. Here, moored yachts bounced around on the water, ropes slapping against masts. Only a few colourful *dgħajjes* were out, the boatmen controlling them deftly as they dipped up and down through the white-tipped waves. It was quiet, hardly anyone around. Most people were at church, he assumed.

He had the feeling he was being watched, conspicuous as he strode along in his heavy suit. A few men stood at the corner of the marina, talking loudly and smoking. As he walked past, he heard a guffaw of laughter. He whipped round, ready to respond, but saw that one man was thumping another on the back; it was a joke, nothing to do with him.

He had learned to trust his instincts, though. He kept checking from time to time but couldn't see anyone behind him. Leaving the marina, he approached the outskirts of Sliema, with its shops, hotels and bars. Spotting an opportunity, he stopped suddenly in the doorway of a tobacconists, watching the reflection of the street behind him in the window. *Yes, he was sure he saw a dark shadow dodge swiftly out of sight.* He *was* being followed.

He continued walking until he saw a bar that appeared to be open. An old, disreputable-looking building, with "Neptune" written across the front. The kind of establishment that had been serving fishermen and sailors for centuries. He ducked inside the front entrance and waited, hidden behind the door. The handle turned. As it started to open, he yanked the door hard and grabbed the person behind it, pulling them into the room.

'I knew it!' he said, as a dishevelled creature with a black cap struggled to get out of his grasp. It was the seedy-looking guide who had taken him to the hotel on his arrival. 'You've been following me all along, haven't you?'

'Leave me alone,' his captive said. 'I do nothing. Let me go.'

'You're going nowhere,' McQueen said, 'until you have told me what is going on.'

'No!'

'Yes.' McQueen twisted the man's arm behind his back. 'What's your name?'

'*Ahh!* Camilleri.'

'Who do you work for, Camilleri? Why are you following me?'

'I not tell you.'

McQueen sighed. Perhaps a drink would loosen the man's tongue.

It was dark inside, a few candles providing meagre lighting. Six men were seated at various small tables around the room. As McQueen had arrived, they had looked up, curious. Then, sensing trouble, they had all turned their backs and resumed their drinks and conversations.

McQueen dragged Camilleri towards the bar. 'I'll get you a drink,' he said. 'What do you want?' He asked the barman for a quarter gill and whatever Camilleri wanted, which looked to be an Italian grappa. He tasted the whisky. It was fairly rough, but not watered down.

He sat Camilleri down at a table. The man was uneasy, shifting on his seat and looking at the door as though ready to make a swift exit at any moment. He would not meet McQueen's eye, but took quick sips of his drink and waited for him to speak.

'Who are you looking out for?' McQueen asked.

'Cauchi – I hide from him. He tell Captain Borġ.'

Police Adjutant Cauchi. Borġ's right-hand man. McQueen downed his whisky and turned around to ask the barman to refill their glasses.

'Is that who gives you your orders?' he asked. 'Cauchi?'

'Yes.'

'How long have you been following me?'

'Monday, Tuesday – every day.'

So, Borġ had been tracking his every movement since arrival. The villa, the hospital, the hotel, the Officers' Mess, the newspaper office, Sarah Hawthorne's apartment. *He had thought as much. He wondered how he could turn this to his advantage. How much could Camilleri tell him?*

'You're working for Borġ?'

Camilleri nodded, keeping an eye on the door.

'Pay you well, does he?'

Camilleri shrugged, his face blank.

'Have another drink,' McQueen said, and watched as the little man took a few more sips. 'Look, you can help me here. If you give me information, I will not tell Borġ that I caught you spying on me. He won't find out how you failed.'

'But I not know anything.'

'You must know something. What is it that Borġ doesn't want me to find out? Is he covering up for someone?'

Camilleri shook his head. 'I not know.'

'Is it something to do with the lady who lives near here? Mrs Hawthorne? Do you know anything about her? Who is she involved with?'

Camilleri looked around, then leaned forward. 'How much?' he asked. 'How much, to say?'

'What do you mean, how much?' he said. 'I am not going to pay you.'

Camilleri shrugged.

'I can buy you another drink, and that's it.'

Camilleri handed over his glass, holding up two fingers.

McQueen turned to the barman, his temper flaring.

'Two more,' he said. 'For both of us.'

Two new glasses of spirit were lined up in front of McQueen and Camilleri. He took the first one and stared hard at Camilleri as they both drained their drinks. He carried on staring as they then simultaneously picked up and swallowed their second.

'Right,' he said, when they had finished. 'Speak.'

Camilleri smirked. 'I hear there are two men who visit her,' he said.

'All right – get on with it!'

'One man, very rich. *Notabile*. His name Count San Pietro.'

That was the second time in two days he had heard that name. *The nobleman from Città Vecchia? Why would he come to Valletta?*

'And the second?' he prompted.

'That man I not tell you. Too important. British. If Borġ finds out I speak to you, I die.' Camilleri drew his forefinger across his throat.

'I go now,' he said. 'Too much danger.' He got up from the table, put his cap on, and disappeared out of the back of the building.

McQueen was left in the bar, with six men turning to look at him. He twisted his glass around on the table, thinking. *Someone British – important? This could be hugely significant. He had to find out more. Time to pay Sarah Hawthorne another visit.*

Buoyed up by the whisky, McQueen walked briskly up to Sarah Hawthorne's apartment and rapped at the door. After a few moments, he heard the maid's voice.

'Mrs Hawthorne wants to know what you want.'

'Tell her I need to see her now. I know who she has been seeing and if I don't talk to her myself, I will broadcast the names at the police office.'

He heard the swish of a dress as the maid turned away to report back to her mistress. A few minutes of silence ensued, then she returned, and he heard the door unlock. She led him inside. 'This way, please.'

He followed her in through the main door and into the drawing room. As he went in, he could see a police constable on the opposite side of the street, leaning against a lamp post, looking bored. Sarah Hawthorne was by the window, fanning her face. The sunlight reflected a becoming shine on her hair. He thought she had positioned herself very carefully, for maximum effect.

'Inspector,' she said, softly. 'How good of you to come and see me again. I'm very popular at the moment, am I not?' She nodded in the direction of the constable.

'We want to know about all your visitors,' he said. 'You are very discreet, but I have found a source who has given me some answers.'

She folded her fan up and tapped it on her left hand, looking at him intently as if considering how much he knew, and how much she could admit to him.

'Is that so? And does your source tell you that one of my visitors is a *notabile*?' she asked, eventually.

'Count San Pietro, yes.'

'The count, indeed, a charming man. He is a great friend of Lord Collingwood. They have known each other since the admiral last lived in Malta.'

A great friend indeed, thought McQueen. *Quite a lot in common.*

'I see,' he said. 'And how long has he been visiting this establishment?'

She unfurled the fan. 'Oh, just under a year, I would say. The occasional visit, every few weeks. He lives with his beautiful wife and family in Città Vecchia. But, Inspector, you will never be able to prove it. The count is very careful.'

'Is he, now? And the other visitor?' he said.

'Oh, I cannot possibly reveal *his* name.'

He did not feel like playing any more games. 'You'd better tell me,' he said. 'I could always have you arraigned on a charge of prostitution. You can dress it up as coyly as you like, but that is what it is, and I will do it.'

Her eyes flashed. 'Oh no you won't,' she said. 'I always make sure I have friends in the highest of places. I feel sure you have already guessed who it is, haven't you?'

He stared at her, trying to gauge what she meant. *The highest of places. Who could that be, in Malta? Not Sir Thomas himself, surely? The governor?*

'Well, haven't you?' she asked.

'Perhaps.' He did not want to give anything away.

'Then scuttle off back to the police office,' she said, no trace of the former softness and seduction in her voice. 'You know you will never arrest me, and I don't care to see you again.'

At that point there was a hammering at the door. The maid went to unlock it, and it burst open with a loud thump. Police Adjutant Cauchi was standing in the doorway.

'Inspector McQueen,' he said, his moustache twitching. 'You're to leave now. Captain Borg's orders.'

'No surprises there,' McQueen muttered as he picked up his hat and pushed it onto his head.

'Mrs Hawthorne,' he said, bowing politely as he left. 'I look forward immensely to our next meeting.'

CHAPTER TWENTY

Maria had received a note from Sonia, letting her know that the next meeting of the Anti-Reform Party was going to be held that night, during the festa. Members of the group had been instructed to enter from the side of the tobacconist's shop beneath Dr Marsat's offices, so that people would not suspect the meeting was taking place. It would be held at seven thirty in the evening.

She was determined to find out who would attend, and what it was they were planning. She was convinced that Lord Collingwood's death was the first violent action they had carried out, but that more would follow. *If she could find out what it was, and expose them, it would prove how capable she was as a journalist. Just think what a great story that would be for the newspaper. People would be clamouring to buy it.* She would write articles telling people the truth about what was happening in Malta. Far better than insipid accounts of polo matches and visiting British gentry. She felt full of energy, inspired.

She took her maid Roži into her confidence, asking her to find out about any servants who worked for Dr Marsat. Roži disappeared for an hour and came back with good news. A young lad who had been taken on six months ago as an office boy turned out to be Rożi's sister-in-law's nephew. There were times when it was useful you could find a connection with most people in this community. Maria had arranged to meet him after work and had bribed him with enough money to make his eyes widen. He was a biddable boy, with an innocent-looking face that would serve well. Yes, he could let her in the building in advance of the meeting and yes, he could find her a place where she could hide and yet hear what was being discussed. There was a storeroom in a corner of the office; he could smuggle her in there before the meeting and let her know when she had a clear path to get out afterwards.

In preparation for her mission, Maria chatted loudly all afternoon about how she was looking forward to the festa, and how she was going to go with Rożi to Strada San Dominica to see the procession. Luckily, *Zija* Paolina detested the crowds and had no desire to go with them. Her father set out for the board meeting at around six o'clock.

At six thirty she dressed herself in an old black gown, slightly short so the skirts were well clear of the ground and made from a fabric so old and soft it made little noise. She covered herself with her *għonnella*. She always made much of hating the cloak and how much she resented that women should be expected to wear it, but now it would be useful for hiding her identity. Then, after calling out that she would return later and wishing *Zija* Paolina a happy festa, Maria and Rożi set out together, wending their way through the crowd.

She loved the atmosphere of the festa, the colourful banners, the bells ringing, the band playing, the people standing out on the street, watching, laughing and talking. Tonight, it was imbued with an added edge of excitement. She enjoyed the anonymity of walking with Rożi; to any passers-by they would look like two ordinary women wearing *għonnielen*, on their way to see the statue being paraded through the streets.

As they walked past Strada Mercanti, she saw Giorgio coming out of his house. He looked so smart and businesslike as he headed up the street. She smiled to herself, thinking how much he would disapprove of her being out like this, and of her plans to spy on the Anti-Reform Party.

Maria had hidden in cupboards before as a child, enjoying the thrill of waiting to jump out and surprise her Papà, or her playmates. But nothing could have prepared her for the terror she now felt. It had seemed such an easy thing to arrange, arriving at seven o'clock and being smuggled into the storeroom at the back of Marsat's office. She had locked it from the inside, and had the key in her hand, so it was extremely unlikely she would be discovered... *but what if she sneezed, or knocked something over? What if the group became aware that someone was spying on them?* If she was found in this ridiculous, compromising position, her life would not be worth living. She would be mortified, unable to bear it if her father was disappointed in her.

It was hot and stuffy in the storeroom. She was surrounded by shelves of files, books and papers. She found a footstool and sat down behind the door. A faint glow of light spilled in through the cracks around the door frame and through the keyhole. She waited for what seemed an age, fighting an overwhelming desire to get out and run away before she was found out.

Eventually, she heard men beginning to arrive for the

meeting. With her eye to the keyhole, she could just about see the table at which they began to assemble, helped by the lamplight illuminating their faces.

She could recognise Dr Marsat easily, with his bald head and rotund figure. There were several other men gathering around, whom she half recognised but could not have named. They greeted one another, talking in low voices. It was difficult to make out what anyone was saying, from behind the door.

Eventually, Marsat rapped on the table with a short gavel. He called the meeting to order, speaking in Italian, which she strained to understand. 'Welcome, friends, to this third meeting of the *Gruppo Militante Pro Italiano*.'

Maria felt a jolt of excitement. *What was that? A militant group? Was this a breakaway from the Anti-Reform Party?*

'We have made progress, my friends,' Marsat said. 'The rally brought 2,000 people to protest. All people who want to see change. We must build on that, spread the word. This is our time; we must act to make it clear what our demands are and what we will do if they are not met.'

A murmur of assent went around the table.

'Since then, the police have acted illegally and aggressively. After Trapani was arrested, he was falsely accused of the murder of Lord Collingwood. He was beaten and badly treated. I know the governor was aware of this and fully sanctioned Captain Borg's actions. We have to hit back hard, make it clear we will not stand for such treatment.'

Maria heard the door to the office open and a dark shadow of a man joined the group, greeted as he arrived, and clapped on the back. He sat down and as he raised his head; the lamplight revealed the gaunt features and unruly long hair of Guiseppe Trapani. His right eye was shadowed by dark bruises.

'Welcome, friend,' Marsat said, switching to Maltese, to

Maria's relief. 'We salute you for your courage and for the pain you have endured for our cause. I see you are determined to keep fighting.'

'Yes, I hate them all,' Trapani said, his voice harsh and bitter. 'If it wasn't for you – and that detective – I would have been hung for a crime I did not commit. Borġ is a corrupt bastard who colludes with the British against his own people. I will never forgive him.'

So, he wasn't guilty, she thought. *And McQueen exposed Borġ's violent methods.* The inspector went up in her estimation, although she wished he had paid her some respect and told her what had happened.

'This adds a new dimension to our grievances against the government,' Marsat said. 'Do not fear. We have been giving thought to our next actions, which we want to share with you tonight.'

Maria pressed her ear to the door, listening intently.

'Our aim,' he continued, 'is to draw attention to our cause at the planned visit of the Duke of Edinburgh in September. There will be another demonstration, a big one, at the military parade.'

'We should go further,' Trapani said, thumping the table. 'We should make a bomb, set it off next to the governor. That will shake things up.'

Without thinking, Maria pressed a hand to her mouth. Her elbow knocked against the underside of a shelf, causing some papers to slip from the top of a pile and float down to the floor. She held her breath.

'Did you hear that? What was it?' an unknown voice said. 'There was a noise over there.'

She could not see what was happening. She sat motionless, her breath escaping in tiny bursts through her fingers, her heart thumping so loudly she was sure the whole room would hear it.

Footsteps approached the storeroom and worked the handle.

'It's locked. Does anyone have a key?' she heard. It was Trapani's voice. She nearly passed out with fear.

If he discovered her, she dreaded to think what he would do. She prepared herself for the moment when the door opened and she would be exposed.

The moment never happened. Maria was saved by the arrival of one of Marsat's servants, who banged on the door of the office, shouting that there were police all over the place, searching for two suspicious men and asking to check the buildings. That there were police all over the place. She strained to hear as the men all got up, chairs scraping, and left the room. For a while she stayed put, desperately waiting to find out what was happening, then there was a tap on the door.

'*Sinjorina* Tanti?' the office boy said. 'You can come out now, they have all gone.'

She unlocked the door and emerged, grateful for the fresher air. She pressed a coin into his hand.

'I will pay you more soon,' she said. 'You are an absolute darling.'

Crossing the street, she went to join Roži, who was still anxiously waiting in the doorway.

'Thank goodness you are all right,' Roži said. 'I was so worried when the lights went out.'

'What's going on?' Maria asked. 'Everyone left in a hurry and there was talk of police.'

'I don't know, but I think something bad has happened. I heard screaming – over in that direction – a short while ago.' Roži gestured towards the cathedral. 'I've been so frightened for you!'

'We'd better get back; we shouldn't be here,' Maria said.

Much as she wanted to find out what had happened, this

did not feel like the right time to go with the crowd. She wanted to get back home. She needed to work out what to do with the information she had just uncovered.

CHAPTER TWENTY-ONE

M cQueen had been standing at the corner of Strada San Dominica with Antonio for what seemed like an age. The noise from the church bells, which had been clanging loudly and insistently since the morning, was getting on his nerves. Was it really necessary, all this din? He looked at his pocket watch – coming up to seven o'clock. They had been there for nearly an hour, when the march was supposed to start at six.

'Don't worry,' Antonio said. 'Is always like this – always they are late.' The lad was hopping from one foot to another, looking out for the band to appear.

Everybody was out for the festa. Whole families were on the street, waiting with great anticipation, grandmothers sitting on chairs in the doorways of houses, mothers with troops of children gathered around them. A father stood right in front of him with his small son on his shoulders, the wide-eyed boy looking apprehensive at all the noise, but keeping his fear in check.

At last, McQueen could see the band assembling: clarinets in the front, percussion in the middle, trumpets and trombones at the back. A signal from the bass drum, a single thump, and the players started up a loud march. Dressed in smart uniform with caps, the musicians had small sheets of music attached to their instruments so they could play and walk at the same time. They began to swagger along the street.

McQueen watched the people around him as they focused on the band playing. Relaxed and happy, they talked to each other loudly, men clapping each other on the back, joking and laughing. Families were gathered on the wooden balconies, windows open, cheering the band and dropping confetti paper down onto the street. Although it was hot, the people seemed to think nothing of it, all dressed up in their finest clothes.

'Look, Mister McQueen, he comes!'

Antonio was pulling at his sleeve and pointing up the road. From a distance he could see the statue of the saint, lurching along above head height. A great cheer arose from the crowd around him as it slowly made its way towards them. Life-size. The hand of Saint Dominic held high, seeming to bless the people he moved amongst. Watching the expressions on faces around him, McQueen saw genuine adoration, as if the saint had come out of the church in real life. And as he watched the tilting movement of the statue, even to him, Saint Dominic's face looked nearly alive, as though he were smiling, happy to be amongst his people. When the procession passed by, though, McQueen could see the priests carrying the saint were under no illusions. Every pound of the statue's weight was etched on their faces as they shuffled along.

Antonio jumped up and down next to him to get a good view.

'Is good, Mister McQueen, yes?'

The best he could come up with was a nod. Truth to tell, he was feeling oppressed by the crowd around him and the loudness of the music, especially the bass drum, which seemed to hammer right into his head, along with the sharp crashing of the cymbals.

He was turning to say something to Antonio about going back to the lodgings, when he caught sight of Guiseppe Trapani. It was the furtive way he was standing in an open doorway, talking to two other men, that caught his eye. Deep in conversation, Trapani gave both men a small package each. McQueen watched as the men split up and started to make their separate ways through the crowd.

Concerned Trapani might be plotting violence, McQueen decided to follow him. He pulled Antonio around the corner of Strada Mercanti. 'Here, Ninu,' he said, loud enough for the lad to hear, but not so other people could tell what he was saying. 'We are going to follow a gentleman. It's the man with the long hair. I'll point him out to you with a nod. You go on the other side of the street. Keep watching me and keep watching the man. If you lose me, and you can't see me anymore, go back home. You hear me, lad? If anything happens go back home, yes?'

Antonio nodded, his face a picture of seriousness and deep honour at being given his first detecting job to do. 'Yes, Mister McQueen – I will do this.'

They moved back into the melee. McQueen indicated which one was Trapani, who had gone past them by now and was pushing his way through the crowd. Antonio slipped away across the street. The throng of people followed the band and the statue of Saint Dominic, singing loudly and jumping up and down. They were heading along Strada Reale in the direction of the Governor's Palace. *What has he got in mind?* McQueen wondered. *Surely not some kind of attack on the governor?* He kept a watch on Antonio's red neckerchief, as well as Trapani's determined movement through the fringes of the crowd.

Up on the roofs there was a sudden sequence of shots

ringing out, sharp reports and flashes of light. Smoke rose up. *What was it, pistols? Flares?* McQueen looked around, but everyone was carrying on as if nothing untoward was happening. A cheer erupted. *Firecrackers, not guns.* Another set went off from the same roof. He saw Trapani duck around the side of a shop – a tobacconist. Keeping a safe distance, he approached the shop carefully, then peered in through the front window. Nobody could be seen inside. He tried the door handle. It was locked.

The band was passing by; the trombonists at the back were blaring out the tune right next to him. McQueen scanned the crowd to see if he could find Antonio. He wanted to tell him he was going to go into the shop. A loud set of firecrackers cut through the noise of the band and the cheering voices. He could not see the boy anywhere. *He should not have left him on his own.* As the band and the people moved on up the street he hesitated. As a detective, he knew he should follow Trapani, but would Antonio have the sense to go home?

Just as he decided to slip around the side of the shop a different kind of sound made him stop. This was not the sound of people enjoying themselves. It pierced through the hubbub, a series of terrified screams. A chilling sound. He knew beyond doubt that something terrible was happening. He tried to work out where the noise was coming from: a good three hundred yards away, the opposite direction to where the band was disappearing out of sight. People started to spill out of a side street, shouting for help. He sprinted towards the commotion, turning the corner into a narrow street of slippery stone steps. He ran down, at one point almost losing his footing, to find a group of people gathered around a bundle at the foot of the steps.

He was relieved to see Antonio there, white-faced and

hovering around the edge of the group. The boy ran over to McQueen as soon as he saw him.

'What is it, lad?' he said. 'What's happened?'

'A girl,' Antonio said, tears running down his face. 'Someone hurt her.'

McQueen's instincts took over. 'Police!' he called. 'Let me through.'

As the crowd parted, he could see the bundle was a girl, slumped over against a wall. He knelt next to her and checked her pulse. It was irregular and weak. He assessed her condition. Her bodice was black, tight against her tiny frame. He felt warm, sticky blood saturating the dark cloth on her left side. He ripped the material away to see a narrow but deep knife wound, sides gaping and blood seeping out. He quickly took off his jacket and pressed it into the wound. The girl moaned. He looked over his shoulder and shouted at the onlookers who were edging closer to see what was happening. 'Get away! Give us room.'

He called to Antonio, who was watching from the edge of the crowd. 'Go, lad, run to the police office, tell them to send some policemen and a doctor. We need a doctor. Go – as fast as you can, then come back!'

He turned to the girl and lifted her face gently. His jaw tightened as he recognised her. The sharp features were etched with pain, but he could see it was the maid he'd spoken to at Lady Collingwood's villa, Ċensa. Her eyes were closed. Then they flickered open. She looked straight at him, seeming to realise who he was. She reached up and clutched at the sleeve of his shirt. 'Pag-oon,' she said in a weak voice, then urgently, more strongly, 'Pag-oon.' The effort made her cough, and her mouth filled with blood. Her eyes pleaded with him for help as the blood bubbled up and ran down her chin to her neck.

'It's all right,' he said. 'It's all right. Help is on its way. You'll be all right. Keep looking at me, stay awake.'

He held on tightly, one arm around her shoulders, the other pressing on the wound. He willed her to keep breathing. *If he could just keep her alive until a doctor arrived, she might have a chance.* She coughed again, dark blood spilling out, and he gently wiped it away. Her breathing became more erratic and she whimpered, '*Ma.*'

'Ċensa!' he urged. 'Help is coming. Please, stay awake.'

But her eyes closed and gradually she sank back into his arms.

He felt hemmed in. People pressed close, clamouring to know what was happening. A woman started up a loud wailing. More women joined in, the terrible sound cutting right through him. A priest came hurrying up. *No surprise there. Far more important that her soul be saved than that she got medical help.*

'Keep away,' McQueen warned. But the priest hovered beside him spouting Latin, his black eyes full of self-importance at the role he had to perform. McQueen could have kicked him. In a few minutes, Sergeant Galea and a couple of constables appeared.

'Get the crowd away, you two. And Galea, get this priest out of my sight before I do something stupid. I mean it.'

Bonniċi appeared, moving as quickly as he could down the steps, using his cane. McQueen felt relieved to see someone he could trust. The doctor hobbled over and knelt next to the girl. He checked the pulse in her neck and shook his head slightly.

'She's gone,' he said to McQueen under his breath. 'You can lie her down, she's gone.'

McQueen found he could not let go of his jacket pressing into the wound.

'McQueen – let go,' Bonniċi said. 'Lie her down so we can cover her up.'

Mechanically, he allowed Bonnici to take Ċensa's body from him and stood up as she was laid out flat on the ground. Her eyes were closed and she looked tiny, like the child she really was, her face drained of colour. *He stepped back, feeling useless. How had this happened?* While he had been chasing a phantom, this poor girl had been knifed to death. The festa was still going on. He could hear the band playing in the distance and the sounds of people shouting. He found it hard to take in, the sudden vicious violence. His inability to save the girl.

Sergeant Galea came and stood next to him. 'I will go and get the superintendent, yes?' McQueen was brought back to reality, realising how hard this must be for the young sergeant. Ċensa was his cousin.

'Aye, you do that,' he said, putting a hand on his shoulder.

Galea hesitated.

'Sorry, sir,' he said. 'You have to let the priest anoint her, sir. You have to.'

McQueen sighed and turned away.

'All right. Do what you need to. Let him through.'

Galea signalled to the priest, who came scuttling back. He knelt over Ċensa's body, praying loudly and marking a cross on her forehead with holy oil. Finally, a woman covered Ċensa's face with a shawl, weeping. He had heard wailing before, but never at this level. Started by one woman, it was picked up by others, a despairing outpouring of emotion that he hoped never to hear again. He felt like a stranger to this culture, out of place and alone.

From a few yards away, McQueen saw Antonio edging back towards him, eyes glued to the body on the ground. He beckoned him over. 'Well done, lad. You did a grand job.'

Antonio sniffed loudly and he could sense the boy was on the brink of tears.

'Go home, see your mother. I'll be back as soon as all this is sorted out. Listen, we couldn't have done anything else. You got help as quickly as you could.'

He watched Antonio running off in his bare feet, feeling an intense disquiet that he had taken the boy so close to danger.

Bonniċi ordered one of the police constables to get a horse and cart to move the body to the hospital mortuary. It took around a quarter of an hour to appear, moving slowly through the crowd. News of the murder had spread quickly. The band had stopped playing. The festa was abandoned. A mass of people elbowed each other to try and get a glimpse of what was going on. Around twenty constables had been sent from the station, led by the police superintendent himself, employed in holding back the onlookers.

McQueen explained to Borġ what had happened, leaving out of his account the fruitless pursuit of Trapani. *The last thing he needed was for Borġ to come up with some theory that the agitator was at the bottom of this.*

The superintendent looked grim. 'This is bad,' he said. 'A murder, of such a young girl, in the middle of the festa.' He called out to Bonniċi. 'Doctor, what did you find? How did she die?'

'Single stab wound to the chest. It's very deep. She died quickly.'

'I will talk to the magistrate. He will order an autopsy tomorrow.'

Borġ instructed two police constables. 'You can put the body on the cart now.' They lifted her up, carried her up the steps and placed her onto the cart. Her corpse was covered with a canvas sheet, changing her into an amorphous shape. McQueen watched as the driver clicked at the horses and they clopped away, their hooves heavy on the flagstone paving. *What had happened to Ċensa? Had she been coming to tell him what she had seen? What was it she had said? Pagoon? What did that mean? Who had she seen in those last moments?*

Bonnići was standing next to him, holding his jacket, which he had retrieved from the body.

'You are covered in blood, my friend,' he said. 'Come, I will walk back with you to your lodgings.'

McQueen looked down at his shirt and waistcoat. They were soaked a deep crimson red.

CHAPTER TWENTY-TWO

Monday, 9 August 1880

M cQueen woke with a jolt in the middle of the night, his heart thumping. In his dream the garish colours, the noise and the exuberance of the festa had been jumbled up with images of Ċensa, reaching out to him with bloody hands and imploring eyes. Then her face had dissolved, changing to a vision of another dying woman, a recurrent nightmare that had visited him for twenty years.

In this dream, he and his father and his brother were visiting the poorest tenements of Fountainbridge. They heard a scream and a sickening thud, running to find the body of a young woman at the foot of a stairwell, her head twisted at an unnatural angle, lying white and still. He knelt by her side, calling for aid, wanting to save her but not knowing how. He begged his father to help, but all the minister did was stand over her, preaching. 'You see, brethren, Satan has been here, and has led this family to destruction. They have listened to his call and been persuaded to the demon drink. Let this be a lesson to you.

You must pray – pray to God to give you strength, to help you take the righteous path, the path that leads to Heaven.' He turned to his brother, but Andrew was standing by his father's side, mimicking his posture, and mouthing words of prayer. He watched in horror as the woman died.

He sat up in bed, staring into the darkness, damp with sweat. The dream had emanated from a real event, the time when he lost faith in the world his father had represented. His father was so sure he knew the truth, so convinced that by preaching and persuading he could turn all people on to the right path. But in the city, there were so many who simply laughed in his face. Drunks, thieves, cheats, men who lived by exploiting women, men who thought it was their right to beat their wives. This young woman, after months of abuse, had been killed by her husband, who would never have stopped, no matter how hard she, or anyone else in the community had prayed. Sam had felt his father, his family, the Church had betrayed her. It made him want to take direct action against violence, to find justice for victims. It had set him on the path to becoming a police officer.

Now, once again, he was faced with the murder of a young woman who should not have died. The guilt was overwhelming. He kept thinking of Ċensa's face as she fought to give him a message. *He should have tried to talk to her sooner. She had seen something on the night of the admiral's death, he was sure. Why had she not told him what it was? Had she been too frightened?* If she had decided instead to speak to the murderer, she had made a terrible mistake. Whoever it was had dispatched her ruthlessly and efficiently.

He got up early, having failed to get any more rest. His eyes burned with lack of sleep. It felt as though they had been roughed over with sandpaper. Rubbing them made it worse. He did not know how he was going to survive the day. It was only the thought of Ċensa, of finding the bastard who had killed her, that gave him the resolve to keep going. He went to the washstand to wash and shave, the cold water helping to jolt him back to life. Opening the door to his room, he found a pressed linen jacket and trousers in a neat pile outside. He tried them on – a little on the short side, but a fair approximation of a fit – then he joined the rest of the household for breakfast.

'Thank you for the clothes. Where did they come from?' he asked. There was a tense atmosphere in the room. *Sinjura* Caruso would not look at him. 'Dr Bonniċi brought them from the hospital,' she said coldly, passing him some bread. She did not look as if she had forgiven him for what had happened to Antonio. Her lips were pressed tightly together and the creases between her brows looked deeper. Antonio was fidgeting in his seat. Child as he was, he had clearly slept well and had bounced back from his terrifying experience.

'What are you doing today, Mister McQueen?' he asked. 'Can I come, too? I can take messages, yes?'

'No!' *Sinjura* Caruso said sharply. 'You will not go.'

'Oh, but *Ma*, please? I am helping Mister McQueen. I am useful, yes?' Ninu turned hopefully towards him.

'Not today,' he said. 'I don't need you today.'

It was the last thing he wanted, having the boy hanging around him, jumping around and asking endless questions.

'I will help. I will run for you, please?'

'No!' he said, standing up. It came out much louder than he intended. 'I said, no. Leave me alone, child, I have work to do.'

He threw down the last crust of bread and scraped the chair back from the table. He could see Antonio cringing away from him, his head dropping in disappointment and fear. *Damn it! Why should he have the boy on his conscience? It was not his responsibility.* He gave *Sinjura* Caruso a black look as he left the kitchen. Let her deal with him; he was her son.

The magistrate's court was on the ground floor of the Auberge d'Auvergne, a dark, claustrophobic room with a heavy mahogany table at the front, faced with six rows of wooden chairs. The magistrate, looking mournful in his white wig and voluminous black robes, conducted the proceedings from an ornately carved high-backed chair behind the table. It all felt strange and unfamiliar to McQueen, especially as the language used throughout was Italian.

McQueen was asked to recount his part in finding Ċensa, wounded and dying. He spoke in English, his words translated by an interpreter. Bonniċi was called up to speak, describing the stab wound and the cause of death. He also told the court that he had recently seen her and her fiancé at his clinic, and that he knew she was with child. The magistrate concluded that McQueen should take charge of the investigation, with Captain Borġ's full support, and asked the police surgeon Dr Girello to carry out a post-mortem examination immediately, with the assistance of Dr Bonniċi.

As they left the court, McQueen went over to speak to Captain Borġ and Sergeant Galea. The superintendent had been subdued during the inquest and now regarded him with narrowed eyes.

'A bad business, Superintendent,' McQueen said. 'I don't know about you, but to me, this changes the nature of the investigation. We have someone dangerous out there, who is prepared to kill to protect themselves. We have to work together to stop them.'

'What about Trapani?' Borġ said. 'He was free, because of you.'

'Forget about him,' he said. 'He was in my sights at the time of the murder. I can swear to that. I think it must have been someone else the girl knew from the villa.'

'She was a maid at Lord Collingwood's, yes?' asked Borġ.

'Aye. I think she knew something – but she wouldn't say what it was. We have a statement from her – Galea wrote it and she signed with her mark.'

Galea took his cap off and ran his fingers through his hair, looking younger and more vulnerable.

'I knew she wasn't speaking the truth,' he said. 'I was angry with her. Now I wish I had been more patient.'

'I doubt it would have made any difference, Sergeant. Don't be hard on yourself.'

McQueen turned to the doctor. 'Bonnići, can you establish where Ċensa's fiancé lives, and find out what he knows? See when he can come to the office for a formal interview.'

Bonnići nodded and left to go back to the hospital in Floriana.

'Captain Borġ – can you call everyone together?'

The superintendent growled his assent.

An hour later, twenty policemen – constables, sergeants, inspectors and the adjutant – were gathered in the police office. A quarter of Valletta's police department. Now at least McQueen felt he was in a position of full authority. The superintendent was letting him have his say.

'Yesterday, a terrible crime happened here in Valletta,' McQueen said to the assemblage. 'A young girl called Ċensa Mifsud was murdered on the streets during the festa celebrations. It's possible she knew something about the murder of Lord Collingwood and that she was killed as a result.

'This is extremely serious. There is a murderer out there who needs to be stopped. This is a small place. It may be someone you know. Do not talk to anyone about the case.'

He turned to Captain Borġ.

'I am going back to the villa to talk to the servants again. Someone must have been close to her. I'll need Galea with me.'

Then, addressing the rest of the officers, 'Go out and knock on all the doors in the area. Talk to everyone. We are looking for any witnesses to the murder. There must be someone who saw something.'

McQueen arrived at the villa to find that Lady Collingwood was out, but that word of Ċensa's death had already reached the staff. He went straight to the kitchen where they were gathered to support each other. The atmosphere was subdued. Williams had lost his air of self-importance; he looked greyer and reduced in size. It seemed they were all fond of Ċensa. Although not the brightest little thing, she had been a hard worker and a happy soul.

McQueen asked who had seen Ċensa the day before, and if anyone knew what time she had gone out. According to Mrs Trapani, who was sitting next to a young maidservant, arm around her shoulder, Ċensa had completed all her duties in the morning and should have reappeared in the afternoon. Various people had been calling for her, but it had been shrugged off when they couldn't find her. Sometimes she could be a little distracted. It was when she did not turn up for afternoon tea that they really began to worry. They had tea and bread and butter at half past five, which had to keep them going until eight o'clock when they had an evening meal. Ċensa was always so hungry, it was strange that she didn't appear. Then a messenger had arrived late that night with the news.

McQueen asked Williams if any of the servants were close to Ċensa and he said she shared a bedroom with the scullery maid, Luċija. The maid looked up when they said her name.

Her face was swollen and blotchy with crying. 'Can we talk to her on her own?' McQueen asked. She looked sick with worry when Williams ordered all the other servants to go and get on with their work, leaving her in the kitchen with the policemen. Mrs Trapani stayed with her, holding her hand. The housekeeper gave Williams a look as if to say, 'Don't you dare order me to leave as well,' and he took the hint, clearing his throat noisily and leaving the room. *Sensible man*, thought McQueen.

They asked Lućija if Ċensa had acted at all differently recently. She nodded. Ċensa had told her that she was seeing a young man. She had been excited; she was talking about getting married. No, she had no idea who it was, she thought his name might be Wiġi, but she did know Ċensa had been happy, that he had a good job, he was a clerk.

'How long had she been meeting him?' McQueen asked.

'About six months,' Lućija related. But she wasn't sure if things were all right, because Ċensa had been worried, not herself, for several weeks.

He told Galea to take statements from Lućija and Mrs Trapani about when they had last seen Ċensa, and what her frame of mind had been. He walked out of the kitchen onto the terrace and lit up a cigarette, reflecting on his next steps. He went back through his pocketbook to find the list of all the guests at the soirée. *If he was right, and one of them had killed Ċensa because of something she saw, he needed to establish their whereabouts last night. Had any of them been near those streets at that time?*

CHAPTER TWENTY-THREE

M cQueen and Galea were still at the villa, interviewing the servants, when Lady Collingwood and her son Edmund returned home. He could hear Williams explaining what was happening and was not surprised when the butler opened the kitchen door to announce that Lady Collingwood would like to see him straight away. Leaving Galea to continue taking notes, he made his way to the drawing room.

He could see that she was agitated. She was standing by the door to the veranda, looking out into the garden. Edmund was sitting sprawled on the sofa, holding his hat in his hands and turning it around by its brim. When she heard McQueen, Lady Collingwood whipped around, concern etching lines on her face.

'Inspector, this is too ghastly,' she said. 'The poor girl, I can't believe it. Is it true that you found her? In the street?'

He nodded.

'This is so bad. What on earth had she been doing? How could something like this happen, almost under our noses? It's like living in a nightmare. Is there anything I can do to help?'

He explained that they were checking the whereabouts of all the men in her household so they could be sure it was not any of them.

'Well, don't be ridiculous, of course it isn't anyone from this house!' she said.

'Then you won't mind me asking Lord Collingwood where he was yesterday evening at seven o'clock.'

'Lord Collingwood? Edmund? Really! Well, he was out, of course, but nowhere near the festa. You were at the concert, weren't you?'

Edmund sat up straight, staring at his hat rather than meeting his mother's eyes.

'Ah. Yes. Last night. Ah. Perhaps not at the concert. A bit difficult to say exactly where I was.'

'Edmund!'

'It's complicated.'

'Edmund, what are you talking about? You were at the concert with Lieutenant Greening, weren't you?'

Lord Collingwood sighed. 'Look, Mama, I'll talk to Inspector McQueen and tell him where I was, but I can't tell you, I really can't.'

'Oh, for goodness' sake! Where were you? Floriana? We all know what goes on there. Do you really think I care what kind of trollop you've been seeing?'

'I am not saying another word, Mother.'

'Very well, talk to the Inspector then. Mr McQueen, I feel this whole situation is out of control. I cannot believe we have had another murder. There is something evil out there, and we are none of us safe anymore. I am going to my room, Edmund. I will speak to you again later.'

When she had gone, the young Lord Collingwood stood up and asked McQueen to step outside. He walked with him down the stone steps and into the garden. McQueen could see he was thinking hard, not wanting to speak until he had worked out what to say. They walked to the end of the garden, into a shaded area where a seat had been set under a tree. Collingwood sat down.

'I – ah – was with Lieutenant Greening last night at seven o'clock,' he said. 'We were in Floriana. And we were visiting an apartment. It's one Lieutenant Greening has rented.'

'Fine.'

'Ah, yes, but – we were alone,' he said, meaningfully.

There was silence, as McQueen absorbed this information, and its significance. Collingwood was entrusting him with a secret that could lead to imprisonment, and certainly lose him his reputation. *Naturally, he would not want his mother to know.*

'I understand,' he replied, carefully.

He remembered Greening from the voyage to Malta. *Hardly surprising that when they spoke, the Lieutenant had withheld the fact that he knew Collingwood so well.* He would immediately have been drummed out of the Army.

'Do you see? We can't have anybody knowing.' Collingwood's hands were shaking as he took a cigarette out of a silver case and offered one to McQueen. He tried unsuccessfully to strike a match.

McQueen took the match from him, struck it, lit his own cigarette and then the baron's. They smoked in silence for a few moments. *It wasn't in anyone's interests for this new information to be broadcast.*

'We will record you were in Floriana, simple as that,' he said, finally. 'As long as Lieutenant Greening can vouch for you.'

Collingwood drew on his cigarette, his pale eyes looking watery.

'I thank you,' he said. He got up and loped back into the villa.

It all made sense to McQueen, but it also left another possibility. He made some notes in his pocketbook against Edmund's name. *Was the admiral aware of his son's proclivities? And had anything happened between them that made Edmund determined to be rid of his father, to lead the life he wanted?* He could imagine the late admiral being adamant that Edmund should marry and produce an heir to the baronetcy, insisting that it was his duty.

McQueen made his way to the Auberge de Castille. The wind had died down and the air was close and humid. They did have a point with these linen suits; distinctly cooler, although his seemed to have crumpled terribly. He vowed to go back to the tailor.

Lieutenant Greening appeared in the lounge, his red tunic smartly pressed and fitting him perfectly. 'Inspector McQueen! We meet again.'

His handshake was firm, his smile friendly. He was undeniably handsome with his high cheekbones, even features and unusual, teal-coloured eyes. They sat down and Greening ordered some drinks. He had a gin and tonic, McQueen a beer.

'How's the investigation? Any nearer to finding out who killed the admiral?'

McQueen wondered if Edmund Collingwood had managed to get a message through to him.

'You know I am here on official business, Lieutenant? There was a murder during the festa; a young maid was killed. I have to ask you some questions.'

'Absolutely. Go ahead.'

He seemed to have the easy confidence of the land-owning English gentry, but McQueen thought he could detect an underlying London twang to his speech. This was someone who had worked hard to make his way up in the world.

'Where were you last night, at around seven o'clock?'

Greening affected a light, unconcerned manner and pretended to think for a few moments.

'Well, Inspector,' he said. 'I do believe I was with my very good friend Edmund, Lord Collingwood.'

'And where was that?'

'We have a place in Floriana. We have a housekeeper who brought us some food. We had a few drinks, smoked a few cigars, talked... We didn't stay late, must have been ten o'clock? We both had to get back.'

'I need to have the name of the housekeeper, to confirm this.'

'*Sinjura* Ċilia, Livia Ċilia.'

McQueen jotted her name down in his pocketbook.

'Turns out you were a wee bit shy of the truth when we spoke on the voyage,' he said. 'You knew a great deal more about the Collingwood family than you let on.'

Greening shifted uncomfortably in his seat. 'Well, I'm sure you can't blame me for that,' he said quietly.

'Did the admiral know about your relationship with his son?'

'Of course not, no!'

'Were you ever at the villa?'

'Well yes, card games, suppers and all that. But with a crowd, always. Never alone.'

McQueen wondered at that. Sometimes a stolen glance was enough to tell the tale.

'And how has Edmund Collingwood been, since his father's death?'

'Well, you know, up and down. He wasn't fond of his father, but it's brought on no end of pressure. He's finding it all rather hard to bear, if you must know.'

Greening fidgeted as he spoke, twisting his glass one way then another, whilst looking around to check who was in the room.

'Look, Inspector, can I just sign a piece of paper or something? I can't be seen talking to you for too long; people will wonder what's going on.'

'Certainly, you can come to the police office and make your statement there if you like.'

'Absolutely not! Believe me, I have nothing to do with this. It's just Edmund. We... I've known him a long time, you know.' All attempts at nonchalance were forgotten and he leaned forward, speaking in a low, earnest tone. 'McQueen, you must keep this quiet. You know the score.'

McQueen relented. 'Of course,' he said, getting up to leave. *He could turn a blind eye. The situation was dangerous for all concerned.* He liked Greening and understood why he had been less than truthful.

'But it does leave me wondering if there's anything else you're not telling me,' he said, putting on his hat. He looked back when he reached the door. The lieutenant was sipping his gin and tonic, deep in thought.

———

McQueen's next stop was at the home of Giorgio Micallef. It was a smart town house on Strada Mercanti, with a shiny brass knocker in the shape of a dolphin. He rapped on the door and after a few moments it was opened by a tiny woman, dressed entirely in black. She had an open, friendly air and the kind of good looks that carry well into middle age: an attractive oval-shaped face with wide-set eyes, high cheekbones and a neat, square chin.

'Can I help you?' she asked.

'Is this the home of Giorgio Micallef?'

'Yes, but he is not here. I am the housekeeper. Please, come in.'

McQueen explained who he was and why he was there, and the housekeeper was happy to help him. She invited him into the parlour. It was dark inside, with sombre furnishings and a muted atmosphere. There were religious paintings on the wall and a large gilt crucifix hung above the mantlepiece. The housekeeper seemed comfortable with him, chatting about the weather, how maybe there was a storm coming. He complimented her on her English.

'Thank you! I worked for a noble family in Città Vecchia,' she said, proudly. 'We all learned English as well as Italian.'

'Very good,' he said. 'I wonder, would you know where Mr Micallef was on Saturday evening?'

'Well, yes, Inspector. He was here, in the house. I bring him drinks, he read his books. He has supper at nine o'clock. It is always what he does.'

'And are you positive he was here at seven o'clock?'

'Oh yes, Inspector. All evening. In this room.' She looked at him brightly.

He made notes in his pocketbook.

'Do you know when Mr Micallef will be back?'

'Soon, soon,' she said. 'He is with Maria, his fiancée. Do you know her? Such a lovely girl. But of course, she is lucky to be marrying him. He is so clever, he will be very rich one day, I am sure.'

McQueen felt a surge of irritation. He left, feeling like he was wasting time, tramping round checking alibis. It helped him to keep going, though, to have a list in his head that he could work through methodically. And, of course, he was used to pounding the streets.

CHAPTER TWENTY-FOUR

M aria was in the drawing room, sewing with *Zija* Paolina. She was trying to finish a hem on a pocket handkerchief, but she had a knot in the thread. It would not go through the material and it had left an unsightly loop behind. Annoyed, she tugged at it a little too hard, and the thread broke.

'Oh, for heaven's sake!' she exclaimed. 'I can't do this. You know I don't have the patience.'

She threw the sewing to one side, sighing loudly.

'Now, Maria!' said *Zija* Paolina. 'You need to learn perseverance. You'll never be a good wife if you don't know how to sew. What will your husband think if you can't even do the most basic of stitches?'

'I don't know, *Zi*. I don't think I am going to be a good wife. I want to work with Papà on the newspaper. I'm hoping Giorgio will understand. We can always pay someone to do the sewing.'

Zija Paolina tutted. 'Really, dear, I don't think that's the answer. Do not forget how lucky you are. Your fiancé is a fine young man. He is already a highly regarded lawyer, one of the best in Valletta. You will need to take care of him.'

Her aunt would never understand; in *Zija* Paolina's world

the whole object in life was to find a husband, and then to spend your days ensuring his happiness and comfort. Maria was intent on finding a better way, where she could have some independence, some respect, her own status in the marriage.

She jumped up and went to the window, looking for a distraction. She could not settle to anything that morning. She could not stop thinking about the meeting at Marsat's office, but she also could not work out what she should do with her information. The news of Ċensa's murder had flown around the city, dominating everybody's thoughts and conversations. It made it even harder to decide who to talk to about the *Anti-Riformisti*.

She could hear a carriage arriving outside the house. *Thank goodness, it was Giorgio.* She felt sure he would know what to do.

'Oh, he's here,' she cried. 'Giorgio's here to see Papà.'

She ran out of the room and down the stairs to greet him. She watched as he handed his hat and his gloves to the housekeeper, and then as he turned towards her, she quickly ran up and kissed him on the mouth. His lips were firm and soft at the same time. She lingered, pulling in close. His coat was warm from the sun. She wanted to kiss him again, but, taking her by the shoulders, he gently pushed her away, a flicker passing over his light-green eyes.

'Maria,' he said. 'You are much too bold.'

She felt he had discomfited her on purpose. She studied his face. *How did he really feel about her?* His eyes were looking past her, and she felt a twinge of insecurity. *But he was so handsome and had promised her so much. It would be all right, wouldn't it?*

At that moment, her father came into the hall from his study, holding a newspaper in one hand, his spectacles in the other.

'Ah, Giorgio,' he said. 'I'm glad you're here. Thank you for coming. I wanted to ask your opinion on this account of that poor girl's death.'

He pointed at one of the articles with the arm of his spectacles.

'Of course, sir,' Giorgio said. 'I've had a look at the magistrate's report from the inquest. The police have started their investigation, but that article is pure speculation.'

They started to walk into the study. She noticed how at ease they were together. He was a natural addition to their household; her father respected him and approved of the match. She tried to put her doubts to the back of her mind.

'I've been reading about that, too,' she said loudly. 'That poor girl. I used to see her at Lord and Lady Collingwood's. It's horrible that your stupid rival at the *Gazzetta di Malta* is speculating on her life and why she was killed in this way.'

She followed them into the study.

A few minutes later another knock on the door interrupted their discussions. Maria listened out for the visitor's voice and straight away caught McQueen's Scottish burr. Sure enough, the housekeeper opened the door and announced the inspector's arrival. He walked in right behind her. It was immediately apparent he was not there on a polite visit.

Maria was taken aback by his appearance. He looked as though he had not slept for days, his suit crumpled and ill-fitting. His mouth was set in a hard line. He nodded a greeting, but any attempt at affability was gone. He took out his battered pocketbook and explained why he was there. It was about Ċensa; he was checking where people were on the night she was killed. Maria could see the murder had affected the inspector. There was a different air about him.

Her father explained he had been at the monthly board meeting. 'There were six crotchety men there asking me many difficult questions from six thirty until eight o' clock in the evening,' he said. 'They will all confirm I was squirming under their gazes at that time.'

She smiled to herself, knowing full well that he had the board eating out of his hand, and had all his decisions ratified, as he wanted.

'Thank you, Mr Tanti,' McQueen said, making a note of all their names as her father spelt them out. Then he turned to Giorgio. 'And I heard from your housekeeper that you were at home the whole evening, is that right?'

'Absolutely, Inspector,' Giorgio said, with the polite smile she recognised as his most charming. 'I had a lot of reading to catch up on, so I hardly moved from my chair.'

The way he so blithely answered McQueen made Maria catch her breath. She tried not to move, or to show any indication of the turmoil she was suddenly feeling. Her fiancé had lied to the police, right in front of her. She looked away from him, trying hard to breathe normally, forcing her mouth into a smile.

'You work so hard!' she said, her tone sounding false to her even as she said it. 'I'm sure it's not good for you. Do you need to know about me as well, Inspector? I can answer that easily: I was with my maidservant Rożi. We were out at the festa. We weren't close to where the murder happened. We were home by seven thirty and I didn't know about Ċensa until later.'

McQueen closed his pocketbook, looking even more weary. 'That's fine,' he said. 'I needed to check.'

'Inspector, would you like a glass of whisky?' her father asked.

'I'll not say no.'

Her father poured the men a whisky and they chatted a little. Tanti explained that he wanted to write a piece countering some of the "stupid speculations" in the rival newspaper. Would it be allowed for him to reference the police investigation? To say that it was foolish to point the finger at Sicilian incomers when there was no evidence? McQueen shrugged and said he could write what he liked, as long as it was within the law. He drank another whisky when it was offered and then left them, saying he had a lot to do. Maria followed him out into the hall, a tumult of thoughts in her mind. She found his hat and handed it to him.

'Goodbye, Inspector,' she said. 'It was good to see you, even though the circumstances are so awful.'

He put his hat on. 'Aye, well,' he said. 'It's my job, it's how it is.'

Impulsively, she decided to say something about the meeting, speaking in a low voice.

'I found out something about the Anti-Reform Party. There's a breakaway group, a militant one. They met at Dr Marsat's office – do you know him? The lawyer. It was seven o'clock yesterday. I've got something to tell you...' She tailed off, realising he was not listening. 'Sorry, I thought it might be useful.'

McQueen gave her a searching look, noticing the edge in her voice. 'Another time,' he said. 'You can see how busy I am.' He added more quietly, 'Come to the police office tomorrow morning?'

She nodded. She would have to think about how much to say and how much to leave out of her explanations. She watched McQueen leaving, the gravity of his position seeming to weigh heavily on his shoulders. *This was not a game. She still wanted to help the detective. She wanted to see approval in his eyes. But she had to be very careful.*

Maria could not face going back into the study. On the other side of the door, she could hear her father and Giorgio talking amicably together. She slipped into the library and paced up and down. She knew that Giorgio had been out on the night of the murder. She had seen him coming out of his house.

She had watched him disappearing to the right, thinking he was probably heading to his offices, perhaps to pick up some papers. He had not looked any different to normal. *If he had gone to fetch something, why had he not said so? Why had his housekeeper said he was there all evening when he clearly had not been?* She did not know what to do. She could not say anything without revealing where *she* had been.

After a quarter of an hour Maria heard the men's voices in the hall, and her father called her name. Reluctantly she answered that she was in the library, and then she heard Giorgio ask if he could be allowed to go in and say goodbye to her. 'Of course, son,' her father said.

Standing with her back to the window, she saw the door open. Her fiancé came in. Carefully, he closed the door behind him and stood silently looking at her. The quietness of his movements unnerved her. She looked back, waiting for him to speak first.

'You were very talkative with the inspector back then, Maria,' he said, softly.

'I don't think so. I tried to be normal, but it's difficult. A girl I know has been killed. It's made me feel strange, uncomfortable.'

He crossed the room and stood in front of her. She felt conscious of his height and strength. He gently lifted her chin so that she had to look into his eyes. With the light reflecting in them from the window, the turquoise colour looked cold and glittery, like the deep waters within a cave. She wanted to pull away.

'Now, Maria. You know I don't like you speaking to him, don't you?'

His voice was barely above a whisper. She did not dare move. He ran his finger down her neck from her chin, hesitating for a moment at the base of her throat. She was conscious of her every breath, watching his face closely, but he betrayed no emotion. He traced along her collarbone with a feather-light touch, then moved his hand behind her head. He drew her in for a kiss, longer and deeper than any they had shared before. Her body responded and she pressed close to him. This time he did not seem to find her too bold. Moments later, as they moved apart, he whispered into her ear, 'You're mine, Maria, and you do as I say. You do not speak to McQueen again, is that quite clear?'

She stared at him. *Was that all he had wanted from her? Her obedience?* She could find nothing to say. It was all she could do to nod, but he seemed satisfied with her response. She watched him walking away, opening the library door, then closing it softly behind him. She waited until she heard him call out a farewell to her father and leave the house. Then she sat down in her father's favourite armchair and tucked her legs up, wrapping her arms tightly around herself. She had to think about what to do. *Should she go and see the inspector, to let him know that Giorgio's alibi was false? Why was Giorgio so insistent she should stay away from McQueen? What was he not telling her?*

CHAPTER TWENTY-FIVE

L ater that morning, McQueen stood outside the door of
Henry Arbuthnot's house. His day was not getting any
better. It appeared that Arbuthnot was not at home. He had
knocked several times, but there was no answer. He stood on the
front step, banging loudly on the door with his fist.

A window opened in the wooden balcony to the right of
where he was standing. A man's head appeared. He was large,
overweight, with tousled black-and-grey hair. He shouted at
McQueen in Maltese, then switched to English when he got no
response.

'What you want? Stop that noise!'

'Colonel Arbuthnot – is he at home?'

'I don't know. Shut up with that noise!'

'I need to see him – police.'

The man muttered under his breath, then said, 'I ask my
wife.' He pulled his head back inside and McQueen could hear
arguing. Then he appeared again. 'She is coming down,' he said.
'No noise, yes? I am sleeping.' He closed the window with a
bang.

The door next to McQueen opened and a sharp-looking

Maltese woman came out. Her grey hair was badly dyed a sepia colour, her clothes were black and dowdy, and she looked as weary as he felt. 'Colonel Arbuthnot is home, in his study,' she said. 'He don't hear too good. I keep house for him, I can open door.' She was holding a big bunch of keys and sorted them to get the right one. She unlocked the door, then motioned McQueen to go inside. 'All right?' she asked. 'Sorry – my husband. He work nights.' She shouted into the house, 'Colonel! Police is here,' then went back into her own home with an air of martyrdom.

McQueen stepped into the dark hallway and immediately sensed that something was wrong. It was too still. Too still and airless, and had a hint of a bad odour. With a heavy heart he walked up the staircase in front of him, hand on the banister. He was used to the geography of Valletta town houses now. The study would be on the first floor, the room at the front with the balcony. He called out, 'Arbuthnot? It's McQueen.' But he was not expecting an answer. The smell was getting stronger, and he could hear a faint humming sound. He got to the door and opened it slowly.

The room was dark, the blinds all closed. He felt in his pocket for a match and struck it against the wall. The humming intensified as hundreds of blowflies flew around each other, jostling to settle back on a dark heap in the centre of the room. Keeping close to the walls, he moved across to the balcony and opened the blinds. The light flooded across the room, revealing Arbuthnot, lying prone in the middle of the floor. It looked as though he had been sitting in his armchair and had fallen forwards. His arm was stretched out as though grasping for something, his head thrown back. The smell was unbearable – the acrid stench of vomit.

McQueen approached slowly and stood looking down on the body of the old man, feeling an intense despondency settle upon him. *Yet another death.* He felt the corpse – it was cool. The head was lying in a pool of vomit. By the grim look on Arbuthnot's face, he must have died in agony. His eyes were showing milky white, rolled up under raised brows, his mouth pulled wide into an horrific grimace. His body was stiff, his back arched.

Had someone disposed of Arbuthnot, too, or had he – God forbid – taken his own life? The smell and the flies were overpowering. McQueen backed off to the doorway. He tried to take it all in, to see if there was anything that could tell the story of what had happened.

He took out his pocketbook and quickly sketched the scene in front of him. Then he left the room, shutting the door behind him. He needed to inform the police superintendent as soon as possible, but he did not want to leave the body. He went back to the neighbour's house and banged on the door. He could hear the husband erupting with rage, then the wife opened the door. She looked weary and suspicious. 'What?'

'Your neighbour is dead,' he said. 'I need you to send for the police. Now.'

She gasped, supporting herself against the door as her knees buckled. '*Ommi Madonna!* What happen?'

'Never you mind,' he said. 'We'll deal with it. Find someone to run to the police office. I will stay next door.'

'Yes, *sur,*' she said. She turned and ran up the stairs, shouting to her husband, her arms flailing clumsily, reaching for the wall and the banister to steady her.

McQueen went back into Arbuthnot's house to walk through all the rooms. The shutters were open in the kitchen downstairs and all seemed normal, quite clean. There was no sign of any recent meals eaten. He prowled around, looking at the tidy piles of crockery and stacks of pans. The housekeeper was performing her role well. Everything looked to be in order.

He went upstairs, past the door to the parlour and along the corridor to the adjacent room. Again, it was in darkness, but he could just make out that it was a bedroom. He opened the shutters. This room was untidy, the bed unmade, and a trail of clothes lay on the floor. A sheet of notepaper lay on the bedside table, folded over. He picked it up and unfolded it. The writing was weak, the ink alternatively scratchy or blotted, as if written in a hurry. *I am sorry for my actions, for all the pain I have caused. I can take it no longer. Henry Arbuthnot.* He had taken his own life.

Loud shouting and heavy boots heralded the arrival of the police. He joined them at the top of the stairs. Sergeant Galea was at the front. He felt relief at seeing the young man's concerned and determined face.

'The body's in there,' he said, opening the door. 'Not a pretty sight.'

'We've spoken to the magistrate, and he said we could get Dr Bonniċi. He's on his way,' Galea said.

'Then no one should touch the body until he arrives.'

Galea approached the corpse and batted some of the flies away. Then he clamped his hand over his mouth and moved away. McQueen pulled him back to the door, putting a hand on his shoulder.

'Go downstairs for some fresh air,' he said. 'It's the smell.'

Galea crossed Bonniċi on the stairs, his hand still over his face. The doctor was making his way up as quickly as he could, leaning heavily on his cane. He smiled slightly when he got to the top. 'We meet again,' he said.

'Yes,' McQueen said. 'It's a sorry scene, Doctor.' He motioned him into the room then followed him inside.

'*Ġesu Kristu*,' Bonniċi muttered as he knelt next to the body. He swiftly got to work, checking the pulse, the temperature, feeling the back of the neck, then the muscles down the rest of the body. He looked up.

'What do you think of the expression on his face?'

'I've not seen it before, but I think I know what it is.'

'*Risus sardonicus* – the rictus grin. It's strychnine. I am sure of it.'

'There's a glass with some remnants in it here,' McQueen said, picking it up carefully from a table next to the armchair. 'Can you test it?'

'I will have to take it to the laboratory.' He wrapped it up in a cloth and put it in his medical bag.

'The superintendent will have a field day with this. There will have to be another inquest.'

A loud voice could be heard coming up the stairs, barking out orders in Maltese. Captain Borġ appeared in the doorway, his bulk blocking out all the light.

'Speak ill o' the devil and he'll appear,' McQueen said under his breath.

'What is this, Inspector? What is happening? Everywhere we find you, we find a dead body.'

'It looks like suicide,' McQueen said. 'There is a note.'

He passed the sheet of paper to Captain Borġ, who read it, then looked up in triumph.

'Aha!' he said. 'This time we do have our man! See, here, he says he is sorry for his actions. He has killed Lord Collingwood, and he has killed the maid, too.'

'No,' McQueen said. 'You are jumping to conclusions. He could have killed himself for many other reasons.' He took the note back and slipped it inside his pocketbook. He would examine it again later.

'Sir, sir!' Galea pushed his way through. He was holding a tall metal canister.

'What is it, Sergeant?'

'I found this in the kitchen, sir, in the flour tin.' He pulled out a bottle labelled Rat Poison, shaking off the flour. Bonniċi took it from him.

'I will take that for analysis,' he said.

'And there's more,' Galea said. He turned the flour tin on its side. Nestling inside the white powder was a steel handle.

McQueen reached over and pulled it out. A kitchen knife appeared. It had a narrow nine-inch blade.

'You see!' said Borġ. 'The murder weapon. We have found the killer.'

CHAPTER TWENTY-SIX

By the time McQueen returned to his lodgings, after the body had been taken away and details of the scene recorded, it was past two o'clock. The sky was still dark and the air oppressive. If a storm was on the way, he hoped it would bring some relief from the intense heat. As he walked up the stairs, he could hardly put one leg in front of the other. Sweat was dripping down from his hair onto his collar, and his shirt was completely soaked. All he could think about was getting to his bed and collapsing into it. He got into the room, pulled off his boots, his jacket and his shirt, and lay down. As soon as his head touched the pillow, he felt himself yanked into a deep, black sleep.

It could have been minutes or hours later when a voice pulled him back into consciousness. For a second, he had no idea where he was. He lay there, trying to remember. The voice was calling from outside his door. 'Mister McQueen, Mister McQueen?' Then a knock, softly, as though lacking in confidence. Then the voice again, sounding tearful. 'Mister McQueen, please!' *Sinjura* Caruso. He wondered what time it was and what she wanted. He sat up, his head thumping as he moved. He got up and went to the door, pulling his braces over his undershirt. It sounded urgent.

He opened the door. *Sinjura* Caruso stood outside, her eyes troubled. She stepped back when she saw him, looking away as if embarrassed. He knew he must look a sight. 'What is it?' he asked. 'What's the time? I fell asleep.'

'It's Ninu,' she said. 'He's gone. Do you know where he is?'

'No,' he said, running his hand over his hair. 'I haven't seen him since this morning. I didn't send him out with any messages.'

He felt a pang of guilt for his sharp words at breakfast.

'I know,' she said. 'But I am worried. He did not come home for lunch or siesta. He is not in the house. He is gone.'

McQueen was concerned. He remembered the way the boy had turned away from him. And he knew how Antonio liked to be out and about on an adventure. *Had he got himself into trouble out there?*

'Don't worry,' he found himself saying. 'I'm sure he will be fine. He's a sensible lad. I'll go out and look for him.'

'But he never did this before. You must find him, soon, please?'

'Of course. You stay here in case he comes back. I'll go out now. I'm sure I will find him. What time is it?'

'Four o'clock.'

'I'll be back by dinnertime,' he said in a tone he hoped conveyed confidence. She looked terrible, her face pinched, and her eyes dark and troubled.

'All right, I wait here,' she said, turning away and going back downstairs.

He looked at himself in the mirror. He did indeed look rough. He splashed water on his face and pulled a comb through his hair. He pulled a new shirt over his head and fixed on a fresh collar. After he had pulled on his boots, waistcoat and jacket, he felt for his pocketbook before setting off. His jacket felt strangely light. He patted the pocket. Nothing there. He sat on the bed and looked under it. Nothing there either. He scrabbled around the room. *What had he done with it?* He remembered staggering in and taking his clothes off before he went to sleep. *Had he done something strange, put his pocketbook somewhere else in the room?*

He felt sick. There weren't any other places. Either he had lost it on the way back from Arbuthnot's house, or someone had taken it. And the only person who knew about it and could easily get into his room was Antonio. *What had the stupid lad done? Had he taken the book?* Everything was in there – every thought, idea and piece of information about the investigation – Arbuthnot's suicide note, even. *Surely, Antonio wouldn't have done that... would he?*

McQueen left the lodging house and tried to think where Antonio would go. He walked down to the English curtain wall, where the road ran along the water's edge. He thought perhaps Antonio had gone to the fishing shacks, where his father used to keep his boat. He walked over to a couple of fishermen who were standing by, gloomily looking at the water, and asked them, but they shook their heads. He checked in the bakery and the grocers on the other side of the road. No one had seen the lad.

He decided to head back to the police office through the city. He would look for Antonio on the way. As he walked, the black clouds scudding across the sky, he felt as if everything was beginning to fall to pieces around him. He had not followed up on questioning the maidservant and she had died as a result. Henry Arbuthnot's body was laid out on a mortuary slab. The superintendent believed they had found Lord Collingwood's murderer, but that did not feel right. And now both the boy and the pocketbook had disappeared. He felt furious with himself; he had allowed the case to slip out of his control.

He scoured the streets. Every time he saw a skinny barefoot boy he would speed up, but it was never Antonio. When he got to the police office, he found Galea and pulled him into a corner.

'Sergeant, can you get the word around for constables to look out for my landlady's boy? He's gone missing. Small, scruffy. Name of Antonio Caruso – also answers to Ninu.'

'How long has he been gone for?'

'A few hours, but it is out of character for him – he's a good wee lad.'

Galea nodded and went to talk to a group of police officers who had come in from the street.

———

The inquest was called for five o'clock. The second in three days. McQueen felt a strong sense of déjà vu as he walked into the room. The magistrate was deep in conversation with Captain Borġ. They stopped and looked at him for a second before resuming their discussion. He sat down next to Bonniċi, who was with the police surgeon.

Bonniċi nodded at him. 'This won't take long,' he said.

The general hubbub in the room died down as Captain Borġ went to sit in the front row and the magistrate stood up. He picked up his gavel and looked gravely around the room ready to start proceedings, when Carstairs came bursting in, papers under one arm and the familiar attaché case in the other.

'*Scusa, scusa,*' he said, smiling genially at everyone. He sat down next to McQueen, plonking the papers on the table. He said something like '*in ritardo*' – no doubt apologising for being late.

The magistrate glared at him then brought his gavel down. As he began proceedings, Carstairs leant towards McQueen.

'Sorry, old boy. Can't believe we're here again. Grim business. Poor old Buffy. The governor's beside himself.'

After a long preamble, McQueen was called up to describe what he had found at Arbuthnot's house, with an interpreter brought in to translate his English into Italian. *This constant need to have everything to do with the law in Italian when most people could understand English!* He was beginning to find the whole situation a farce.

He described the scene in the study, and everything he had found at the house, including the suicide note. He said that the note was vague, that it referred to "actions" and not to murder.

He saw Borġ lean close to the magistrate and mutter something in his ear. The magistrate raised his eyebrows, looked at McQueen intently, then asked another question, translated as, 'His Honour wants to see the suicide note.'

He felt a rush of anger and glared at Borġ.

'I regret that I don't have it with me.'

'And why not?'

'Because,' he said, 'I have left my pocketbook at my lodgings.'

A murmur went around the courtroom.

The magistrate waved a hand for him to stand down and called for Captain Borġ. The superintendent reported that the suicide note clearly stated that Arbuthnot was guilty of two crimes – the murders. And, what was more, the knife that had been used to kill Ċensa was found hidden in his kitchen.

Bonniċi described the state of the body. He also reported that the rat poison found in the kitchen was likely to be the source of the poison. Finally, the magistrate ordered an autopsy for the next morning, and asked Bonniċi to investigate the contents of the glass found near the corpse.

He finished by announcing, 'We will reconvene after the post-mortem examination. And, Inspector McQueen, I expect you to bring all evidence with you. It is not acceptable to forget things. It is not how the police operate here in Malta.'

Captain Borġ was smirking, looking like a toad that had recently lunched on a dragonfly. McQueen fought the desire to reach across and throttle him. He could not bear for the superintendent to have the upper hand. *He had to find his pocketbook. And he had to find the boy.*

CHAPTER TWENTY-SEVEN

Coming out of the law courts, McQueen decided to head to Barrakka Gardens. He had seen groups of scruffy young urchins gathered around the entrance before, daring each other to run up to smart visitors and ask for pennies. His hope was that Antonio was lurking amongst them. He scanned the children's faces but could not see him. He asked one of the boys, even gave him a coin, but no, the lad shook his head.

The sky was now a deep, lowering grey. As McQueen turned the corner back into Strada Mercanti, he felt a few spots of rain and turned his collar up. Before he had gone twenty more paces, rain was pelting down. He dodged inside an open doorway and found himself in the entrance to a church. Taking his hat off and brushing the water from his jacket, he stood inside for a while, waiting to see if the rain would ease.

The church was sombrely lit and cool. Hardly anyone was inside, only two women dressed entirely in black, seated at the front. Something about the atmosphere drew him further in and he sat down heavily on a dark oak pew. At the altar, two priests were lighting candles, laying out cloths and preparing the wine and the bread. Their movements were practised, unhurried. Despite the hammering of the rain on the high, domed roof, the atmosphere was subdued.

McQueen breathed out and sat forwards, trying to clear his head. A cushion was tucked into the back of the pew in front of him. He picked it up and turned it around in his hands. It was old and worn, intricately stitched with Latin text. He put it back and looked around the church. It was not large; it looked as if it would hold around two hundred people. Nor was it particularly ornate, though it did have its fair share of gilt and baroque decoration. Behind the altar was a large painting showing a robed figure, holding a staff in his right hand. Above the painting, a golden scallop shell. He knew the Bible well enough to know this must be Saint James, patron saint of travellers.

The rustle of clothing and muttered voices from the church entrance indicated that more people were arriving for the service. Richly dressed couples with unnaturally quiet children went to the front, along with elderly widows and their dowdy companions. He watched as they walked up the aisle, stopping to dip their knees and genuflect, eyes lowered, before moving to the right or the left and sitting down. A deep reverence was etched on their faces. Once seated, they pulled out a rosary and began to mouth silent prayers. Gradually the church filled up with people. Nobody looked at him or paid him any attention. Not having much idea of how a Roman Catholic service would unfold, he felt uncomfortable, thinking perhaps he should leave before it started. But his legs felt like blocks of lead, making it impossible for him to get up and walk away.

He closed his eyes, but that instantly brought up a succession of unwelcome images: Ċensa's face, her eyes imploring as she clutched his arm; Arbuthnot's twisted body lying prone on the floor; Antonio looking up at him fearfully in the kitchen. He felt he had failed in every way since arriving in Malta. *He had let so many people down.* Time and time again he had come up against a brick wall in the investigation, and through his negligence a young girl had lost her life.

He shook his head and opened his eyes. The priest had begun the service, extending his hands and intoning, '*In nomine Patris, et Filii, et Spiritus Sancti.*' The Latin was unfamiliar and yet familiar, echoing the words he had known throughout his childhood. As the priest continued speaking, a latecomer scurried in, taking a quick curtsy in the aisle before making her away along his pew and sitting down in the middle, a few seats away from him. A middle-aged woman, in a black *għonnella*, with an energy about her that he recognised from somewhere. She took off her *għonnella*, folded it and put it on her lap, her head now covered by a black lace veil. She joined in with the congregation, which was chanting words they had known all their lives, yet probably didn't fully understand: '*Mea culpa, mea culpa, mea maxima culpa*'. As the prayer finished, with '*Dominum Deum nostrum*', she sat down, giving him a quick sideways look. She tucked the folds of her skirt around her. The way she moved, with tiny almost nervous actions, reminded him who it was – the housekeeper from the young lawyer Giorgio Micallef's place. He gave her the barest of nods.

He sat back and let the service wash over him. It felt so different to the plain, pared-back worship he was used to. His father would hate the fripperies and extras; he would say they were "designed to add mystique and keep the common people from a true understanding of faith". The incense burner wafted around on a chain, the ornate silver paten and chalice for the bread and wine, the ringing of the altar bell. The Mass went on for a long time; muttered streams of Latin from the priest punctuated by responses from the congregation. Prayers were sung as well as chanted and at one point he thought he could pick out the words of the Lord's Prayer.

Eventually, the members of the congregation made their way to the front to receive communion. He stayed in his seat, watching the priests going through the practised rituals, the people going along with them, convinced by their meaning. *If only it were as simple as it seemed.* He thought about the meaning of *'mea culpa': through my fault, through my fault, through my most grievous fault.* So much had happened through *his* fault. *If only he could go to confession, receive penance and be absolved of his sins.* He knew he would find the world an easier place to live in. But he had rejected the tenets of the Church – any church – a long time ago. He shifted forwards in his seat and leant his arms on the back of the pew in front. Sitting here was not going to solve anything. *He had to get back out into the streets.* And yet he did not seem to be able to move.

His eyes were locked on the wall behind the altar; thirty feet of marble stretching up to the top of the domed roof. Dully, he registered the gold leaf ribbons and swirls around the sides and tops of the pillars; the gold scallop shell and hideous white plaster cherubs sitting above the painting of the pilgrims' saint. It was ridiculous that those romantic angels and clouds were expected to make you believe in Heaven. But the painting itself, that was different. It was a simple picture of Saint James standing in front of a rocky background. Dressed in white robes, looking up at a stormy sky, his staff and his bare feet firmly planted on the ground.

There was something about the painting that reminded him of his father, the way the figure stood so strong and firm, reaching out to the people. The Reverend John McQueen. His congregation loved him; thousands of pounds had been raised for the new church to be built for his parish. A church large enough to seat a thousand people. He remembered them piling in, talking excitedly, looking forward to hearing his father preach. He and Andrew would be standing at the church entrance, handing out pamphlets. Dressed in simple corduroy, so as not to be seen as any better than the working men and women they welcomed in.

He could picture his father standing tall at the pulpit, preaching with so much conviction, showing off his deep knowledge of the scriptures. At that time, he had mocked him, despaired of him, thinking he was wasting his time, giving people false hope in a miserable world. Hated him for being so narrow in his beliefs and for the endless, tedious preaching. Yet, here, the priests did not even look at the congregation. They did not seem to make the Bible come alive with stories that could be understood, in the words of the people; they ran through the motions in a dead language that had no meaning.

The sound of the rain drumming on the roof had died down, and a shaft of sunlight managed to break through the cupola window, lighting up the front of the church and making the pillars glow white. For a moment, he wished himself back at the church in Edinburgh, if only to acknowledge for once that his father was doing some good. At least he cared about his parish, bringing people together through the church and offering them help and support.

He realised that he – Sam McQueen – was in many ways his father's son. He might not be a paragon of virtue, but he cared just as much about the community he worked amongst. There were times when he, too, had picked up the pieces when people's lives had taken a wrong turn. He had helped them to stay off the drink or the laudanum, or found them a job to keep them from thieving and cheating – if he felt they deserved a second chance. He had done it not in the name of religion, but in the belief that there were good people in the world.

He sat upright. He had to accept he could not always be right, that he made mistakes. He had to stop looking backwards and blaming himself. *He had a job to do.* He felt energy returning to him. He would wait a moment longer, then get back out onto the streets, find the boy and get the damned pocketbook back.

He watched the supplicants as they walked back from taking communion and sat back in their seats. Several of the women dropped to their knees in silent prayer. He wondered what it was they were asking of their God. *Were they thinking of husbands lying grievously ill at home? Or were they praying for lost souls?* He could see Micallef's housekeeper, her head bowed, praying fervently. There was a tension in her, the way she held her body, that was very different to the person he had met earlier. He wondered what was troubling her. He watched her closely. As if she sensed it, she turned her head and looked directly at him. Fear flickered across her face and he knew in that instant she had something she was hiding.

The Mass was drawing to a close. After final prayers, blessings and mutterings of *Amen* and *Deo Gratias*, the congregation began to file out of the church, talking quietly to each other on the way. He got up, keeping his eyes firmly on the housekeeper. She pulled her *għonnella* over her head and darted out of the church. He decided to walk after her, to ask a few more questions. There was something she had said last time, something about living in Città Vecchia, that he remembered he wanted to follow up.

Out in the street, the brief glimpse of the sun had already been chased away by the clouds. McQueen watched the tiny figure of the housekeeper, swathed in her black cloak, crossing the road and disappearing into the house a few doors down, her movement reminding him of a swooping bat. He waited a moment or two then approached the front door and rapped loudly with the brass knocker. He could hear some muffled noises, before the door was opened a crack. The housekeeper looked unhappy to see him, which convinced him to push the door open further and step inside.

The hallway looked darker and more oppressive than he remembered. She backed away from him.

'I saw you in the church,' he said.

She nodded, glancing towards the staircase and then back towards the front door, as if wanting to disappear.

'I wanted to ask you something. It's about something you said last time we spoke,' he continued. 'I have to follow everything up; it's important.'

'Then you leave?' she asked, quietly.

'Yes. I want to know which house you worked at; you mentioned a place in Città Vecchia?'

'Oh, yes.'

She hesitated, as if she did not know what she should say. She studied the floor.

'Look, I need to know!' He raised his voice. 'Was it Count San Pietro's house?'

She jumped and looked up, tears gathering in her eyes.

'Yes,' she whispered.

'How long ago? How long did you work there for?'

'Many, many years. From when I was a girl. I am from Rabat. Many people have work there with big families in the Old City. First, I was a maid and then a nursemaid, until five years ago when I come here.'

'What do you know about the count? Did you know he was friends with Lord Collingwood?'

'Yes, but a long, long time ago.'

'Do you know if he saw him again recently?'

She shook her head.

'I don't know. I haven't seen the count for five years. He is a good man, Inspector, he always be kind to me. Believe me, he never do anything wrong. Now go, please go. Mister Micallef will be back soon and I have work to do. Please go.'

As she stepped backwards again, he heard a key in the lock, then the door swung open. Micallef strode in and threw his hat onto the hall chair, before stopping abruptly, looking from McQueen to the housekeeper and then back again.

'Back here again, Inspector?' He had adopted a pleasant smile, but McQueen could see from his eyes and the small lines by the corners of his mouth that he was feeling some strain.

'I had some questions for your housekeeper. About Count San Pietro.'

'Oh, yes?' Micallef said. His smile remained fixed, his voice smooth. 'I hope you were able to help, Sulina?'

'Of course, sir,' she said.

'I cannot imagine why you would be asking about the count, Inspector.'

McQueen noticed Micallef's eyes flick towards the housekeeper. It was a tiny, almost involuntary movement. And he saw a connection between them, which he felt sure was significant.

'There appear to be a few links between the count and the late admiral,' he explained. 'I need to find out more about him.'

He looked closely at the housekeeper. Her eyes were spaced wide apart, like Micallef's, and the shape of the face had similar proportions – from the cheekbones down to the square chin. *If he was right, then why were they hiding their relationship?* He decided to say nothing until he knew more.

He turned away, put on his hat and stepped towards the door.

'Thank you for your help,' he said to the housekeeper. 'I'll see myself out.'

He left the two of them standing in the hall, feeling certain that they were more than merely housekeeper and master: they were mother and son.

CHAPTER TWENTY-EIGHT

'So, you've come back, you little tyke!'

Arriving back at his lodgings, McQueen had walked in to find Antonio sitting at the kitchen table.

The boy looked at him with a sullen expression.

'Oho, it's like that is it?'

'He is bad boy,' *Sinjura* Caruso said. 'I told him, never do that. Never disappear without telling me.' She said a few more harsh-sounding words in Maltese.

The boy shovelled his food into his mouth, pushed his plate away and started to get up from the table.

'Stop there,' McQueen said. 'I want a word with you.' He could not let him go without asking about the pocketbook.

Antonio stood by the table, eyes darting from McQueen, to his mother, to the door. He looked like a rabbit, hesitating before deciding which way to run.

'This is serious, lad. I need to know if you have stolen something of mine? Something important that is missing?'

'No!' the boy said, loudly. 'I no steal.' He started to edge away from the table.

'Antonio!' *Sinjura* Caruso said.

He looked at his mother pleadingly, explaining himself in a torrent of Maltese, then ran out of the room in tears.

After he had gone, *Sinjura* Caruso cleared away Antonio's plate, taking it into the kitchen. McQueen could hear a clattering of pots and pans. He sat back, waiting. Eventually she came back and slammed a plate of food down in front of him.

'My son is not thief,' she said. Her eyes flashed with anger. 'He told me he stole nothing.'

McQueen shrugged. 'I had to ask. I have lost something, something important. My pocketbook. I need it back.'

'Is not Antonio. Maybe you lost it somewhere, not here.'

'No, I think it was him. He looks guilty, surely you can see that? Perhaps he didn't mean to *steal* it, but I do think he took it away.'

'He not steal. I teach him good!'

McQueen understood that this was hard for her, but she had to realise the gravity of the situation.

'This is serious; it is important police evidence,' he said. 'I will have to talk to him again tomorrow.'

A pained expression crossed her face. She pulled out a chair and sat down opposite him, as if forgetting that he was her lodger. He noticed how pronounced her cheekbones were. She looked exhausted, dark smudges under her eyes.

'I worry. About Antonio,' she said. 'He never act like this before.'

Her hands were resting on the table. He remembered when he first saw her, her hand holding the taper, lighting a candle in church. The dark sorrow in her eyes, revealed by the dancing flame. Wanting to offer support, reassurance, he moved his hands towards hers across the table. She ignored the gesture.

'I don't want him to work for you anymore,' she said. 'Is not safe. I don't like it, what is going on.'

'I understand,' he said. 'Don't worry. I really won't ask him again.'

She looked down at her lap. All her energy seemed to have drained out of her. After a moment, she tucked a stray hair behind her ear, took a breath.

'Is difficult. Without husband,' she said. 'I have to be father and mother. Ninu is good, but – you know – he is growing up. Now he run around city, has secrets. Is not right. He should be in school, learning.'

McQueen felt his face go red. He was ashamed that he had brought trouble to the house. *He should not have encouraged the lad; it was a foolish thing to do.*

'He'll be fine,' he said.

'You are good with him, Mr McQueen. He likes you very much.'

He wondered what was coming next. *Already, he regretted reaching out to her. He should have kept his distance.*

'Can you help?' she asked. 'Talk to him for me? Please.'

So that was it; she wanted him to help her keep her own child in check.

Clumsily, he picked up his fork and started to eat, looking intently at his plate.

'I'll do what I can, *Sinjura* Caruso. But it's his choice.'

Harsh, he knew, but so it had to be. He carried on eating, keeping his head down.

Sinjura Caruso sighed, got up and went to the back of the kitchen. She returned with a pile of laundry; the blood-stained clothes from Sunday now washed, dried and pressed.

'Here,' she said. 'Two shillings. It was hard to clean.'

He ate his meal silently, then went upstairs.

Later that night, McQueen went up to the roof and smoked a cigarette, leaning over the balustrade. He had invested in a tin of Turkish tobacco and he was enjoying the mild, aromatic flavour. The sky was a dark indigo, the heavy clouds obscuring most of the stars. Far away, he could hear distant laughter from a group of drunken men. He could see and hear shadowy figures on other rooftops, aware of their murmuring voices and the red tips of cigars glowing. A dog barked a few streets away, which started up another dog until there was a chain of responses, gradually dying down. The air was muggy and oppressive.

He thought about Jeannie, 2,000 miles away. He hoped that she was coping without him. *Had she found work? Was she managing to stay away from the laudanum?* He remembered how it would lift his spirits to arrive home from a long night and find her waiting for him; how she would run up, take his hat from his head, throw herself into his arms. He missed the simplicity of their relationship, the trust.

He tried not to think about what had happened, the night when he had come close to losing her, but the memory came flooding back.

It had been a long day. It was late, and he had been at the Fountain Inn, drinking more whiskies than he should have done. As soon as he had let himself into the apartment, he had known something was wrong. It was dark and quiet. All he could hear were voices and noises from the neighbouring rooms. He called, 'Jeannie?' but there was no answer. He thought perhaps she had gone out to meet that friend of hers, the one with the new baby. He was hungry. *She must have left him something to eat.* He walked along the hallway and stood in the doorway of the kitchen. The fire in the range was out; it was cold. The door was open and unlit coals tipped onto the floor.

There would be no hot water, and no dinner. He felt a surge of anger. Stepping forward he picked up some of the coals and threw them into the range, cursing loudly; words he had never used in this apartment while Jeannie had lived there. *Was it too much to ask, to have a warm homecoming with a decent bit of meat for his tea?*

Then, sensing rather than hearing her, he turned around to see Jeannie in the doorway.

'I couldn't get the fire going,' she said, her voice flat. 'It wouldn't take.'

Fury overtook all sense of reason. *What the hell had she been doing all day?*

'It's not that difficult. Jesus Christ!'

Then he noticed how withdrawn she seemed. She looked as she had done when he had first come across her. Blank. Like a two-dimensional painting. As though she were physically present, but her soul had been taken away. His suspicions were raised.

He grabbed her by the shoulders, looking into her eyes. 'Have you been taking laudanum again?'

She twisted away from him, and ran into the bedroom, trying to shut the door on him. He stopped the door with his foot and pushed it hard, sending her flying backwards. She landed on the floor, hitting her head against the bedstead, and lay there looking up at him in disbelief.

'Oh my God, Jeannie, I'm sorry. I didn't mean to. I just wanted to see – to know–'

He tried to help her up, but she pushed him away, eyes blazing.

'Get away from me. You've been at the drink. You promised you'd never do that.'

Her father was a drunkard. She had told McQueen how fearful she had been, every time he returned from the inn. Hoping to God he would not lash out at her mother, or even come after her.

McQueen felt sick.

All the trust he had built up over the past two years had gone. Instantly, he had become a man who could hurt her as she had been hurt so many times before.

'A few drams, Jeannie, just a few.'

'No. You're out drinking more and more. You won't even admit it.'

'Look, I'm sorry. It won't happen again.'

She got up shakily and sat on the bed.

'It's more than that, Sam. I never see you, you're never here. It's too hard, living like this. And now I can't even trust you.'

The memory of those words cut through him. He had helped Jeannie to escape a life of exploitation, but he had not taken good enough care of her. It was not the drink. It was his work that was the problem. His job as a detective had brought her to him, and now it had taken her away. He had not been constant enough for her. He could never be a husband or a father because his time was always spent elsewhere.

Standing in the close heat of the Mediterranean night, his life in Edinburgh felt like another world. There, he knew how things worked. He knew who to talk to, who to put pressure on, how to shake things up to get to the truth. It was all much more straightforward. Even the criminals behaved in a way he could understand. They committed their crime – burglary, theft, yes, even murder – then they tried to get away. They left obvious trails behind them and he could always track them down. However long it took, however far they went, he would find them, usually holed up in some godforsaken lodging house.

Here, he still did not know what was going on. He felt close to breaking through, but the truth was tantalisingly out of reach. He did not believe that Arbuthnot was the murderer. Instinct told him that the old man did not have it in him, and he held the admiral in too high regard. He had taken his own life because of a variety of factors, in part because he was a ruined man and because he had caused others to lose their own savings.

That meant that Ċensa's killer was still out there. Her murder had been planned and carried out with ruthless efficiency; the knife hidden to throw suspicion on the colonel. He had to find the killer before anyone else was made to suffer, and he only had three days left before the governor would send him home. He heard a low rumble of far-off thunder and looked over to the left, in the direction of the sound. There was a flash of lightning. Automatically, he started counting the seconds before another thunder-roll – sixteen. The storm was over three miles away. As he looked to the southern skies, they lit up with a flash of crackling electricity, the dark clouds pierced by white, jagged lightning bolts.

McQueen threw his cigarette over the edge of the roof, and watched it dip and twirl, the glow eventually going out before it reached the ground.

CHAPTER TWENTY-NINE

Floriana, Malta, Tuesday, 10 August 1880

'Scalpel, *Dottore*.'

Bonniċi passed the six-inch curved blade to Chief Surgeon Girello.

It was early morning and he was assisting at the post-mortem examination of Henry Arbuthnot. The small dissecting room was across the corridor from his laboratory at the hospital. It was kept dark and cool, the air thick, tinged with its own peculiar smell: viscera and disinfectant. He liked the methodical process of the examination, taking care to lay out the instruments in the correct order, alongside the dishes and sample jars. All clean and ready on metal trays by the side of the dissecting table.

The dead colonel was stripped of all identity. He was now no more than a corpse lying on a marble slab. Chief Surgeon Girello worked quietly, systematically, muttering under his breath. Every now and then he would bark out his observations for Bonniċi to note. First, he examined the mouth and lips, his head close to the body. '*Risus sardonicus* – the rictus grin. Consistent with strychnine poisoning. Could be tetanus, but unlikely, given the sudden onset. No odour, nothing to suggest any other poison. Do you agree, *Dottore?*'

Bonniċi nodded. 'Yes, that would be my conclusion.'

Girello then moved down the length of the table, observing the corpse. It did not bear thinking about, the intensity of pain that would rack a body in such a way.

As they worked, Girello exclaimed over the state of the old man's body.

'He would not have been long for this world. Look at the liver, at the heart.' The colonel's liver was enlarged, scarred with cirrhosis, the arteries around his heart hardened and yellow. 'Liver failure due to alcoholic poisoning would soon have killed him, if not a heart attack.'

Between them, they removed the stomach and placed it on a large porcelain dish.

'I wonder if he even knew what he was doing! Take a note, *Dottore*, that the victim's movements and cognitive ability would have been impaired by alcohol.'

At the end of the examination, Girello replaced the sternum and sewed the cadaver back together. He shrugged out of his white coat and threw it into the corner of the room. Then he went to the basin to wash his hands.

'As clear as can be,' he said. 'Death from asphyxiation, due to poisoning. I will leave you to complete the notes. And I believe you may have evidence in the form of a drink? I have no doubts that you will find strychnine is to blame.'

He left the room, leaving Bonniċi alone.

The dissecting room was quiet, the only sound the dripping of the tap at the basin in the corner of the room. Normally, he could maintain a sense of detachment, viewing the post-mortem with clinical interest. But this time, he felt uneasy; the horror of

Arbuthnot's last moments had got to him. He called for the assistants to take the body away and clean down the room.

Back in his laboratory, Bonniċi set to work analysing the sample of gin and tonic. There were two tests he could do. The first was the taste test. He dipped his finger in the liquid and tried it on his tongue. It was incredibly bitter – even more bitter than the quinine in the tonic water. He pulled a face and reached for a glass of water to wash away the taste. The second method was known as the chromic acid test. If the drink sample contained strychnine, adding chromic acid should oxidise the solution, producing a rainbow of colours.

He poured most of the remainder of the sample into a flask, keeping a little back in case of error. He added a few drops of sulphuric acid to the liquid, then dropped in a small crystal of potassium bichromate. Holding his breath, he pushed it about in the liquid with a glass rod, watching for any changes in colour. First, the sample turned a deep blue colour. Then, as he stirred, it rapidly changed to purple, followed by crimson, red and orange before slowly fading away. A strong indication that strychnine was present. He let out his breath. It was not concrete evidence, but together with the terrible symptoms the cadaver had exhibited, it was enough.

He examined the small bottle McQueen had given him. Strychnine sulphate powder – used in bait to kill rats or other vermin. He recognised the name of the chemist where it had been prepared: Brown's from Strada Mercanti. A cork top, with traces of powder around the edges as though recently used. The bottle contained three and a half grams of powder, and it was clearly labelled POISON in red letters, in addition to a skull and crossbones. By his calculations, one tenth of the bottle had been used, and that was more than enough to kill.

The gin and tonic had clearly been poisoned with strychnine. *But had the colonel mixed the deadly toxic drink himself? If so, why had he measured and prepared it in the kitchen and tidied the bottle so carefully away before taking it upstairs to drink it in the living room? This was a man who was clearly intoxicated, feeling morose and desperate. Surely, he could not have been so calculating and careful? Besides, if you were going to choose any way to take your own life, why would you take strychnine? It was the most appalling way to die.*

He shook his head at the thought.

Bonnići finished tidying up and washing down the surfaces of the laboratory. The pleasant smell of the phenol returned to him the familiar sense of cleanliness and order he liked in his world.

He exchanged his white coat for his black jacket, and picked up his hat and cane. He would take a *karrozin* to the police office, where he had agreed to meet Carstairs and McQueen. He took with him the bottle of poison. *At least the Scottish inspector was shaking things up.* Bonnići was beginning to have confidence that things would take a turn for the better, and that he had his part to play.

CHAPTER THIRTY

M aria woke early. She penned a note to McQueen and sent it to his lodgings:

I can't come to the police office. Meet me at Hastings Gardens, near the North Gate, seven o'clock.

The previous evening, she had heard the shocking news about Arbuthnot from her father. He had said that the colonel was responsible for the murders and had killed himself because he could not live with the guilt. It was hard to believe. He had seemed such an innocuous person; avuncular, fun, even. She had enjoyed bantering with him on many an occasion at the Collingwoods'. She wondered what possibly could have happened to cause him to kill his long-time friend.

The news had put her mind at rest over Giorgio. He was clearly being ridiculous in his jealousy toward McQueen. She would have to talk to him about that soon, make it plain he had no need to be worried. In the meantime, she still had to speak to the detective about the nationalists' plans.

The wind picked up as she set off for Hastings Gardens with Roży. It was one of her favourite places in the city – quieter than Upper Barrakka Gardens, but still with fine views out across Marsamscetto Harbour, to Manoel Island and Sliema. There were plenty of places to sit amongst the palms, carob trees and acacia bushes. She was reasonably sure they would not be observed.

The inspector arrived soon after they did. He was back to wearing his old suit and his bowler hat, which he took off as he greeted them. 'Miss Tanti – this is very mysterious,' he said with a smile. She liked the way he looked at her, as though he were amused by her, but not in an unkind way.

'Thank you for coming,' she said. 'I didn't want anyone to see us, but I had to tell you something. Let's sit here; it's sheltered.'

She took him over to a bench, under the reaching branches of a carob tree, leaves rustling in the wind. Roži waited discreetly nearby.

'Why all the secrecy?' he asked, sitting down.

'Oh, it's nothing. I'm just trying to keep out of trouble.'

'Your fiancé?'

'Yes. He seems to think I should stay quietly at home. He really doesn't like me talking to you. It's not going to stop me, but it would be easier if he didn't find out.'

'Oh, aye?' McQueen said, raising his eyebrows.

'I have to tell you about the Anti-Reform Party meeting. Sunday night. I was there, I heard them plotting–'

'What do you mean, you were there?'

'I hid in the cupboard, never mind how.' She adopted a more serious tone. 'The thing is, it's a breakaway group – the *Gruppo Militante Pro Italiano*. They're planning an attack on the governor – when the Duke of Edinburgh is visiting – at the parade. A bomb. They were just talking about it, when all the noise outside broke up the meeting.'

'I see,' he said. 'That is serious, indeed.'

'Exactly. They are dangerous.'

He was quiet for a moment, as if thinking through his response.

'That's fine. I can warn the governor, the police superintendent can put plans in place. It's useful to know. But you should not have put yourself in danger like that.'

She laughed. 'I was terrified, but it was fun, too!' Then she remembered the maid and felt a flicker of shame. 'Of course, then we found out about Ċensa. It's all so awful.'

The mood changed in an instant. McQueen looked past her, his eyes focusing on something far away that she could not see. *Was he still angry, reliving what he had experienced?* Instinctively, she reached out and rested her hand on his arm, wanting to reassure him.

'Inspector, I'm so glad it's over now. I heard about Colonel Arbuthnot. That he killed the admiral, and poor Ċensa – is that right? And now he's dead? My father is working on the story, right now.'

McQueen looked back at her, shaking his head.

'No. I'm afraid the case is not closed yet.' He frowned, his forehead creasing. 'I don't think your father should report that it was the colonel.'

'What?' She took her hand away. 'But Captain Borġ has said... I don't understand. Why else would the colonel kill himself?'

'Not entirely clear, but we suspect it was partly because of guilt over business affairs.'

'Have you any proof?'

'We know he caused a lot of people to lose money through some investments. He left a note.' McQueen cleared his throat. 'Unfortunately, I seem to have lost my pocketbook – or someone has taken it – and the note was inside.'

'What? That's terrible!'

'It's not helpful, certainly.'

'But if not the colonel, who could it be?'

'I don't know. I will find out – soon.'

She thought about the last time she had seen him. 'You were interviewing all the men who were at the soirée. But are you absolutely sure it had to be one of the guests?'

McQueen regarded her for a moment, his brown eyes contemplating her as if deciding whether to trust her.

'That's a good question,' he said, carefully. 'There is *one* person who may be of interest, but who was not on the guest list.'

'Please, tell me. I can help. I know everything that's going on. I'm sure I will know him.'

'All right, but this must go no further.'

She nodded, her heart beating fast. Finally, she was able to be part of the investigation!

'It is Count San Pietro. Do you know anything about him?' McQueen asked.

Count San Pietro? She had never considered he could be involved. Giorgio had taken her to Città Vecchia to meet him some months ago, a formal introduction as his fiancée. She had liked him; he was very charming, if a little pompous. Giorgio, of course, thought the world of him.

'The count? Well, he was a friend of the admiral's. A good friend, I believe.'

'Do you know if they met frequently?'

'From time to time. When the count came to stay in Valletta. But he doesn't come often. He's one of the *notabile* – so grand! They keep to themselves in Città Vecchia. They like to pretend it's still the time of the Grandmasters, that the world has not moved on.'

'Have you heard of any disagreement between the count and Lord Collingwood?'

'No. Sorry. But, of course, most people seem to have fallen out with the admiral at one point or another.'

'True.'

She thought for a moment about the newspaper, and recent articles her father had written.

'Perhaps something about the Anti-Reform Party and their cause? The language question, the wheat tax? The count would not have wanted Collingwood to get involved. Perhaps he thought the admiral's letters were fanning the flames of discontent?'

'Why so?' McQueen asked.

'Well, some of the nobles want to keep things the way they are. They think ordinary people should pay the wheat tax, because they don't want to pay any more tax themselves. They are happy for the poor to take the brunt.'

'Interesting.' McQueen was turning his hat around in his hands as he listened.

She did not want to give him the wrong impression; it seemed incomprehensible that Count San Pietro could be implicated in any way. 'But really, I can't imagine the count getting that angry. And he certainly wouldn't want to get his hands dirty by getting involved in anything unpleasant. I just can't see it.'

'Thank you, Miss Tanti, you have been extremely helpful.' McQueen got up, putting his hat back on. 'I have to go. Thank you for the information about the militant group. I'll make sure something is done.'

He nodded at her before walking away. She watched his solid frame, the determination in his heavy tread.

'Let me know if there's anything else I can do to help,' she called out after him. He lifted his hand to acknowledge her, without looking back. As he walked through the gate to the gardens, Maria thought she saw a small boy slipping out from behind a tree. Antonio, the boy who was with him a few days ago. She wondered why they were not together this time, and what the boy was up to. He seemed to be tracking the detective from a distance. *Perhaps it was some kind of game?*

The sky was dark grey, the wind whipping up the dust at her feet. Roży came to stand next to her. 'Shall we go back, *sinjorina*? It is time for breakfast; we will be missed.'

'No,' she said. 'I am not hungry. The inspector just told me he doesn't believe it was the colonel. They still haven't found out who killed Ċensa. I think we should go and talk to people. There were thousands on the streets during the festa. Someone must have seen something.'

Wrapping their *għonnielen* tightly around them, they headed into the centre of the city.

———

Later that morning, Maria was with Roży, deep inside the Church of Saint Paul the Shipwreck. The church was just steps away from the narrow street where Ċensa was found. After questioning many people in the area, Maria had discovered that the woman who first found the maidservant was a cleaner at the church. She wanted to speak to her, to see if there was anything the cleaner remembered that could help.

Saint Paul's Shipwreck was one of her favourite churches. Even its name had appealed to her when she was a child. Attending services there, she would gaze at a richly coloured painting in the domed ceiling, showing the apostle standing on the deck of a ship, the crew fighting a raging storm. She had loved the sense of drama and adventure it evoked, imagining herself on the high seas.

They found the cleaning woman polishing the glass of a cabinet holding the church's most famous relic: part of the wrist-bone of Saint Paul. It was revealed within a golden hand, a snake curled around the base. The woman had a gaunt face with prominent cheekbones, framed by a black headscarf. She replied to Maria's greeting, revealing several gold teeth. When Maria asked her if she had been the one who found Ċensa, she crossed herself several times, saying she wished she had not – the poor girl – and that she could not sleep for thinking of her. How she wished someone could have saved her.

'I'm from the *Malta Post*,' Maria explained. 'We are writing a piece about what happened. I wanted to ask if you saw anything, anything at all, before you found the maidservant?'

'No. It was busy, so many people. I heard something down the steps and I saw the girl. She was collapsed against the wall.'

'Did you not see anyone nearby, running away?'

'I think someone went past, in a cloak. I couldn't say. They weren't running.'

'A man? A woman? Tall? Short? What kind of cloak? Do you remember?'

'I am not sure. Perhaps a man, but not tall. Perhaps a fine cloak, like a silk, black. I don't know. It was dark, there were so many people. I do not know how anyone could be so wicked. She was just a girl.' She shook her head, tightening her mouth, the small creases across her top lip deepening, making her look years older. Her arthritic fingers gripped the cloth tightly. 'May God have mercy on her soul.'

There was nothing more they could glean from her. Maria and Roży left the cleaner buffing the glass with extra energy, as though polishing away the memories of that terrible evening.

Emerging outside, they stood blinking in the light, waiting for their eyes to adjust. Maria was about to suggest to Roży that they went home, when she sensed someone approaching her, coming up close from behind. She smelt a familiar cologne, then felt a tight grip on the top of her right arm, a low voice close to her ear. 'Maria, what are you doing here?'

'Giorgio! I could ask you the same question.'

She tried to shrug his hand off, but he was holding too tightly. 'Come with me,' he said. With his arm around her, he steered her across the street into a humble trattoria. He ordered coffees, which arrived swiftly, the owner looking overawed at seeing such august clientele at his table. Maria, furious at being forced to go with Giorgio, stared steadfastly out of the window. She could see Rożi hovering by the statues at the doorway to the church. She knew her maid would wait for her and felt glad for her reassuring presence.

Giorgio added sugar to his coffee and stirred it, the spoon catching the side of the cup with a clink. 'Well?' he said. 'What were you doing at the church? Tell me.'

'Saying a prayer for Ċensa,' she said. 'Why else would I be in church?'

'Oh Maria!' he said in a mock severe tone. 'What am I to do with you? Somehow, I don't believe you are telling the truth. A little bird has told me that you have been out in the streets, asking questions.' He was watching her closely. She kept her face impassive. *What else did he know? Had she been seen with McQueen earlier?*

He clicked his fingers. The trattoria owner came to the table.

'We would like lunch. Do you have pasta?' Giorgio asked.

'Yes, yes, all kinds.'

'I will have *timpana*, and the young lady will have – what do you want, Maria? The same?'

She nodded, feeling queasy at the idea of eating anything.

'You see, Maria, it's not possible to do anything in this city without people knowing.' He smiled. 'That's the beauty of it.'

He took off his gloves, placing them on the windowsill

behind him. He reached across the table and took hold of her left hand. 'Tell me what you were up to, my love. I think I have a right to know.'

She wanted to pull her hand away, but managed to keep it there, attempting a small smile. She did not want to reveal any more than she needed to.

'All right,' she said. 'I've been trying to find out more about what happened the night the maid was killed. It's for the newspaper. I want to write about it.'

She found it easy to lie, keeping her voice light and unconcerned.

Giorgio was playing with her engagement ring, turning it around on her finger.

'But I told you before,' he said. 'As my fiancée, it's not becoming for you to be out and about on the street, talking to all kinds of people. I have a certain standing in the city, which needs to be maintained.'

He dropped her hand as the food arrived. She watched as he picked up his fork and deftly cut a corner from the pasta pie, raising it to his mouth. She could not bring herself to even pick up her cutlery.

'Do try it,' he said after a few moments. 'It is very tasty. Surprisingly so.'

She continued to watch him, wondering what he was going to say, what he knew.

'The thing is,' he said. 'I don't understand why you are getting involved. I heard last night that the case was over. The police have found the murderer, dead at his home – that colonel friend of the admiral's. Suicide. It's such a relief, don't you think?'

She shrugged. 'I wanted to get extra detail. I'm writing a piece for the *Times*. I want to be a journalist, Giorgio, you know that. Besides...'

'What?'

She decided not to say anything about McQueen's uncertainty about Arbuthnot. *How would she know?*

'Nothing. You're right. It is good news.'

Giorgio had continued to eat, one forkful after another. He cut each piece of pie with great precision, the same size each time, eating swiftly and efficiently. When he had finished, he put his fork down across the plate.

'The thing that I am most delighted about,' he said, 'is that the Scottish detective will now be leaving. I don't like him being here. I don't like the way he walks around here, with his stupid boots and his tweedy suit, asking questions. And I particularly don't like the way he talks to you. The sooner he leaves the island, the better.'

He dabbed his mouth with his napkin, then folded it up and placed it back on the table.

'Go on, eat,' he said.

Reluctantly, Maria picked up her fork and tried a small mouthful.

He sat back a little, watching her.

'I am aware that you are at fault – the way you have behaved towards the inspector,' he said, so softly that she could barely hear what he was saying. 'You have compromised yourself, Maria. I know you have. Meeting, talking in public, unchaperoned.'

She stared at him, putting her fork down. *So, he did know.* She remembered Antonio slipping out of Hastings Gardens. Was he the "little bird"?

'I am in two minds about what to do about you, Maria. Do I break off the engagement? After all, I have every reason *not* to marry someone who has shown themselves to be disobedient, who behaves in an unseemly fashion – and with a foreigner, not even a gentleman.'

'You are being ridiculous,' she said, her temper flaring.

'No, I am not,' he said, leaning forward. 'I can see quite plainly that you have been throwing yourself at him. It is completely unacceptable.'

'We have only been talking about the murders,' she said. 'I have been trying to help. You've got this completely wrong.'

'I do not believe that is the full truth, but no matter. He will be leaving soon. What I have decided, and I have thought about this very carefully, is that we *are* going to go ahead with the marriage. I have worked hard to get to this position, and I am not going to have it thrown away by your scandalous behaviour. I will not be humiliated by you. We will marry in five weeks, just as arranged.'

He stood up and put his gloves on. 'Come on, we're leaving.'

He threw some coins on the table, then taking her by the elbow, led her out of the door.

She pulled away from him as they stepped into the street.

'Perhaps I don't want to marry you,' she said. 'The way you are treating me. I know it's not what my Papà would want for me. He wants me to be happy.'

'My dear, it's all sorted, all arranged,' Giorgio said. 'If it doesn't go ahead, I will have no choice but to ruin your reputation. Completely ruin it. Just think about what that would do to you.'

He leant forward and kissed her on the cheek. 'I cannot wait to see you at the altar,' he said softly. 'And to hear you promise to obey.'

Roži came towards them warily, her eyes flicking from Maria's face to Giorgio's. Maria felt a huge affection for her, knowing her maid would discern the tension and would be ready to take her side.

'Roži, darling, let's go!' she said in a forced, bright tone. 'Thank you for the lunch, Giorgio.'

She linked arms with Roży. 'Quick, let's go home,' she said. 'I need to get back and do some thinking.'

She looked behind her at Giorgio as they walked away. He had stood for everything she wanted, but she knew for certain now that she could never promise to obey him. Their engagement was over, whatever the consequences might be.

CHAPTER THIRTY-ONE

At the Auberge d'Auvergne, McQueen had found a couple of extra chairs and crammed them into the office. He had called for Bonniċi, Galea and Carstairs to attend a meeting to pull together everything they knew about the investigation. He felt full of energy; for the first time since arriving in Malta he had a team around him to work with. Bonniċi arrived first and bowed his head formally as he entered the room, placing his hat and cane by the side of the table. Galea came in and said a few words in Maltese to Bonniċi before sitting down and pulling out his pocketbook, watching McQueen closely, as if ready to take down lecture notes. There was an awkward moment of silence before Carstairs breezed in.

'Sorry, sorry, got caught up with Lady Burbank. She needs forty-two roses for the ladies' event next Thursday. Well, honestly! Anyway, managed to extricate myself and hot-footed it over. Hope I'm not too late?'

'Take a seat,' McQueen said. 'If you can manage to find a corner.' He breathed out, then stepped in front of his audience.

'Gentlemen,' he began. 'We have a great deal to discuss.

Firstly, despite what Captain Borġ thinks, I do not believe that Colonel Arbuthnot was our murderer.'

'But, the knife,' Galea said.

'Yes, I know we found the knife – but someone must have placed it there.'

'And the suicide note?'

'The note did not say he had murdered. Only that he felt guilt for his actions and that he could not face living any longer.'

'It is a strange choice for suicide,' Bonniċi said. 'Strychnine. It is the most terrible way to die. Ten to twenty minutes after taking it, the muscles start to spasm. The convulsions keep on and on coming, getting worse all the time, until the person is either asphyxiated, or dies from exhaustion.'

'Perhaps he did not know, perhaps he just took rat poison on a desperate whim,' Carstairs said.

'I think it unlikely,' McQueen said. 'Suicides are seldom so spur of the moment.'

'We have the poison,' Bonniċi said, putting the bottle of strychnine on the desk. 'We need to establish how he got hold of it. The housekeeper said she had not seen it before and nor had she ordered it. I know the chemist, though – he will be able to tell me.'

'What are you saying?' Carstairs asked. 'That it wasn't even suicide?'

'It is possible,' McQueen said. 'Arbuthnot could have been persuaded to write the note, then unknowingly drunk the strychnine.'

'Although it is bitter to the taste, the mixer, and his intoxication, would have masked it,' Bonniċi explained.

'My word!' Carstairs said, his face paling. 'Appalling. Dreadful.'

McQueen tapped on the blackboard with his chalk. 'So,

gentlemen, let us put together everything we know and see what we come up with.'

He wrote in clear letters:

1. Ċensa

'Going back to Ċensa's murder,' he said. 'I believe the girl was dispatched because she had seen the killer on the night of Lord Collingwood's murder. We need to know more about what she had been up to, who she had gone to meet.'

He turned to Bonniċi. 'Did you find out about the fiancé?'

'I did. His name is Wiġi Scerri. He is eighteen years old, living with his parents. I asked him to report to the police office at one o'clock this afternoon.'

'Good. Please stay for the interview, as he knows you now. We might be able to find out more from him.'

He turned back to the blackboard and wrote:

2. The mistress

'We have identified that the admiral had a mistress here on the island. A mistress whom he shared with two other men. One person is unknown – I have suspicions, but no proof. The other, we know, is Count San Pietro.'

'What?' Bonniċi exclaimed, tapping his cane on the floor. 'That cannot be right. The count is the most correct man I have ever come across. I would never believe it of him.'

McQueen was amused by the doctor's disapproval.

'I'm afraid it is true,' he replied. 'I heard it from the lady herself.'

'Who? Who is she?' Bonniċi asked.

'An Englishwoman, name of Sarah Hawthorne. She lives in Sliema.'

Bonniċi shook his head, muttering, '*Ma nemminiex* – I don't believe it.'

'Yes,' McQueen said. 'Apparently the count and Lord Collingwood were old friends, from the time when the admiral was based in Malta. I don't know how often they saw each other in the last year, since Collingwood's return, but we have evidence that suggests the count had visited him recently. Tell them, Sergeant.'

Galea cleared his throat. 'We found cigar ends on the roof of Villa Porto. They are a type smoked only by Count San Pietro and one other man on the island – Professor Attard. I have seen Professor Attard. He swears he has never spoken to Lord Collingwood and has never visited the villa.'

The young sergeant managed to look both self-conscious and pleased with himself at the same time.

Carstairs was rummaging in his attaché case. 'You won't believe this,' he said, pulling out a sheet of paper and waving it around. 'This is what I found out at the Malta Bank. The bank account. Where Collingwood paid money every year. I found out whose account it was.'

They all turned to look at him.

'It is the same person! Count San Pietro, of Città Vecchia.'

'It can't be! They are rich,' Bonniċi said. 'Very wealthy. Why would Collingwood be sending money to the count?'

'Why indeed?' Carstairs said. 'And why did those payments stop?'

McQueen wrote again on the blackboard:

3. The count

He underlined it several times, in strong white chalk marks.

'Galea, organise some transport,' he said. 'You and I will go to Città Vecchia this afternoon. It seems the count has a lot of questions to answer.'

———

The meeting broke up and McQueen took Carstairs to one side.

'Carstairs, can you give me the details of that bank account?'

'Yes, certainly. I must skedaddle now, got a government council meeting this afternoon.'

'Ah, does that include Captain Borg's brother?'

'Gabriel Borġ? Yes. Fairly ruthless businessman, by all accounts. Charmless fellow.'

'No surprises there, knowing his sibling,' McQueen said. 'Listen, I want to know about his property company. Can we find out how much they've spent, how much money they've made?'

'Certainly, I'll see what I can find out. Any reason why?'

'I have a feeling he and his brother are involved in some interesting business dealings. I'll say no more than that,' McQueen said, aware that the police office walls might have ears.

———

A little after one o'clock, when most of the citizens of Valletta were resting behind closed shutters, the door to the office opened to reveal a young Maltese man. He looked bewildered and overawed at being summoned to speak to the police. He was holding his hat in his hands. His hair was sticking up at odd angles and the shadows under his eyes made them look heavily bruised.

'Come in, come in,' Bonniċi said in Maltese, leading him to a chair. 'My condolences. You have had a difficult time.'

'This is Wiġi Scerri,' he said to McQueen. 'The fiancé of the maid.' He asked Scerri, 'Do you speak English?'

The young man nodded.

McQueen looked at him intently, without saying a word. Scerri sat slumped in his chair, twisting his hat around, his eyes flicking up to the inspector and then back to the floor.

McQueen moved a chair close to him and sat down, leaning forwards in a manner designed to intimidate.

'Did you know,' he said, slowly and clearly, 'that in nearly every case where a woman has been murdered, the police find that it is the husband or the lover who has killed her?'

Scerri seemed to sink even lower in his chair. 'It was not me,' he said, desperation in his voice. 'Not me, never!'

'But you know something, don't you?' McQueen said. 'Why was Ċensa out alone at the festa? What was she doing?'

Scerri began to cry, brushing the tears away from his eyes, but said nothing.

'What was she doing?' McQueen repeated. 'I will find out, and if you are withholding important information, you will be up before the magistrate.'

He handed Scerri a handkerchief. 'We need to know.'

The young man broke down, hiding his face in the handkerchief, shoulders hunched and shaking. Eventually he looked up, and McQueen could see his strategy had worked. Scerri was broken, his eyes reflecting the full extent of his guilt and sorrow.

'We needed money,' he said. He looked meaningfully at Bonniċi. 'We had to get married.'

'What happened?' prompted McQueen.

'Ċensa said she saw a man in the house, before the admiral died. He ran down the back staircase – the one from the roof. She saw him from the servants' landing.'

'Who? Who was it?'

'She did not say. A gentleman. It was dark, but she think she recognise him. She ask me to write a letter – I can write, but she can't.' His voice caught and he corrected himself, '...couldn't. I wrote the letter. She was going to take it to his house.'

'What was in the letter?'

He thought for a moment, then recited, 'Dear sir, I think it is difficult for you if the police find out you were on the roof before Lord Collingwood fell. If you pay me fifty British pounds, I will not tell the police I saw you.'

'But why did she not tell you who it was?'

'I don't know. She wanted to do it by herself. I was at work. I should have gone with her, I know. I should have waited for her, to make sure she was safe.'

There was no doubt in McQueen's mind that Scerri was telling the truth. *That foolish girl, thinking she could get the better of this gentleman.* Maybe the knowledge that she was expecting a baby had made her bolder, the dream of marriage spurring her on. But she had been mistaken, with terrible consequences. The killer must have found out from her that she had told no one else what she had seen, and then simply dispatched her. *The easiest way out, without compunction or regard for human life.*

'Write me a copy of the letter, and then you can leave. You will have to give evidence when we find the killer.' He called Sergeant Galea to take him away.

He sighed. Another life wrecked through desperation and need.

'Bonniċi, I now know it's the same here as in my country. Where money is concerned people do stupid, stupid things.'

CHAPTER THIRTY-TWO

E arly in the afternoon, McQueen and Galea set off for Città Vecchia. The journey seemed to take an age, as the ancient, heavy carriage lurched along stony roads. The rain had not had much impact on the state of the ground. The wheels threw up a white dust that covered their clothes and their faces. McQueen could taste it, at times almost choking on the gritty powder. They passed field after field of crops, divided up by low stone walls: cotton, maize, marjoram. Strange cactus plants with bulbous fruits called prickly pears, which Galea informed him were good to eat. Occasional small villages with irrigated patches of land growing fruits and vegetables, with goats roaming freely in the road. Hardly any people to be seen.

The carriage stopped for the driver to give the horses some water. McQueen stepped down to stretch his legs. He thumped the dust from his jacket and his hat.

In the distance he could see a wide flat hill, rising above the landscape. High walls surrounding fortified buildings and the tall domed roof of a cathedral.

'There it is,' Galea said, standing next to him. 'Città Vecchia. The ancient city.'

McQueen took a swig of water from his flask, then poured some into his hand to splash his face.

'I can see why it used to be the capital – you must be able to see for miles from the top of the hill,' he said.

Galea nodded. 'It's a strange place now. Quiet. Only priests and nobles live there. The streets are empty. Rabat is very close, much more busy.'

'When we get there,' McQueen said, 'I am going to talk to Count San Pietro. I want you to go to Rabat. You know people there. Go and ask about Sulina, who used to work for the count. I want every piece of information you can find out about her.'

'Yes, sir.'

They jumped back into the carriage, which continued its ponderous route, criss-crossing through the villages, until finally they climbed up a steep road, taking them to the gates of the city. The driver stopped at a shady watering place, where other horses stood flicking the flies away with their tails, patiently waiting until their next journey. Scruffy coachmen sat around under the trees, drinking and joking.

McQueen and Galea bought a *ftira* loaf from a roadside stall. It was busy with people milling around, the women covered by their black *għonnella* cloaks, and peddlers shouting out their wares.

'That's the way in?' McQueen asked through a mouthful of bread, nodding towards a gigantic stone entrance guarded by statues of lions holding shields. Above the entrance the Maltese flag was flying on its own, no sign of the Union Flag that dominated Valletta.

Galea nodded. 'No carriages in there,' he said. 'It is forbidden. It is called the silent city. Special place. Very holy. I go this way.' He pointed in the opposite direction, away from the city walls. 'Rabat.' A sheepish smile crept over his face. 'Not so grand, but my home.'

'Along with you, then – we meet here again at five o'clock.'

As McQueen walked over the bridge into Città Vecchia, he felt as if he were entering a different world. Under the principal gateway, he passed a battered statue of the Roman goddess Juno, with peacocks on her breast. The giant wooden doors were open and two guards stood on either side, looking at him suspiciously as he approached. He walked through. Inside the city walls there was a strange hush. Hardly a soul around, although he did see a priest disappearing off to the left, his black robes flowing behind him. McQueen showed his letter of authority to one of the guards and asked where he could find Palazzo San Pietro.

He followed the instructions: left, then right, then left again, through narrow streets. Everywhere he walked, he felt as though people were disappearing into houses ahead of him. Although he saw no one, he sensed a kind of whispering presence. The houses themselves presented flat fronts with firmly closed doors and windows. His heavy footsteps resounded through the stillness of the city. Finally, he emerged from a narrow side street into a large square and saw in front of him the Palazzo San Pietro, a beautiful honey-coloured building of massive proportions. Above the front door, a coat of arms was carved from the limestone. At the centre, a peacock's head, around the outside, cedar trees and peacock tail feathers. He remembered the description of the missing brooch. *Was there a link?*

Handing his card to the servant at the door, McQueen was shown into a grand drawing room. Family portraits filled the walls, together with a Renaissance painting of Madonna and child, and a stirring depiction of the shipwreck of St Paul. He wandered over to a table on which a large cross was displayed between two heavy silver candlesticks. *There was money here, money and privilege.* He picked up one of the candlesticks to gauge its weight, judging it to be well in excess of sixty pounds in value.

'Don't worry, we are well guarded here,' said a voice behind him, and he swung round to see the count, who had entered the room without making a sound.

The count was of medium height and build, although showing a slight tendency to portliness. He was dressed in a neat black jacket with a white silk waistcoat and cravat. His voice was cultured, almost without accent, and he gave an impression of politeness, charm and affability. He smiled and offered McQueen his hand, but the handshake was fleeting.

'Inspector McQueen,' he said. 'Welcome to Città Vecchia. What brings you to our beautiful city? Please sit.'

He indicated one of several chairs, then sat opposite him on the sofa, leaning elegantly into the corner and picking a tiny piece of lint from his pristine black trouser leg.

McQueen knew that the count would have been kept fully informed about the investigation into Lord Collingwood's death, and might even have been expecting his visit, but his expression was one of feigned detachment. He felt his blood pressure rise; he was going to have to dislodge this aristocrat from his perch of assumed superiority.

'I've come to ask you about Lord Collingwood,' he said. 'I am looking at everything that happened in the weeks and months before he died. And I have found a number of threads that link his life to yours.'

'Ah,' said the count. 'An unfortunate business.'

He stood up and walked towards the window, then turned back towards McQueen.

'Lord Collingwood,' he said, 'was a very dear friend of mine. We met at the Governor's Palace over twenty years ago. I was delighted when he returned to Malta for his retirement. He was a fine man, Inspector. Very British, yes, the kind of man who has steel in his nature. He earned his good name through taking big risks in battle. It was not for nothing that he was awarded his knighthood. You could see it in his eyes. You could tell he would do whatever it would take to win. And he had the scars to prove it.'

He sat back down again. 'I myself have never been to war. My father was a general, and my son is in the Army – making a name for himself. But I... I look after the family affairs and sit here in my fine *palazzo*.'

He gestured to the walls and the furniture.

'There is a lot to take care of, don't you think?'

McQueen wondered how much that assumed nonchalance was hiding. *What did he mean by "looking after family affairs"? What was the nature of his business? He would have to get behind the façade.*

He took out his new pocketbook.

'So, where did you meet him, and how often? And when was the last time you saw him?'

'Am I under suspicion, Inspector?' The count laughed. 'How very entertaining.' He thought for a moment.

'All right. I will tell you. We played cards, from time to time, at my club. I last saw Lord Collingwood for a game of whist at the end of June – the thirtieth – then in the morning I saw him again. We had coffee. I have my own apartment in Valletta, you know.'

'Would anyone be able to confirm when you met?'

The count looked at him contemplatively, lightly resting his chin on his elegant fingers. 'No, I don't believe so.'

'How did he seem, the last time you spoke?'

The count's face remained impassive, but the pause before he spoke was long enough to make McQueen think he was working out what best to say. 'He was troubled, Inspector, I must admit. There was something about his son, something concerning him, but he didn't reveal the details.'

McQueen thought of Edmund and Lieutenant Greening, but he said nothing.

'Anyway, he told me he had decided to do nothing about it, that he wasn't going to change his mind. He told me not to worry and said that he could handle the situation. And I must say, Inspector, that I believed him. He always was as good as his word. So, although he wasn't on the best form, I got the impression he would soon have things sorted out.' He looked off into the distance. 'Then, of course, I found out what had happened. And I was shocked. Very shocked.'

'Why weren't you at Lady Collingwood's soirée on the fifth of July? Where were you?'

'I was here, Inspector, with my wife and family. We had our own celebration for my son's birthday. We would not go to such a gathering. It is regrettable, but my wife would not see the connection as quite suitable. There would be people there with whom we would not, as a rule, circulate. I am a great believer in tradition. We have a position to maintain; it is important that the San Pietro family keeps the status that we have had for two centuries.'

McQueen felt a rush of irritation. It made him want to shake the man out of his complacency.

'So, how do you explain this, then?' McQueen asked, pulling out the cigar ends from his pocket. 'Do you recognise the brand?'

The count peered at the cigars and shifted uncomfortably.

'Yes, they are Nostrano del Brenta.'

'And are those the cigars you smoke?'

'Yes, but surely many people do on the island?'

'No. You are the only person connected with the late

admiral. We have proof from the tobacconist. These cigars were found on the roof of Lord Collingwood's villa. The rooftop from which he was thrown. Can you tell me how they found their way up there, if you were not there yourself?'

For once, the count could not hide his feelings. He looked up quickly with a puzzled expression.

'I have never been there,' he said. 'I have no explanation.'

'Come on, man, you were there; don't try to deny it. You argued – most probably about your shared interest in Mrs Sarah Hawthorne! I'm sure your wife would love to hear about this.'

Now the count recoiled, staring at him with hardened eyes.

'How dare you!' he said, the smooth tone replaced by a harsh edge. 'How dare you talk to me like this in my own home?'

McQueen was enjoying himself.

'You cannot deny that you have been seeing Mrs Hawthorne. We know you have visited her at her apartment. She's a fine lady, don't you think? Did you find she meant too much to you, and that you no longer wanted to share her attractions with the admiral? Did you ask him to give her up, only to be insulted by his refusal?'

'I am insulted by *you*, Inspector! If I am involved with a lady – and I say *if* – then that is my own business, and I will handle it with discretion. I was grateful to Lord Collingwood for his help and his advice. He understood.'

The count's eyes watered momentarily, and he pulled out a handkerchief to mop his face. 'We hardly spoke about such matters and we certainly never argued. And I promise you I have never been to the villa.'

'It all points to you. Not only your shared mistress, but also your shared business. We have established that for the past twenty-five years, up until this year, you have received annual payments of £100 from Lord Collingwood. That is a considerable amount of money. How do you account for that,

Count San Pietro? You are deeply involved; you cannot pretend that you are not. You know what happened to the admiral – admit it.'

The count got to his feet, trembling. 'That's enough!' he said. His urbane manner had completely left him now; he was clearly shaken to the core.

'My business affairs are my own. You will leave now. You have no right to insult me in this way.' He pointed to the door. 'Get out!'

'I have every right to speak to you,' McQueen said. 'You will report to the police office in Valletta tomorrow morning at 10 o'clock for a formal interview. And I would advise you to consult with your lawyer. I want answers and I will get them.'

He picked up his hat and left the room, casting his eyes around at the opulence and the gold. He had done exactly what he had intended and successfully ruffled this *notabile's* feathers.

CHAPTER THIRTY-THREE

McQueen had another half an hour before meeting Galea. He stood outside the palazzo for a few moments, wondering at the complete silence in the street and the hidden yet secretive splendour of the world behind the walls. The opulence and sense of entitlement was greater than even the highest echelons of Scottish society. Here was a deep-rooted power, held by a small group of people, which they were always going to be reluctant to relinquish. It came from the descendants and favourites of the Knights of the Order of St John of Jerusalem, who had wielded power over the Maltese islands for nearly 300 years.

A short way up the narrow street, to the right of where he was standing, a door opened and he could hear bristles brushing across stone. He walked towards the sound and saw first a broom sweeping dust from inside a dark doorway, and then an elderly woman peering out from behind it. She was scarcely taller than the broom she wielded, with a deeply lined face, but she looked strong and her eyes were inquisitive and bright. He smiled at her and she nodded, watching him intently. He decided to ask her what she knew about the count and his family.

He showed her his papers, but she mimed that she could not read. He pointed at the palazzo.

'Count San Pietro?' he asked. 'Can you tell me about him? I am with the police – *polizija*.'

She looked up at him quizzically, studying his face, then suddenly stretched out her right hand and grabbed hold of his wrist. '*Idħol, idħol*,' she said, pulling him inside the house. He wondered where on earth she was going to take him, and whether this was a good idea. At the same time, he was amused at this tiny creature leading him with such conviction into her house. The passage from the door led a long way through to a square, dark kitchen. Here, she let go of his arm and pushed him into a chair at a heavy wooden table. She rested the broom against the wall, poured a cup of beer from a jug and set it before him, then went to the back door and called out, 'Publius! Publius!' then a stream of Maltese in which McQueen could only catch the word *polizija*.

A man appeared, wiping blackened greasy hands on a cloth. Dressed in a white undershirt, with coarse trousers held up by a thick leather belt, he was of strong build, with a close-trimmed black beard defining his jutting chin. He stared at McQueen with some ferocity.

'I want to know about Count San Pietro,' McQueen explained, speaking slowly. 'It's about a death in Valletta – Lord Collingwood?'

The man stood looking at him for some moments, narrowing his eyes.

'I am with the police,' McQueen tried again, wishing he had Galea with him to translate.

The man threw down the cloth onto the kitchen cupboard top and fired some instructions to the elderly woman, who busied herself getting him a drink of beer and setting it on the table. Then he drew up a chair opposite McQueen and sat down, peering at him from under fierce black eyebrows.

'Well,' he said, finally. 'You are in luck, my friend. My mother here watches the palazzo all the time. I think there is nothing she doesn't know about the family.'

McQueen felt a fool. 'You speak excellent English,' he said, holding out his hand. 'Detective Inspector Sam McQueen.'

'Publius DeBono,' said the man. His hand was rough and calloused. 'I was in the Army for ten years. Now I look after the carriages for some of the families in the *città*. I like working with anything mechanical.'

McQueen felt at ease with him; here was a straightforward working man who could well provide some useful information. He took out his pocketbook.

'Can I ask some questions?'

'Go ahead,' said Publius. His mother hovered in the background, pretending to be busy with a dishcloth.

'Count San Pietro. How are he and his family regarded here?'

'People who work for the count mostly say he is fair and treats them well. He is respectable, very much the gentleman. His wife, though...' Publius paused and shook his head. 'She is not popular.'

He said a few words to his mother, who launched into a bitter torrent of Maltese, finishing with a flick of the dishcloth on the kitchen surface.

Publius laughed. 'The countess is very religious,' he said. 'She only comes out of the house to go to church – every single day at 10 o'clock and then three times a day on a Sunday. The rest of the time, she complains about the servants. Nobody can do anything right. Always she has priests with her too, telling her how she can get to Heaven by prayer and by giving money to the Church. And yet she never has a kind word for anyone. My mother worked in the palazzo for a while, over twenty years ago, but she didn't like it there. She won't stand for any unfairness, my mother. Very strong principles.'

McQueen could well believe it.

'And the rest of the family?'

'Well, there is the eldest – the heir. He is spoilt and thinks he can do whatever he likes. He is a captain in the Army in Valletta. I have friends still serving, and they say he is well known for his eating, drinking and carousing. Whether he is a decent soldier, I have no idea. There are daughters, too, but they are now married into other noble families. Very traditional.'

If Publius's mother worked there, perhaps she knew the servant who became Micallef's housekeeper. McQueen asked, 'Did your mother perhaps know a maid called Sulina?'

Publius said a few words to his mother and got a nod and a long explanation. 'Yes, Sulina looked after the children. The count was very fond of her and said there was no one better. So fond that he did a surprising thing. When she was young, she had a baby even though she wasn't married, and he let her stay with the family. He even let her boy come with her to the house sometimes, until he was old enough to be at school. It was strange, but the countess had to accept it; the count was adamant. You can imagine what everybody thought.'

'And the boy's name?'

'Giorgio. He was always very good, very quiet. I believe he has done well; he is a lawyer in Valletta.'

So, he was right, Micallef *was* the son of the housekeeper. No wonder everyone believed he was the count's natural son.

'What about Lord Collingwood. Did your mother know anything about him? Did he ever visit the palazzo?'

Publius asked the question, but his mother shook her head.

She explained in some detail, concluding with a shrug of her shoulders.

'She doesn't know their names, but at that time there were some English gentleman visitors. They would stay up late, drinking the best wine. But the countess did not approve and she stopped them coming. Now the count has an apartment in Valletta,' Publius winked at McQueen, 'so he can meet his friends every now and then.'

McQueen smiled. He checked his watch and realised he needed to leave. 'You have been very helpful,' he said. 'Is there anything I can do to repay you for your time and information?'

'No, no. It is a pleasure to help, and it will keep my mother happy for weeks, telling everybody about your visit and that she has helped the police.'

McQueen left, feeling even more sure that the investigation was on the right path. All the pieces were beginning to fall into place. Now he just had to break down that front of respectability put up by the count, to reveal the sordid truth that no doubt lay behind it.

———

Galea was waiting outside the gates, holding a large bag. He held it up as McQueen approached. 'Cakes,' he said, looking embarrassed. 'From my mother.'

'Fine woman!' McQueen said, and dipped in. They were sweet almond cakes, topped with a glacé cherry. He ate one and immediately went in for another.

They found their carriage and set off back to Valletta, the driver clearly in a hurry as they swayed down the steep road away from Città Vecchia. McQueen turned to see the walls of the ancient city silhouetted against the sky. It seemed to loom over the centre of the island, holding close its secrets and its past.

'So, what did you find out about Micallef's housekeeper?' he asked Galea.

Galea was brimming with excitement.

'Well, firstly she is also Micallef,' he said. 'Sulina Micallef. She comes from a small village, outside of Rabat. Very poor.'

'Did you go there?'

'Yes, I did. I found some of her family. Her sister. She said that Sulina did have a child twenty-five years ago, and she called him Giorgio. She stayed working with the family and she left the boy with her parents. She worked hard and brought him many presents – clothes and toys the young marquis had grown out of. And sometimes he went with her to the palazzo.'

'Interesting,' McQueen said. 'I wonder what he was like back then?'

'Well, his aunt was not very fond of him. She said he was proud, very vain. In the village they called him that bird – you know, the one with a big tail, shiny, lots of beautiful colours.'

'Peacock?'

'Yes, that's it. He was a peacock, walking around thinking he was better than anyone else. It was difficult for Sulina's parents. They have passed now, God have mercy.'

'So how did he end up in Valletta?'

'They told me that he was sent to school. A Jesuit school where he lived and studied. He was clever and he did well. He went to university, and as soon as he was working as a lawyer, he sent for his mother to come and look after him. His aunt never sees them anymore.'

'I wonder why he hides the fact Sulina is his mother?'

'Maybe shame? I think he wants to pretend he came from a rich background. He wants people to think he is the count's son.'

'Aye, well, the count admitted no such thing to me. He was all politeness and charm until I asked him about the money and Mrs Hawthorne, then he refused to speak. I've issued him with an order to come to the police office tomorrow morning. If he doesn't come, I will get Borġ to arrest him.'

As they travelled on companionably, McQueen asked Galea a few questions about himself. The lad confessed that his mother was extremely proud of him. She and his father had worked hard to give him and his brother the chance to go to school in Rabat. Now his brother and his father ran a good business together, while he had made a life for himself in Valletta. They were so excited when he was promoted to sergeant.

'The only thing now,' he concluded, 'is that she keeps asking me when I will find myself a wife.' He sighed. 'Mothers, they never give you any peace. She wants me married, she wants to have grandchildren. I keep saying, "Ma, I am too young. I have to work hard. I will marry later when I am an inspector".'

McQueen laughed. 'Good luck to you, lad,' he said. 'You've got the right idea.'

He thought about his own mother, and the moment he had told her he was going to join the police force. The colour had drained out of her face and she had turned away from him to hide her tears.

'Your father will not hear of it, you know that,' she had said, her voice wavering. 'He wants you for the ministry, you and Andrew, working alongside him. The police, Samuel? When God wants you for His work? How can you even think of it?'

The tension had been hard to bear and from that moment, he had seen very little of his parents. The only news about them was whatever he gleaned from Andrew. There was no reaction from them when he became a detective, when he was promoted to sergeant, or even when he became inspector. It seemed nothing was going to change that. The unwelcome feeling settled its familiar cloak around him as he sat in the carriage. As they approached Valletta, the sun going down behind them, the city glowed with thousands of lamps and the low buildings looked purple against the darkening sky. For the first time he felt glad to be far from the austere granite of Edinburgh.

CHAPTER THIRTY-FOUR

Wednesday, 11 August 1880

M aria had slept badly. She was angry at Giorgio – at his high-handed attitude and his lack of trust. He was no paragon of virtue himself. She had heard him tell McQueen that he had been at home during the festa, when she had seen him leaving his house. *What could he be covering up? Where would he have been going, that he didn't want the inspector knowing about? There must be an explanation – a woman he was seeing, or a business deal he was involved in that was not entirely legitimate.* Her mind could not stop racing. She felt she had to know. If she had some ammunition against him, she could potentially negotiate a civilised end to their engagement. It was her only hope.

She breakfasted alone and wrote a note for her aunt to say she was going out to spend the day with Sonia. Then, she had dressed in her shabby old gown again and Roży had looked at her sharply.

'What is it, *sinjorina*?' she asked. 'Why are you dressing so? Where are you going? You shouldn't be going without me.'

'I am fine,' she had replied. 'Don't worry. I have something important to do, but it won't take long, I'm sure.'

As she left the house, Maria covered herself with her *ghonnella*. The wind was getting stronger and heavy rain threatened from black clouds overhead. She walked briskly to Sonia's house and asked her to make up a story if anyone wanted to know her whereabouts that day.

'Oh, Maria, what are you up to?' asked her friend. 'Please don't do anything to get yourself into trouble! I'm worried for you. You are meant to be getting married next month. Promise me you won't do anything stupid.'

'It's all right. I know what I am doing. It's precisely *because* I am supposed to be marrying Giorgio that I have to do this now. I will send you a note later.'

She left Sonia's and walked to Strada Mercanti. She thought she would start by watching Giorgio's house to work out if he was at home or not. She walked slowly up the street, looking in the shop windows, keeping her face turned away from passers-by. She kept glancing over to the house, but there was nothing to see. It presented a blank face, with nobody coming or going and no evidence of people inside or out. She was running out of shops to look into, so she decided to go inside the milliner's, on the other side of the street. She could stand by the window pretending to look at the hats on display, whilst keeping close watch on the front door opposite.

A bell rang as she went in and an assistant – a severe-looking woman of around forty – instantly appeared by her side. 'Can I help you, *sinjorina*?' she asked.

Maria assumed a haughty tone.

'I am looking for a hat for my aunt,' she said. 'I'll ask for your help when I need it, thank you.'

She was relieved when another customer entered the shop, giving the assistant someone else to concentrate on. She picked up a hat, pretending to examine it from all sides, at the same time watching the house. Nothing was happening. She put the hat down and picked up another. A ridiculous affair with a long feather that even her aunt would not dream of wearing. She put her head on one side as if to seriously consider it. Something caught her eye; a carriage drew up outside Giorgio's house. She stepped closer to the window, peering out. There was a crest on the carriage that she thought she recognised. One of the *notabile – was it the San Pietro family?* A servant jumped out of the carriage and knocked on the door. When the door opened, he handed a letter to the housekeeper, then got back in the carriage and drove away.

'Excuse me, *sinjorina.*' The assistant's voice startled her and she almost dropped the hat. 'Let me help you with that.'

The other customer had gone and the assistant was standing right by her shoulder. Maria handed over the hat. 'Perhaps I will just get some ribbons,' she said. 'Do you have any green silk?'

'Certainly, *sinjorina.*'

She carried on watching the house while the assistant went back to the counter and started pulling out lengths of ribbon in different shades. After a couple of minutes, she saw the door open again. Giorgio walked out, carrying a leather holdall. She stepped back instinctively, but he did not look across the road. He seemed focused, walking quickly away in the direction of the city gate. *This was her opportunity.* Her heart was beating fast. *She would give it a few moments and then see if she could get into the house and go through Giorgio's papers.*

She went to the counter and abruptly told the assistant that none of the colours were right, then left hurriedly, thinking that she would never be able to go into that shop again. She could feel the woman's eyes boring into her back as she walked across the road.

Maria knocked at the door of Giorgio's house. After a short while, Sulina opened it. She looked subdued as she peered out, and it took a few moments for her to recognise Maria.

'I'm sorry, *Sinjorina* Tanti,' she said. '*Sinjur* Micallef has just gone out.'

Maria stepped inside. 'That's all right, Sulina. I will wait for him.'

'But I don't know how long he will be. He did not say. He took a bag and he has gone.'

Tension showed in Sulina's face; gone were the usual smiles and the animation. She barely looked at Maria and her eyes kept flicking to the door as if hoping that Giorgio would reappear. But Maria was determined.

'Oh dear! We agreed we were going to meet this morning!' she said. 'How inconvenient. I have something to talk to him about. I will wait in his office.'

She tried her best to seem as bright as usual, to be her normal cheerful self.

Sulina showed her into Giorgio's private room, which was extremely ordered and clean. She did not seem keen to leave Maria there.

'Can I bring you anything?' she asked.

'No, I am fine. I will wait,' Maria replied, taking off her *ghonnella* and handing it over, but keeping hold of her reticule. 'Don't worry, it's nothing serious. It's just about the wedding, you know. About the guest list, and where everybody is going to sit. I'm sure he will be delighted to come back and find me here, ready to bore him with all the details. He must have slipped out for a few moments.'

Sulina hesitated at the doorway, then left to fold up the *ghonnella* and put it away in another room. Quickly, Maria darted over and closed the door, then slipped across to the desk. *What was she looking for? Business papers? What could he be hiding?* There was nothing on the desk apart from the blotter, inkwell and pen holder. There were four drawers on the left side. She opened the top one and rifled through. Nothing; only blank sheets of paper and a small leather book containing names and addresses. She stopped and listened for a moment, but there was silence in the house. She opened the next drawer, and the next, finding folders and legal papers from the law firm Giorgio worked for. Nothing looked unusual or out of place.

She heard light footsteps approaching the room and quickly sat down on a chair, smoothing down her skirts. Sulina tapped on the door and opened it.

'I thought you would like a drink,' she said. She came in, carrying a cup of tea, and placed it on the desk. She looked at Maria with some suspicion.

'I don't think it is worth waiting,' she said. 'I don't think *Sinjur* Micallef is going to be back for some time.'

'It's fine,' Maria said. 'I am quite happy here. I'll wait a little longer to see if he remembers and comes back.'

Reluctantly, Sulina walked out of the room, leaving the door ajar. As soon as her footsteps retreated, Maria jumped up, closed the door again as softly as she could and ran back to the desk. She pulled out the fourth drawer. It was full of envelopes bearing the crest of Count San Pietro – at least thirty of them. She hurriedly put a handful of them in her reticule to read later and delved down further to the bottom of the drawer. Then she caught her breath as she saw something that did not belong there. Underneath all the papers and envelopes she could see the corner of a pocketbook. A battered brown pocketbook with sketches all over the front. It was the one she had seen Inspector McQueen using. *What on earth was it doing in Giorgio's desk?* She pulled it out and started to flick through the pages.

'I knew you couldn't be trusted!'

She looked up to see Sulina in the doorway. She had never heard such anger in the housekeeper's voice.

'Get away from his papers. I am surprised at you, Maria Tanti. What are you doing? *Sinjur* Micallef will be very angry.'

Maria smiled as sweetly as she could.

'I thought I would have a look for the guest list. I left it for Giorgio to look at.' She held up the pocketbook. 'Here it is, you see? Don't worry, I don't need to wait now. When Giorgio gets back, do let him know that I have taken my pocketbook, won't you?'

Chatting all the way about how you can't seat one branch of the family near another because they don't talk, and other nonsense, Maria left as quickly as she could. Now she had something to take to the inspector. Something that he would definitely be grateful to receive. *But what did it mean? How had her fiancé got hold of McQueen's pocketbook?* She headed towards the police office.

CHAPTER THIRTY-FIVE

The interview with Count San Pietro had already lasted over an hour. McQueen sat opposite him, arms folded, irritation building. *How could he break through this polished performance?* Ever since he had arrived, the count had smoothly repeated the same answers. Yes, it was true that he had received regular payments from Lord Collingwood for twenty-five years. It was for a business venture, a company they had set up to invest in local communities. His lawyer produced papers to provide evidence of such a company. Lord Collingwood's name did not appear in the papers because he wanted to remain anonymous. No, it was not true that they had argued, and he had never been to Villa Porto. He would admit to visiting Mrs Hawthorne in Sliema, but there was no disagreement between himself and Lord Collingwood over their involvement with the same lady. They had remained good friends and he was devastated by his death.

Earlier in the morning, McQueen had told Captain Borġ where he was with the investigation, and that Count San Pietro had been called in for interview.

'I do not believe it!' the superintendent had said. 'We have found the killer. Colonel Arbuthnot. Why can you not leave it there?'

'There is evidence that points to the count's involvement in the case.'

'Nonsense. He is a pillar of society,' Borġ said. 'He is from one of the grandest families of all Malta. I will swear that he has done nothing.'

'There are questions he needs to answer,' McQueen said.

'Very well, but he has the best lawyer on the island, I warn you. Also, I insist on being present when you talk to him.'

Borġ had agreed to one of the law court rooms being used for the interview. It was a basement room, cool and dimly lit, with high barred windows looking out onto the street. Count San Pietro had arrived on time, formally dressed in a black silk suit, not a hair out of place. His lawyer was equally smartly turned out, a short figure with slicked-back dark hair, a shiny black moustache and a smug expression that McQueen wanted to wipe from his face. He was getting increasingly frustrated. He knew he was close to solving the case, but he could not get any answers. *Why would nobody here speak the truth?* And Captain Borġ's sanctimonious concern for the count was taking him close to losing his mind. They would never get anywhere while the superintendent toadied to San Pietro's wishes.

After ninety minutes, Borġ had a whispered conversation with the lawyer.

'Inspector, the count is getting fatigued,' he said. 'We must allow him to rest.'

'Fine!' McQueen said. 'Take ten minutes.' He could hardly contain his anger as he left the room, slamming the door behind him. In the corridor outside he found Sergeant Galea waiting for him, looking anxious.

'I didn't know what to do, sir,' he said. 'I didn't want to

interrupt, but *Sinjorina* Tanti is here, and she insists on seeing you. I think it is important.'

What could she want? Not more information about the militant group? He was tempted to tell Galea she should go and pester somebody else with her stupid stories, but something about the sergeant's demeanour made him think twice.

'She's in your office, sir,' Galea said. 'She has some letters for you to see. And something else she says you need for the investigation.'

As they entered the room, Maria was looking out of the window. She whipped round, her eyes gleaming with excitement.

'Inspector McQueen – look what I have found,' she said.

With a jolt of recognition, he saw she was holding his pocketbook. He leapt forward and snatched it from her.

'What the devil?' He flipped through the pages. There were all his notes, all his sketches. The note from Arbuthnot, even. Relief flooded through him.

'Where did you find it?'

'In Giorgio's office, hidden in a drawer.'

'How... what? You have no idea how important this is. What was it doing there?'

'I don't know, Inspector. That's not the only thing. I found this letter. I brought it straight away. There's something in it you need to read.'

Maria handed him a folded piece of writing paper. He opened it and saw that it was headed with the San Pietro crest and dated 20th June 1880.

My dear Giorgio, he read.

It has given me great satisfaction to see your success with your studies and your advancement in life. Your aptitude for learning, and your dedication towards achieving your goal of becoming a lawyer, have been most impressive.

Your mother was a valued member of our household and we were always happy to receive you at home. I am very pleased that we were able to provide you with the financial support you needed to take you to the position in society you have achieved. I thank you for your forbearance, given that I was unable to provide you with information as to the source of that income. I can assure you, however, that the supposition you alluded to in your previous letter is absolutely not the case. I urge you not to pursue any further inquiries. It will not lead to any change in the circumstances.

Regretfully, now you have reached your twenty-fifth birthday, you will cease to receive any monies. I have always made it clear that this was the arrangement. In any event, I feel reassured that you have attained the level of financial stability to render the payments unnecessary from this point in time. I understand, too, that you will shortly be marrying. I am sure that Sur Tanti will be generous in his dowry for his daughter Maria.

I wish you continued prosperity and success in your chosen profession, and a happy marriage with your chosen wife-to-be.

Yours sincerely,

Francesco San Pietro

McQueen whistled. He waved the letter in the air.

'Well, this is just what we need. Now we have him! The count was using Collingwood's money to give Micallef an allowance. I wonder if this means what I think it does...'

He paced up and down, thinking it through – what the letter meant, and how Micallef had got hold of his pocketbook. He wondered why Maria had brought it over. *Why would she forsake her fiancé, betray him, even?*

'What were you doing in Micallef's office?' he asked. 'What were you searching for?'

Maria blinked for a moment, then stood up a little straighter. 'There's something I should have told you sooner,' she said. 'When Giorgio told you he was at home on the night of the festa, he was not speaking the truth. I saw him walking down Strada Mercanti. I didn't let him know. I wanted to find out if there was a reason he lied to you. Perhaps a business meeting he didn't want anyone to know about? Reading this note, I think he may have needed more money.'

'He would need a lot of money, the way he lives. He is a proud man, isn't he, *Il-Pagun?*' Galea ventured.

McQueen stopped in his tracks.

'What did you just say? What did you call him? Say it again.'

The sergeant was confused. 'You mean *Il-Pagun?* It's what I told you. His name – what they called him in Rabat. It means The Peacock.'

McQueen thought quickly; he had to act immediately.

'Where is Micallef now?' he asked Maria.

'I saw him leave his house a while ago – that's when I went into his office. He had a bag with him. I don't know where he went. He was heading out of the city. I came straight here from his house, so he can't have gone far.'

McQueen turned to Galea. 'Sergeant, I want you to get some constables together and go out on the streets. Find out if anyone has seen Giorgio Micallef and can tell us where he is going. Come back as soon as you have some news.

'Miss Tanti, go home and stay there. You have been a great help. You did the right thing coming here. Now, I can go back to the count and wipe that smile from his face. Finally, we can get to the truth.'

———

Armed with the letter, McQueen went back into the basement room. The conversation immediately stopped. Borġ scowled at him. Count San Pietro and his lawyer looked at him with polite expectation.

'I suggest that if you have nothing else to ask my client, we cease this pointless interview,' the lawyer said.

'Oh, but I do have something,' McQueen said. 'And before we proceed, I would like to remind the count that he would be wise to tell the truth.'

The lawyer looked at his client, who nodded.

McQueen showed Count San Pietro the note.

'Do you confirm that this is your handwriting, and that this letter comes from you?'

The count's face became a frozen mask.

'Where did you get this from?' he said.

'I ask the questions. Did you write this letter?'

'Yes, I did.'

'And for the purposes of these other people present, could you read it out?'

The count pulled out a pair of spectacles and read the letter with an air of detachment. Silence fell when he had finished.

'So, you have been funding Mr Micallef throughout childhood and up until his twenty-fifth birthday,' McQueen said.

'Yes.'

'And how much money have you given him?'

'One hundred pounds a year. Initially I paid for his education. Since he completed his studies, I have paid him the money directly.'

'And when was the last payment?'

'It was June, this year.'

'Which coincides with the last monies you received from Lord Collingwood, yes?'

'Yes.'

'So, therefore, I think we are safe to conclude that it was Collingwood who forwarded the money to you for Mr Micallef?'

'Yes,' said the count, with some reluctance.

'And, finally, in order to clear up this matter completely. Was Lord Collingwood in fact Giorgio's father?'

The count hesitated, looking at his lawyer, who shrugged his shoulders.

'Yes,' he said, finally. 'He was.'

He took his spectacles off, polished them and put them back in his waistcoat pocket.

'Collingwood stayed with us from time to time,' he explained. 'Especially when we had card games lasting late into the night. I had no idea that he had intentions towards Sulina. She was such a good girl. Wonderful with the children.' He sighed. 'But Collingwood never could resist a pretty face.'

Once again, McQueen found himself loathing the admiral, who felt he could take whatever he wanted, no matter what happened to others. He imagined how devastated Sulina would have been when she discovered she was with child. She would have feared losing her position.

'Carry on,' he said. 'How did your arrangement with Lord Collingwood come about?'

'When we found out about the baby, my wife was very unhappy. She wanted to dismiss Sulina at once, but I persuaded her that we would not be able to find such a perfect maidservant to look after the children. We kept it as quiet as we could. Collingwood agreed to pay for the boy, but on the condition that we never told him of his true parentage.'

'And did Giorgio believe *you* were his father? Is that what you're referring to in the letter?'

The count nodded.

'This is the worst of the matter,' he admitted. 'The boy was so interesting, so clever, I did not mind that he thought it was the case. He is highly thought of in society, you know. He looks so fine and has such impeccable manners. He will go very far. However, he was pushing for an answer. I think the upcoming marriage was making him think he needed to know where he stood. He wanted me to acknowledge him as my natural son – and to include him in my will.'

'How did he respond to the letter?'

San Pietro looked at his lawyer, who nodded.

'He came to see me at my apartment in Valletta,' he said. 'I have never seen him like it. He was so angry.' The memory of it seemed to genuinely pain the count. 'He accused me of all kinds of things. Of ruining his career and his place in society. He should have known that even if he were my son – which would have been impossible – I would not be able to acknowledge him. The San Pietro family is one of the oldest in Malta and my wife is the daughter of the fifth Marquis Montagna di Scelleri. It would never have happened. I explained this to him as patiently as I could.'

The count broke off to cough then took a sip of water.

'Then, I am sorry to say, he threatened me. He said he would tell people that I *was* his natural father, unless I told him the truth. He was very insistent. So, I gave in and admitted that it was Lord Collingwood. He was shocked because of course Collingwood had not been around for twenty years. He scarcely knew who the admiral was. Micallef left my apartment soon afterwards. I sent a message to Collingwood to let him know what had happened, and went back to Città Vecchia, where I have been ever since.'

'And when you heard of Collingwood's death, you did nothing about it? You didn't even think to tell the police?'

'Oh, but I did!' said the count. 'I told the superintendent that Micallef may have wanted to talk to Collingwood about his discovery.'

There was a momentary silence, then Captain Borġ cleared his throat.

'There was no evidence that Micallef did contact him,' he said. 'It was not relevant to the investigation.'

McQueen slapped his hand down on the table, making the count and his lawyer jump.

'Have you any idea what you have done?' he thundered at Borġ. 'He *must* have caused Collingwood's death. You let him believe that if he covered his tracks, he could get away with it. It's because of your incompetence, your reluctance to expose the count and his family, that an innocent girl was murdered. It was Micallef who killed her. I know it now. How the hell can you live with yourself, Superintendent? How can you look at your face in the mirror each morning?'

Borġ did have the good grace to look uncomfortable. McQueen turned back to Count San Pietro.

'Did you send Micallef a message this morning to say that you had been summoned to the police office?'

The count nodded again. 'I thought he should know.'

'Well, thanks to your warning, he's gone. We have men out looking for him now. We need to stop him. He's dangerous.'

McQueen ran back up to the foyer of the police office, taking the steps three at a time. At the top, he found Galea deep in conversation with two police constables.

'Sergeant – any news?'

'Micallef's been seen riding away from the city,' Galea said. 'He has someone with him... a boy, they think.'

'What? No!' *It couldn't be, could it?* The pocketbook could only have come from Antonio; the wee lad must have been bribed by Micallef to steal it. He had probably been told it would help with the investigation. *Had Micallef now picked Antonio up, to use him as a hostage?*

'Quick, run to my lodgings. Find out if *Sinjura* Caruso knows where Antonio is,' McQueen said.

'No need,' Bonniċi's voice came from behind him. The doctor had just entered the police office, accompanied by *Sinjura* Caruso. They were both sopping wet, their clothes dripping with rain.

'I was on my way here to see you,' Bonniċi said. 'We met on the street. The boy has gone missing again.'

'I sent him for bread,' *Sinjura* Caruso said, in tears. 'But he didn't come back. We have to find him. Storm has come. Is danger!'

'Damn and blast it! Which way did they go?' McQueen asked Galea.

'I think they are headed for Rabat. And the constable said something else.'

'What?'

'Micallef has a gun.'

CHAPTER THIRTY-SIX

'Why would Micallef head to Rabat instead of the coast?' McQueen asked.

'It's the storm,' Bonniċi said. 'No one would go out in this weather. All boats will stay in harbour until the winds die down. He's taken the boy for a reason. He's going to use him to try and negotiate his way out.'

Sinjura Caruso looked stricken, her eyes travelling from McQueen to Bonniċi and back again, trying to work out what they were saying.

'Please, Inspector, please. You have to help my boy,' she said.

McQueen imagined Antonio, tucked in front of Micallef on horseback, hanging on for his life, terrified of what might happen. He had to get to him fast and get the lad out of danger.

Borġ had joined them from the basement. 'Superintendent, do you have any revolvers?' McQueen asked.

'We have two.' Borġ dispatched one of his inspectors to issue the firearms.

'Galea, you come with me,' McQueen ordered. 'We'll take horses and head to Rabat as fast as we can. Bonniċi, you take a carriage and follow with *Sinjura* Caruso. I'll take one revolver, you take the other – you know how to shoot. Borġ, you stay here and await further orders.'

There was no way on God's earth he was going to allow the superintendent to take any part in the ensuing negotiations.

McQueen and Galea arrived in Rabat first, water streaming down their mackintosh capes. They had ridden hard through gale-force winds and rain. They stopped in the centre of the town, in a square dominated by an immense church. It looked deserted. They tied up the horses next to an inn, opposite the church.

'Any ideas where Micallef might have gone?' McQueen asked Galea, shouting to make his voice heard over the roaring of the wind.

'No. There's the village where he lived. But I don't think he would go there.'

'We can ask in here.'

The inn was shuttered up for siesta. McQueen banged on the door, which opened immediately. The innkeeper pulled them inside from the storm. Galea asked if he spoke English. 'Yes. What you want?'

'Police,' McQueen said. 'We're looking for Giorgio Micallef. Do you know him? Have you seen him? He would be travelling by horse, with a small boy.'

'Yes, yes, I see man on a horse. With boy, or bag, I don't know. Could be him.'

'When was it? Where did he go?'

'Perhaps two hours ago, I don't know. Beginning of siesta. I clear tables here and I see him from window. He come from that way – but then he go that way.' He pointed to the right.

'Do you know where that road goes?' McQueen asked Galea.

'Yes, not much down there. Fields. It leads to Dingli – and the cliffs.'

'We'll have to go, see if we can find them.'

McQueen opened the door again, ready to step outside, but halted when he saw a two-horse carriage rattling up. It stopped outside the inn. Bonniċi and *Sinjura* Caruso – and then Maria Tanti – climbed down, their clothes whipped by the ferocious wind.

'This way, quick!' McQueen called, motioning to them to come inside.

The innkeeper showed them into a cluttered room, opening the shutters to let the light in – what light there was.

Bonniċi helped *Sinjura* Caruso to a chair. She was shaky, clearly distressed. Maria was last to walk in, her chin held high in a determined manner.

'What are you doing here?' McQueen asked. 'I told you to go home.'

'I want to help,' she said. 'I couldn't stay behind and wait.'

'There was no way of stopping her,' Bonniċi said, shaking his head. 'Is there a plan, Inspector?'

'Not as such. We think Micallef has ridden off in that direction.' He gestured towards the cliffs.

'I might have an idea where he has gone,' Maria said.

'Where?'

'The catacombs. He used to explore them as a child. I think he would go there to hide.'

Sinjura Caruso cried out, 'No, my boy!'

McQueen's heart missed a beat. Catacombs. Underground. *The lad would be so frightened.*

'I thought they were walled up,' he said.

'Giorgio knows a secret entrance. In *Tad-Dlam* – the field of darkness. He told me.'

'Where the hell is that? How can we find it?'

'I don't know, Inspector. I'm sorry.' Maria's eyes were troubled. 'I wish I did.'

He turned to the sergeant. 'Galea – do you know it?'

'*Tad-Dlam* is close, but there are many blocked entrances. It could take a long time to find it, especially in the storm.'

'Damn it. Can we get in any other way?'

'I only know one entrance that's still open. In Vicolo Katakombi.'

'Where?'

'Here in Rabat, but we'll never find them, sir. The catacombs go on for miles underground; we'll get lost.'

McQueen weighed up the options. They could contact the local police and wait for guides. They could roam through fields in the storm, looking for a hidden entrance. Or they could get into the catacombs now and start the search. They could not afford to waste any more time. *Micallef needed to know they were on his track.*

'Let's go,' he said. 'We have to. Bonnići, you come with us. Maria, stay here with Mrs Caruso. I mean it. It's too dangerous. Micallef has a gun.'

The innkeeper brought them lanterns and ropes.

'You will need these,' he said. 'Be careful. Many places full of stones, difficult to get through.' He drew them a rough map on a piece of paper. 'When you get down there, you find one corridor through the catacombs. This one, here. Many crypts, left and right, but you go straight until you get to big chamber, thirty, forty feet long. There is altar there, ancient place of worship. From there, many different ways to go.' He drew arrows out from each side of the room. 'You need luck to find them.'

As they set off, Maria reached out and touched McQueen's arm. 'Please, take care.'

He shook her hand off. He only had one thought in his head. *Find the boy.*

Galea led them across the square and down an alley behind a row of town houses – Vicolo Katakombi. He stopped in front of a heavy wooden door with an old iron ring for a handle. 'It's in here,' he said. The door was locked. McQueen assessed it: it was old; it would easily give way. He put his shoulder against the wood and pushed hard until he heard a splintering sound. It swung open. He held the lantern up to reveal worn stone steps leading downwards into blackness.

McQueen felt sick. *How could he do this? The last place he wanted to go was deep underground.* He swung the lantern back to the others' faces. Galea was pale, his eyes pleading. *Just as terrified as him, perhaps even more so. This was no time for panic; the young sergeant would be a liability.*

'You stay here, Sergeant,' McQueen said. 'Find the local police. Let them know what's happening. Get them out into the fields. If Micallef escapes, I want constables out there to stop him.'

Galea nodded. 'Yes, sir.'

Bonnići's features were set, determined. McQueen knew he could rely on him.

'Doctor, have you got your revolver?' he said. 'Come with me. Be ready to shoot, but only on my orders.'

Bonnići cast aside his cane. 'I am ready,' he said.

McQueen gripped the lantern. The steps were dusty and worn, the walls on either side roughly hewn out of stone. He counted fourteen steps. They were perhaps twelve feet down at this point. As they moved further underground, the air became musty and cool. At the bottom, they entered a small chamber. The light from the lantern gave out an orange glow, which melted into the darkness beyond. He could only see a yard or two in front of him. Everything was a sandy brown: the floor, the walls, the ceiling.

'I think this is a family vault,' Bonniċi said. 'Empty now, ransacked.'

McQueen held up the lantern, looking around at three dark archways. *Which one to choose?* 'This way, I think,' he said, thinking of the rough map. 'Straight ahead.'

They crossed the chamber and entered a narrow winding corridor. The walls were soft limestone, pickaxe marks showing how they had been dug out centuries ago. The silence was unnerving. McQueen led the way, holding the lantern up to throw light onto small sepulchres glimpsed through arches each side of the passage.

They kept going, the passage winding and sloping downwards. McQueen was acutely aware that every step was taking him deeper underground. Unable to see anything further than a few feet ahead, he had to keep pressing on. His every instinct was screaming at him to turn the other way, to get back to the fresh air and the light. The air was getting denser, making it harder to breathe. After thirty yards or so, just as he thought the passage was never-ending, he saw a set of steps, which led them down into a small chamber. Three tombs were cut out from the rock, with canopied roofs. Shining the light into the spaces under the arches, he could make out a jumble of rocks and, unmistakeably, human bones. *Tibia? Possibly a humerus?* He could sense Bonniċi close behind him, his intake of breath as he, too, saw the skeletal remains.

It was still silent. 'This is not the big chamber,' he said softly. 'Which way now?'

Bonniċi shone his lantern in front of a low archway leading away to the left. 'I think it's this direction. After you.'

McQueen had to crouch down to get under the arch, then squeeze himself up several steps on his hands and knees, to emerge into a much larger chamber – two rooms separated by a central pillar. It was at least thirty feet in length, with a ten-foot-high ceiling. At last, he could stand up straight again. He walked around, taking in the detail. The first room had a raised plinth at either end, with a circular table and a semi-circular bench hewn out of the rock. To the left, he went down a couple of steps into what had been the chapel, with an altar. He could see rows of long, low tombs. Some were for single bodies, some for families, then there were small tombs cut as recesses out of the walls, for children. It felt like a strange world, all to itself. The light from his lantern revealed skeletons lying on stone beds, eye sockets staring out blackly from silent skulls.

How were they ever going to find Micallef? There was no way of knowing where he was hidden.

'They may still be close by,' he said. 'They can't have got far; Micallef will have been carrying Antonio, remember. We have to find them.'

He called out, his voice loud, breaking through the silence.

'Micallef!'

Nothing.

'We know you are here. Give up the boy.'

Again, nothing.

He tried calling for the boy. 'Antonio! If you can hear me, shout. I will find you.'

This time, he heard a faint echoey sound in response.

He clutched Bonniċi's shoulder, pointing to the right.

'It's that way; they're through there. Stay close to me.'

He took out his gun and headed towards the noise, scrambling under an archway, his shoulders bruising against the stone. Four steps led down into a low corridor, keeping him nearly doubled up.

'Antonio. Ninu. Stay where you are; we will find you.'

He heard a muffled cry in response, as if someone was holding a hand over the child's mouth.

'Micallef, give yourself up,' he shouted, his voice resonating through the passage. 'Let the boy go. It will be the better for you if you do.'

He could see a faint light ahead, perhaps twenty yards away, and started to edge towards it. The passageway opened up to just under his head height. It was similar to the one they had come through earlier, with dark doorways leading to interlinked crypts on either side.

'Micallef. Come out. I warn you, I have a gun.'

A tall, black shape appeared at the end of the corridor. Micallef's voice rang out. Gone were the smooth tones of the clever lawyer; he sounded tense, harsh.

'How did you find me?'

'You can't get away.'

'Was it Maria?'

'Let Antonio go.'

'No. The boy stays with me. Allow me free passage from the island, or I swear I will kill him.'

McQueen could hear the determination in his voice. Micallef had already killed two, perhaps three people. *He was not going to give himself up. He had nothing to lose. He would not hesitate to dispatch the youngster to save himself.* The image of Antonio's resolute features flashed into McQueen's mind, swiftly followed by the pinched white face of the young woman lying at the foot of the tenement steps. *It was not going to happen again. At all costs, he would get Antonio out alive.*

Bonniči was right behind him.

'I will keep him talking,' McQueen said, speaking as softly

as he could. 'See if you can get closer without him hearing. Try and get to the boy.'

Bonniċi nodded, the dark circles under his eyes accentuated by the dancing light of the lantern. McQueen felt an absolute assurance that he could trust the doctor, watching him disappear through an archway on the right.

'The boy does not deserve to be involved in this, Micallef,' he called out. 'You've been using him from the start, haven't you? You got him to spy on me, to take my pocketbook. He's done enough for you; let him go.'

'Do you think I'm stupid? Of course I'm not going to let him go. I took him for a reason. He's been so useful, haven't you, Antonio? He thought he was helping you, but he was giving me all the information I needed.'

'Mister McQueen. I – I so sorry!'

McQueen could hear the confusion and shame in Antonio's voice.

'Don't worry, Ninu, I know it wasn't your fault,' he said.

He heard scrabbling noises as Antonio struggled. Then a slap and a sob, which cut right through him.

'Micallef, stop,' he shouted. 'What are your plans? Tell me. I will do what I can.'

'I want a boat ready at Fomm ir-Riħ Bay and I want a horse to get me there. I am taking the boy with me, and if you try anything – *anything* – I will shoot him. Do you understand?'

'But where will you go? What will you do with him? How can we have assurance you won't harm him? Unless we know that, we have no reason to help you.'

'I will leave him with the boatman when I get to Italy. Once I am there, I will disappear. You will never find me.'

There was no sign of Bonniċi. McQueen kept talking.

'I know why you killed the admiral,' he said. 'You couldn't stand the thought of him being your father, could you? You didn't set out to murder him. You sent him a message saying you wanted to talk. When he left the party, you followed him, went to share a cigar on the roof. You told him you knew he was the one who had been giving you money all those years, that you were thankful. But that you wanted him to face up to his responsibility, to own you publicly. And – let me guess – he refused. You must have hated him at that point. Did you want to see him suffer?'

'He deserved to die,' Micallef said. 'He said he would never acknowledge me. That he valued his family too highly to besmirch its name. He called me a bastard, called my mother a whore. I tried to get him to take the words back, but he collapsed. I had to dispose of him, tried to make it look as though he fell.'

McQueen started to move towards Micallef, revolver in hand.

'I understand that,' he said. 'Anyone could understand that. But the girl, Micallef. How could you kill the maid?'

'I had to!' Micallef said, his voice high and tight. 'She was trying to blackmail me. I had to silence her. She was stupid, so stupid, to come to me. Enough talk. Leave now. Get me my boat.'

Perhaps he loosened his grip on Antonio at this point, perhaps the boy managed to wriggle away. There was a rustling and a cry of annoyance from Micallef, then Antonio's treble voice rang out. 'Mister McQueen, I am free.'

'Bonniči, get the boy!' McQueen shouted. 'Give up now, Micallef. You will not get away.'

He edged towards Micallef along the sides of the corridor, but the silhouette had melted back into the darkness.

A shot rang out, a deafening explosion, reverberating underfoot. Micallef was shooting at them. *He had to be stopped.* McQueen rushed blindly towards him to get the gun. As he ran, another shot sounded. He felt a hard punch to his shoulder, but kept going. He could see Micallef's shadow disappearing through an archway on the right.

He scrambled through, then stopped short. In front of him, Micallef was standing in the middle of a crypt, Bonniċi holding a pistol to his head.

'It stops here,' the doctor said. 'Drop your firearm.'

Micallef hesitated, then threw his revolver to the ground.

'I am sorry, my friend,' Bonniċi said, looking over at McQueen. 'I was not in time to prevent you getting injured.'

'I'm fine,' McQueen said. Indeed, he could hardly feel it. 'Never happier to see you, Doctor. Where's Antonio?'

He looked past Bonniċi and saw a small shape emerging from the darkness. 'I'm here, Mister McQueen!'

He saw a pair of shining eyes under a shock of black hair and smiled in relief. He reached forward to pick up Micallef's revolver. He was not paying enough attention, too pleased to see the boy was safe. Before he knew it, Micallef crashed into him with his full weight, and everything went black.

CHAPTER THIRTY-SEVEN

M cQueen slowly regained consciousness. He opened his eyes to find that he was in total blackness. He could see nothing, nothing at all. The air was cool and oppressive. He realised he was still deep underground in the catacombs. The darkness pressed in on him and he felt a rising panic. He lifted his right hand. He could not see it, even right in front of his face. He tried to get up, fear overwhelming him. His left shoulder burned like hell. A wave of nausea swept over him. He sank back, cursing. Warily, he touched his shoulder. It was soaked and slightly sticky with what he knew must be warm blood.

To his relief, he heard the scratch of a match against rock. He was not alone. The flame from the match was used to light a lantern, revealing Micallef on the opposite side of the chamber. He sat on a semi-circular table, cut out from the stone, his revolver next to him. His eyes glinted in the flickering flame of the lamp.

'Back with us, Inspector? Thought you had gone; your breathing was getting so ragged.'

McQueen raised himself onto his right shoulder and looked around. They were alone.

'Bonniċi? The boy?' he asked.

'They got away while I was dealing with you. The doctor did well. But frankly, it's easier with the boy gone. It makes matters simpler, just you and I.'

'You can't get away.'

'I can. I've had time to think. If I stay any longer, a search party will find us. If I leave the way I came in, no doubt there will be constables waiting. So, I will find another way.'

Micallef sighed. In the shadows, his face looked older than his years, gaunt and sallow.

'You have caused so much trouble for me, Inspector. Each time I thought I had tidied everything up, there you were. Why didn't you accept that the colonel was responsible? Why did you go after the count?'

'It didn't fit,' McQueen said. His mouth was dry. He was finding it hard to speak. 'Too much didn't add up.'

'I thought if you found the knife, with the suicide note, that would be the end of it. The old man would take the blame and I could get on with my life.' He laughed, without mirth. 'I knew you had questions about him, that he'd been involved in a financial scandal. It was so easy. I brought him the poison, gave it to him in a glass of gin and tonic. He was so easy to persuade, so racked with guilt. It was perfect! Nobody knew I had been there. I went straight to the Tanti house afterwards, where you saw me!'

'That's three people you killed, Micallef. How could you think you would get away with it?'

'I nearly did, didn't I?' he said. 'And even if I get caught now, there isn't enough evidence to convict me. All you have established is that I knew Collingwood was my father. Everything else is circumstantial.'

'What are you going to do?'

'I'll take my chances in the tunnels. The catacombs go on for miles. Nobody has ever reached the end. There's a tale of animals – pigs – released here, who emerged in a village by the coast. There must be a way. I'll find it.'

Micallef stood, picked up his revolver and started to walk towards the arch leading out of the chamber.

'I'd take you with me, McQueen, but you wouldn't make it. Better that you stay here. You will soon bleed to death. And you will be in good company.'

He waved his gun at the skeletons lying in the tombs. He turned, the light from the lantern dancing over his face as he stepped out of the gallery.

'Goodbye, Inspector.'

McQueen felt a surge of fear. *He could not, would not, be left underground, in this chamber of death.* Already, he could feel the darkness closing around him as the lantern moved away. Micallef had miscalculated, thinking he was incapable of action. There was plenty of life in him yet.

He lurched to his feet, adrenaline cancelling out the pain. With his right arm he instinctively reached into a tomb, his fingers closing around the nearest missile, a skull. He made it to the gallery and called after Micallef's retreating figure.

'There *is* evidence,' he shouted. 'Doctor Bonniči traced the poison bottle to the pharmacy. Your mother bought it, on your instructions. We have proof. And she is in custody, right now.'

Micallef looked back over his shoulder, fear etched on his face. 'You can't do that. You must leave her alone!'

'Too late for that.'

McQueen drew his arm back and threw the skull as hard as he could. It hit Micallef squarely on the forehead and he fell backwards.

McQueen could only watch in horror at the scene that then unfolded. The lantern smashed to the ground, the kerosene exploding into a ball of fire. Micallef's eyes were wild with shock as flames caught the folds of his cloak. He tried to bat them out, but the fire took hold fast. He screamed, flailing his arms.

'Stop, lie down, roll,' McQueen shouted, but Micallef was too caught up in panic. His wild movements fanned the flames, and they engulfed his body. He succumbed to the smoke in a matter of seconds, collapsing to the ground.

By the time McQueen managed to reach him, Micallef had stopped breathing, asphyxiated. The smell was intense: kerosene, smoke, burnt hair and flesh. McQueen put out the few remaining flames, covered Micallef's blackened face and slumped down next to him. There he remained, in the darkness, hoping to God a search party would find them soon.

At the end of the week, as he checked the shoulder injury at the hospital, Bonniċi took the opportunity to ask McQueen a few questions that had been bothering him.

'Has the coroner recorded the verdict?' he asked.

McQueen winced as he took the dressing off.

'Yes,' he said. 'It has been recorded that Micallef was fully responsible for the murders of Collingwood and Ċensa, as well as the death of Colonel Arbuthnot.'

'That's good.'

Bonniċi swabbed McQueen's shoulder with an antiseptic solution, causing his patient to wince again. 'I wanted to ask you about the brooch – the one we found by the body. Did it belong to Micallef?'

'Ah, yes. But Captain Borġ assumed it belonged to Count San Pietro. Knowing about the count's links to the admiral, he wanted to protect him, thinking he could gain from this, both financially and in terms of power. So, he conveniently "lost" the evidence.'

'And what about the cigars? The ones found on the roof?'

'They were Micallef's. He had a box of them as a gift from Count San Pietro. I think he wanted to show Collingwood how well he was doing, was trying to impress him. They talked for quite a while before he realised he was not going to get what he wanted. If the admiral had not been quite so cold, so unbending and then ultimately so cruelly dismissive of Micallef's mother, it might have been a different story.'

'The tie between a son and his mother is very strong, no?' Bonnici said as he proceeded to wind a new bandage over the big man's shoulder.

'Aye, it is. Sulina Micallef is devastated. She has lost everything. But there is some comfort, in that Count San Pietro has agreed she can work for his family again.'

'Micallef must have thought he'd got away with it. No one raised the alarm until he was back in the drawing room, so he was able to mingle with the guests. He even offered to fetch the police.'

'Yes, he had a cool head. But Censa had seen him on his way down the stairs. The poor wee lassie. If only she'd spoken to me and not to him.'

Bonnici folded a sling around McQueen's arm and tied it on his right shoulder. 'We all did what we could, Inspector. Good news: you are well on your way to recovery. We need to have you fighting fit for the visit of Prince Alfred in three weeks' time.'

'Oh, yes. The Queen's son, another admiral. I cannot wait,' McQueen said.

CHAPTER THIRTY-EIGHT

Thursday, 26 August 1880

McQueen had arranged to meet Sarah Hawthorne at the Customs House before she embarked on her voyage back to England. He walked down through the ancient stone archway of Porta del Monte to the harbour front. Comfortably cool in his new linen suit from Ellul's, he enjoyed the warmth of the sun. He saw Mrs Hawthorne as he stepped into the hall, standing amongst dozens of boxes and trunks, talking to her maid. When she caught sight of him, she gave him a warm smile.

'Inspector McQueen. How good of you to come and see me.' She waved at her luggage. 'As you can see, I am ready to leave the island.'

He was disappointed she was going. He had enjoyed meeting her and thought in some ways they could have been friends. He had admired her frankness and her strength of character.

'I am sure there are quite a few gentlemen who will be sorry to see you go. I wonder if I could talk to you alone for a moment or two?'

'Certainly. Shall we step outside?'

She said a few words to her maid, then he offered her his arm and they walked out and around the side of the Customs House to the water's edge. They stood side by side looking across the flat, calm water to the three cities. The fort of San Angelo stood watching over the busy harbour where countless ferries and fishing boats were crossing to and fro. The sky was once again a bright, clear blue. McQueen felt that Malta was starting afresh after the unsettling storm.

After a few moments of quiet contemplation, he broke the silence. 'Have you seen Count San Pietro recently?' he asked.

'I have,' she replied. 'That is partly why I decided to leave. With all the attention on his family, the count has decided he is unable to see me anymore. His wife is devoting all her time to prayer at the cathedral and insists that he stays as much as possible in the Old City. She has spies everywhere and he doesn't dare to make the business trips to Valletta that he used to.'

'So, you have lost two admirers – him and Lord Collingwood?'

'I have. I confess I am much saddened. The admiral and I were friends for a long time, and the count I found utterly charming. He is very upset, you know. He cared about Giorgio and he was so shocked that he could have carried out those horrific crimes. He feels some of the blame, for encouraging the boy in his belief that he was connected to the San Pietro family. He thinks he should have realised how Lord Collingwood would react if Giorgio confronted him. He is a kind man, Inspector, but perhaps a little weak.'

Her tone betrayed that the count had dropped considerably in her estimation. McQueen could imagine that once she had lost respect for a man, that would be it. She would not be able to maintain a relationship with him.

'What about the other gentleman?' he asked. 'Is there anything you would like to tell me about him?'

'Oh, I don't think so,' she said airily. 'I don't think that would get us anywhere, Inspector, do you?'

'You were pleased to allude to his influence when I spoke with you last.'

'I was. I wanted you to leave me alone. But whoever it was, that is also over.'

'Oh, is that right?' *Not that he was surprised.* The governor must have felt relieved that nothing had been revealed through the investigation. *Discretion was definitely the better part of valour.*

'It is. I find I'm not as popular as I once was. Tell me, Inspector, are you not going to leave Malta soon, now that the case has closed?'

'You never know, I may stay a wee while longer. The island does have its appeals.'

'Oh, yes?' She arched her eyebrows. 'I wonder who that might be?'

'It's not a person,' he replied. 'Just the place.' *Did she mean Maria? He was fond of the girl, but no, she was far too young.*

'Look, Inspector – may I call you by your first name? I don't even know what it is.'

'Sam.'

'Sam, there is a lot going on here that you don't know about. You've only been here a few weeks, and I have stayed for over a year. It's a complex country, Malta.'

'I've learned a great deal. I'm aware of the Borġ brothers' business dealings and I think things are changing. The superintendent is already in trouble for withholding evidence.'

'Just be careful, Sam. The Borġs will make life very uncomfortable for you if you stay.'

'Aye, well, I never seem to make friends, wherever I go. It makes no odds to me.'

'Well, I feel *we* could have been friends in different circumstances,' she said, looking at him with a mischievous smile. 'It's been fun meeting you, Sam. And you never know; perhaps our paths will cross again one day.'

She put her arm through his and he felt her head lightly pressing against his shoulder – just for a moment – as they walked back to the Customs House.

Maria was on her way to the newspaper office. It was late afternoon and the heat had subsided a little, but she still felt irritated by the return of the hot summer weather. Her clothes felt tight and itchy, and she was annoyed by the dry dust covering her skirts. She did not know why her father had sent her a message to meet him. She had hardly seen him over the past few weeks as he had been so busy covering all the stories resulting from the Anti-Reform Party's recent activities – and of course, the truth about the murders.

It could be to do with the article she had written for the *Malta Post*. Trying to keep herself busy, and following up on the story about Guiseppe Trapani, she had begged her father to be allowed to interview him. Her father had agreed, and Trapani had been surprisingly willing to talk, perhaps feeling he would get fairer representation from her than from her less-than-even-handed father. She had indeed listened carefully and wrote what she felt was a considered piece. It explained not just why the Anti-Reform Party was so vehement about keeping Italian as the official language, but how its members saw the language question – and the recent reports threatening higher taxation and fewer jobs for the Maltese – as symptomatic of high-handed, prejudicial treatment from the British. She remembered the glint in his eyes, the fervour with which he described the absolute need for the Maltese people to resist, that if they did not act, with violence if necessary, their whole identity would be lost. Her father, she knew, would never condone violent opposition, so perhaps he was not happy with the conclusion of her article. She had said that although the newspaper's stance was one of supporting the teaching of English, nevertheless there was a principle at stake in terms of listening to the will of the people.

Despite throwing herself into the writing, she had been struggling with her feelings for Giorgio. She could not believe how cruel he had been, and that for so long she had not suspected it. She also felt betrayed. He had never wanted to marry her; their engagement had purely been for convenience. She felt she had been foolish, allowing herself to fall for him. The signs were there, in his coolness and desire to control her, but she had kept hoping she could win him over.

The cheery bell rang out when she opened the door to the newspaper office. She felt a surge of affection for her father as he looked up at her over the top of his spectacles. He smiled broadly and held up a page of copy.

'This piece of yours, Maria. It's so good! Come here, let a proud father give you a hug!'

He stood up and gestured for her to come over so he could put his arms around her. She rested her head against his chest, feeling reassured and safe, soaking up the familiar scent of cologne, tobacco and printer's ink. After a moment he held her away from him, his eyes crinkling up at the corners.

'I am going to put this interview on the front page,' he said.

'Goodness, I'm flattered,' she replied. 'I thought it was far too balanced for your tastes. You don't agree with anything the Anti-Reform Party is saying.'

'Well, I don't understand their infatuation with all things Italian. It's a modern world, and anyone can see that English is the language of the future. It's already spoken in a quarter of the globe. We have to move forwards, be a part of the commercial and industrial world! We have our own identity. We are not Italians. It's just nonsense to say we should stick with our antiquated use of the language.

'Don't worry, I am making all these points in my editorial. But one thing they talk about is true – we must not let the British just walk over us. We have to be at least an equal part of the government.'

'We do, Papà. Rizzo is calling for an election – he wants all the council members to be from the Anti-Reform Party. And they will keep fighting for fair representation, although they are distancing themselves from Trapani and the *Gruppo Militante Pro Italiano*.'

Her father smiled. 'We will make a newspaper editor of you yet!'

'But *you* are the *Malta Post*, Papà!'

'Yes, but I have been thinking. About your education, and what you told me you want from your future. One day I will need a successor. You never know – if you are as good a writer as we all think you are, it might just be you.'

'Oh, Papà, that's wonderful!' she said, her spirits soaring.

'And the first step, Maria, is that tonight you will attend the annual general meeting, during which I will recommend that you join us on the board.'

Café de la Reine was the smartest café in Valletta. Here, the best of society could be found drinking their afternoon tea, either outside at tables under the orange trees, or in the sparkling interior. McQueen walked inside and weaved his way through the tables until he reached the back of the café, where Captain Borġ sat with his brother. Their heads were together as they talked in low voices. Gabriel Borġ was even shorter and wider than the superintendent, filling up the whole of one side of the table.

As McQueen approached, they both sat up, looking at him with open hostility. He found it amusing to see two sets of similar features, with almost the same scowl.

'What are you doing here?' asked the superintendent.

'We're having a private conversation,' growled his brother.

'Now then, gentlemen,' McQueen said, drawing up a chair and joining them at the table. 'Let me hazard a guess at what you have been discussing. Could it be about what you're going to say when the governor calls you in to talk about your building contracts? The contracts you obtained fraudulently from the government?'

'You don't know anything about our business,' Captain Borġ said.

'Ah, well,' McQueen said. 'That's where you are wrong.'

He stood up and waved cheerfully. 'Over here, Doctor!' he called. Bonniċi acknowledged him with his cane, then made his way over to join them. He also sat down at the table, giving the Borġ brothers a charming smile.

'I have been to see the Chief Medical Officer,' Bonniċi said. 'I have detailed my findings from recent visits to the *Kerrejja* in Strada Cristoforo and Strada Mezzodi, where I have discovered families living in the direst of conditions. My notes include reference to the company that leased and developed the buildings – GVRB Property Associates. The Chief Medical

Officer has commissioned a full report. A petition is being made to the House of Commons in London, drawing Her Majesty's Government's attention to the situation in Malta and the plight of the people.'

'And,' McQueen chipped in, 'I have done a little research myself, with the help of Lieutenant Carstairs. We have identified that GVRB Property Associates is in fact owned by your two good selves. Which is going to look very bad, considering that you – Mr Gabriel Borġ – are on the council that rubber-stamped the sale of government property. Tut, tut, gentlemen.'

'I knew you would cause trouble from the moment you arrived,' Captain Borġ said. 'You should not get involved in our affairs.'

'We are not worried,' said his brother. 'We have nothing to fear. The governor and the crown advocate are happy that everything has been done legally.'

'Oh, but you *should* be worried,' McQueen said. 'Times are changing. The voice of the Anti-Reform Party is starting to be heard. Rizzo is calling for an election, before the end of the year. The Colonial Office is under pressure to grant more autonomy to the Maltese people.'

'You should put these things right before the report is published,' Bonnići said. 'Here, I have drawn up a list of improvements that I suggest you make over the next few months. Water pipes, proper disposal of waste, better ventilation. If you do this now, there is a chance to show that you are not completely heartless. You may even avoid prosecution.'

Bonnići laid the papers down on the table. McQueen watched the Borġ brothers' faces, which grew darker and darker. The police superintendent banged his fist on top of the papers.

'You have no right to threaten me,' he snarled. 'I am still the chief of police. I demand that you leave now. This is a private meeting.'

'Certainly,' McQueen said, politely. 'We are very happy to do so. We just thought we would give you a friendly warning.'

As the two men left the café, McQueen glanced over his shoulder towards the table at the back.

'Well, well, well,' he said to Bonniċi. 'Looks like you may have struck a chord.'

The two Borġ brothers were poring over the papers, reading the police physician's recommendations in minute detail.

CHAPTER THIRTY-NINE

Floriana, Malta, Thursday, 5 September 1880

It was McQueen's first visit to the Parade Ground at Floriana – the heart of the British military presence in Malta. He had passed it and seen a flat expanse of sandy soil, about the size of five football pitches. Now, it was packed with 4,000 troops marching in close formation. He stood on the officers' platform on the western edge of the parade ground, feeling hot and irritable. The persistent yelling from the sergeant majors was grating on his nerves. The dust from the sirocco wind, together with the sand whipped up by the soldiers' feet and the horses' hooves, was making his eyes feel gritty. It did not help that he had a headache from last night's drinks with Bonniċi, and his shoulder was throbbing under his linen jacket.

He had received a missive from Carstairs, saying the governor insisted on his presence at the Grand Parade. It was all in aid of the much-anticipated visit of Prince Alfred, Duke of Edinburgh. He had heard a great deal about the Queen's second son; a Navy man, he had lived in Malta with his young family up until a few years ago. Now a rear admiral, Prince Alfred was visiting Valletta on his way to Alexandria.

Naturally, all the British had turned up for the event. The mere mention of royalty had them scuttling out in their best clothes and they were now standing in the full sun, protected by their parasols and panama hats. McQueen wished he had not bothered. He could not think of a less useful way of spending his time.

Carstairs was standing next to him, clearly enjoying explaining every last detail of the drill.

'This is the march past, where the troops salute the prince. Look at them, they are absolutely spot on – well done, men. Look at that tight formation. How splendid.'

He was practically jigging up and down with excitement. 'Wish I was down there with them.'

McQueen stifled a yawn. His thoughts drifted to the letter that had recently arrived from his brother, now crumpled up in his jacket pocket. It was full of news about family, about the youngest bairn, Jonathan, who was thriving, and how busy they were in the run-up to the Harvest Festival. But it was two sentences which had jumped out at him and kept turning around in his head. Andrew had written: *I have enquired about Jeannie in Leith and she continues to do well. She is now employed at a milliner's and by all accounts has taken to attending St Stephens, so you have no need to worry about her, I can assure you.*

Of course there would have been pressure from his family for Jeannie to find her way to the Church. He could imagine the glee with which the news would have been greeted by his father. His hopes for returning to her felt as though they were slipping away. Surreptitiously, he pulled his hip flask from his pocket and took a nip, whilst mopping his forehead with his handkerchief.

When the parade was finally over, McQueen gratefully headed over to the Officers' Mess with all the other guests. The dining table in the big hall was laid out with a ridiculous array of luncheon dishes, from which people were serving themselves on large dinner plates. For the royal visit, they had pulled out every conceivable type of fish, salad, cold meat and jelly dessert. His stomach churned at the sight of a giant salmon mousse in aspic. Instead, he went for the cold chicken and game pie, and a glass of beer. This went down very well and he was reaching for another when Carstairs approached, looking flustered.

'I say, Inspector, the governor is asking for you. He's with the prince, who wants to talk to you about Admiral Lord Collingwood. Come with me, if you don't mind.'

He put down his plate and glass. He *did* mind, but he supposed he could come back for some more.

'Oh, now, McQueen – protocol!' Carstairs said. 'You might want to take a napkin and... your beard... Ah, yes, that's it. You can call him "sir" and you don't need to bow; he's not too stuffy. A Navy man, you know. But manners, decorum, you know.' Carstairs fussed alongside him as they made their way towards the royal presence.

Sir Thomas Grant, the governor, was standing alongside the prince, his white eyebrows and mutton-chops as bushy as ever. Prince Alfred was a small man, with dark hair parted in the middle and a full naval beard. Like the governor, he was wearing dress uniform. He resembled his mother and carried about him an air of quiet authority.

'Ah, Inspector,' said Sir Thomas. 'Your Royal Highness, may I present Detective Inspector McQueen?'

'McQueen, good to meet you,' said the prince, shaking his hand.

'Sir.' The light blue eyes were disconcerting. They seemed to look beyond him rather than at him.

'I wanted to thank you for solving the case. Edward Collingwood was a splendid man, a true hero. I am glad justice was done – thanks to you, Inspector.'

McQueen felt a flash of anger coursing through him.

'Lord Collingwood might have been a war hero,' he replied without thinking, 'but he was a *poltroon* in his private life. It was the mess he made that led to his own death, and that of two other innocent people. Aye, justice has been done, but you'll not find me extolling the admiral's virtues.'

'McQueen!' the governor said sharply, stepping forward.

'It's all right,' Prince Alfred said, waving him back. '*Poltroon*, a coward – fine Scottish word. You're from Edinburgh, are you not? Wonderful part of the country.'

'Yes, sir.'

'Terrific police force. I stand by what I said. Well done.'

The prince and the governor shook hands and moved away, with Carstairs looking nervously over his shoulder as he went with them.

Back in amongst the melee, McQueen picked up another glass of beer and a new platter of food, wondering how soon he could get away from this gathering, when he was approached by Lady Collingwood and her son. *The widow was looking a little drawn*, he thought. Her eyes were less fierce than they had been and her colour paler than he recalled.

'How do you do, Inspector,' she said. 'Did you enjoy the parade?'

'Not my favourite pastime,' he replied. 'The food is good, though. And the beer.'

He took a sip, looking at her over the top of the glass.

She laughed. 'I don't know if you've heard, Inspector, but

we're leaving Malta. Very soon. Just as soon as we can make all the arrangements.'

'There's nothing here for us,' said Edmund. 'We're going to go back to England and live on the estate.'

He swept his hair away from his forehead in a nervous gesture.

'Edmund's going to be married,' Lady Collingwood said. 'Louisa Grosvenor, daughter of Sir George Grosvenor, of Russell Square.'

'Is that right?' McQueen said drily. 'I wish you every happiness.'

There really was no end to the hypocrisy in these grand families. He felt he had had enough.

'I've got to be going,' he said, putting down his glass. As he started to move away, Lady Collingwood put her hand on his arm.

'I want to thank you, Inspector,' she said quietly, with unexpected sincerity. 'It's not been easy, not for any of us, all those things you found out about my late husband. I'm not condoning him, not at all. But I am still convinced it was right to find out the truth about who had murdered him. And for true justice to be carried out.'

'Well, at least his by-blow has been removed, eh? No chance of any further claims on the hallowed estate from an illegitimate child.'

'Inspector! That was uncalled for.'

'Aye, well, too many people died as a result of this case. It doesn't sit right with me. Look, I hope you'll all be very happy on your return to England.'

Good luck to them, he thought. They would be fine, of course they would be. But happiness, well that was another thing.

When McQueen arrived back at his lodgings, he could hear voices in the kitchen. He went in to find Bonniċi sitting at the kitchen table, looking relaxed and comfortable. He was wearing what looked like hunting clothes: khaki green breeches, stockings and a jacket. A flat cap was lying on the table and a shotgun leaned against the wall. *Sinjura* Caruso was at the kitchen counter and as he came in, she turned around, holding up a dead rabbit. A further pile of rabbits lay on the counter next to her.

'Look what Dr Bonniċi has brought us! We can have *fenek* every day this week. You like casserole, yes?'

McQueen had never seen her look so happy. Her eyes had softened and she looked younger, more animated. He looked over at Bonniċi, who raised his eyebrows very slightly, a small smile crinkling the edges of his mouth and his eyes.

Antonio came running in from the back door.

'Mister McQueen, come and see. Dr Bonniċi has a dog – look!'

The lad grabbed him by the hand and dragged him outside, where the strangest looking dog he had ever seen was sitting upright in the yard. It was tall and slender, with short chestnut fur and huge ears sticking straight up. It looked at him expectantly, with amber eyes. He reached down to pat it, while Antonio threw his arms around the dog's neck.

'He is lovely, isn't he?' said Antonio. 'He's called Pepi. Dr Bonniċi has been hunting with him. He's going to let me go with him next time. I can help him.'

McQueen had no idea Bonniċi had a dog. 'Daft thing, with those ears,' he said. 'Makes him look like a bat.'

'Don't listen to him, Pepi,' Antonio said, covering the dog's ears up. 'You are very handsome.'

McQueen went back into the kitchen and sat down

opposite the doctor. *Sinjura* Caruso fussed around them, bringing them glasses of beer, and plates of bread and cheese.

'How was the parade?' Bonniċi asked. 'Did you meet Prince Alfred?'

'I did. We didn't exactly hit it off,' he said. 'I thought you were going to be there.'

'I hate parades. I tell them I can't go because of my leg.'

'Then you go hunting instead. Very good.'

Bonniċi shrugged and smiled. 'Well, we all need to eat.'

'You must eat with us tonight, *Dottore,*' *Sinjura* Caruso said. 'I will make you special, special dinner. We will celebrate. Ninu, come and tell Inspector McQueen your news.'

The lad appeared in the doorway with the broadest grin across his face.

'Guess what, Mister McQueen?' he said. 'Next week I am going to school! Dr Bonniċi got me a place. I go on Monday.'

'Very good, lad, very good.'

It was clear to McQueen that an understanding had formed between his friend and his landlady, and he smiled to himself. *It was probably the moment that Bonniċi had brought Antonio back to his mother. Her gratitude had melted her reserve, the barrier she had built around herself since her husband's death.* The doctor seemed quietly content. He hoped his friend would take his time, go carefully, and build a lasting relationship. They would suit each other, he was sure.

He pulled out his hip flask and poured out a couple of drams. 'Let's drink to that,' he said.

'So, McQueen,' Bonniċi said. 'What's next for you? Are you going back to Scotland, now this case is well and truly over?'

McQueen pictured the grey clouds and buildings of Edinburgh in the biting wind and rain of autumn. He thought about Jeannie – how difficult it would be, to be near her and yet unable to see her, as she continued to rebuild her life. He imagined himself going back to his family home, reconnecting with his father, trying to build a bridge of understanding.

'Well, no,' he said. 'I've been asked to stay on. A new police chief is being appointed. There's work to be done to set up a detective department. I think I might just stay here a wee while.'

THE END

AUTHOR'S NOTE

Although this is a work of fiction, I have attempted to reflect some of the events and concerns of the day.

In 1880, Malta was an important strategic part of the British Empire. 6,000 troops were stationed in Malta and it was a key naval station. Around 7,000 ships of all types would have stopped in the harbours each year, taking on coal and provisions. Governors of Malta were generally military men without experience of civil administration. The Council of Government included elected members representing the Maltese people, but these were outnumbered eight to ten by members appointed by the governor.

A petition from the Maltese people for representative government and a civilian administrator, signed by 9,000 people, was sent to parliament in 1879 and again in January 1880. The reply from Lord Kimberley, Secretary of State for the Colonies, published in August 1880, was very badly received. It said that as Malta was an 'Imperial Fortress and a Naval Station', it could not be treated as a normal colony.

A new nationalist movement emerged in 1880 in the form of the Partito Anti-Riformista, under the leadership of Dr

Fortunato Mizzi. The party protested against a series of reforms announced in 1880, following reports commissioned by the British government. The proposals included the reform of taxes and public administration, and the Anglicisation of the educational and judicial systems, starting with English being taught at primary school instead of Italian. In 1883 the Partito Anti-Riformista became the Partito Nazionale.

It was at a protest outside the Governor's Palace in 1885 that Dr Zaccaria Roncali reportedly shouted the words 'Malta e' dei Maltesi, non degli Inglesi. Fuori lostraniero!' – 'Malta belongs to the Maltese, not to the English. Out with the foreigners.'

Poverty was a real problem within the Maltese population. Overcrowding and insanitary conditions in the Mandraġġ – an infamous area of Valletta – and in common dwelling places, had also been highlighted in petitions to the British government.

Maltese language

At this time, Italian was an official language of Malta. It was the language of the wealthy, the law courts and the university. Maltese was the language of the common people, but written Maltese was still in the process of being established. The modern Maltese alphabet and grammar systems were published in 1921 and 1924. I have used Italian versions of the first names of most Maltese characters, as this was the norm for the time, although for the servants/working classes I've used Maltese names. I have used the Maltese spelling for *Singer* and *Sinjura,* although sources from 1880 mainly use Italian spelling. In Valletta in 1880, street names were written in Italian. Any errors are entirely my own.

Maltese pronunciation

There are some different pronunciations of letters and extra consonants in the Maltese alphabet, for example:

Ċ = ch, like church

Ġ = j, like jump

J = y, like yes

Għ = silent

H = silent

Ħ = h, like hat

Ż = z, like zebra

Z = ts, like pizza

Examples of how to pronounce characters' names:

Bonniċi = Bon-eechee

Borġ = Borj

Ċensa = Chen-saa

Rożi = Roh-zee

Luċija = Loo-chee-yaa

Other vocabulary:

Għonnella – On-nel-la

Dgħajsa – Dye-saa

ACKNOWLEDGEMENTS

My greatest thanks go to my husband Colin for his endless support, especially the many long walks talking about Sam McQueen. Also, huge thanks to Daniel, Tasia and Anya Taylor, to Simon, Mark and Ruth Tudge and to Siobhan Brennan, for their support and unwavering belief in me; to Margot White for a wonderful place to stay in Edinburgh (with countless cups of tea!) and for being my research partner in crime in Malta; to Richard Tudor, Lesley Barros, Jo Taylor, Sara Miles and Maurice Vella, who all read manuscript drafts and gave me faith to carry on; to Charlotte Wolff, Alison Roxburgh, Toni Chappell, Laura Kohonen, Jason Hill and Irene Large from the MA in Creative Writing Course at Bath Spa University, for their insightful comments and encouragement; to Amber Duivenvoorden for reading the MS and advising on questions of Maltese language and culture; to my manuscript tutors Celia Brayfield and Jack Wolf, and to Gabrielle Malcolm, who helped me every step of the way.

I could not have written this without a huge amount of help from people in or from Malta. Thank you to Liliana Wood, for helping me get started. I owe the greatest debt to Publius Debattista, for his expert knowledge and help with Maltese history and language, and to Joann for welcoming me so warmly into their home in Rabat. Sadly, Publius passed away in 2023. I wish he could have read the finished novel, which benefitted so much from his wisdom. I would also like to thank Trevor

Calafato from the University of Malta, Melvin Caruana from the National Archives of Malta, Denise Falzon, and Annamaria Gatt, who all kindly helped me with my research.

Finally, of course, a big thank you to Betsy Reavley, Rachel Tyrer, Tara Lyons and all at Bloodhound Books.

A NOTE FROM THE PUBLISHER

Thank you for reading this book. If you enjoyed it please do consider leaving a review on Amazon to help others find it too.

We hate typos. All of our books have been rigorously edited and proofread, but sometimes mistakes do slip through. If you have spotted a typo, please do let us know and we can get it amended within hours.

info@bloodhoundbooks.com

Printed in Great Britain
by Amazon

41434372R00192